About the Author

Kerry Barnes, born in 1964, grew up on a council estate in the South East. Pushed by her parents to become a doctor at a time and in a place where women only dreamed of having a professional career, she started off as a microbiologist and then went into medicine.

She began writing when her daughter was born and she had free time, and by the time her children were grown, she had written four novels.

Ruby's Palace is the second to be published, following *Ruthless*.

Also by this author

Ruthless (ISBN: 978-1-84897-497-5)

Ruby's Palace

Kerry Barnes

Ruby's Palace

Olympia Publishers
London

www.olympiapublishers.com

OLYMPIA PAPERBACK EDITION

ISBN: 978-1-84897-801-0

This is a work of fiction.
Names, characters, places and incidents originate from the writer's imagination. Any
resemblance to actual persons, living or dead, is purely coincidental.

First Published in 2017
Olympia Publishers

60 Cannon Street
London
EC4N 6NP
Printed in Great Britain by CMP (uk) Limited

Dedication

I grew up in a truly loving family and I would like to dedicate this book to those who are no longer with us.

My grandmother Isobel Barnes (Nanny Barnes), the epitome of a strong woman.

My Uncle Bill, Uncle Howard, Uncle Terry and my Aunt Kath were taken too soon and left a big hole in our hearts.
You may be gone but you will never be forgotten.

Acknowledgements

I would like to acknowledge all the people that supported my first book, *Ruthless;* without them believing in me, there would be no *Ruby's Palace.*

My Uncle Trevor for helping me to bring the story to life, by keeping it real.

Robert Wood – my co-pilot.

Dannie Pleasants for her tireless proofreading.

Regan Lockhart – the face of Ruby.

Deryl Easton for her enormous support.

Colin Gillon for the photo of Regan.

Chapter One

Dan looked at the bar staff standing in line ready for inspection. It was the opening night of *Dan's Palace*, the latest in a string of clubs owned by the Vincent brothers. Dan's club was the grandest. He had taken the concept from his brother-in-law's casino in New York. He divided the club into sections: a pole dancing area, big dance floor and a poker room. The other two clubs had been above board for years, and so the authorities allowed him his first gambling licence.

The men were rigged out in black suits and purple shirts – nothing tacky – and the women dressed in slinky purple dresses. It gave the club a classy edge. There would be no riff raff.

"'Ere, Jody or Joanne, what's your name?" Dan pointed to the scruffy-looking blonde, who had a fantastic figure and looked great in the dress. However, without makeup and with unwashed-looking hair, she resembled a hooker.

"Me name's Jady, what's the problem?" she asked, bouncing her hands on her hips and chewing gum like she had a rubber ball in her mouth.

Dan laughed, as everyone turned to stare at her. "Well, Jady, I do have a fucking problem, and it's you! All of you, take a good butcher's at Jady. Make a note that if you ever turn up to work looking like you couldn't give a shit, then spin around on your heels and fuck off home."

Cassandra, a barmaid from his first club, was admiring Dan as she always did. He had never looked her way, no matter how hard she tried. He was the sexiest man she had ever met and grew more handsome with age. He kept himself trim two nights a week at the boxing club. He liked to take his nephew, Jack, and spar himself. The holidays abroad ensured he had a decent tan which set off his steely-blue eyes, the family trait. It was easy to spot a Vincent as they had an uncanny resemblance. Dan, the eldest, was in his forties, but still pulled younger women in their twenties due to his looks and cool exterior.

Jady felt uncomfortable now as, with youth on her side, she was used to getting her own way.

"There's nothing wrong with how I look, darling. Perhaps you need to go to Specsavers." She laughed, hoping the others would join in, but they wanted their jobs.

Dan lit up a cigarette and pulled a deep drag. Everyone remained silent, waiting for the explosion. He looked down at his brand new black patent shoes and slowly lifted his head to glare at Jady. "You're still here?"

Her eyes darted around, searching for support. There was none.

Choked up and humiliated, she asked, "So you really want me to go then?"

"I think it's a good idea that you leave of your own accord. You see, it's like this. When you gaze around and realise that every inch of my club reeks of class and money, and, quite frankly, you don't, it's not difficult to work out, is it? One other thing, and a note to you all. Unless your surname is Vincent, then don't ever get cocky with me. So, Jady, I'm gonna politely ask you to fuck off."

The rest of the staff watched and learned. The Vincents were hard, but fair on their employees, who were paid well but had to toe the line. Anyone caught with their fingers in the till faced a serious hiding and the sack. No one had the balls to cross the line. Not once they had heard the rumours.

Jady spun on her heels and ran from the bar, blubbering like a schoolgirl.

"Right then, girls, no flirting with the customers. You look good, but that's all. I've got the dolly birds on the floor to do that, all right?"

The girls nodded eagerly. Dan had employed sexy women with long legs and big tits to flirt with the older men and entice them to buy the champagne, which was another good little earner.

"And, boys, anyone gets too pissed, you nod to security. Any problems, you ask Cassandra. She knows the ropes." He glanced her way and winked. It was the first time he had ever made a gesture to her. In fact, she hadn't been confident he knew her name.

Cassandra blushed, which was very out of character. She was older than the others, being in her early thirties. Joe, Dan's younger brother, had taken her on when they opened the first club called *The Purple Palace*. Joe was the least clever of the bunch, but his decision had been a good one. Cassandra looked good and worked hard: tall, slender and model-like, but she was also streetwise and tough. He watched her one night in the local pub fly kick a punter who had grabbed her tits and squeezed them. She had been polite enough to say, "Do that again and I'll fucking floor ya." The idiot laughed and did it again. Before he blinked, she had swung her leg around and, with a huge blow, knocked him clean off his feet. Cassandra continued to collect glasses, stepping over the concussed punter, who never returned to the pub. So, Joe snapped her up by offering more money and status. Of course, she grabbed the opportunity with both hands.

Dan clocked Cassandra's embarrassed glow and had a sudden urge to give her a hug, but he had a club to open and no time for fussing. As he walked away, he caught her staring at him and, without thinking, he winked again.

The punters arrived in their droves, filling *Dan's Palace* with Faces, footballers and wannabe WAGS. Women dressed to impress – fake tans, fake nails, and little more than a ribbon covering their fake tits. He proudly gazed around. It was just how he wanted it to be. *Dan's Palace* was buzzing with classy, rich customers.

Sam and Joe showed up together, dressed in sleek designer suits, crisp and polished.

"'Ere, what's with the flash Rolex and Armani whistles?" Dan gently punched Sam in the chest. "And you, Joe, what do ya call this ol' bit of rag?" he laughed. Of all the brothers, Joe was teased the most, being the softest natured and not the sharpest knife in the drawer.

"Fuck off, Dan, this ain't off the peg. Handmade, this is." He opened his jacket to show the lining.

"Ooh, yes, it's Primarkos," he giggled.

Dan hugged Joe. "You look great and it's good to see ya."

"I've left Ol' Sid running *Sam's*," said Sam. It sounded funny, saying his own name, but each brother had a club named after them.

"Cor, I bet he loves that, aye?"

Sam laughed and nodded. Sid was their father's best friend. He'd helped run the scrap business when they were kids and they looked up to him as an uncle. Since their father had sold the yard, he'd gotten bored – and turned to the drink more than he should – so a few sessions in the clubs acting as manager kept him straight, much to the relief of his wife, Shirley.

"And what about *Joe's*? Who's taking charge in there tonight?" asked Dan.

"Adam. He's over here for a while. His boy's running a summer camp in the States and he offered, so all sorted."

Dan had faith in Adam. He was employed as his sister's protection when she was in the country. If she trusted him with her life then he could certainly be trusted with the club. The Vincents kept their relationships tight. Authority was only given to a select few.

"Fine and dandy. Let's get ourselves a fucking good drink and watch the money come rolling in." The three brothers walked to the bar, stared at by hungry women and intrigued men. Everyone wanted to know who the owners of the *Palace* were. They weren't the usual ageing wannabes. All eyes were on them – with the women eager to impress. Their status meant respect and wealth.

With the dance floor in full swing and the bar staff flat out, the boys sat back, grinning from ear to ear. As the evening moved on, the confidence in some of the women grew until one, by the name of Sophie, dressed in a white shirt and a leather belt, brazenly walked over to Sam and asked if, at the end of the night, he would be interested in a twelve-hour shag.

Sam had the hardest look of the brothers, accentuated by an American GI crop, yet he had the steely-blue eyes and long eyelashes which the women loved.

Joe and Dan waited to hear his reply. He laughed with embarrassment. It was a reaction very different from Dan's who, after waiting a few seconds, jumped in. "Well, sweet cheeks, if he doesn't fancy a marathon shag, I can't stand by and see a good session go to waste, now can I?"

Dan had the charm and sexy grin to go with it.

Sophie, taken in by his interest, tried to sit on Dan's lap. He laughed and moved his leg to the side, and she slid helplessly to the floor.

"'Ere, hop it, darling, and you can come and find me, if you're still sober at the end of the night."

She composed herself, smiled sweetly and left.

"You're a cruel bastard, Dan," said Joe.

"Leave off, I ain't having no tart sitting on me new fucking whistle. For all I know, she might have pissed herself."

Sam nearly choked on his Bacardi and Coke.

Just as the three brothers were eyeing up the girls, in came a stunning-looking woman. They stopped talking and smiled. She headed their way. Her figure was perfect. She walked with confidence and reeked of money. Kitted out in a black slim-fitting dress, her hair was pulled tightly away from her face, defining her high cheek bones and large, steely-blue eyes.

All three jumped up to greet her.

"'Ello, sis, glad you could come!" Dan beamed with excitement.

She hugged each one and laughed with them. "Well, boys, you have done a great job. This place is rocking."

They looked at their sister with complete admiration. As tough and hard as they were, she was the queen bee.

Living in the States with her husband, a very wealthy Italian named Sergio, she came back to London every couple of months to visit her family. She helped with their businesses, in particular the legalities. She had trained as a barrister and was always on hand if needed.

Cassandra spotted Francesca and poured her favourite drink, brandy on the rocks.

"Hello, Cassie. It's lovely to see you again." Francesca stood to greet her and Cassandra felt honoured.

"This is a pleasant surprise, and I must say, you look stunning in that beautiful dress."

Francesca gave her a soft, kind smile, thanked her for the drinks, and watched as Cassie walked away.

"She has an eye for you, Dan, and don't pretend you haven't noticed."
He grinned and his whole face lit up, showing a tiny diamond planted in his back tooth.

"You could do a lot worse!" Francesca was trying to play the match maker.

"Look, sis, I know Cassie likes me, and that's why I keep me distance. She ain't an old slapper, and I have too much respect for her. I couldn't go there. She's not my type. I'm not into all that heavy stuff." He knocked back his vodka and laughed. "I'm content on me own. No one telling me what to do." He grinned at his brother.

Joe smiled. "Well, I'm happy with my Belinda and our little Alfie. That will do me fine, thanks very much!"

"Yeah, Chubs. You need a woman bossing you around. Who else will tie up your shoelaces?"

"Leave our Chubs... I mean Joe, alone. He could put you on your arse, Dan." Francesca laughed and pinched Joe's cheeks.

"Too true. He knows I'm only joking."

"And what about you, Sam? Isn't it time you found yourself a woman?" She looked adoringly at her brother and wished he could meet someone who would love him. He had devoted the last twelve years to his son and daughter and she was proud of him. Most men would have run a mile, but he didn't. He doted on the children and made a good life for them. "Sam, don't you think it's time our Ruby and Jack had a mother figure? Someone nice and warm to cuddle up to in bed at night?"

"Aw, fuck me, sis. You've only been away from Sergio a night, and you're missing him already."

She laughed and sipped her brandy.

"Anyway, sis, Jack and Ruby have got you."

She rolled her eyes. "But it's not the same."

Dan kept one eye on the family gathering and one eye on the club. He didn't need any trouble on the big opening. It never went down well in the local rag. Any fights would scar the reputation and he wanted a good name.

"So how's our Fred then, still chasing the Yankee birds?" laughed Sam.

"Isn't he here?" She looked at the bar.

"No, he ain't, and he didn't say he was coming either," said Joe.

"He is definitely here. We flew in together. In fact, I was supposed to be the late one. Fred and Dom were suited and booted before I had even had a shower."

Dominic was another minder who looked after Francesca and Fred.

"Well, where is the little fucker?" asked Sam excitedly. The brothers loved it when they got together. They didn't need mates as such, as they had each other. Dan and Fred were the most alike in their cheeky ways. They could both charm the birds out of the trees. Fred was Francesca's twin brother. He had moved to the States to be with her – after a serious episode in England had left him with no choice. Once he had had the taste of

American living, he decided to stay there. He followed in his sister's footsteps by returning every month or so.

"I bet he popped in to see Mum and Dad. You know how he misses them."

Dan nodded and Sam sighed. Joe was quiet: something was obviously bothering him.

"'Ere, what you sulking about, Chubs?" asked Sam.

Ignoring Sam, he turned to his sister. "Fran, do you think this suit looks like it's come from Primark, or what?"

Sam had just taken a swig of his drink and nearly choked with laughter.

"Fucking 'ell, Joe, how old are you? Gawd, mate, you must know by now we're winding you up!"

Joe pursed his lips together and Francesca pinched his cheeks again. Joe, the second eldest, was treated like the baby because at times he was so daft. As a young lad, he had been the muscle. If there was any hard core lifting to be done, he did the job. Even in the boxing ring, where they all trained, he was hard pressed to find an opponent who could make him wobble.

He liked the slower pace of life. He had put a stop to the nights out and settled down with his girlfriend.

Dan watched from the bar and clocked a group of men in the corner passing what looked like drug wraps.

He recognised one of the men, a gypsy by the name of Levi, and felt the hairs on the back of his neck stand on end. He knew Levi from the boxing club and had heard he was a big supplier of skunk and cocaine, slyly peddling it wherever he could.

"'Ere, Sam, check that cunt over there. If he thinks he's gonna come into my gaff and start dealing, then I'm gonna —" Before Dan could finish, Sam jumped up.

Immediately, Dan grabbed his arm. "Sit down, boy! I've got heavies to sort them out. Don't make a scene."

Sam was livid. He hated drugs and had every reason to. He had served three years for possession of a large stash of cocaine, courtesy of his girlfriend. He took the rap because she was pregnant with their daughter and because of their son, Jack, who was only a year old.

Dan called over Jason and Johnnie Lee, two brothers born in the East End. They were built like brick shit houses and hard as nails but without a full brain between them. They had worked the clubs for the Vincents for years and were chuffed to be part of the new one.

"See those 'do as you likeys' over there? Get fucking rid of 'em, and make sure the boys don't let them back in. I'm running a decent joint, not a two bob gaff!"

"Do as you likeys?" Johnnie was dafter than his brother.

"Pikeys, Johnnie. Fucking pikeys," shouted Dan. The music blared out Shaggy's 'It wasn't me'.

"Oh yeah, got ya. The problem is, guv, the pikeys are getting themselves done up and it's hard to tell them apart from everyone else!"

Dan stood up and Johnnie stepped back. "Listen to me. I can smell a gypsy a mile away. Togged out or not, a pikey looks like a fucking pikey. Now, I don't wanna see another one in my club."

Johnnie hated being shouted at but he had fucked up. "Shall I put Farley on the door?"

Dan screwed his face up. "Who the fuck is Farley?"

"He's a gypsy, but he's straight as a die." Johnnie pointed to the fit-looking lad, no more than twenty, dressed in the black suit and red shirt. All security wore red shirts. He appeared smart. His hair was slicked back but Dan spotted the sovereign on his little finger and then looked at his dealer boots, the giveaway signs.

"Johnnie, don't tell me he is straight as a die. All pikeys are born bent!"

"He really wants to do a good job and is eager to please. He might look small but he is fast with his fists. A fucker sometimes, but he tries hard, and he can spot a pikey, being as he is one."

Dan chewed the inside of his mouth. "All right, put him on the door, but you watch him. Make sure he talks to no one. The first sign of shenanigans, and you're gonna personally beat the crap out of him."

Johnnie nodded furiously. He liked the boy, and had promised him a job, but he respected the Vincents.

"Now, see those over there? Get rid of them. Any lip, take them out the back and fuck 'em up!" Johnnie grinned, showing his new false gnashers. Being a hard case was the reason he was hired – and he was good at it.

Sam and Joe listened to the conversation but didn't interfere. Dan knew what he was doing – and had made a success of their businesses – so the others took his lead.

Fred arrived at the club with Dominic. He was another one of Francesca's men. She didn't need protection but, since her husband and family were worth a fortune, they felt safer having her guarded.

Immaculately dressed, Fred was the most handsome of the brothers with his long wavy hair and a smile which displayed gleaming white teeth. He moved very swiftly and was excitable at times, which often got him into trouble. His white shirt was open and his tie was still in the pocket of his new grey suit. His face and the tiny glimpse of chest showed off a golden-coloured tan. He looked like a celebrity.

As he walked past the queue to the door, young Farley stopped him in his tracks and put his hands on his chest. "Oh no you don't, sunshine. You have to wait like the rest. As you can see, Mister, everyone has the same ticket." He thought he was being clever in front of Jason, the other bouncer.

But Jason knew who Fred was. He grabbed Farley's hand and before he could explain Fred had gripped him around the throat.

Farley wasn't quick enough and realised he had messed up as Jason stood rooted to the spot.

"Listen, you little prick, don't ever touch me like that again or I'll take your head off your fucking shoulders. This is me brother's club, and I don't need a ticket. Your job is to keep order out here, not give any fucking lip. Got it, sunshine?"

Farley nodded and shut his mouth. Dominic stood beside Fred, towering above all of them. "I'm with him," he said, with his Italian accent.

Jason turned to Farley when Fred was out of sight. "You knew he was a Vincent, you dipstick."

Farley grinned. "Yeah, of course I did. Just trying me luck."

"You are taking liberties, firstly with me brother's good nature, offering to take you on, and secondly with the Vincents. Not a good idea, mate. Not if you know them like I do!"

A cheeky grin spread across Farley's face. "So, who is the one you really wouldn't fuck with?"

Jason shook his head. "I watched this programme once, David Attenborough, I think. Anyway, it was about wolves. You see, I like those wildlife documentaries…"

"What's this got to do with the Vincents?" asked Farley, impatiently.

"Wolves work as a pack. Each one has a job to do, and you think that the one calling the shots is the alpha male. It ain't, it's the alpha female – and when one's in trouble, the others appear from nowhere."

Farley rolled his eyes. "Yeah, so what has that got to do with anything?"

"Figure it out yourself, clever bollocks," replied Jason.

John approached the men in the corner as Dan had ordered him to.

"Right, lads, do you want to follow me." Not a question, more of a statement.

Levi sat back, held up his hands and said, "What have I done, boss?"

Johnnie stood with his feet apart and his fists clasped together in front of him.

"What's up?" asked Levi with an exaggerated grin, showing his missing back teeth.

"Just come with me. I want a quiet word in your lug hole." His voice was deep. With a real rasp, he sounded menacing.

Levi guessed he had been caught and tried to shove the remainder of the cocaine down the back of the seat.

Johnnie leaned forward and whispered, "You can try to hide it, but I ain't the fucking filth. I don't need evidence. I can fuck you up any way! Now, move your arse."

Levi eyed the giant up and down and then noticed two other bouncers walking towards him. He stood up, looked over in Dan's direction, and winked.

Dan was livid. Piss-taking little shit, he now wanted to dish out the hiding himself.

Levi followed Johnnie and the other bouncers out the back. Once outside, they were joined by Dan. Usually, he would let the men do their job – but not this time. It was the cocky smirk on Levi's face which Dan took personally.

"So, you must be Dan Vincent? You own this club, then?" asked the cocky gypsy.

Dan hated scummy little small-time coke dealers. They had the audacity to swan into his *Palace* and deal like a gangster.

"I ain't come out here to socialise with you. I came to give you serious advice. If I wanted Charlie in me club then I'd 'ave one of me own fucking mates shifting it, right? You see, I'm territorial, what's mine is mine, and I call the fucking shots. I am highly offended when the likes of you think you can walk into my establishment and try to make money out of my business. Now, the advice is this: fuck off! Don't ever come back, and tell your pikey mates. You can carry on using the boxing club and the gym, but you stay away from here, got it?" Dan lit up another cigarette.

Levi, high on cocaine, was hopping. His eyes as wide as saucers, he flared his nostrils, or what was left of them. The cocaine gave him the confidence to get lippy.

"Who are you to tell me that I can still use the boxing club and the fucking gym?" Before he could continue, Sam was there with his hand around Levi's throat and his arm up the drug dealer's back.

"The fucking owner, you knob head!"

Dan laughed. "All right, Sam, let the mackerel go!"

Levi coughed and retched. The throat clench was too hard for a mere warning.

"Go on, catch your breath. Any more questions, before you leave?" Dan didn't want bloodshed on his first night.

After looking them over, Levi walked away quietly with a smirk on his greasy, pit-holed face.

Luckily, Fred missed the action. His fiery temper would no doubt have led to Levi dragging himself away or, worse, being scooped up on a shovel.

Back inside the club, Francesca chatted to Joe, who was totally unperturbed by the fracas and was pleased to see Fred arrive. It was important for them all to be there for Dan's big night.

Joe watched Fred and Francesca together and giggled.

"Ya know what, you two may look different, but you still act the same. I can't get over the way you two drink the same drink, eat the same food, and even screw your faces up in the same way when you don't like something."

Chapter Two

The opening night was a huge success. The takings were far over and above what Dan had expected, and the customers left with smiles on their faces. The family stayed until the end, enjoying a celebratory drink.

"'Ere, Dan, what do you think about that black beauty with the fucking great long pins, spinning round that pole? Cor, she must have made a fortune tonight in tips," said Sam, entranced by the dancer.

"Yeah, and I bet she had half your fucking money down her drawers," said Fred, on form. He had only had a few drinks and enjoyed the banter with his brothers. They had more fun and laughs when relaxed in each other's company than at any other time. Those outside the family were simply that, outsiders.

"So, sis, how long are you here for?" asked Dan.

"I'm here for a week, but I'll be back for three weeks at Christmas. I take it you are all still coming for the holidays?" Her brothers, who were all sitting around the low table, nodded in unison.

Christmas was a special time for them. Since Francesca had the biggest house, with plenty of bedrooms, it was at her home that they spent the holidays. She never celebrated it in the States and even her husband's family would come over and enjoy the festivities.

Joe rubbed his hands together like an excited child.

"I can't wait. I've gotta tell you something." He beamed from ear to ear.

"Fuck me, Joe, you've decided to come out of the closet," laughed Fred.

Joe pushed him off the stool. "No, my Belinda's expecting again. It's early days but, all going well, we will have another little 'un come June."

The boys patted him on the back and Francesca kissed him. "That's lovely news, Joe, and little Alfie will have someone to play with." There was a silence for a minute as they now stared at their sister, thinking their own thoughts. She was born to a large family and yet had to grow up an only child. But the circumstances of her childhood brought them together, tightening their bond.

"Yeah, I want a big family, but my Belinda hates being pregnant." Joe nearly choked on his words. He had forgotten for a second that Francesca couldn't have children and she would give anything to be expecting a baby.

"Well, two's plenty, Joe, and besides, remember you had the easy job of putting it there; getting the baby out is the hard bit."

Joe was relieved his sister was so kind. The boys giggled at their sister's humour. She looked so sophisticated, any hint of a dirty joke was hilarious.

As they finished up, Fred caught the eye of a young-looking woman who was dressed in a skimpy silver dress, wearing too much makeup and with wild hair. As she passed them Fred stared and she winked back but without a smile.

"Who was that, Dan?" Fred nodded in her direction as she left the club.

"That's one of the strippers, Kizzy or Kezzy." Dan gulped his Jack Daniels and stood to let the girls out of the side door, where the cabs waited.

"Why do you ask, Freddie, fancy her or what?"

"No, I thought she looked a bit young. You wanna be careful you don't get nicked for having underage girls stripping."

"Don't worry." Dan ruffled Fred's hair. "The girls give us a copy of their birth certificate and passport. I'm all above board here, boy. I can't afford to fuck up or they will take away all my licences."

Fred smiled, but he still felt uncomfortable. That girl made him go cold.

"Where does she come from?" he asked.

"I don't know, a local girl. Why? What's the fascination?" Dan downed the last dregs of his drink.

"None, but she kind of looks familiar." Fred stared into space. He couldn't get her face out of his head. There was something uncomfortable in the way she winked at him – as if she knew more about him than he did her.

Francesca said her goodbyes and left with Dominic, her minder. Sam headed off with Joe whilst Fred stayed behind to help Dan to close up.

They locked the doors, set the alarms and left via the back. The air was warm. November was not the chilly month it should be. Fred observed two bouncers, still hanging around the door.

"Hey boys, it's time to go home, or are you kipping here the night?"

It was Farley, the new doorman, who spun around first, ready to give a mouthful back. He stopped in his tracks. He was already in the Vincents' bad books, and he couldn't afford to risk his little scam being discovered. He needed to get in with them, and stay tight.

"Goodnight, Mr Vincent!" waved Farley. "Wanker," he whispered under his breath.

Fred stared for a second and then remembered the doorman from earlier that evening. He had tried to stop him coming in. He recalled the stripper. She looked familiar because she resembled Farley.

Fred hurried to catch up with his brother, Dan, who was getting into his new Mercedes. He jumped into the passenger seat and was instantly taken by the new car smell.

"Cor, mate, this is a tasty little number, fucking cream suede." Fred stroked the roof and ran his hands along the seats. "Nice."

"Yeah, gave meself an early birthday present."

"Listen, Dan. I know I haven't been around to help with the clubs but I want to give you some advice." Fred waited to see his brother's reaction.

"Yeah, go on then, mate."

"I noticed you had a pikey on the door – and that stripper, Kizzy, or Kezzy. Well, I thought I'd seen her before. I'm sure she's one of the O'Connells. You know, that fucking gypsy family. That Albi and Billy, right nasty bastards! You know who I mean? They used to do business with the McManners. They were right tight with that cunt Charlie McManners!"

Dan frowned as he tried to remember.

"Fucking hell, Dan, the brothers used to go down the gym!"

Dan guessed then who he was talking about. "Oh yeah, I know who you mean now. They did a bit of digging when the McManners went missing. I recall that Albi asking a lot of questions and that fat fucker, Billy, throwing his weight around, but that was years ago."

"Well, all I'm saying is, watch those fuckers. No one wants to go to a club full of pikeys. It makes you kind of uneasy and, besides all that, they'll have their hands in the tills, or worse."

Dan listened and agreed. He wanted celebrities, footballers, footballers' wives, and the odd wealthy villain blowing their money.

He employed a successful marketing company to advertise the club to the right people and attract the right crowd. It was money well spent.

"I get what you're saying, Fred, but unless the doorman and the bar staff are pikey-trained, I don't know what to do. Even John reckons they are hard to spot when they're dressed up."

"You know how it works, Dan. If you clear them out from the beginning, they don't come back. It's when they feel it's their turf and they get their feet under the table that we've got a problem."

Dan was still nodding. He hoped Fred would return to the manor and give him a hand as he had missed his little brother since he moved to the States.

"Look, Dan, I can come home for a while. I only help run the casino, and they don't really need me."

Dan would usually have said 'not to worry' but he wanted his brother back in the business.

"Fred, I need you for a while, just to get the club up and running. You know me. I can't trust anyone except me own family, and Joe and Sam are busy working the other two clubs."

Fred was pleased his brother had asked him. He loved the States and his easy way of life but, after spending the evening in the new club, he realised how much he missed working with his brothers.

"Settled then. I'll be on the door, Wednesday."

Dan grinned. It would be like the old times, when they had the first club.

Chapter Three

Francesca had brought presents for her niece and nephew over from New York. She was always spoiling them. As far as she was concerned, they could have anything they wanted.

Not being able to have children herself, she treated them as the next best thing.

Sam was resting on the sofa when Francesca arrived.

"Hey, you, lazy bones. What's all this, lying on the couch? It's twelve o'clock. Where are the kids?"

He looked shattered. He had left the club at the same time as her.

"Well, sis, her fucking royal highness is still in bed and Jack is at the gym."

Francesca detected a disapproving tone.

"What's up, mate?" she asked, seating herself opposite her brother, waiting for him to spill the beans.

"Sorry, sis, it's nothing. Just kids being kids." He jumped up. "Fancy a coffee?"

Francesca followed him, taking due notice of the untidiness of the very attractive house.

Whenever she visited the house, it was always spotless. Sam had bought the four-bedroom detached house in Kent not long after he was out of prison. His sister had given him the deposit and he earned enough from the club to pay a decent mortgage so he could give his kids a lovely, clean and respectable home, a far cry from their mother's shit-hole. Jack had been four and Ruby only three years old when their mother, a drug addict, had gone to prison. They were handed to Francesca and her brother to take care of them.

Francesca adored them and so she paid for their private education, their trips abroad, and their holidays with her in the States. Jack was sixteen now and Ruby fifteen. They looked very much like the Vincents, particularly Ruby, who was the image of her aunt when she had been her age yet, unbeknown to Francesca, her character was very different. As a child she had been adorable, sweet and loved by everyone. Not now, though.

Francesca had been a very kind-hearted young woman when she was fifteen and she hadn't lost her sparkling and well-rounded personality. She was still very attractive, with jet black hair tumbling down her back and the brightest steel-blue eyes.

Ruby had the same eyes, but they weren't as open and honest-looking as her aunt's.

Sam poured his sister a coffee and they returned to the living room.

"Tell me to mind my own business, but is your cleaner on strike or what?"

He laughed. "I never had a cleaner, never needed one. Sis, I have always kept this house clean and tidy. The kids picked up after themselves, and we mucked in together, but now it's like I've asked for the earth. If I ask Ruby to empty the dishwasher, she huffs and fucking puffs, then storms out."

He paused, lighting up a fag. "She's a different kid and I don't know her anymore."

No sooner had he spoken than she walked into the room. "All right, Fran?" Her voice was flat and ugly.

"'Ere, madam, it's Aunty Fran to you, young lady!" snapped Sam.

Ruby stood in the doorway, rolling her eyes. She was wearing a crop top and baggy sweatpants.

"Hello, Rubes," replied Francesca, who was surprised to find her niece looking so grown-up. "Have you had your belly button pierced, or is it a stick-on one?"

Her niece tutted.

"Don't be silly, it's real. As if I'd have a stick-on belly bar!" With that, she flicked her long fringe out of her face and walked into the kitchen.

Francesca looked at Sam in disbelief. He shrugged his shoulders as if to say, 'I told you'.

"I guess it's hormones and the dreaded teenage years." She tried to laugh it off but she could tell Ruby had developed a nasty attitude, along with big tits and a fake tan.

"I bought Jack those trainers they are all raving about. They came out in the States first, and you know what he's like with the latest fashion. He put his order in. I couldn't remember which ones he wanted so I got all three colours."

"You spoil those kids. I hope he is grateful." Sam knew his son would be. He was no trouble: he was so helpful, polite and kind.

"Don't worry, Jack appreciates everything, and I love to see his face light up."

Ruby could hear talk of trainers and remembered her aunt always brought her a present. She entered the living room, expecting to be handed a gift. Instead, she got nothing.

"So, Aunty Fran, did you get me trainers?" asked Ruby, full of fake smiles.

She stared for a moment at her niece. "You didn't ask for any." An uncomfortable silence lingered between them.

"Oh, I see, so I have to ask now, do I? Jack just gets it all then, does he?" She stood with her hands on her hips.

"Ruby, Jack calls me at least twice a week for a chat. You haven't called me in a month, and I look around the room and notice all your messy shit.

Then, I listen to your mouth and how you speak to me and your father." She got to her feet. "Now then, my girl, you can change your attitude for a start and show the people that love you some respect." Her sinister glare unnerved Ruby and she shuffled uncomfortably. Francesca was never nasty, quite the opposite in fact. She was kind and caring, but there was an edge to her. Ruby was aware her uncles and dad treated her aunt with paramount regard. There was always a nagging feeling that, outside the comfort of her family, she was a dangerous woman.

In a flash, Ruby ran out of the room and back upstairs.

Sam shook his head and puffed on his cigarette.

Francesca pulled out a box. "When she behaves herself she can have this, but only when she changes her shitty attitude."

Sam took the small parcel and smiled. "What is it?"

"Open it," she whispered.

He opened the black box to find a shiny silver watch.

"Gucci is all the rage with the teenagers."

Sam laughed. "Sis, this watch is too much, she's only fifteen!"

"So? I want her to have it. I bet her posh friends have all the latest gear."

He adored his sister. She had been the one who rescued his children from the clutches of their mother and gave them back their dignity. She had taken responsibility for their future and made sure they had the best.

Ruby came back in the room with a sweatshirt on and a sweeter smile.

"Sorry, Aunt Sisco." Sisco was short for Francisco. Both Jack and Ruby couldn't say 'Francesca' in their younger years so they had called her Sisco and the name seemed to have stuck.

"Right then, love. I have something for you." Ruby's eyes lit up. Her aunt never gave them shit presents.

"But it's yours only when your dad thinks you have earned it!"

Ruby bit her lip.

"So, my girl, buck your ideas up, or you won't be wearing a Gucci watch on your wrist."

Ruby squealed with delight. "A Gucci watch?" She clapped her hands together.

Francesca waved her finger. "Not yet, madam – when you prove you can be more helpful."

As she smiled, her dimples appeared and she looked more like the little three-year-old who Francesca found twelve years ago.

Minutes later, Jack arrived. He was tall – like his dad – but his face was the double of her twin brother, Fred. He rushed over to his aunt and kissed her on the cheek.

She smiled with pride as she looked her nephew over.

"Look at you! You must have grown a foot since I last saw you!"

He laughed. "Yep, another growth spurt. I'm just trying to bulk-up now, I've got my big fight next week."

Francesca never liked the boxing club. She hated violence for fun, or as a sport, and their history contained more than most.

Jack opened his boxes with a huge smile. He never asked for much but he loved a pair of fresh trainers.

Eager to please, Jack straightaway offered to make tea. Next, he presented his school report and his latest boxing pictures. Francesca was so proud. He was well liked by his teachers and his grades were good.

"Where's your school report, Rubes?" she asked, peering over Jack's photos.

Ruby glanced over at her father who, without a word, gestured for her to tell her aunt.

Instead, she stared at the floor. Jack jumped in. "Rubes, your mate Jenny's outside. I forgot to tell you."

It was a quick way to get Ruby out because he guessed she would be so embarrassed if she had to tell their aunt about her exclusion.

"Oh yeah, sorry Sisco, I've got to rush." With that, she left.

Sam looked at his son and decided not to tell his sister now that the headmistress had excluded Ruby for fighting. He admired the way his son protected her. It had always been the same. Ever since they were small he would run to Ruby's defence and vice versa.

Francesca wasn't stupid. In fact, she was extremely intelligent, and fathomed straight away that Jack was defending his sister. So she waited for him to have his bath before she tackled the situation.

"What's going on, Sam?"

"I didn't want to tell you because I didn't want you to worry," said Sam with a flat, resigned tone. "Our Ruby has got herself excluded from school for a week because she gave one kid a black eye."

Francesca cocked her head to the side in disbelief. "What did the girl do to her?"

"By all accounts it was just a bit of verbal and Ruby landed her one. I've gotta say, it ain't the first time. That little prat is quick with her fists."

Francesca was astounded. The last time she saw her niece had been in America, and she was a perfect little angel. What could have changed so much?

"How long has she been acting like this, Sam?"

"It's been getting worse over a period of about six months, sis. I don't know what to do…" He stopped to light up another fag. Francesca looked closely at her brother and he had definitely aged. She could see the silver streaks in his hair and he was looking a touch haggard.

"Sis, I've stopped her training at the gym. At first I thought it was okay for her to get fit and learn to defend herself, but she punches harder than Jack and, when she loses it, well, fuck me, sis, she can fight."

She listened intently. She was dumbfounded to think her sweet, little Ruby was a street rucker with a bad attitude.

"Why is she like it, Sam?"

He stood up to go to the kitchen. "I have absolutely no idea."

*

Francesca left the house, hugging her brother. "Listen, Sam, I will be back in the week to have a chat with Ruby and, if she gets too much, I'll take her home with me for a while, just to give you breathing space." He nodded, but in his heart he knew his daughter was on the long road to self-destruction. He prayed she wouldn't turn out like her mother.

Francesca had driven herself to Sam's. Dominic, her driver as well as her minder, was enjoying the Sunday rest. As she turned the corner, she spotted her niece sitting on a bench with four other teenagers. She was punching the air and laughing as if she was re-enacting a fight. The other kids looked on intently. She was the centre of attention and she was loving it. Then Francesca noticed her dragging on a cigarette. She pulled up across the road and watched for a while, disappointed that Ruby had taken her sweatshirt off, revealing her midriff.

She decided to leave Ruby for now. Besides, it was just a cocky phase she was going through. After all, she had grown up with a brother who was a boxer and four uncles, all as tough as old boots. So having a brassy attitude was, no doubt, high on the agenda. But her smile soon turned to horror when she observed Ruby take a small bag from one younger man and roll a joint. Not a clumsy affair either. Ruby rolled that spliff with accuracy, as if she was an old hand at it. And Francesca would bet her last dollar she was!

Without thinking, she jumped from the car and, before Ruby could look up from her tobacco, Francesca had grabbed the lot. The others stepped aside.

"Fuck off, lady, and give me my gear back!" spat one spotty little teenager.

Ruby gripped her seat with her mouth wide open in horror. She stared at her aunt, who looked like the devil herself.

"It's not mine, Sisco, I was just rolling it for him," she said in a panic.

The spotty teenager realised that Ruby knew the woman and then agreed. "Yeah, Misses. It's my gear!" He held his hand out, assuming Francesca would give it back, but instead he got the shock of his life. Francesca, still clutching the skunk, gave the boy a nasty back-hander which, to her own surprise, sent him on his arse.

"Fuck off, you little prick, or I'll 'ave ya nicked!" She spoke in a language he understood. In a flash, he was on his feet and running down the road, followed by the rest. Ruby, still in shock, didn't know whether to defend her statement that it wasn't her skunk or to say sorry and that it wouldn't happen again. Before she could do anything, Francesca grabbed her by the arm and marched her to the car.

"Get in there, you little cow," she screamed as she threw her onto the back seat.

Ruby had never heard her aunt speak like that before. She had always been so sophisticated and graceful, full of nice posh words.

She felt angry that Francesca had damaged her street cred and humiliated her.

The house was only around the corner but Francesca would not risk Ruby running away.

After they pulled up, she dragged her from the car and frog-marched her through the front door.

"What the fuck is going on?" said Sam.

Francesca pushed Ruby into the living room and handed Sam the bag of skunk.

Sam's eyes widened. The one thing he hated more than anything was drugs. He had served time over drugs and his children had been neglected by their mother because of them. Both his children were well aware of his feelings.

Sam looked at his daughter, who sat with an expression of spite, staring at the wall, with no remorse whatsoever. He waved the bag in front of her nose. "What the fucking 'ell do you think you are doing, my girl?" he shouted at the top of his voice – an inch away from her face.

She didn't even flinch. "Like I told *her*," Ruby pointed to her aunt with venom in her eyes, "that gear ain't mine, it's Craig's. I was just rolling a joint for him, that's all!" Ruby's temper increased. "She has just gone and shown me right up…" Before she could finish her words, Sam, in a fit of rage, slapped her across the face. He never hit his children, but she had gone too far this time.

Ruby stood up, holding her stinging cheek, and stared into Francesca's eyes. "See what you've done. Happy now, are ya?" She pushed past Francesca to go upstairs.

"Oh no you don't, my girl. Get down here now or I'll fucking give you another slap!" yelled Sam.

Ruby stopped at the foot of the stairs. Her face was throbbing but she didn't care. Her anger was bubbling up and she turned on her aunt.

"Look at you! Coming in here as if you own the place, acting like you're my mother, just 'cos you can't 'ave kids of your own, fucking thinking you know best. Paying for us don't mean you can control me!"

Francesca was mortified. It was hard to believe those words had left the mouth of the girl she had given everything to. She thought she had done the right thing by the kids but those cutting remarks absolutely shattered her.

Jack, hearing the commotion, ran down the stairs, near to tears. "Ruby, stop it. Don't be so nasty, you love our aunt. Why did you say those wicked things?"

"Cos she ain't our muvver, all right! She took us away from her and now I don't even know who she is. Thanks to *her*!" Ruby was still angry and it was obvious to Francesca that this wasn't just a spur of the moment, spiteful few words. No, it was much more than that.

They stared at each other, long enough for Ruby to see the hurt she had caused, and for Francesca to recognise the hate her niece felt.

Sam, stunned by his daughter's outrageous outburst, looked at his sister, hoping she'd laugh it off or shout back, but she didn't. It cut him deep to see the first sign of a tear in Francesca's eyes. If it hadn't been for her, his children would have been living in squalor with their mother.

Trying to stay calm, he grabbed Ruby's arm and marched her upstairs.

Jack was crying, which looked so out of place – a strapping lad, bawling into cupped hands. Francesca put her arm around his shoulders and whispered, "It's okay, Jack, she is just a hormonal teenager."

He gazed up at his aunt and shook his head. "She's more than that, the fucking nasty bitch." He wiped his nose on his sleeve, between sobs. "She is getting right out of hand." Francesca admired her nephew for the way he was at such a young age. Most brothers would have let their wayward sisters get on with it, but Jack showed real concern.

They both heard a door slam shut and Sam storm back down the stairs. His expression was one of sheer anger. His face was white and his lips were tight. Francesca had seen her brother get annoyed but he never looked angry. It was a shock to her. In fact, the whole Ruby tantrum was alarming. Her supposed near-perfect family were far from perfect. The issues here were more than teenage tantrums. She could see that Ruby had a problem and that she herself had been part of it. Ruby was angry her mother wasn't in her life and maybe, since she had been responsible for that, she should be the one to put matters right.

Sam was embarrassed by his daughter's behaviour and found it hard to deal with, so he went to the kitchen and lit a cigarette. Francesca joined him, ushering Jack to stay in the living room so she could speak with his father alone. She put her arm around his waist; he was too tall to put it around his shoulders. "Listen, Sam, I'm thinking that maybe she could meet with her mother." Before she could continue, Sam stopped her.

"Are you mad?" He stubbed out the fag. "No fucking way is she going anywhere near that junkie. I know she has said horrible things to you and, trust me, I couldn't feel more hurt, listening to the venom coming from my own daughter's gob, but, sis, there's no way she's gonna have anything to do with her!"

Francesca was used to people agreeing with her, but now she understood her brother had the right to call the shots. If he was adamant that Ruby was to stay away from her mother, then so be it.

"Sis, even if she met up with her, not that she even knows where she lives —"

"I do," interrupted Francesca.

Sam frowned. "How do you know?"

Francesca looked at the floor. "I should have been straight with you – years ago."

Sam never got annoyed with his sister. The respect ran too deep. He waited for an explanation.

"When she was released from prison, I paid her a visit."

She sat at the kitchen table, followed by Sam, who was intrigued to know more.

Francesca had made it her business to find out the date of Jesse's release. That was easy back then, since her days as a lawyer gave her a good insight into the loopholes where you could get hold of this kind of information.

*

It had been nine years ago when Francesca waited at the prison gates. The air was cool for September, so she had sat in the comfort of her limousine. Dominic, her driver-come-bodyguard, was in the front, reading the newspaper. Francesca remained in the back, wrapped in her long cashmere sweater. The gates opened and out walked a skinny, bedraggled-looking woman, wearing the same clothes she wore the last time Francesca had clapped eyes on her. That was a meeting both women would never forget.

Jesse was the mother of both Jack and Ruby and had just served three years for drug offences.

She looked over at the black limo and guessed it was Francesca's. She waited for her to step out of the car, hoping that the six months spent in the prison gym had given her enough strength to give Sam's sister the hiding she deserved. When she gazed in the mirror, she saw a skinny runt, but when she stared into her own eyes, she saw strength. The day Francesca had set her up with cocaine on a prison visit had haunted her for three solid years. She fell asleep in the dark cell every night, reliving the horror of being found with Class A drugs in her bag and that sadistic grin on Francesca's face as she had slipped away with her two children.

35

Francesca remained in the back of the car and Jesse stood apprehensively on the edge of the pavement. She had agreed that Francesca should meet her on her release in order to give her a good kicking but, seeing the flash black car and the huge driver, Jesse now had a nasty taste in her mouth and felt nervous. There was something stopping her.

The door slowly opened and she could just make out the silhouette of a woman in a long fitted dress.

She walked forward, looking up and down the road in case she had the wrong car. There wasn't another soul in sight. She shivered as she peeked inside.

"Get in, Jesse!" came a stern voice.

The blood rushed through her veins as she awkwardly clambered in. Instantly, the car tore away. There was no escape. Francesca smirked and confidently took a drag on her cigarette.

She looked the girl over. She had changed very little. She was still thin and unattractive. Her mousy brown hair, pulled away from her face, showed her gaunt features, sunken eyes, and lines around her mouth from too many fags. Her niece and nephew, thankfully, had got their looks from their father.

"Do you mind if I 'ave a fag?" asked Jesse, who was fumbling in an old plastic Tesco's carrier bag, looking for her tobacco.

Francesca handed her a Benson and Hedges.

Jesse's hand shook, noted by Francesca, who assumed it was the effects of drug-taking. Then she cringed at the girl's nails, bitten to the quick, and the unsightly yellow stains inside her forefinger.

Jesse dragged on the fully loaded Benson and Hedges, so unlike the thin roll ups she was used to. The intention to duff her up and bounce her face off the curb was gone. Francesca was intimidating. Jesse wasn't sure if it was the cool, stunning exterior of the woman or the hardness in her eyes which emanated so much power. Conscious her bowels were moving, she knew she would shit herself if they planned to do away with her.

"Kind of you to pick us up," Jesse smiled, showing her crooked yellow teeth.

Francesca had, for a second, a twinge of guilt, but she thought back to the sorry state of the children and decided it had been for the best. If she hadn't put Jesse away then, well, God knows what would have happened to Jack and Ruby.

"So, how's me kids, then? Getting big, I s'pose?"

Francesca felt anger welling up. Who the fuck did she think she was, 'her kids'?

"They are fine, Jesse, and that's just how they will stay, so here are the rules."

There was no way she would get her hands on Jack and Ruby again. But she could use the threat of custody to get out of the Vincents as much as she could as, in her eyes, they still owed her.

"Jack and Ruby are happy, healthy, and in good schools. I know you abused them. I saw the scars, the bruises, and heard their night terrors. You were a cruel cunt, Jesse, but, mark my words, you will never see them again," said Francesca, so matter of fact she could have been reading a restaurant menu.

Jesse wasn't shocked, but she was prepared to barter.

"Yeah, but they are still me kids, and I 'ave a right." Her face was white and her lips dry. She was afraid but she wanted some type of pay off. She was leaving prison with nothing – not even a fiver – and going to a hostel.

Francesca leaned forward and calmly clarified that there would be no argument. She would be the one calling the shots.

"You gave up that right when you abused them!" she said, glaring coldly into Jesse's eyes.

Jesse slumped back in the seat. She hated her children. They must have exaggerated the odd smacks to get their own way and to make everyone feel sorry for them.

"I am their mother and the law will be on my side." Jesse couldn't believe she had just said that. She realised she was pushing her luck.

Francesca pulled out her gun and pushed it up to Jesse's throat.

"Now, you fucking listen to me, and listen well!"

Jesse's bowels were off again. She had been in a few scraps in her days but this woman was ruthless.

"You will never see those kids again, and if you so much as ask after them, I'll have you skinned alive." She smiled and put the gun back in her pocket.

Jesse was still in shock. She had never looked down the barrel of a gun before.

"Now then, let's start again. First, they are not your children anymore, so get that thought out of your head!"

Jesse nodded.

"Secondly, since I was the one who put you away, I think it's only fair I make sure you are taken care of, now you are out."

Jesse assumed her days were over.

"So, there you are. Take this, and never come looking for those kids again. If I find you anywhere near any member of my family, I will fucking brutalise you. Try anything stupid, Jesse, and you will wish you had a gun in your hand to blow your own fucking brains out. I will dismember your body, one limb at a time, then burn the stinking remains."

The words echoed around Jesse's mind – dark and foreboding. She stared in horror, knowing this woman meant every word.

Jesse gingerly took the packet from Francesca and nodded.

"What's this?" she whispered.

"I have been paying the rent on your council flat so you have the keys to move back in. It has been cleaned and furnished, and there's two grand to get yourself decent clothes and to find a job. If those kids want to see you when they are old enough, well, you'd better be clean, sober and a fucking pillar of the community."

Jesse couldn't believe her luck – a home and two grand. That should buy her the best gear in town: skunk, coke, even a rock. Her eyes widened.

"There is a condition, though, and I fucking mean it. You stay the hell away. If they ever want to see you, they will find you. But, be warned – what you put them through – don't expect a bunch of roses. You may find a damaged kid, with revenge as a gift."

Jesse was on a high and nodded furiously. She didn't want the fucking kids. Two grand and a furnished flat was worth the labour pains – and the stint inside the clink.

As they drove into the estate, Francesca shuddered to think that her dear niece and nephew had once lived here, amongst the dirt and debris. The East End of London wasn't pretty by any means, but there were parts a damn sight worse than others. This estate was in South East London and made up of blocks of flats and smaller blocks of maisonettes. Both were dark and dreary. The dullness of the estate matched the mood of the people. In the earlier days, when the buildings were new, the residents enjoyed the community spirit, but not now. It was run down and ready to be demolished and rebuilt. A council plan was already in place for the revamped luxury apartments.

No matter how polluted they looked, Jesse was pleased to be back in her familiar surroundings.

The whole estate couldn't have been more run down; the blocks were covered in graffiti, the walk-ways still stunk of piss, and there was washing left on the balconies, green and mouldy, because the druggies couldn't be bothered to bring it in. It was the same old story. They started off with good intentions, getting the washing done and the floors vacuumed. But then, after a heavy drinking session or a night on the pipe, the wet clothes were forgotten about and the vacuum cleaner was left in the middle of the room. The little children lay sodden in their nappies with a small tot of whisky in their bottles to keep them quiet.

Francesca looked at the small, run-down play area. Not a blade of grass in sight – just concrete, and the remains of a swing, with dangling chains and no seats. She noticed two children, too young to be out of nappies, playing alone in the square. Francesca bit her lip. It still hurt not being able to have children herself and there, amongst a concrete jungle, were two youngsters who were barely clothed and running around, whilst their parents were getting stoned. She imagined Jack and Ruby doing the same.

The car came to a sharp halt outside Jesse's flat. A scruffy dog had shot across the road, causing Dominic to brake suddenly.

Jesse nearly fell to the floor whilst Francesca remained composed.

As she opened the door to leave, Francesca grabbed her arm.

"We understand each other, don't we?"

Jesse looked into her eyes and smiled. "Yes, we do." She held out her hand to shake on a deal but Francesca looked away. She wanted to show her that, no matter what, she would always be in charge.

Jesse knew there would be no messing with this woman – that was for sure.

The rain poured and she hurried to see her flat, not new, just refurbished. It was as she had said and, seeing all the furniture and how clean it was, it lifted her spirits to a height they had never been before. It didn't stop her from running to the first dealer to score some draw and a rock, though. Within an hour she was as high as a kite and had already burnt the new settee with what was commonly called a black attack – where the red, hot marijuana droplets burned through any soft furnishings. Already, Jesse was on the downward spiral to self-destruction. When the money was gone she would have a habit so bad she would be on the streets selling her arse for a joint or two.

Jesse had gone to prison with no one waiting for her on the outside. There was no bloke, no kids, not even her mother, but she didn't care. She had her dope.

*

Jesse had had the chance, just once, to have it all. She had met Sam Vincent, a handsome man and a real catch. He was the middle brother in the Vincent family, with a reputation for being kindhearted. Still a hard bastard, but fair. He took to Jesse when he first met her – but this was before he found out about the drug taking. She had put on a different persona to capture his heart, and, by the time he realised how sly and sneaky she was, it was too late. She was up the duff with their first baby. Speed had kept her slim, long before she had met Sam. She was a looker then, too. Her hair had been long, thick and the brightest blonde, and her teeth were straight and white but, over the years, the hard core shit had changed all that. Now, she was a wreck.

He was not short of a few bob and so when she hooked up with him, the drugs were easy to get. The money flowed and so did the cocaine. When he put his foot down, she bought and sold it herself. She was expecting their second child when the raid happened.

Sam had been putting their son to bed when the police bashed down the front door. The noise was so loud he nearly dropped his son, Jack. They stormed the house with such force that Sam didn't have time to grab a weapon, which was lucky for him since he hadn't realised he was up against the law. He thought some local thugs from the club were trying to rob him. He often took the nightclub takings home before banking it in the morning.

The police were up the stairs and on him, throwing him to the floor. He had no idea what the hell was going on.

"Leave it out, I ain't done nothing!" shouted Sam, as the policeman handcuffed him. Jack screamed hysterically as the coppers tore all over the house, pulling out drawers, and emptying the wardrobes.

"What the fucking hell's going on? Let me go, you cunts!" Sam was struggling to get to his feet. "Look at me boy, Jack! For fuck's sake, he's screaming!"

One policeman pushed him down on the bed.

"Shut up and sit still. We have a warrant to search the premises for drugs," said another copper, who was the size of Big Daddy and looked like he should have retired years ago.

Sam shouted for Jesse to come and get the baby. He assumed she was downstairs but there was no answer.

"Your missus has scarpered out the back but, don't worry, our officers will have her in no time."

Then he realised it was about her. The penny finally dropped. The fucking bitch had been dealing. Sam stared for a second at his little boy who was sobbing. His tiny face was soaked and snot was running down his lips.

"For Christ's sake, have some compassion. Look at me baby!" Sam was looking at the fat copper, who nodded to the other officer.

They removed the handcuffs but guarded the door. They were not letting him escape until they had thoroughly searched the house.

Jack hugged his father tightly, burying his face into his neck. He was terrified.

Eventually, a younger police officer came into the bedroom with two carrier bags. "Found it, guv." He was as pleased as punch. The smug face said it all.

Sam shook his head in disbelief.

He kissed the baby and handed him over to the policewoman, who cradled him gently and tickled his cheek. He was grateful she had been kind to his son.

The other policemen left the room.

"I'm surprised at you, Samuel Vincent." The old copper sat next to him on the bed. "I mean, you Vincents are big-time. Nightclubs, boxing clubs. What the fuck is it with the pills?" He looked for a second like a father figure, telling his son off.

Sam ran his hands through his hair and shrugged.

"These ain't yours, are they, Sam? Do yourself a big fucking favour – turn her in. Between me and you, I like your lot, you run the clubs and sort out any aggro yourselves. We don't go near, or by, and that suits me."

The words were going around in circles, and it was a few seconds before he realised he would go down for a long stretch with the amount of drugs in those heavy-looking carrier bags.

The need to vomit made him swoon.

"Just hit you, has it, boy? You know you are looking at seven years." The copper wasn't winding him up.

Sam nodded.

"Samuel Vincent, I am arresting you on possession of attempting to supply Class A drugs…" Sergeant James looked at Sam with a sorrowful face.

"Class A? Fucking hell! What was in those bags?" The blood drained from his face.

"Sorry, mate, you had cocaine, amphetamines and it looks like a bag of heroin." The sergeant felt Sam's pain and he guessed this was Jesse's filthy work. He recognised that a family like the Vincents were brought up with that old moral code: you don't grass.

Sam took the rap without a thank you or an apology from his bird. She had him where she wanted him all the while she had his kids. Sam would die for his son and Jesse knew he wouldn't let the mother of his child serve time, especially since baby number two was on the way. She promised to wait for him and bring their son and the new baby to see him regularly, as long as she got her bit of poke from the clubs to feed them. Sam agreed, and that was how it was for three years until Sam's sister, Francesca, came over from America. In one prison visit she managed to set Jesse up good and proper, putting her behind bars, and taking the kids away forever. Jack and Ruby had only been a means to an end for Jesse. They were her meal ticket and nothing more than that. In fact, she despised them. After her daughter was born her body took a bashing, leaving her with stretch marks which looked like the London underground map. Her tits had shrunk to nothing and the continued drug abuse, along with the pregnancy, had turned her teeth black. She blamed the kids for all of it. Everything that went wrong in her life was their fault. Every cry, every moan, want or need, was just an irritation. She knew that if they went into care she wouldn't get her weekly poke – her puff money. She kept the children in tow and managed them, by a slap or a kick, if they got in the way. She sold the furniture and spent the rent money for their lavish house until eventually she was evicted and moved into a council flat with nothing.

Sam served his time with no real aggravation. He was already a Face. The Vincent brothers kept their nightclub business between themselves and so no one had anything on any of them. They were shrewd businessmen and were not easily intimidated. They had the boxing clubs too and each brother had a reputation in the ring. So, when Sam arrived at Downview Prison in Surrey, the inmates looked after him. There were some older Faces, nearing the end of a large lump, and they knew Sam's father. They gave him respect and saw he was all right.

He wasn't a druggie, and it wasn't long before the screws realised he was taking the rap for someone else. When Jesse came visiting they guessed it was her, since she looked like the typical waster. In fact, she was so rough that the other inmates, who had the bottle to be so bold, said as much to him.

She was an embarrassment to him, turning up as if she had just got out of bed and clothing the kids in clothes even the charity shop would throw out. But he still said nothing. All he wanted was to see his children and ensure her regular money encouraged her to bring the kids to the nick. Ruby, until the age of three, had only ever seen him in prison. She loved him as a dad, not a stranger. Jack adored his dad and the only time he was happy was at nursery school or on a visit.

Sam knew Jesse had him in the palm of her hand when he had kicked off about how she dressed the kids. She came on a visit in a new pair of Levis, leather boots, a smart leather jacket, and her hair highlighted. She walked into the visiting room like she owned the place. Sam was initially pleased she had made the effort, until he noticed the state of his children.

Ruby, who could barely walk, had a faded T-shirt with stains down the front. She had on a pair of pyjama bottoms, which were so small the elastic was leaving a deep purple mark around her tummy, and Jack's old trainers but no socks. Dangling from her mouth was a baby's bottle which had the remnants of old tea. Sam then looked at his son. His tracksuit bottoms fitted but he had no jumper – just a T-shirt and plimsoles. More distressing than that, though, he had a bruise on his cheek and sadness in his eyes.

He hugged his children and watched their mother. She was in ecstasy on cocaine, chatting for England about nothing, telling him how much she missed him and how the kids were her life. He wished she would just be honest. She was so full of shit.

"Jesse, shut up for a minute and listen to me. I ain't sending you cash each week to stick it up your fucking hooter. That money is to get my kids some decent clothes. Look at the fucking state of them. I'm warning you, Jesse! The next time I see them, I want them looking smart and I fucking mean it!" His voice got louder. The screws would normally approach an inmate and ask him to keep the noise down, or escort him off the visit, but they knew he was right and left him to it.

With that, Jesse jumped up from her seat, grabbed the kids and headed for the door.

Without any pride, she shouted, "Fuck you, Sam. Stick your measly pennies where the sun don't shine. You won't see your fucking kids again!"

Sam put his head in his hands and silently cried.

The other visitors watched in disgust. Billy O'Connell was a lifer on Sam's wing and watched as Jesse left. He knew where she lived, since Billy had come from the same manor. It was his time to get in with the Vincents; he wanted a piece of what they'd got. He whispered to his new girlfriend, "See that bitch? Do you see her about?"

She nodded. "Yeah, she lives on the estate, a junkie she is."

"Pay her a visit, make sure the kids aren't around, and give her a fucking good kicking. Evil cunt, she is."

"Yeah, no problem, Bill, but why are you getting involved?" Julie bit her lip and no sooner had the words left her mouth he was on her.

Through gritted teeth, he spat, "You fucking women are too fucking nosey. Just do as I say." Then he gently kissed her on the lips. "There you go, my sweetheart. Now, don't say who it's from or why, just give her a decent clump. I want you to keep an eye on her for me, all right?"

Julie nodded again. This time she kept her mouth shut. She could have a good fight herself and so the likes of Jesse weren't a worry for her.

Sam had gone back to the wing, deflated. He looked forward to his visits with the children. But a shiver ran through him as he remembered the cold, evil look on Jesse's face. How could she do this to him? He was the one who was serving time for her.

He sat on the lower bunk bed in his cell and was surprised to find that Billy O'Connell had followed him in.

"All right, Bill. What's up?" His voice flat, he wasn't in the mood for small talk.

"All right, Sam. I came for a chat."

"Sorry, mate, no offence but I wanna be alone."

Billy took up the whole doorway. Sam almost laughed. He was a funny-looking man with a huge body, a small bald head, and no neck.

Ignoring Sam's comment, Billy sat himself next to him.

"I know how ya feel, mate. I been there meself."

Sam turned to face him. He wasn't mates with Billy. There wasn't a connection. It just happened that Billy was on the same wing, serving the last lap of his sentence.

"S'pose they are talking about me?" He nodded towards the landing, suggesting the wing was having a good gossip.

"Nah, mate. I saw her on the visit, but don't worry. Me missus is gonna give her a slap," stated Billy.

Sam digested those words before he stood up. "What the fuck do you think you're doing, getting involved in my business?"

Billy had a reputation for throwing people off the balconies – after he had given them a good hiding. So he was surprised that Sam had so much front. He jumped to his feet to be on guard, since he also knew that Sam and his brothers could have a tear up.

Sam was nodding his head and flaring his nostrils. The anger was welling up. Billy could feel the tension and sensed at any second it would go off. He moved away from the bed and stood firm, facing Sam.

Sam stared for a while and then he threw his head back and laughed until the tears rolled. Bill didn't know what to make of him.

"You crafty fucking bastard. I ain't stupid. Think I'm gonna owe you anything, Billy No Neck? Think on. You fucking muppet!"

Billy's eyes widened. He felt humiliated and by now there was an audience. The loud laugh drew attention, since there wasn't too much aggro these days.

"As if I would have you, a fucking thug, sort out any of my problems. Don't you think that I could have the slag dead and buried if I wanted?" His expression was serious again.

Billy watched Sam's demeanor change from one extreme to the other. A sure sign of madness.

"I know what you're after and, if you think I would have you anywhere near my clubs, you can dream on. Now, do yourself a huge favour and get out of my face." Sam was calm now. He had said what he needed to say and then turned to face the small window, heavily barred.

Billy was still in shock. He couldn't believe that Sam, who was usually quiet, had just coated him. There were a few muffled comments and then the wing cleared. The only screw in the prison given respect was Mick, who was seen as consistently fair and approachable. After he moved the spectators on, he put his head around the corner to see Sam with his back to Billy. Not a good position to be in. Mick had witnessed Billy frequently, over the years, batter people near to death, and he didn't want Sam to end up the same way.

"All right, lads?" he said, with a soft tone to his voice.

Sam spun around. He was well mannered and had respect for his elders. Now in his thirties, he was he was a kind and caring man and always very courteous to everyone. Mick liked Sam. He knew he was serving time for his bird. Most drug pushers were dabbling in drugs themselves, but everyone knew Sam was clean.

"Hello, Mick, sorry for the noise, only Billy and I got a bit excited over something, that's all."

Billy glared: he was still not sure whether to give him a good kicking or try to reason with him. A fight was easier than reasoning, since all his life he had just taken what he wanted, with brute force if needed. Right now, he was on edge. He was due for parole and didn't want trouble but Sam had also pissed him off. His intentions were sussed out and he hated looking the fool.

Mick flicked his head, a gesture for Billy to leave. Sam expected Billy to indicate he would have him later but, to his surprise, he left without a word or a sneer.

"So, then, Sam, I heard about your visit." Sam shook his head and plonked himself on the bed.

"Look, son, this happens a lot. I see it all the time, and you know what? They find it hard on the outside, when their ol' man's banged up. It ain't easy for 'em. She'll be on the next visit. Give her time. She'll have a twinge of guilt and be up 'ere, kids an' all." His words were kind.

"Thank you, Mick. I needed to hear that. I miss me children."

Mick rubbed Sam's shoulder. "No problem, but a word of warning. Keep away from Billy. He's a nasty piece of work."

Sam smiled. He wasn't the least bit bothered by Billy O'Connell.

The prison's lock up time was nine o'clock and Sam was for once looking forward to the blackness. He lay awake, waiting for the last inmate to be silent, and he thought about how he would get his children and leave the country. Take them far away from England. He would go to his sister in the States and start a new life. As the hours ticked by, his body ached from tiredness and his mind went to a dark place. He visualised taking Jesse by the throat and strangling her until her lips turned blue and the vessels in her eyes burst. He saw her foaming at the mouth and her lips curling at the edges as the life left her body. Then he saw his children: with black and blue rope marks on their skin and bottles taped to their mouths. Suddenly, he gasped for breath and sat upright. He was sweating and his heart was pounding. He realised he had been having a nightmare, but it was so vivid. His children in the dream looked too real, with their tiny, round faces and big eyes with that look of terror in them. He cried – from frustration, bitterness and anger.

The mail arrived. As usual, there were letters from his family and a couple from some old friends. As he read the letter from his mother, his anger turned to blind fury.

Dear Sammy,

I managed to see Jack and Ruby today. They were playing on the estate. I'm so glad they recognised me. It was so cold and they didn't have a coat between them.

Sammy, I don't know what she does with all that money you give her but it ain't spent on clothes for the little ones. Anyway, not to worry, I went to Arding and Hobbs. They have a lovely kiddies department and I bought them coats, jumpers, boots, socks etc. I gave them to Jesse. I was hoping

that she would let me have the kids for the weekend but she said she was
taking them to the museum.

I do miss you and I miss those babies, they look so much like you and
Fred and Francesca.

Anyway send a VO for next week and me and your dad will come up.

Take care, son
Love, Mum x

Sam looked at the date of the letter. It was sent the day before Jesse's visit. He couldn't believe that even though his own mother had bought them new clothes, they were still in rags. The fucking bitch had sold them, just like she sold all the kids' things. He tried to calm down but his whole body shook.

Billy O'Connell had lain in his bed, getting angrier by the minute. He had never been humiliated like that and he would not take it. After all, he'd seen it as a favour and he shouldn't have been snubbed.

As Sam got up from his bed, Billy appeared in the doorway. He slipped inside and shut the door. Sam knew Billy was about to start. Sam looked at Billy's hands and spotted the fat, sausage-like fingers wrapped around a blade. He was so angry he didn't care, blade or no blade. If Billy wanted a straightener, then that's what he would get.

Unbeknown to Billy, Sam and his brothers all held a deep anger, which was one of the reasons why they all went to the gym – to try to keep a lid on their temper. The lid was about to be lifted. Sam was fit, his body was trim, with not an ounce of fat, and he had the height at six foot three. Billy was heavy, and a punch from him could crack a cheek bone in half, but his size slowed him down.

Billy gripped the blade tightly and took a deep breath. He was often out of breath these days. The doctor suggested that he lost weight, but he liked to look heavy.

Sam gave a sarcastic grin, almost laughing at him.

"What's up, Billy, not man enough to do me with your bare hands? Need a little weapon, I see?" Sam was goading him.

"I'll fuck you up blade or no blade, but I wanna make sure you're fucking hurt bad. Think you can take the piss out of me and get away with it?" He lunged forward to stab Sam, but as Sam moved to the side the weight of Billy's body carried him on and Sam gave him a hard elbow clump to the back of his neck and he fell to the ground. He kicked him hard in the face, cracking the pig-shaped nose. The blood flowed and Billy knew he was in trouble. He took a while to ease off a bed, let alone get up off the floor with Sam kicking him in the head. Sam was in full swing now; the anger was overwhelming, and Billy was his target. Another blow and almost instantly Billy's face was a purple balloon.

Louis Summerfield, a well-known lifer in the jail, had heard a whisper that Billy O'Connell was after slicing Sam and he was having none of it. Louis had served twenty years and in his time he had shared a cell with Bill Vincent, Sam's father, and that made him Sam's uncle as far as he was concerned.

An old man now, but with a lot of clout, he marched down the wing and pushed open the door. He found Sam foaming at the mouth and pulverising Billy O'Connell. "Stop now, son, before you're on a fucking murder charge!" He grabbed his waist and pulled him away.

Sam snapped out of his frenzy and stared down at the bloody mess.

But Billy had been unconscious long before Sam stopped the beating.

Louis took Sam out and pushed him into the cell next door. There, Lenny Fisher and Joey Salter, two bank robbers who had been planning their next job, had been tasked with looking after Sam.

"Stay there, boy," he said, taking control.

"What's up?" asked Lenny, who, at the time, had his back to the door.

"Get him cleaned up, and he was in here with you two, all right?" stated Louis. No one would argue with the older man, widely respected by the other prisoners.

They both nodded. They got to work cleaning off the blood from Sam, who was still in a daze.

Charlie Lucas, a young lad on a murder charge, was given the job of wing orderly. This was a more interesting job as it meant he wasn't banged up all day. Louis called him over.

"Get your mop and wash out Sam's cell."

There was no question and it was done. Louis got two other inmates to carry out Billy's limp and heavy body onto the landing. No one saw a thing. The wing was quiet, with everyone keeping themselves to themselves.

The doctor confirmed that Billy had suffered four broken ribs, a snapped femur, and his cheek bones were like mashed potato. The screws found Billy alone on the landing. It took two days before he regained consciousness and by then even he didn't know who had done it, so he said. But he hadn't forgotten. He remembered every blow which had hit his face and head before God gave him grace, letting him drift off into a state of sleep.

He had never had a kicking like that before in his whole life. He resigned himself to the fact he had messed with the wrong man.

Sam lay in his empty cell, feeling sick. He had smashed a man's face in over a stupid disagreement. He wasn't worried about being a name or having any kind of reputation for violence. He could fight, but only if and when he needed to. There was no bragging and no threatening, and he never glorified his wins. He had always been that way, from a lad at school. If he got picked on, he would fight back and then walk away. His mates would try to rub his head and pat him on the back but he hated all that.

Louis liked Sam a lot. He was a man of integrity, but when wronged – as Billy had wronged Sam – he was a man of justice. The inmates were more than happy to protect Sam, as Billy O'Connell was a bully; he loved to pick on the weaker, timid inmates to make himself look good. He had thrown Charlie Lucas over the balcony when he'd first arrived, just because he forgot to put sugar in Billy's mug, so Charlie was only too pleased to mop up Billy's blood. It was his small taste of revenge.

The O'Connells were a large gypsy family. Most of them were serving time. Those who were not, bragged about their uncles who were. That was until word got around that Uncle Billy had been beaten by a Vincent.

The O'Connells thrived on feuds, whether it be family feuds or with the neighbours; it was their way of life. Some grievances went on for decades, even carrying on through generations. But the ways were changing. Younger gypsies had their own ideas of a moral code which were frowned upon by their elders.

Chapter Four

Ruby sat on her beanbag as she looked around her beautiful bedroom. Spoilt with material things, the most expensive satins covered her bed and her carpet was lush and thick. She had a walk-in wardrobe and a dressing table surrounded by spotlights, with enough room to have a party. But it meant nothing. Her world was a lie, a big cover-up. Unlike her brother, who accepted their life, she didn't, and it played on her mind every day.

Her family had been through some serious problems and sometimes she felt so distant from them. Even her own father hid from her the truth. She had never forgotten what she had witnessed when she was three years old. Her uncles and her aunt were in a big warehouse, with men tied up and blood everywhere. This was not a vision which usually haunted her because, oddly, she had felt safe and secure. When she had asked her Uncle Dan one day about the incident, he had playfully ruffled her hair and laughed, telling her she had a vivid imagination. There was a close bond between her family, much closer than normal, to do with the dark secrets they shared, but what those secrets were she would probably never know. The unknown excluded her from the pack.

Torn between the love from her family and the grief of not knowing her mother, she became agitated and rebellious.

Jack never wanted to speak of Jesse, his mother; the vile memories of abuse disturbed him. He was a year older than Ruby and he remembered an enormous sense of relief when he had been told he would not be living with his mum again. Ruby didn't understand abuse and had been too young to store those thoughts. Instead, she painted a romantic picture of a woman destitute and penniless who gave her children to their father's family, who were far better off than her. This was a selfless act, undertaken by a special person. Ruby was content to think her mum lived a modest life, as a waitress, perhaps, or a check-out girl.

Even when they explained to her that Jesse went to prison for drug offences, she defended that accusation and even rationalised it, by believing she did it for the right reasons, to earn money for her and her brother, Jack. She dreamt about her mother as a woman staring into the playground, searching for her children. It was those days at school, when the lesson bored her, that gazing out of the window seemed more appealing. She drifted off into a world where her mother would be. She imagined her soft face, with big blue eyes and long golden hair, wearing a flowered smock dress. She pictured her making her own Christmas cards; she would write a sweet message in the card and then place it in a box with the other fifteen she would have written, saved for the day when she could be reunited with Ruby.

When she tried to talk to her father about her mother, he changed the subject. Ruby mistook this reaction for guilt. In her eyes, he was wrong for not giving Jesse the chance to visit her children, but Ruby didn't push the matter too far because she loved her dad.

Sam had cooked shepherd's pie, an old family favourite. The smell wafted up the stairs and Ruby realised how hungry she was. She had behaved appallingly. She knew it and was reluctant to go downstairs. It was humiliating, but it was of her own doing.

"Rubes, Dad wants you to join us for dinner in the dining room." Jack had popped his head just inside Ruby's bedroom door.

"Who is down there now?" asked Ruby, somewhat sheepishly.

"No one. Only me and Dad." He winked. "Come on, Rubes, I'm starving."

Jack adored his sister. He was well aware she had acted up but he hated to see her sitting alone and upset.

Like a coiled spring, she leapt from her bed and onto the thick pink carpet.

Sam had the table laid and it looked like Christmas with wine glasses and the best china square plates. He placed the pie in the middle of the large ebony wood table and the vegetables in smaller dishes.

Sam nodded for Ruby to sit down. They dished the food up but the tension persisted.

Ruby decided to keep quiet and hope the whole incident would be washed over, so she'd get to wear her new Gucci watch.

*

They ate in silence, with Sam looking over at his only daughter, who had changed so much in the last few months, and then at his son, who hadn't changed at all. More concerned now than disappointed with her behaviour, he wondered how he should deal with it.

The knife and fork came crashing down, making both of his kids jump.

"Tell me, Ruby, be fucking honest with me, what is going on? Why are you being so rebellious right now?" His voice rose to the point of shouting. With his elbows on the table, he clasped his hands together and waited for a response. She just shrugged her shoulders.

"Answer me, Ruby. I want a good explanation. What the fuck is wrong with you?"

Ruby, furious, felt the anger welling up again. This was something she struggled to control these days. Deep in her heart she guessed that maybe the cannabis was part of it. The school lectured on the paranoia and mood swings which were an effect of smoking drugs.

"All right then, if you must know, I've had enough of being a Vincent!" She, too, slammed her cutlery.

"What the fuck are you on about now?" Sam tried to stay calm; lately, Ruby had a knack of winding him up.

She looked at Jack to help her but he was as dumbfounded as his father.

"Look at me! I'm surrounded by boys; the boxing club, uncles, a brother, but there's no girls in my life!" Ruby wasn't being sweet. Her face tightened with rage, making her appear ugly.

"Well, madam, ain't you fucking lucky? Most young ladies would love to have all you've got; a big family that damn well care, even though they are men."

Ruby didn't leave the table. She sighed and gave her father a filthy glare.

"Ruby, I don't buy your pathetic excuse for your shitty behaviour. You'd better give me a proper reason, 'cos this is how this family works. You have a problem, then tell me about it, and I'll do me best to help ya. Come out with cock and bull, and I will get pissed off. So, shall we start again?" he shouted.

"I want me mum!"

Sam's eyes widened and glanced Jack's way. Jack shook his head in disbelief.

He took a while to get his thoughts together. "You can't, Ruby, I can't put you through that."

Ruby jumped up from the table, red-faced. "I fucking hate you! You sent my mum away and you all pretend she was scum! Well, fuck all of you! I'm gonna find her meself and you can't stop me!"

Sam wanted to slap her, but he had already done that once today and it hadn't made him feel any better then. Like Sam's younger brother Fred, Ruby's movements were quick, along with her temper. Her face, once so full of charm and sweetness, had changed. She looked spiteful and hateful, pursing her plump lips and narrowing her big, blue eyes. It wasn't a Vincent look but it was certainly her mother's expression. Sam bashed the table so hard the china jangled and Jack nearly left his own skin. Ruby stormed out of the room, stamping her feet as she headed back to her room.

*

Jack cleared away the plates and started cleaning the kitchen. He was in the middle in this family. He felt sorry for Ruby, but he also loved his dad, and could tell his father was protecting her. She was so strong-willed, believing, come what may, she would find Jesse. One thing was for sure, she'd be on her own. Jack shuddered at the thought of meeting her again. The memories of his mother were not exaggerated, nor were they illusions, but scarily vivid. The scar on the top of his leg gave him a permanent reminder.

He had only been four years old and Ruby three. It had been raining continually outside, and so they were playing hide and seek. With no toys or board games, they had to amuse themselves. The small run-down flat contained little furniture, and few places to hide, but they made the best of it. Jesse had dossed in her bed most of the day; this was a usual occurrence because she often entertained friends through the night, drinking and smoking. Jack didn't understand it all at four-years-old but now, at sixteen, he knew why his mother lived the way she did. It was the drugs and her so-called scag-head mates.

They were hungry that morning, more so than usual, because Jesse hadn't fed them the night before. Ruby tried to take her mind off her hunger pains by singing 'Itsy Bitsy Spider' as she ran around the flat. Jesse was hungover and the child's voice echoed around her head and each exaggerated lisp fuelled her annoyance. "Ruby, get in 'ere, you fucking little prat!" she croaked harshly, and Ruby stopped dead in her tracks. She hated her mother shouting.

Jesse shrieked again. "Ruby, I said get 'ere!"

Jack ran to Ruby's side and together they walked into their mother's room.

He scanned the room and saw his mother, half-naked, in the middle of the bed. There was sick on the floor. The rancid odour of the vomit, mixed with the smell from the overflowing ashtrays, made Jack gag. Their mother propped herself up. Ruby shook as Jesse curled her finger. "Get here, you little bitch!" she spat.

Jack hated his mother's spiteful expression; her hair was stuck up in all directions, her teeth were coated in a yellow film and her eyes looked a devilish red. Ruby stood rooted to the spot, fearing she would get hit, or worse.

"Sorry, Mummy, we will be quiet, I promise," said Jack in Ruby's defence. He was desperate for her not to set about his little sister.

Ruby stared at the floor, trying not to cry or wet herself.

Jesse slid her legs around and sat upright on the edge of her bed. She looked like a skeleton. Her sunken eyes made her mouth appear big. Jack smelt her sour breath from twenty inches away. He gazed at her feet, with the black, overgrown toenails, and then at her unshaven legs. Jesse reached forward with her long, thin arm and snatched Ruby. Then, with the other hand, she slapped her across the mouth. It was a hard slap, which would cause a grown woman to yell.

"Now then, what have I fucking told you? Keep your noise down. I'm trying to sleep!" She fell back on the bed.

Ruby, too afraid to cry loudly, held her throbbing mouth with her two little hands. Jack gave his mother an evil stare, wishing her dead. In that moment he knew that he hated her, and his blood ran cold when he thought of how Jesse systematically hurt Ruby.

He walked Ruby to the living room, with his arm around her shoulders, whispering that one day their daddy would come to get them.

Her tears fell with no sound, just silent sobbing. Unable to console her, Jack went in search of food. In the kitchen was a fridge full of mould because the door wouldn't shut tightly. He found nothing there to eat, only sour milk. All the lower cupboards, with no doors, were bare. Jack climbed onto the work surface to have a look in the top cupboard and, as he opened the cabinet door, he couldn't believe what he saw. There were cakes – about ten. He looked around, to check if his mother was there, but no, so he grabbed two and shut the door. He scrambled off the side and into the living room where Ruby sat, with her nightdress pulled over her knees, sucking her thumb. He showed her the cakes and she smiled. They hid behind the settee and ate them, hoping that their mother wouldn't find out what they were doing.

"I like these cakes," whispered Ruby as she tried to cram another piece between her swollen lips.

"Um, me too," said Jack.

They scoffed them fast, leaving no crumbs. Jack was still hungry, and thought about going back to the cupboard. He figured his mum wouldn't remember how many she had baked, so he climbed on the side again. As he went to open the cabinet door he swooned, but he held on until the dizziness passed. There seemed to be so many cakes. He grabbed as many as he could carry and rushed back to Ruby, who was hiding behind the sofa. She was smiling. They sat and ate more. "Mummy can make nice cakes," said Ruby. Jack nodded. He had never felt so ravenous. When they had finished the last morsel, Jack looked up at the opened cupboard door, but he couldn't seem to find the energy to get up to close it. He felt sleepy and dreamy.

Ruby lay on the floor but a wet patch appeared on her turquoise nightdress. She had wet herself. When he tried to wake her she didn't move. It was then he noticed her body twitching and that there was puke at the sides of her mouth. He couldn't understand why she couldn't open her eyes. In a dazed state, he attempted to pick her up but she was too heavy. He moved her onto her side and the vomit came out. His mum would be mad. Ruby always got a smack if she wet herself. Afraid that Jesse might hurt her again, he knew he must do something as Ruby was ill. The room spun and his sister's face turned a deathly grey.

"Mum!" he screamed – no answer. He waited.

"Mummy!" he cried louder.

"What now?" she shouted back.

Jack was unable to put his words together. His mind was jumbled. He shouted, "Mum! Help!"

Jesse was livid; she needed more sleep. The anger made her leap from her bed like a woman possessed. She grabbed a stiletto shoe and marched into the living room, where the children lay slumped behind the sofa, out of sight.

Her aggression gained momentum, thinking they were playing a game. She stormed into the kitchen to discover no kids, the cupboard door wide open and the cakes gone – just an empty, crumb-filled plate.

"Where are you? Get here right now!" Jesse hollered at the top of her voice.

Jack tried to get to his feet but they felt like mashed potato.

Jesse saw Jack behind the couch and, with her arm pulled back clutching the stiletto, she plunged the heel of the shoe into Jack's leg.

In a fit of rage, she pulled him from the floor and threw him onto the sofa, slapping him hard across the cheek. There was no expression on her face – just a cold and spiteful bottom jaw protruding, which caused her lips to tighten. He sensed the pain and saw the anger in his mother's eyes, but felt it was happening to someone else. She shouted in his face but he couldn't make out the jumbled words. The deep gash in his leg bled heavily, but in his confused state of mind he wasn't sure if it was real or not.

Jesse fled the room and Jack tried hard to focus. He still felt dizzy and sick but his little sister lay by the side of the sofa, looking as if she was dying. His fear so great, he crawled off the couch and sat by her side. Tears trickled down his throbbing cheeks as he touched her cold, clammy forehead.

"Ruby, wake up," he whispered, staring at her limp body.

It seemed as if he had sat there for hours, with his sister's head on his lap, still confused and worried for her. He could see better now and he looked down at his leg and saw the blood still oozing from the deep hole. Ruby was sick again and Jack wiped the hair away from her face. Although his mind was in complete turmoil, he knew he had to overcome his own suffering to protect her. She was all he had and he loved her. He whispered in her ear, pleading with her not to die.

A commotion outside startled him but through the muffled sound he recognised Gloria's voice. She was a Jamaican woman who lived in the end flat. As she appeared through the door she seemed huge. A big woman anyway, Jack saw her as enormous and yet, at this moment, he was so relieved by the sight of her.

Gloria's husband and older sons often sat with Jesse in the evening and smoked but Gloria always stayed in her own flat, keeping herself to herself.

She had met them a year before when she'd dropped a plastic bag and her fruit had rolled down the hill. The two children had chased the runaway apples and proudly handed them back to her. A pitiful sight they were; skinny, half-dressed and certainly too young to be outside unaccompanied. So, every chance Gloria got, she gave them a treat such as a doughnut or sausage rolls. Watching them tuck into a small helping of food made her heart ache and often, on the bitter cold days, she invited them in to warm themselves up.

They loved to go to Gloria's flat. It was cosy with carpets, cushions on the sofa and flowered curtains at the windows. They laughed at her deep, Jamaican accent and took comfort in her hugs. They only ever had cuddles from their father on a prison visit.

"Where are they?" Gloria's voice was deep. Jesse pointed to the sofa as if she had disclosed a rat's nest.

Jack saw Gloria's huge caramel arms reach forward, grab him from the floor, and cradle him. The warm, sweet breath on his face soothed him. She placed him on the sofa. Then she bent down and picked up Ruby, laying her next to him. She knelt down beside the couch and shouted orders at the people in the doorway.

"Jesse, get some blankets!" She glared at their mother, but she just looked unperturbed.

"Joseph, fetch water!" Joseph was her eldest son. He often hung around the flat, smoking and drinking. But right now, he didn't seem his usual self; his eyes were large and frightened.

Jesse left the room. She returned with a smelly cover, which most reasonable people would have thrown out. She was still undressed, in just a stained nightdress, with her breasts practically hanging out. Gloria looked at the faded, old rag which Jesse had tried to pass off as a blanket. She sucked her teeth in a typical Jamaican gesture of disdain.

"Joseph, get me some blankets from me bed and leave the water there," ordered Gloria, with her thick Caribbean accent. Joseph had put the cup with no handle on the floor. Again, Gloria tutted. She lifted Jack's head and made him drink. "Come on now, me precious child, sip a little for Aunty Gloria." Her voice was like a song. Each word had a gentle harmony. Next, she tried to sit Ruby up. She was gradually coming around – to the relief of Jack, who had thought she was dying.

She covered them in the blanket which Joseph presented, and encouraged them to drink more.

Gloria had trained as a nurse back in Jamaica. She checked the children over, including their pulse. Luckily, they would be okay.

As she tucked them in the blanket, she saw the blood and quickly she searched for a cut. There, like a black hole, she found the wound at the top of Jack's leg.

"Oh my God! How did this happen?" Her voice had notched up a few decibels.

Jesse shrugged her shoulders, "I don't know. I guess he fell onto something when he climbed up to steal me dope cakes."

Gloria jumped up and walked towards Jesse, who was backing away.

"All right, Glor, it wasn't me, I didn't fucking do it."

"You don't deserve these little children. If I see you harm them again, I'll call the police meself and don't think, me girl, I won't!"

Gloria returned to Ruby and Jack, kissing their foreheads. She scooped them in her arms and walked out of the flat, followed by Jesse, who was in a panic. If she called the police or social services then her weekly money would be gone. Those kids were her earner.

"Where are you taking me babies? I can look after them here!" cried Jesse.

Gloria pushed past Jesse and carried on walking with Joseph and her husband, Daniel. They knew, only too well, that when Gloria was on a mission you didn't get in her way. Joseph opened the front door and she stepped sideways into the hallway, still clutching both children. She took them to her bedroom and laid them on her bed. There were no complaints. Jack felt safe with Gloria and he smiled at her, although tears streamed down his white cheeks.

"There you go, me little ray of sunshine. Aunty Gloria's going to make you feel better." The pain was excruciating, because Jack was slowly coming around from the effects of cannabis, making it all the more real. Gloria reached for the phone beside her bed and called her best friend, Massie, a nurse at the Hackney and Homerton.

"Massie, I need a favour." Never before had she asked for help but, in her younger days, she was everyone's angel and Massie owed her a few good deeds.

"I need you to have a look at a little boy. He has a nasty cut on his leg and he is hurting bad."

Massie was leaving work just as Gloria had called.

"Does it need stitching?" replied another Jamaican accent down the phone.

Gloria looked at Jack, hoping he couldn't hear.

"Yes, it does, and some antibiotics. Massie, he is only four or five years old, and he is in a lot of pain."

"I'm on me way, so just keep the child warm and put a clean cloth over the wound."

"Thank you, Massie."

Jack was in shock. The cannabis cakes had had a serious effect on him and his blood pressure had dropped. The sight of all the blood and the gaping hole in his leg was too much for him to handle. He passed out. Gloria pulled him onto her lap and rocked him. Jesse stood in the doorway and stared. There was fear and panic written on her face. Gloria misjudged the look, assuming it was compassion for her children. Jesse had to keep the children with her. If the Vincents were ever to get wind of this then her weekly poke would be history.

Gloria's face softened. "Now, don't you worry, me friend is on her way, and she will get the babies well."

Jesse burst into tears and Daniel put his arm around her shoulder.

She fooled everyone with her crocodile tears. Inside, she was angry with the kids. They had eaten the cakes she had saved for the weekend, and now they were making a big fuss, leaving her looking the bad guy.

When Massie arrived, still in her nurse's uniform, Daniel showed her to the bedroom. Massie looked so much like Gloria they could almost have been sisters. But Massie had braids and wore purple lipstick, whereas Gloria had short hair and didn't wear makeup. Difficult to tell their age; they could have been thirty or fifty.

She marched past Jesse and practically pushed her out of the way.

Ruby sat up and the colour returned to her cheeks. Massie concentrated on Jack, who was pale and semi-conscious.

She realised, straight away, his condition was more than a cut.

"Gloria, what is wrong with this child?"

Not one for lying, she answered, "He has eaten cannabis cakes."

Massie turned to face Jesse. "If Gloria wasn't a friend of mine, I would have called social services. My God! How can this happen?"

Jesse wanted to have a go back but thought better of it.

"Look, it wasn't my fault. I turned me back for a few minutes and he climbed up to me top cupboard and ate the dope cakes." Jesse was worried now.

"The state of these little mites, they look like they have never had a decent meal in their tiny bellies. No wonder they ate your precious dope cakes. Now get out of the room and let me fix them up."

Jesse didn't argue. She sat in Gloria's living room with Joseph and Daniel.

"Wanna fag, Jess?" Joseph offered his packet of Marlborough. Jesse snatched one and sucked madly on it.

Gloria and Massie stitched Jack's leg and got his blood pressure back to normal without a fuss.

The two Jamaican women were now in the doorway, away from the children's earshot.

"You know, Gloria, these children are used to abuse. I have just stitched his wound with the least amount of anaesthetic and he didn't flinch. Please, my friend, keep an eye on them because they need help."

Ruby fell asleep again, sucking her thumb, but Jack sat upright, now awake. Massie had given him a painkiller and bandaged the gruesome wound, which helped him to feel much better. In his little mind, he was mended.

"Aunty Gloria, can we stay with you tonight?" whispered Jack.

He knew how his mother would react to all the commotion and he hoped that, by the time tomorrow came, she would have calmed down and forgiven them for causing so much trouble. He wondered if other mummies were like his. Gloria seemed a nice mummy. He wished she was his, with her soft hugs and gentle kisses, and the way she bent down to tickle their cheeks or give them a surprise ice pop or chocolate curly wurly. Just how a nice mummy should be.

"Me little angels, you can stay with Aunty Gloria for the whole week, and you can go back to your mummy when you're better." Again, she kissed them both on the top of their heads. Ruby heard those words in a sleepy state and smiled. She loved the smell of the clean bedroom and the bright, pretty colours. The children giggled at each other. They knew they would be warm, safe and comfortable, if only for a week. Yet a week in their lifetime seemed forever.

Massie had suggested that Gloria feed the children as much as possible, because for sure they were malnourished. Gloria was in her element. She loved to fatten anyone and had tried for years to put weight on her very thin husband and four sons. Whilst they remained slim she, on the other hand, got bigger. Fried chicken with rice and peas was their main diet but, no matter how much they ate, their weight remained the same.

The following week was a holiday for Jack and Ruby. Gloria fed them morning, noon and night, with cakes and biscuits in between each meal. They watched cartoons on the television and drank milkshakes through coloured straws. At the end of the week, Jesse arrived to take them home, full of smiles and sweet words – but it was all an act. Gloria had, in the meantime, visited her flat every day to check it was clean and tidy, and stocked up with food for when the children returned home. Jesse did as Gloria ordered. She knew that if her kids went into care she was well and truly fucked.

A deal was agreed on. If she kept her end of the bargain, Gloria wouldn't turn the children over to social services.

Jack glared at his mother. He despised her and she knew it. Even though his leg was better there would always be a scar, and a haunting memory of that terrifying day. He would never, ever forgive her for her cruelty. The thought that one day his father would come and rescue them kept him going and gave him hope still for them both. He also had another thought – he would grow up and murder her while she slept.

Chapter Five

Sam decided not to mention the conversation which had taken place at the dinner table to his sister. He had so many mixed emotions. His daughter was interested in meeting her mother, but he wanted to save her a real heartache because he knew what her mother was – a selfish junkie. Francesca had given his children everything they could want, including an abundance of love. She had rescued both Jack and Ruby from Jesse's clutches when their little lives were so bleak and sad. He recalled their faces when he'd told them they never had to go back to her again. They had clung to him so tightly and made him promise. He knew then that his two children had suffered in more ways than he'd ever imagined. He'd seen the scars and he'd heard some of the stories but had assumed there was more than they'd cared to say.

Jack came into the living room with a mug of tea for his father. Sam admired the way his son looked. He had a man's body, big and strong, with olive skin, blue eyes, and long, black eyelashes. He was the image of Sam's youngest brother, Fred. He was placid, unlike his live-wire sister, Ruby. A sensible lad. A son to be so proud of.

"'Ere you go, Dad, get your laughing gear around that," Jack giggled.

"You're a good boy," said Sam.

"Not really, Dad. I made it to put you in a good mood, before I ask you for a fiver."

Sam laughed.

"I want to talk to you, Jack, about your mother."

Jack put down his tea and his expression turned sour. "What mother? I don't have one, and I don't want one, thanks!"

"I know you don't want to see her, but you heard your sister, she does." Sam sipped his hot tea, hoping that Jack would help him with the whole situation.

"Well, what do you want me to say, Dad? I hate her! If only our Ruby remembered the abuse, then she would stay well clear!"

"It might do her good to see what a cunt she is. Then, she may change her tune and snap out of her hard-arse attitude."

Jack's eyes widened. "Dad, you can't be serious? The woman's a nutcase. Fucking hell, even I'm scared of her, and I'm sixteen and a champion boxer!"

Sam felt his stomach churn. Jesse must have been a cruel woman for his strapping lad to still fear her, all these years later.

"Well, if it's not arranged properly, Ruby will go by herself, and God knows what she may walk into."

Jack didn't answer. He was still unsure about it all. But he had noticed his father looked bedraggled these last few weeks and assumed that it was his sister's behaviour dragging him down.

Ruby stomped down the stairs, with her bag slung over her shoulder and her high-heeled boots on. As she went to go out the door, Sam shouted, "Come here, Ruby, please!"

She marched into the living room. "What now?"

"Where are you going?" Sam asked, with his voice lowered.

"Out!" She stood with her hands on her hips.

"Don't push it, Sunshine. I asked where you are going. If you won't tell me, then you ain't going out!" Sam wanted to shake his daughter.

"I told you already, I'm going to find me mother." She folded her arms now, curled her lip and glared at her father as if he was a piece of shit.

"And how do you know where to find her?"

Ruby rolled her eyes. "I ain't thick. I'm gonna go to the estate and ask."

"Don't be fucking ridiculous, Ruby!" Sam got up from his seat and grabbed her by the arm. She tried to shrug him off. "Sit down, Ruby!" he demanded.

"Oh, for God's sake, let her go – then, maybe, she will find out for herself!" piped up Jack, fed up with his sister's carryings-on. Both Ruby and Sam were surprised at his outburst. Jack stood up and walked to within two inches of her face. "If you really think our mother is so special, then go and find her. But, just remember one thing. I'm older than you, and I didn't imagine she was a fucking no-good scumbag. I remember it only too well. I still have the fucking scars to prove it!" he screamed.

Ruby stared defiantly, leaving Jack fuming. He grabbed her by the back of her jacket and dragged her to the front door, so angry and disappointed with his sister. Sam watched. She needed a firm hand and this was the first time he had witnessed Jack give it to her. She didn't struggle as he opened the door and pushed her out.

"Now, find your precious muvver and, when you do come back, I want an apology for calling me a liar!"

Ruby straightened her jacket and marched off along the drive.

Sam remained tight lipped as Jack stormed back into the living room.

"Come here, son, and sit yourself down. I'll go after her." As he slipped his feet into his Italian leather shoes, Jack snapped at him. "No, Dad, fuck her, the little bitch! Leave her to look for her mother and, when she finds her, she will be back, with her tail between her legs!"

Sam wanted to listen to his son but she was still only fifteen and it was close to nightfall. She would have to get a train to London and then walk around the estate in the dark – alone.

"No, I'm gonna bring her home and then, tomorrow, I'll take her to her mother's. It's late, and I don't want anything bad happening to her."

Jack sighed. His father was right. "Okay, Dad, but how do you know where she lives?"

Sam flicked the side of his nose, telling him to mind his own business.

He found Ruby, before she jumped on a train, and explained he would drop her off tomorrow. She agreed and spent the rest of the evening in her room. Jack went back to the gym; he needed a way to keep his anger under control. Ruby was excited. However, she had imagined meeting her mother alone, not holding her father's hand.

At seven o'clock, the sun shone through her pink voile curtains, casting rainbows around the room. The smell of bacon and eggs wafted up the stairs. Yesterday's events must be forgotten, she thought, since her father was singing along to music blaring from the kitchen radio.

She smiled to herself. It was going to be such a memorable day, and now she had her dad's blessing to find her mum. She took her time getting ready. Her mum had to be impressed. It was important she looked a nice person, whatever that was. Her dad was always moaning about the layers of makeup she wore, and the lack of covering around her stomach, so she guessed it would be more appropriate to dress modestly, with just a hint of blusher and a dusting of mascara.

"Well, look at you, Ruby, you look like an angel. I'm glad you're dressed respectably for a change," said Sam, with a big smile across his face.

Ruby looked him up and down, wondering why, on a Monday morning, her father was wearing a suit. Surely, after slating her mother, he wasn't planning on impressing her now.

"So, Dad, what's with the whistle? In court, are ya?"

Sam laughed at his daughter's lack of charm.

"No, babes, we are off to your school. I forgot we have a meeting there this morning. Get this down your neck while I clean me teeth."

Ruby stared at her fried breakfast with no appetite. How could he be so cruel? He knew how much she wanted to meet her mum and yet the whole time he had made plans for her to go to school.

When Sam returned from the bathroom Ruby had gone. He rushed to open the door but there was no sight of her. He couldn't believe she had just left with no word. She must have thought he had changed his mind about taking her to Kidbrooke. He hadn't, of course, since he had always been a man of his word. He had intended to drive her to school, meet with the headmistress, and then take her to the estate and show her where her mother lived. He called her mobile but it was switched off.

As she stepped on to the train at Sevenoaks, she was about to start a fresh chapter in her life. The train stopped at the station right next to the estate. The moment Ruby walked onto the platform, her heart pounded. This was it. This was the new beginning. She might even move here, especially if her mum wanted her to. Maybe it would be a good idea to get to know her and rekindle a long-lost relationship.

*

Ruby was appalled by the half-derelict concrete mess called Kidbrooke. She walked gingerly along the road which split the estate into two halves. Each block of flats had the doors and window frames painted a primary colour. Her heart sank. It was so ugly. There were blocks with boarded-up windows, and signs stating a redevelopment programme was taking place were in evidence everywhere. The whole estate was decorated with random graffiti, grey nets blew in the windows from smashed panes, and passers-by walked with their heads low and their hands in their pockets. This was a far cry from the streets in Sevenoaks. She hoped that when she turned a corner the view would be more civilised. It wasn't – only sights of deprivation caught the eye, everywhere she gazed.

She passed a small park with two swings and saw a child playing with a skateboard bigger than him. An overwhelming sense of familiarity swept over her. She walked over to the small playground and tried to absorb the sense – it might help her remember where she'd lived. The little boy came over to her and asked if she could push him on the swing. He looked sweet – with caramel skin and an enormous afro. Ruby laughed and agreed. She tried to remember more as she pushed the child. She was so engrossed that she didn't notice the boy's minder head her way.

"'Ere, what are you doing with me boy?" The voice was a deep Jamaican and partially put on. Ruby stopped and spun around.

"Hey, it's all right," he laughed at her reaction. "I was just pulling your leg. Me name's Jacob."

As he sat on the other swing he looked Ruby up and down, puffing on his joint. He offered her a go.

"It's good gear!"

She shook her head.

"You don't smoke, no?" he said, his accent now South East London.

Ruby didn't want to come across as a childish school girl.

"Yeah, I do, but I've got business today."

She looked Jacob over. He was light-skinned, had unusual green eyes, his hair was cane rolled, and he wore the latest Nike tracksuit.

"So, you're not from here, are you?" he asked.

"I might be," replied Ruby. She wanted to act hard and yet she also knew how to flirt.

"I know you're not, because I'd have your number by now."

Suddenly, the grey, dull depressing estate seemed exciting and fun. The foul odour of piss had gone and the graffiti looked a work of art.

"I've come to see me mum."

Jacob nodded. "So where does she live then?"

Ruby shrugged her shoulders. The little boy hopped off the swing and tried to ride his skateboard.

"I see. You don't want to tell me!"

"No, it's not that. She lives here on this estate, but I don't have an address."

Jacob laughed. "I didn't think you was from here, you know." He stood up and held out his hand. "Me name's Jacob." He kissed her cheek.

Ruby lapped up the attention.

"I'm Ruby," she blushed, as she stared into his green eyes. "Who's the little boy then?" she giggled, knowing only too well he couldn't be his. He was too young.

"Me sister's," he nodded. "So, how are you gonna find your mum? This is one ginormous, big estate, and I don't know everyone. Nearly everyone, but not everyone."

Jacob clocked Ruby's clothes and the bling around her neck. She was loaded. Hard to imagine who her mother could be.

"What's her name?"

Ruby, pleased he cared enough to want to help, replied, "Well, her first name's Jesse, and I think her second name's Right."

Jacob screwed his face up and frowned. Knowing exactly who Jesse was, he found it difficult to believe that Ruby was related in any way to her.

"Are you sure someone ain't sent you here on a wind-up? I mean, look at you, babe, you're clean and fresh. You don't belong 'ere!"

Jacob was a rogue. He dealt puff, sold counterfeit Rolexes, and shagged as many women as fell for his charms, but he wasn't the worst kind of crook when compared to other lads his age who lived there. He felt for this young girl. She had come from a decent home, so why would she want to meet Jesse?

"Jacob, I haven't seen my mum in twelve years, and now I want to see her. If you know where she lives, please tell me." She put on her sweetest voice. It was the voice which usually got her what she wanted, time and time again. Even Jacob was sucked in.

"Listen, sweetheart, I don't know you, but you seem a nice person and, take it from me, babes, you don't belong here."

Ruby had a temper, and, if she didn't get her own way, she could lose it. She was sick of people telling her what was good for her – Jack, Francesca, her father, and now a stranger.

"Fucking 'ell, mate, I don't need to be told where I belong. I just want to find her. Now, do you know, or not?"

Shocked by the change in Ruby's tone and look on her face, he recognised that expression and, sure enough, she was definitely Jesse's daughter.

He pointed to a row of flats across from the park.

With a dull tone in his voice, he said, "She lives in number thirty-one."

Ruby walked away, without another word.

He had initially felt sorry for her because he knew Jesse only too well. So did most of the estate but the little rich kid had that same malicious spite he had seen on Jesse's face and his view had now changed. She could get on with it. It was a shame, though, because she was a good-looking girl, with dimples and thick, wavy dark hair. Her eyes – grey-blue, with lots of eyelashes – had captivated him. He sat on the swing and rolled another joint, reflecting on the girl.

*

Ruby stood at the front door of her mother's flat. Her mouth was dry and her stomach churned. This was it; the moment had arrived! The door had been partially boarded. The pane of glass had wire running through it, with cracks everywhere, and a hole where the letter box should be.

She looked up to the end of the row of flats and remembered running with Jack up and down the cold stone steps. Her memory still vague, she recalled a big woman who gave her curly wurlys – or was it only a dream?

After taking a deep breath, she banged on the door. An eerie groan came from inside the flat. Ruby waited.

"Who is it?" Jesse shouted in a gruff voice.

Ruby assumed whoever was shouting must have the flu.

"I said, who is it?" Jesse stood in the hallway, waiting for an answer before she opened the door. No one came knocking this early – unless it was the Ole Bill.

There was no gear in the house so she didn't give a shit.

Ruby pondered over what to say: 'It's me, Mum,' or 'It's Ruby Vincent'. She shuffled from foot to foot.

Jesse was nursing toothache and a split lip. Her punter had cracked her one on the side of her head, which had left her in agony, so she wasn't in the mood for silly games.

"I'm looking for Jesse, err, Jesse Right!" shouted Ruby through the hole in the door, hoping the voice shouting back wasn't her mother's.

"Well, you fucking found her. Now what do ya want? Make it quick, I'm busy," Jesse shouted, assuming it was a teenager from the estate, trying to score draw.

"Can I come in?"

Jesse was looking in the hallway mirror at her swollen cheek. *How the hell am I going to earn any money tonight with a face like a balloon?* she asked herself. Still wearing the long T-shirt she wore to bed, she pulled open the door.

Ruby stepped back in bewilderment. She didn't recognise the haggard woman standing, half-naked, in the doorway. Her face was puffy, half her teeth were missing, and the skin on her neck was wrinkled. She looked so old. Her hair was thin and almost bald in parts.

The smell of drains and fags hit Ruby and she took another step back.

"I'm Jesse. Now, what do you want?" She leaned on the doorframe with no pride at all. The T-shirt was see-through, leaving nothing to the imagination. Ruby was staring in disbelief. There was no way this wretched-looking woman, stinking of all sorts, could be her mother.

"I ain't got all day, girl, what the fuck do you want?" Her voice was croaky, like an old man's. Ruby wanted to turn away and run, but she didn't.

"I'm Ruby," she said in her sweetest tone, hoping that the angry expression on her mother's face would soften and she'd invite her in.

Jesse shrugged. "Is that supposed to mean something to me?" Her eyes were cold and hard.

"It's me, Mum. Ruby!" she said.

Jesse, sizing her up, spotted the jewellery around her neck and the designer handbag. There, before her, stood her meal ticket. She had to put on an Oscar-winning performance to pretend she had any feelings for her daughter.

"Oh, my Ruby, is that really you?" Her voice softened. She watched to see the girl's face. Was she going to buy it?

Jesse flung her arms around Ruby's neck. "My baby girl's come home!" The acting was over the top.

Her mother's bony arms almost crushed her. The reek of sweat and whisky made Ruby gag.

The vision of her mother in a Laura Ashley smock dress, and the perfume of lavender or sweet peas, quickly diminished – or had that just been an illusion?

"Come in. The flat's untidy, but I wasn't expecting any visitors."

Ruby shrugged. "It's all right, you should see the state of my house." She was trying to make her mother feel more comfortable but Jesse thought otherwise as, dressed like fucking royalty and covered in diamonds, how could her daughter possibly be living in a shit-hole? Never mind, one day she would have the same. Besides, the Vincents owed her.

She was right. The flat was a shit-pit if ever Ruby had seen one. But she was sure she had remembered coloured curtains and cushions with flowers. The smell was bad enough and it was evident why. The carpet was sticky and the heavily stained couch was devoid of proper covers, with an old bed sheet flung over the back. In the corner of the living room there was a table covered with pizza boxes and chip wrappers. Beside the sofa, overflowing ashtrays and beer cans added to the mess. The curtain was grey, not fitted properly, and the window had a crack across it. Ruby cringed as Jesse invited her to take a seat.

"Let me get you a drink," offered Jesse as she hurried into the kitchen.

Ruby was heartbroken. This wasn't the vision she'd had at all. Closing her eyes, she tried to remember how her mother was back then, but it was blank. She didn't recognise the flat inside but she recalled the outside and the park. Perhaps this wasn't her mum. Jesse returned with a mug of tea. As Ruby peered into it, she saw white blobs of sour milk floating on the top, which turned her stomach over.

She had the urge to be sick. She breathed deeply and held it back.

"How's Jack? Is he all right?"

Ruby nodded. She concluded then that this vile woman was her mother.

"Hey, I know! Let me get dressed and we will go for a coffee. How about that? And then we can catch up." Jesse was desperate to win her daughter over and she could tell, by the look on her face, that the flat disgusted her. Jesse wondered how long she could keep the pretence up. It was hard not to jump off the chair and punch her in the mouth. She had a hatred for her kids which was burning away, day by day.

"Does your dad know where you are?" asked Jesse, as she stood up.

Ruby nodded. She thought about how he was a good dad and she couldn't imagine him living with this woman. She was so rough-looking. He was smart, clean, and handsome for a dad. In fact, he looked so young that her friends fancied him – which she found gross. But Jesse was the complete opposite. She seemed older than her grandmother.

"What happened to your face?" asked Ruby.

Jesse needed to suck Ruby in, one way or another. "Oh, well, I get these dizzy spells. The doctors think it might be a brain tumour, as I fell over and smashed me mouth. Listen, I don't want you to be worrying about it now. You've found me, and we are gonna have a good time." Jesse forced her eyes to water.

Ruby changed her opinion of Jesse. That's why she looked so thin and raggedy. It was the brain tumour. In her naivety, or longing to find an explanation for her mother's sorry state, she accepted the story.

Jesse returned to the living room, wearing a velour tracksuit. Her hair had been pulled back into a pony tail and she had on a pair of sunglasses. They were perched on her bony nose to hide the brown rings, but they did little to improve her appearance.

"Let's go then!" Jesse grabbed the keys off the table, along with a packet of fags, and they left the flat, much to the relief of Ruby, who was nauseous and eager to leave.

As she slammed the door shut, her neighbour, Pat, a huge man, with two pit bulls, who was walking up the path, shouted, "'Eh, Jesse, what's up with you? Did you shit the bed?" He laughed.

"Get lost!" she shouted back, in obvious annoyance.

"Who's your friend?"

"She's me daughter, Ruby." Jesse had now put her arm around Ruby's shoulders.

Pat looked at Ruby and laughed. He didn't believe it for a minute.

"Oh, yeah, sure. Anyway, Jesse, all right tonight for a draw?"

She hurried past him, nodding, as she tried to get Ruby out of earshot before he said any more – and gave her secrets away.

The estate looked gloomy again. Clouds hung heavy and that was how Ruby felt too. As they walked towards the café, centred in the middle of the estate, Jesse tried to be friendly. "You aren't 'arf pretty, Ruby. I am so proud of you!"

She smiled sweetly but felt oddly uncomfortable that an adult, her mother, was beneath her. She had hoped instantly to form a bond but there was nothing.

"Ya know, you look just like me when I was your age." Jesse was trying hard but she could sense the awkwardness.

Ruby cringed again, praying that this was some kind of joke, as there was absolutely no resemblance whatsoever.

*

The café was cleaner than the flat but still grotty-looking. Ruby slid along the red plastic seat. It was meant to replicate an American diner.

Jesse sat opposite. "Now then, honey, what do ya fancy? How about a nice bacon sandwich and a cup of coffee?"

Ruby didn't feel hungry – she was still in shock – but agreed anyway.

"I can't tell ya how pleased I am ya came to find me. I was sure you would one day, ya know, when you was ready." Jesse was squeezing Ruby's hand. This wasn't how it was supposed to be. She stared at her mother's fingers and felt so much shame. The nails were bitten to the quick with tiny scabs and, to make matters worse, they were filthy. She wasn't sure now if she wanted to hear her mother's side of the story. Could she even handle this kind of poverty? She had a lovely house, with beautiful things, and she could never imagine living with her mother for one single day. Ruby's lifestyle was a million miles away from this and she had taken it for granted, every bit of it.

The coffee and bacon sandwiches arrived and, despite Jesse's sore mouth, she tucked into them as if she had never eaten before. Ruby broke off a small piece and popped it into her mouth, but she didn't like it. She saw the fat swirl around, mixed with the soggy bread, and couldn't eat any more. The coffee was bitter but she drank it to wash away the remnants of the bacon.

"So how's your dad and your Aunty Francesca?" It grieved her to ask but she needed to stay calm and pretend she cared.

"Yeah, Dad's got his own nightclub, called *Sam's Palace,* and Fran lives in the States with Uncle Sergio." She said it so matter of fact.

Jesse knew Sam had his own club and was fully aware that the Vincents were minted. "Did they treat you well, babe? Was you happy?" Jesse guessed she was just by her appearance.

"Yeah, but it would have been better if you had been there." Ruby couldn't believe she had said that because the vision she had had of growing up of her mother, sadly, wasn't at all accurate. She realised that now and she felt sorry for her. This pathetic waif of a woman was stirring feelings of guilt.

"They must have looked after you well, babe, you look beautiful." She stroked her daughter's face. Ruby didn't want her mother touching her.

As Jesse picked up her cup of coffee, her hand shook and she nearly spilled its contents.

"Why are you shaking like that?" asked Ruby.

Jesse grabbed this opportunity to work on the sympathy vote. "Oh yeah, that's the brain tumour. It makes me shake." She looked down.

"But I thought you said the doctor only thinks you have a brain tumour. It could be something else!"

Jesse was gritting her teeth, *cocky little madam.* "I didn't want to tell you, really, but I have brain cancer and the doctors are not sure how long I have to live." She tried desperately to force out a tear. "So, it's so special to me that you came back into my life, Ruby." At that point she felt sorry for herself, believing in her own bullshit, and the tears came – full-force. Ruby panicked. She wasn't used to seeing adults crying. Her family had always been strong and in control. Even her Uncle Joe, who was the daft one, she had never seen in an emotional state.

"Don't cry, Mum, I'll help you." She wasn't sure how, but she was stronger than her mother.

Jesse was excited. Now she had her daughter right where she wanted her, she would milk it for every last penny.

"Oh, sweetheart. You're such a lovely girl, but there ain't much you can do. There ain't much anyone can do, except one of those special surgeons abroad. Only the rich and famous get that kind of treatment. All I want is me girl around, and then I'll be the happiest mum in the world." Jesse didn't mention Jack. She knew he hated her. The disdain on his face, the day he came home from Gloria's, had said it all. Ruby's mind was working overtime. If her mother needed a lifesaving operation, then, with a little persuasion, she could get her aunt, who was a millionaire, to organise it. She kept that thought to herself.

"Now then, enough about me. Tell me about you. Have you got yourself a nice fella?" asked Jesse, now she was done with the tears. Most mothers in her situation would ask about school and hobbies, not act like a mate.

"Yeah, one or two, but no one special," Ruby laughed.

"That's my girl, keep them on the go. I can see 'em drooling over you. Like me, at your age. Always had two on the go, too much for any one fella. Just you make sure, babe, you ain't the one doing the chasing."

Ruby giggled. She guessed what Jesse meant but it was strange to talk about relationships. She was only fifteen.

"So, what music do you like?"

"Garage, house and R and B. That kinda stuff."

"Yeah, me too," replied Jesse, much to Ruby's surprise.

They sat for hours talking about boys, parties, the things that Ruby chatted over with her best mate – she even admitted she smoked weed. She then decided that this was what was missing in her life. This was what having a mum was all about.

"You don't mind, then, that I've smoked pot?" asked Ruby.

"Cor blimey, Ruby, I won't condemn you for a little fun. I was young once meself. Weed don't hurt, as long as you don't get on heroin. And, besides all that, look at you. You're grown-up for your age, and you know what you're doing, a sensible girl like you. No, I'm not worried, I trust you." Jesse was saying the right words to get her daughter on her side. She planned to become her friend and just let her do what she wanted. That was the one thing she had over Sam. She could allow Ruby to let her hair down because, in reality, she didn't give a shit. If Ruby ended up on crack cocaine, became a prostitute, or even ended up dead, she didn't care, as long as she got what was owed to her.

The café owner, a greasy-looking Turkish man called Farez, came over to the table with the bill. "Listen, Jesse, your tab has now gone over the limit. I'll come around tonight, and you can settle it then!" His voice wasn't loud, just firm.

Jesse hoped he wouldn't say any more. She nodded and he left.

They headed back to the flat. Ruby decided she should go home. It was getting late and she had a lot to think about.

"Mum, you don't mind if I don't come in, do you? Only, Dad will worry if I'm late." She felt guilty but the need to get away was greater.

The sky was now dramatic. The clouds were heavy and black.

"Ruby, my babe, please, please, promise me you will come back. I can fix your room up and make it really nice." She looked down at the floor and attempted the fake tears again. "You don't know how happy you have made me today. It was like fate or something. I mean, me being ill, and you turning up, just when I needed ya." A tear fell, and Jesse wondered if she was still believable. She hugged Ruby again, who this time returned the gesture, although it was awkward and embarrassing.

"Yes, Mum, I will come back!" She gave her mum a huge smile which exaggerated her deep dimples.

"When, babe?" Her voice was pleading.

"Two days or so." She walked off, waving, with Jesse nodding furiously as she hoped and prayed she had sucked Ruby in enough for her to return.

Suddenly, the heavens opened and Ruby ran towards the station. The estate looked dark and haunting. Some of the flats were empty and the wind howled through the broken windows. The rain made a racket as it crashed onto the overflowing steel dustbins.

*

Her home was so much more inviting. The grand Victorian lamps lined the drive to her front door and, in the leaded light window, there was a golden glow from the tiffany lamp which sat on the hallway table. Ruby paused for a second before she put the key in the lock. She stood still, wet from the downpour. So many thoughts had gone through her mind before she had reached home. Guilty feelings were coming at her from every angle: running away from her father that morning, being so cold towards her brother who, after all, was so kind to her, and, most of all, not feeling the way she should about her own mother.

Jack opened the door, before she had a chance to, and stepped back. He looked her up and down and, although he had anger on his face, she could tell he was relieved to see her, and he was. The worry of her going missing, assuming she had gone to Jesse's, made him fret and anxious.

"Get inside. Dad's driving around looking for you. Your phone's switched off, and you didn't even say where you were going!" Jack was red in the face and expected his sister to give a mouthful back but, instead, she half-smiled and apologised.

"Well, Ruby, where did you fuck-off to then?"

"You know where I went. I told you and Dad yesterday where I was going" Her voice was calm and she looked tired.

"Are *you* all right?" He emphasised the word 'you'. He didn't care about his mother, just as long as his sister was okay and safe back home.

"Yeah, I'm fine, Jack, apart from getting soaked and suffering a pounding headache."

70

Jack let her go upstairs to her bedroom. He could see she wasn't up to talking and he wasn't going to push her.

The full beam lights from Sam's Jaguar shone through the living room window as Jack picked up the phone to call him. Sam rushed in, shouting, "Jack, is she back yet?" There was panic in his voice. The evening was drawing in and it was cold and dark. He knew the estate and had visions of Ruby wandering aimlessly around the hell-hole.

"Yes, Dad."

Sam ran into the living room, expecting his daughter to be perched on a chair, ready to be lippy, but there was only Jack.

"She's up in her room. Looks like she got caught in the rain," said Jack softly. Sam went to go after her.

"No, Dad, leave her."

He looked puzzled. "What's going on, son?"

"I think she's seen her, but she's quiet. She doesn't want to talk about it."

Sam nodded. There had always been a special bond between Jack and Ruby. They had an exceptional understanding of each other and for a long time after Sam's release from prison – when they had lived with Francesca – he'd felt an outsider to them both. They loved him, and they showed they did every day but, if either of them were sick, they would tell each other first. They'd confide in each other and had even shared the same room until they were teenagers. He had understood and accepted it. So, taking Jack's advice with regard to Ruby wasn't always an odd thing.

Sam opened the brandy bottle and downed a large glass. His mouth was dry from worry and his head ached from the traffic. He had driven to the estate himself and looked for Ruby. The sights he had seen had worried him even more; there were the dealers, half-hidden in the doorways of the flats, and then he had seen a gang of teenagers, hanging around in the park, even though it was chucking it down. When he had pulled over to ask a young woman directions, he'd been surprised to find she was a street girl touting for business. Of course he was used to seeing this, as he owned a London nightclub, but he was taken aback to see it on a council estate. He imagined his daughter being dragged into the alleyways and beaten up, mugged – or worse, raped. The relief was enormous in the knowledge that his naive, little girl was here, safe in her bedroom.

Thoughts had crossed his mind that maybe Jesse had changed her ways and sorted herself out. In which case, Ruby might have met with a woman she could have looked up to. He snapped the idea out of his head. It wasn't only his sister who kept an ear to the ground. He had too. It was common knowledge Jesse was still on drugs, and he'd also heard she was selling her body for money. He believed that after meeting her mother, Ruby would be back with her tail between her legs. His daughter detested everything that looked 'gross', as she would put it. She might have been an untidy mare at times, especially lately, but she couldn't handle filth. Any programmes on the TV which showed vulgarity, she switched off. Ruby was at the age where appearances were a major factor in her life and she would make comments like 'err, minging' or 'get a life'. Even Jack thought she was too hard, especially when Ruby was rude to her friends and to one in particular, called Heidi. A very pretty girl, she was cursed with the dreaded spot outbreak, and could be clear one day and covered the next. When she was smothered, Ruby wouldn't sit next to her at lunch time. She said it put her off her food.

Sam sat heavily on the sofa and chortled to himself. Ruby must have had a shock when she walked around that estate. What a shit-hole. If Jesse was half as bad as everyone said she was, his daughter would have spun on her heels and legged it home. He laughed out loud.

"What's so funny, Dad?" asked Jack, who had just got off the phone from ordering a curry takeaway.

"Just imagine the look on Ruby's face when she first set eyes on Jesse. She must have nearly puked, you know what she's like." He was doubled over laughing now and Jack was joining in. It was the relief she was home that heightened their mood.

Sam imitated his daughter's voice. "'Err, me muvver's a minger.'"

Both men were hysterical when Ruby entered the room.

"What you laughing at?" She hadn't heard what they had been saying, just the chuckling. They stopped instantly. Sam ignored her question and got up to greet his daughter. He hugged her and she hugged him back. That didn't feel strange. She had a natural affection for her dad. She loved him very much. With her mother it was different. Perhaps she was expecting too much too soon. Besides, it had only been their first meeting. She had gone over the day's events on the way home on the train and concluded it was good to have a mum you could talk openly with about anything; subjects she could never talk with her father about, such as sex, fights, and smoking puff. Her mother understood her way more than her dad did. She didn't mind talking about boyfriends – and she felt more at ease discussing the more taboo areas, such as the times when she would enjoy a spliff or try ecstasy with her mates. Her mother had shown interest when she spoke of her triumphant fighting victories, and she'd enjoyed the pat on the back for it. It was always Jack who got the fuss when he had won his fights. Fair enough, they were in the ring, but her dad and uncles always gave her a hard time when she got rucking.

She asked her dad again, "So, what were you laughing at?"

"Nothing, Rubes." He shrugged it off. "Now then, where have you been? I was worried sick, not being able to contact you. When I cough up over a hundred quid for a phone, make sure I can get hold of you on it, yeah?"

Ruby stood back and rolled her eyes. He was off again, moaning.

"My battery is flat and I told you where I was going."

He was silent for a moment as he stared at her. "Did you see Jesse?" His tone had changed and he was cold and distant. She nodded.

Jack left the room. He didn't want to hear anymore.

"And was everything all right?" What he wanted to say was, *'Still on drugs, is she? Still selling her arse, is she? Still a selfish bitch, is she?'* But he didn't.

Ruby nodded again. She wasn't going to discuss it with him. She wanted her relationship with her mother to be separate from her father. The Vincents had secrets – and now she did too.

Chapter Six

The second open night at *Dan's Palace* was heaving with customers, and Fred was on hand as promised. Sam again asked Sid to manage his bar, which allowed him to help out. There were always teething problems with any new club and, until this one was firmly established, Dan and his brothers would be a little on edge. The pole dancers were the main attraction and, as the night went on, their popularity increased. The gambling segment was partitioned off for a more serious clientele than the stripper audience.

His staff, especially the girls, were more or less handpicked by Dan. Impressed with their positive attitude and flirting skills, they were worth their weight in gold. He had sold more bottles of champagne in two nights than he had in a month at *Sam's Palace*.

Sergio, Francesca's husband, had taught him enough to make sure that the new *Palace* was a good money-maker.

Dan and Fred surveyed the club. They made sure that everyone was in their place and the bar was stocked to the brim. All the girls were heavily made-up, with their nails manicured, and they wore skimpy dresses. Flawless. The men had their hair fashionably styled and their shirts crisp. Coloured lights danced around the room as the music played. Bouncers were positioned in every corner, croupiers were at the ready to deal, and the strippers were knocking back the brandy for confidence.

"Who is on the door?" asked Fred, remembering the cocky doorman from last week.

"I don't know, I left John in charge, but I have warned him, no pikeys."

"I'm gonna go on security for a while. Keep an eye on them. I don't trust that fucker Farley."

Dan nodded, pleased his sidekick was back and ready for action. Fred, being lively and quick-witted, kept Dan amused. He trusted him to sniff out trouble a mile away.

As Fred opened the main doors, he was taken aback by the amount of people waiting to come in. Then he clocked Farley, talking to one man in the queue. It was hard to see who but, as Farley turned to face the entrance, he jumped when he saw Fred standing there.

He headed back to the door with the cheesiest grin across his face.

"All right, guv, so what's happening then? You on the door with me tonight?"

Fred cringed at the voice; he was a pikey through and through. He didn't answer his question.

"Who was that fella you were talking to?" asked Fred accusingly.

"Oh yeah, just one of me old mates from school."

Fred hated lies. Gypsies never went to school.

"So then, Fred, ready for the rush are ya?" Farley was excitable and hopped around. He didn't look at all like a standard doorman. He was so unlike the other strong, beefy and calm men working there. Fred ignored his question and instead sized him up and down.

Farley realised he was on the go – fidgeting constantly. It must have been the small toot he'd had earlier.

"You'd better be clean, or you are gone!" said Fred in an icy voice.

"Of course, mate, it goes without saying." He knew he needed to keep Fred on side. He couldn't afford to get elbowed right now.

"Stand still and show the customers respect, except any gypsies. No excuses, do what you have to, but they ain't coming in, got it?" Fred was acting the governor now.

"So are you the boss, or what?"

He took umbrage at Farley and Farley knew it.

"Of course I'm your fucking boss!"

"Look, sorry mate, I only meant, who do I go to if there's a problem?"

"It ain't that difficult. You just take direction from any one of us Vincents and, when we are not around, you listen to John who, I hope, has told you what your fucking job is."

Farley was nodding. "Oh yeah, guv, I know what I'm doing."

"Well, stop dancing like a fairy. Stand like a doorman, and less lip."

Farley had hoped that Fred would warm to him but it wasn't happening. Then again, the Vincents weren't in the habit of trusting outsiders. Farley's job was to get at least one of the Vincents in his pocket, but they stuck together like glue. No chance of spreading a Chinese whisper or turning one against the other.

The doors officially opened and in they came, two by two. The bags were checked and the youngsters had their IDs verified. Fred wanted no mistakes, no underage drinking, and no weapons, even if it held up the queue. He watched as two travellers approached. They were smartly dressed but not enough to disguise who they were. He kept a close eye on Farley. The men were frisked but, luckily for him, they weren't wearing a tie.

"Sorry, boys, can't let you in. Strict dress code!" He looked over at Fred, who made no bones about the fact he was watching Farley.

The two travellers knew Farley well. They lived on the same site as his mother. They pulled out ties from their suit pockets and began to put them on. Farley was now shuffling uncomfortably. He had to get rid of them but anticipated a row. Fred was still staring, waiting for Farley to step up, but what excuse did he have? He looked at the wrinkled ties and he found grounds for refusing entry.

"Sorry, boys, they are creased. Strict dress code!"

One gypsy, a twenty-three-year old called Noah and built like Noah's ark, took offence. The worst of it was, he had been snubbed by his own kind.

He sized up the other doormen, four in total, and decided not to argue but walk away. The other gypsy followed Noah in silence.

"The fucking little ponce, I'll not forget that one, Ash. When that little cokehead, Farley, comes visiting his dear mother, then I'll fucking 'ave 'im. On me mother's eyesight, I'll 'ave him." Noah was a real Romany. If you weren't a gypsy, his accent was hard to understand. He grew up on the Kent site, living with his mother Mary Anne and his brothers, but often came over to London to stay with his Aunty Lacy who had moved after she'd got married. Getting wed was not done in a church. It was running off together and jumping the broomstick. Then it was a lifelong commitment.

Noah, big enough in the prize fighting scene, had a reputation, and planned to have his next fight with Farley on the Kent site – for all to see what would happen when you disrespected your own kind.

Fred grinned. He knew who Noah was and guessed Farley was in for a beating, but what he didn't realise was that it was worth it to Farley just to get in with the Vincents. There was so much to be earned in the clubs and they needed to be in there to take it. Either that, or get it closed down and taken over by the Nappers.

Kizzy, the stripper, walked around to the back door. Her hair was piled high with sequins glued in and her face was heavily made up. Fred saw her from the corner of his eye but, before he got to her, she was through the door and heading for the changing room. He wanted to stop her. It was an uneasy feeling, having a traveller in the club. But he decided to see how much money she could bring in, and most importantly, if she was worth the risk. Cassandra was checking the bottles and glasses just before the mad rush.

"Hello, Cassie, how's my long-legged beauty?" Fred laughed. He was always kind to Cassandra. He had known her for years. She was the most loyal member of staff and he knew she was totally in love with Dan.

"It's good to see you and Dan together again. I think he has been a bit lost without you," she said freely. She could always be open and chatty with Fred, but she clamped up when it came to Dan.

"Cass, I know you do a brilliant job running the bar, but do you think you could look after the girls?" He pointed to the pole.

Cassandra was gutted. She thought he was asking her to leave the bar and manage the strippers.

"Look, only for a short time. I'll tell you why. See that girl with the long, black hair, a youngster by the name of Kizzy?" She nodded, knowing exactly who he meant. Kizzy had been eyeing up Dan and making no attempt to be subtle. She was out to have him herself, or so she thought, and so Cassandra had taken an interest.

"Yeah, I know the little slut!"

Fred took a step back. "Not keen on her, then?" he laughed.

"No, struts around she does, thinks she fucking owns the joint, winking at Dan. As if he is going to be sucked in by a two-bit of brass."

Fred didn't like the sound of it.

"Well then, Cass, I guess you will enjoy being her boss for a while until I find out what the fuck she is up to."

Cassandra was flattered. It was the first time she'd felt included in the Vincents' business. She had always been part of the club, but only so far as managing the bars. They never discussed plans or concerns with anyone except their own.

"Well, I'll keep an eye on her, that's for sure, but who will run the bar?" She loved her job and hoped it wasn't handed over to someone else.

Fred grabbed her hand. "Don't worry, I'll sort that, and it's not a long-term thing. I need the strippers watched. I don't trust that Kizzy."

Cassandra nodded and, with great pride, she introduced herself to the girls, explaining she would be managing them. She glared at Kizzy and then questioned her age.

Kizzy rolled her eyes. "I already showed Dan me ID, all right?" she said with a gypsy accent. Leaning on the wall, chewing gum, she showed she didn't want to take orders from Cassandra. Her cousin had stipulated, *'Take no shit off anyone, just work your charms on Dan Vincent'*.

Fred walked into the changing room to find Cassandra laying down the rules. Two of the strippers, ex-circuit girls, tutted in annoyance at the way he'd just entered without knocking. He sized them up right away. "Listen, girls, you've had your first night with no manager, and you have all tasted the water, to see if *Dan's Palace* is for you. If you like it, great, as long as we like *you*!" He emphasised the word 'you' enough to put the girls on their guard.

He pointed to the two girls who had tutted. "If you think you have any privacy here, then think again. The only people in the club who have that luxury are the owners and your manager, Cassandra!" He smiled at Cassie, who was beaming with pride. Not only was this the second time he had treated her as part of the family, demanding respect from the girls, but she now saw herself as having greater status in the club.

"So, no fucking lip, no trying it on with management. You stick to flashing your ass, tits, and eyelashes at the punters!"

That comment was aimed at Kizzy and she knew it. Cassandra had obviously said something.

"And, by the way, any funny business and she will fire your arse. Plenty more girls where you lot came from." He was nodding at Cassandra.

As soon as he left the room, there was a silence.

"So, like I said, Kizzy, how old are you?"

"Oh, for fuck's sake, what is it with you? I told you I already showed Dan me ID."

"I didn't ask you if you have ID, I asked how old you are, and it's Mr Vincent to you. You heard Fred, clear as day." Cassandra's voice was hard.

Kizzy frowned. "What do you mean?"

"Your job is to dance that fucking pole and remember your place. Don't get familiar with the Vincents, that's what he was saying. Now then, I'll ask you again. What's your fucking age?" Cassandra was a tall woman and could look vicious when she was annoyed. Kizzy knew, then, she was getting too big for her boots.

"I'm twenty-two."

"Well, so we don't get nabbed by the Old Bill, because you look under age, you'd better give me your ID. I will have it checked out, and then no one can shut us down over a silly mistake like you, eh?"

Kizzy swallowed hard. She had to keep this job at the club because if she got booted out the plan would be fucked.

"All right, I'll fetch it with me next week!" She tried to sound sweet but it wasn't working. "On me muvver's life, I'll 'ave it Saturday!"

Cassandra nodded. She felt she had put Kizzy well and truly in her place.

The other girls had thought they were special, until Fred had just burst in without knocking first. Just like the other clubs, they were to be treated as whores. But they would not complain; the money was good, the club was clean and fresh, the punters were younger, and the tips were plentiful.

Kizzy looked around the room, her stomach in knots. She was young, but this was the life she aspired to. She couldn't have hoped to get a classier club to flash her assets. The dressing room was adorned with mirrors which lit up, the chairs were pink leather, and the floor had soft carpet. She had seen the inside of other strip clubs and you were lucky if you had a dirty toilet to get changed in. As she did the splits up the pole the punters cheered, and each of them slipped a twenty in her knicker elastic. She was blessed with a fantastic figure. At fifteen, her breasts were huge and her arse neat. With a tiny, flat stomach and bronzed skin, she would be the main attraction, and the other girls knew it. But, tonight, she was nervous, as the thought of losing her job made her feel sick.

"What's up, Kiz, you look worried about something?" mocked Cassandra.

"Nah, I'm all right. You know how it is, before you get on that pole. The nerves get to you." Kizzy was being careful.

"No, actually, I don't know what it's like. I've never lowered myself!"

Kizzy looked down. She knew she didn't stand a chance with Cassandra. It was over and done with unless one of her cousins could find her a better

ID – this time a fool-proof one. She put the worry behind her and straightened her tassels.

*

Sam arrived late. The club was already full and people still queued to get in. He used the front entrance like Fred and was just about to be stopped by Farley for not wearing a tie. Sam looked the new bouncer up and down and then glanced at John. It was odd, seeing three big bouncers and then Farley, who was a runt in comparison, but he guessed there was a reason. Farley smiled and let Sam pass. He wasn't going to piss him off too.

The customers were two people deep at the bar so Sam poured himself a brandy and started serving. There were so many people that the lesson from this evening was that they needed more staff. Once the initial rush was over, Sam was joined by his brothers in the poker room, where they had peace and quiet.

"You look rough, Sam. What's up, mate?" asked Dan. He had noticed over the last few weeks that his brother had lost weight and looked tired.

He took a deep breath. "I guess you're gonna find out soon enough. Ruby has been to see her mother." There was a silence while both Fred and Dan tried to take it in.

"What the fuck did she do that for?" Fred sounded almost hurt, as if she had insulted him personally.

Sam shrugged. "She thinks that she missed out, not having a mum, and so she took a fucking train to that poxy shit-hole and found her!"

Dan knocked back his Jack Daniels. "So then what happened?"

"I don't know. She won't say no more except that she is visiting her again this weekend." He looked resigned.

Fred was angry. "What's the fucking matter with her? Don't she remember what that scumbag did to her?"

"She doesn't believe any of it, and I don't know what the attraction is now, but she is definitely going back."

"Listen, Sam, I wouldn't worry. Our Rubes, she's a good girl, and once she sees her mother for the waster she is, she will be home and that will be an end to it!" stated Dan, who meant what he'd said.

Fred shook his head and wiped his mouth with the back of his hand. "We should have buried her years ago."

"Our Ruby should have been a boy. The mare is so cocky. She's not like our Dolly, is she, and yet, when Rubes was little, she was the image of Fran. Maybe it's just a phase," replied Dan. They referred to Francesca as Dolly. It was her nickname because, as a baby, she had looked like a china doll.

"Well, let's be honest, we didn't know our Dolly when she was a teenager. She may have been a rebel, who knows? Fran ain't mouthy or stupid, but she has nerves of steel and is harder than us." Sam raised his eyebrow. "And speaking of Fran, Ruby was fucking rude to her…"

Before he could finish, Fred jumped in. "You what, rude to our Dolly?"

"Yep, fucking hurtful cow. I slapped Ruby across the face. I didn't want to, but by Christ she deserved it! To see our sister's eyes well up gutted me."

Both Dan and Fred were wide-eyed in shock. It was hard to imagine any family member hurting Dolly. She was their angel. She saved them all, including Ruby. As a child she was sent away for her own protection. It was years later, when she returned as a woman, that their family was complete and didn't have to live in fear. They adored her and, in their eyes, she could never do any wrong. This situation was difficult because, as a family, they had an unwritten code which glued them together. No outsider could ever comprehend this, but now their niece was testing that bond.

"You shouldn't have slapped her though, Sam. She is still our baby," said Dan, in a quiet voice.

Fred didn't agree but, then again, he was Francesca's twin and couldn't handle the idea of his sister in tears. "Well, Dan, sounds to me like she needed it. She is a Vincent and, fuck me, we all toe the line. You know how it is. Look around at what we have. We sure as hell wouldn't be where we are today if we tried it alone. Our Ruby needs to understand this. If she carries on the way she is, by the time she's twenty, she could take this family apart."

"You're right, Fred. Sorry, Sam, she does need guidance and to be shown the error of her ways. That slap might do her good. If not, lock her in her room until she's twenty-five." He tried to laugh it off but Sam changed the subject. "So, where's Cassie then? I thought she was running the bar?"

Fred shook his head. "No, I put her in with the strippers to manage them. I don't trust that Kizzy, or that fucking Farley!"

Dan smiled. "Well, all I can say is there's been no pikeys in here tonight, and that Kizzy is drawing in the punters, so don't be too tough, Fred."

He had a free hand to do as he liked because Dan trusted him and his management decisions were good. If his little brother was concerned, then there was probably a good reason.

"I agree with ya, Dan, but let's keep a keen eye. Besides, there's plenty of good-looking girls that would love to work here. Fuck me, bruv, look at the joint, it's five star!"

"Who are you talking about anyway? Who's Kizzy?" asked Sam.

They finished their break and, as Dan went back to the main bar, Fred took Sam to the pole section to watch. Kizzy was in full swing. He stared for a while. Suddenly, he grabbed Fred by the arm and pulled him to one side.

"Jesus, Fred, get her out of here!"

Fred struggled to hear with the music blaring. They walked upstairs to the office.

"What is it, Sam? You look as though you've seen a ghost?"

"No, mate, only I know that girl's face. She used to spar at the club with our Ruby. She's only fucking fifteen!"

"What?"

"Go and fetch Dan up here now," said Sam, distressed.

The three of them sat, dumfounded. How the hell could a fifteen-year-old get away with that, and who in their right mind would let their teenage daughter pole dance?

"I'm telling you, Dan, something is going on here. First of all, you've got Farley on the door to stop the pikeys coming in, then you had Levi trying to deal, and now there's a gypsy kid showing her fanny for scores on the pole," said Fred.

"Well, just sack them. It's no big deal." Dan couldn't understand the issue.

"That's not what concerns me. It's why they are here. What the fuck are they up to? Let's face it, a fifteen-year-old dancing will close us down."

Dan's eyes widened and his anger welled up. "Little slut!"

"Come on, Dan, it ain't her. She's been put up to it, but fucking why?" Sam bit his nails in thought. "Bring her up here."

Dan smiled as Fred went to fetch her, knowing that gypsies are the best for keeping quiet.

Cassandra was watching Kizzy dancing on the stage when Fred caught her attention.

"Cassie, do you know whose bags are whose in the changing room?"

She nodded.

"Good. Sift through Kizzy's and grab her mobile phone. Hide it. Call her off the pole and bring her up to the office."

Without any questions, she did as she was told.

*

Kizzy was surprised when Cassandra called her off the stage, but she wouldn't argue – not now.

"Mr Vincent wants to see you in the office," said Cassie, her voice sounding friendlier.

She looked down at herself – just a pair of white hooker boots, a cerise pink thong, and a tiny tasselled top, barely covering her nipples. "Shall I get changed?"

Cassandra shook her head. "No, it's fine, he won't mind."

She wasn't worried about how he felt, she was more concerned with her own dignity. It was okay on the pole, because it was a game, but to have a conversation dressed like a hooker was another thing altogether. Cassandra walked behind Kizzy, making sure she got to the office without scarpering. The door was open and Kizzy gingerly stepped inside. Cassandra closed it behind her and headed back to the bar.

Kizzy was nervous, seeing three grown men. Her heart raced when Fred locked the door.

"Take a seat," said Dan coldly. He sat behind a huge desk, joined by Sam, who towered over him. Kizzy glanced around the room. It was a big office, with book shelves, coloured leather sofas, thick rugs, and a long fireplace built into the wall. She thought that maybe Dan lived here. It was so homely and cosy. She fancied a pad like this for herself, instead of her cramped caravan. Her thoughts returned to reality. She was half-naked and sitting in a locked room with three men. Stripping was easy but having sex was not on the agenda – and not with all three of them. Her heart was pumping again. What had she gotten herself into? Instantly she regretted flirting the way she had with Dan, but she had been told to by her cousin. She started to push herself deeper into the padded chair, trying to cover herself as much as she could. She felt exposed more than ever, but what she didn't realise was that the men knew her age and didn't look at her that way. The Vincents were brought up right – with no kinky perverted ideas. They had loads of good-looking women but none underage. Their aim was to find out what the gypsies were up to – nothing else.

"So, did you think it would work, your pathetic plan to shut us down?" shouted Dan, who went from calm to manic in two seconds flat. He was on his feet and leaning across the desk, red-faced and foaming at the mouth. Fred was surprised. Even he didn't move that quickly. Sam, on the other hand, had seen Dan act like this before, but it had only been in the last year and he blamed the stress of setting up the new club. Fred had become more laid back now. But he didn't have full responsibility of a club.

Kizzy was shaking. She knew they were on to her but, being only fifteen, she didn't have the savvy to follow through. Although they were unaware that they didn't really know about the plan, they were very clever manipulators when it came to dragging the truth out of people.

"What?" she said coyly.

"You fucking heard me, you dirty little tramp. Think you can get my club shut down, you and your fucking gypo mates, eh?" He was still screaming as he reached over the table and grabbed her by the hair, pulling her off the chair.

Sam wanted to stop him hurting the girl However, this was a serious threat to the business and she was going to be taught a valuable lesson.

"So, you want to play the big girl's game? Then you can take what's coming like a real woman." His anger had reached its pitch and he slapped her hard across the cheek. She didn't flinch – too afraid to speak. He

82

slapped her again and threw her back in the chair. She began to blabber. "Please don't hurt me!" She was afraid of the unknown; the fear of what was coming her way made her feel sick and she shook from head to toe.

Fred grabbed the leather swivel chair, with the crumpled Kizzy, and spun it round to face him. He leaned on the two arms and coldly said, "You're a pretty little thing. If you want to remain that way, you had better start answering our questions because if you don't, I will become your worst nightmare."

Dan laughed, intimidating Kizzy. "Ah, Fred, you wouldn't cut her boat race would you? Look at her lovely painted fingernails. That's more your style, bruv, chopping up body parts."

Sam was grinning and Fred laughed out loud. As if they'd hurt a fifteen-year-old. Their aim was to put the fear of hell into her to get her to talk. She was a child, and they were known Faces. They only intended to scare the shit out of her, that was all.

Kizzy began to cry and Sam swallowed hard, but he knew it had to be done. The tears streamed and she covered her face.

"Look at me when I'm talking to you!" spat Dan.

Her makeup was now smeared across her face, snot bubbled from her nose, and she sobbed as a teenager would. Her cheeks were stinging but she was afraid, and so the slap was nothing compared to the pain if they cut off her fingers.

"So, Kizzy, who put you up to it?" Dan was back in his seat, with a blade in his hand. It was a diver's knife – an evil-looking, jagged blade, eight inches long. Kizzy gasped and her mind raced. It was her boyfriend, Ocean, another gypsy from the site, who had forced her into it, but he was just the messenger. She had seen the men gathered around Billy's caravan talking – sometimes through the night. She only heard bits and pieces and never took much notice. As far as she was concerned, she had to secure a job in the club and, when she got the nod, she had to be on the pole ready for the police raid.

"Mr Vincent, I don't know what you mean. I'm sorry, I just wanted to earn some dosh, is all. I ain't got family of me own, ya see." She was choking over her words.

Dan hated the pikeys. He never believed a word they said. "Lying cunt! Who set you up for this?" he shouted.

"No one, I swear on me muvver's grave, Mr Vincent!"

Dan couldn't stand oaths they took. Every other sentence was *'I take an oath on me muvver's life'* but they were always lying through their back teeth.

Fred grabbed her tiny wrist. "You think we're daft? No family, eh, Kizzy O'Connell. 'Ere, Dan, give us the knife!"

Kizzy almost fainted as the blood drained from her face and the vomit sat at the back of her throat. They had sussed her.

"Please don't, please, I swear to ya, I tell ya the truth. It was Ocean, he made me do it."

The words were out and Kizzy was as shocked as they were that she had blurted out a name.

The men frowned. They hadn't heard of anyone called Ocean but they guessed it was another traveller.

She knew she had done wrong and the whole site would call her a grass. She had assured them she could handle it all. In fact, she had been looking forward to it but now her world had fallen apart. She loved Ocean with a passion and the thought he would fuck her off, after this, was worse than losing a finger.

"You had better tell us why, or I'll cut your fucking tongue out," said Fred.

She looked into eyes that were blank and she assumed he would do exactly that.

"He wanted me to earn money so that we can get us married!" She stopped crying.

"You have one more chance to tell the truth. If you don't, I will strip your pretty cheeks, then cut out your tongue." Fred ran the blade across her cheek, careful not to cut her. He only intended to frighten her into spilling the beans.

She held her breath while the knife went back and forth. She was terrified he would destroy her face. It was all she had going for her. Without her looks, Ocean would find another girl. Besides, he could have anyone he wanted. He was so handsome, with the brightest of green eyes.

The immense fear grew, but she couldn't think quickly enough, so she told the truth.

"I was told to work here until the place got raided, that's everything I know, I promise!" They could see she was being honest. It was the resigned tone in her voice and the way she looked to the floor in shame.

"So who's behind it?" questioned Sam, who had kept quiet until now.

She shrugged her shoulders. "I don't know, that's the truth. All I know is I get paid a bundle when yous get shut down."

The men knew she was being truthful but were puzzled by the name. They felt uncomfortable having an unknown on their case.

"Who is Ocean, then?" asked Dan, who was instantly calm again, and seated back in his chair.

"He is my boyfriend, and someone told him to set me up, but I don't know who, I swear on me muvver's —"

Before she could continue, Dan jumped in.

"Yeah, I know, on your muvver's life." He rolled his eyes.

Fred unlocked the door and Kizzy ran as fast as she could. Leaving the office, and all its luxury fittings, she fled towards the comfort of her caravan and into the arms of her man, Ocean, and prayed to God he would forgive her. She didn't even stop to get changed. She just grabbed her bag and left. The other girls watched in surprise as the top stripper – red-faced, tear-stained and in a blind panic – raced out of the building. It caused the changing room to become just like a chicken coop, with the girls gossiping excitedly about what had just happened.

Cassandra walked in and the room was silent. She nodded. "That's better! Now, get on with the job and mind your own business!" She left with the hidden mobile and took it up to the office.

Sam and Fred had left to check up on the club and Cassandra was alone with Dan.

"'Ello, babe, come in!" said Dan, who was still trying to be cool himself.

"Oh, hi, Dan. Sorry to disturb you, only I thought Fred was here. I've got Kizzy's phone."

He gestured for her to take a seat.

Dan admired her. It was funny because, in all the years she had worked for him, she hadn't aged. Her skin was tight and her eyes sparkled. She should have been a model, with those legs.

"How's it going down there?" Dan was treating her like a manager.

"Well, we need more staff on the bar, and obviously a new girl on the pole, but the atmosphere is great." As she smiled he noticed just how pretty she was, with perfect white teeth and heart-shaped lips.

"Tell me, Cassie, do I pay you enough?" he asked coldly.

Cassie's heart sank. When he asked this to a staff member, she knew he was going to fire them for having their hands in the till.

She nodded.

"You never grumble, you do whatever I ask, and you are the only person in this club, other than me brothers, that I can trust." He put his hands together. "I want to say thanks for everything you do. If you ever need anything, you only have to ask me."

She looked into his deep blue eyes and had the urge to say out loud, '*I want you, Dan*'.

He got up from his chair and walked around to her. She handed him the phone and he kissed her on the cheek. As she stood up to go, he stopped her by cupping her face in his hands. Her cheeks flushed. She closed her eyes and held onto the kiss he planted so tenderly on her lips. As she opened her eyes, he was staring lovingly with a kind expression. For years she had dreamt of this moment and now she was living it. But did he honestly like her, or was she to be just one of his conquests? Either way, she still loved him.

85

"How about tomorrow night me and you go out for a nice meal and catch a movie?"

Cassie wanted to pinch herself. Was she dreaming or had he just asked her out?

"Yeah, that sounds a good idea. I thought you'd never ask!" She was surprised that those last words came out of her mouth.

He laughed. "Yeah, about time." Dan had surprised himself. He had kept Cassie at arm's length, knowing she fancied him, as he hadn't ever seen her as his type, really. He was more into a quick shag, and he knew that Cassie wasn't like that.

*

Fred and Sam agreed to drag Farley around the back and kick the answers out of him.

The door was quiet. Only a few drunken stragglers came along, and they were refused admittance. Farley had been true to his word and hadn't allowed any gypsies entry. So, when Sam and Fred summoned him to join them at the rear, he was confused. As he hadn't seen his cousin Kizzy flee the premises, he had no idea that the plan had been blown.

He now had to face the Vincent brothers and he turned cold. He was on his own and they were after his blood. Their expressions said it all.

Fred flicked his head and he knew then he had to follow. There was nowhere to run.

"What's up?" Farley was so calm it must have been the first time he wasn't jumping around on cocaine.

"So, when's the raid supposed to take place, then?" asked Fred, who was ready for a brawl.

Farley felt the heat rising up from his feet to his head. He couldn't believe their plot had been rumbled.

"I don't know what you're talking about," answered Farley, trying to look composed. Inside, he was shitting himself.

"Yeah, you do. Come on, tell us why, and we might let you go with your bollocks intact." Sam's voice was gruffer, more menacing.

"Oh, come on, guys. Give me a break. I've already said, I have no idea what you're on about!"

Fred threw the first punch, which cracked Farley in the side of the head, sending him to the ground. Sam booted him hard in the ribs. He curled into a ball as both men kicked and punched. They stopped for a few seconds and watched to see if Farley was moving. The blood was seeping from Farley's nose and a nasty lump was growing from his chin, but he didn't move.

Fred grabbed him by the arm and tried to stand him up but his feet gave way; he was barely conscious. Sam grabbed a chair from inside the club and they plonked Farley on it.

He slowly opened his eyes and stared at Fred. "You cunt, Fred, I don't deserve this!" The blood seeped from his nose into his mouth, one eye was closed, and he could hardly move his jaw.

Fred kicked the chair away and Farley fell to the floor.

"Who's behind it? Cos it sure ain't you, ya fucking little weasel!" Fred lifted him up by his collar and shook him like a rag doll. "Tell me now and I'll let you live."

Farley was suffering. Gripped by pain, he drooped his head and whispered, "Please, Fred, believe me, I don't know!"

Fred dropped him like a sack of shit and watched as he squirmed around on the floor.

"Don't fucking lie, you little shit! Now fuck off, back to ya campsite, and make sure you, and your scummy pikey gang, don't come here again. That little beating was a taster. Come back – and you'll get the real thing!"

Farley hated Fred, for many reasons: he was rich, a looker, had respect, and had beaten the crap out of him. The only thing that kept Farley going on the way home was the thought his brothers and cousins would trash the club once they saw the state of him. He imagined truckloads of men, tooled up with flame throwers, taking down the Vincents, torturing Fred and burning the *Palace* to the floor.

The evening's takings were over and above expectations. While Fred and Sam locked up and paid the wages, Cassandra helped Dan to count up the money. It was a cosy affair. Fred was pleased to see Dan opening up to Cassie and letting her have more responsibility. It was a sign that they were starting to trust others.

As the club emptied, the doormen left for the night. The cleaners came in. It was an unusual arrangement, but one that Dan was a stickler for. He never wanted to walk into any of the clubs the next day and see it untidy. That was how it had always been.

The cleaners were taken on through an agency and Dan paid them well – as long as they did a good job.

Fred and Sam checked the toilets and store room for drunk strays. As the cleaners began vacuuming, Fred smiled and they grinned back. The hairs on the back of his neck stood on end – he noticed the Creole earrings, the dark creased skin, and the thick gold around their necks. More fucking gypsies.

"'Ere, Sam, do us a favour. Get rid of those gypos. I don't trust any of 'em."

Sam laughed. "They're all right, Fred. They've been cleaning up the clubs for the last five years. That's old Daisy and Maggie."

Fred smiled. He let them carry on but kept a close eye as he continued checking over the place.

When the clearing was done and the money counted, the brothers sat down and enjoyed a glass of champagne. Cassie got up to put on her coat, and was on the verge of leaving when she was invited to stay by Dan. "'Ere, babe, have a glass of plonk. We took more than last week, and I'm fucking happy!" Cassie sat as part of their family and enjoyed the fuss. The cleaners looked over and smirked, but only Fred clocked them.

Chapter Seven

The campsite was only a bus ride away from the club. It had been there for thirty years, no matter how many times the council tried to house them, or move them on. They came up against human rights' acts and then appeal courts. So it became a permanent fixture. There were roughly thirty caravans in all; some were so big they couldn't be towed. Dotted, here and there, were new 4x4 cars. It would look odd to anyone not understanding the gypsy way, but it was almost customary to have a caravan and a luxury car today. Even their horses were worth a great deal of money. They had land. Half of Kent was owned by travellers, but they lived their life differently and didn't care how the outside world, or gorgers, as non-gypsies are known, viewed them.

Kizzy was still in shock as she fled the club and got up the road. She managed, with a struggle, as her hands shook so much, to put her jeans and jumper on. She fumbled through her bag for her phone to call a taxi but it had gone, so she assumed she had lost it when making a mad dash to escape. She jumped on the night bus and tried to sort herself out before she reached home. Her mind worked overtime, trying to think of how she would tell Ocean what had happened. Again she cried. The thought that the Vincents had threatened to chop her fingers off conjured up all those images in her mind of her sitting in that club, and it made her feel sick again.

As she headed for the site, her stomach spontaneously emptied its contents and, before she could brace herself, half of it covered her clothes. She stood at the entrance and gazed around. Tiny lights from some of the caravans gave a cosy feel to the site but, as the dark enveloped her, she shuddered. In the distance a fire burned and she could make out a group of men gathered there. They always had a fire – it was tradition. She loved to sit there as a youngster, listening to the stories, and watching the women tie ribbons on the lucky heather or making lucky bead necklaces. The orange flames burned high and bright. She saw the silhouette of Ocean, there with the men, some dogs, and a few wandering cockerels. A tear stung her sore cheek.

She loved him so much, but he played such a cool character and didn't rush to her side when she appeared. He didn't visit her at the club either, and sometimes it seemed as though he only wanted her when he felt horny. She struggled to understand why he was so cold towards her. She knew she was good-looking. She earned more money at the *Palace* than any of the other girls. She had to – so why didn't he pay her attention like most boyfriends would? He never said she was his girlfriend, but he often shagged her when no one was around.

Kizzy grew up in a caravan. When her father went to prison and her mother ran off with a gorger, she was left with her Uncle Johnnie, her father's brother. Her father, Albi, refused to have anything to do with her, as he was convinced she wasn't his. He had black hair and green eyes and his wife was fair with brown eyes. So where did the blue eyes come from? He tried to bond with the child but, in the back of his mind, he believed she belonged to someone else. When his wife ran off to Spain with a gorger, he realised then that she was a slut and probably screwing everyone. Albi, and probably half the campsite, knew it but Johnnie O'Connell continued to raise her and no one dared argue. Johnnie's wife had died of pneumonia and so he raised Kizzy alone. It was difficult, though, because he only had sons and they were older. Although he treated her well, he was also hard on her and so she grew up being tough. She had her own tiny room and, being the prettiest girl on the site, she got away with a lot, especially with the boys. It was not a matter of opinion but fact that Kizzy was a beauty. The younger men all tried it on but she only wanted Ocean.

Ocean, an Irish gypsy, was not into the boxing game like the O'Connells. He was more into horses. What he didn't know about cobs and shires wasn't worth knowing. He rode before he walked and he never went to school. His mother, a hard-faced woman called Moira, raised her three daughters and her son the old ways, and that didn't include mainstream education. "I'll teach me chavis what they need to learn." Moira was softer on her boy than her girls and so he often got away with murder. They were an old travelling family, going back generations. When her father got sick, they had sold the wooden caravan and bought a modern six berth van. He died shortly afterwards and took with him some of the traditions. In the 1960s their ways changed. A gypsy was not a gypsy unless he owned a horse and that horse was, at one time, a vital part of his family. But, when lorries and trailers took over, it affected not only their culture but how outsiders viewed them. Back in the old days, before they would move on, the caravan would be scrubbed down, the harness cleaned and the horses groomed. It was a beautiful sight as the sounds of the hooves and the wooden vardos painted in very striking colours, passed through a village. Moira's father, a proud man, enjoyed sitting up at the front of his wagon, trotting through the country villages in Ireland. It was not so much the lung damage which killed him but more the dismal existence without horses which finally finished him.

The farms relied on the gypsies working the fields – hop picking in September, apples and pears in late autumn, and potato harvest in early winter. But, with the introduction of motorised machinery, farmers didn't need their help anymore so they had to source other means of income.

The tradition of storytelling around the camp fire, which helped to keep the gypsy ways alive, also changed. Now it was full of plots and plans of deception – of how they would rip off the next person.

With the scrap metal business dying a death, the younger gypsies dealt with some of the big London boys, selling drugs. Cocaine could be easily hidden on a camp. The Ol' Bill, or gavvers, as the travellers called them, never entered a gypsy site, not unless they were mob-handed. It would cost a fortune to arm so many police in riot gear, and they would need protection. Even the kids, as young as five, would pick up a brick and launch it at the police. After all, the gavvers were the enemy. The children, taught from babies not to talk to any strangers, didn't give their real names and told no one where they lived. The old ways were dying and the younger men, finding ways to make a living, didn't all sell drugs. Many turned to landscaping, new driveways and patios. Johnnie missed the traditions. He never sat by the fire and listened to the bullshit. He hated the idea of serious wrong doings, so he stuck to scrap metal and the odd bit of fencing and made enough money to look after Kizzy and himself.

Moira loved her son, Ocean. He was the image of his father who was serving a long stretch over in Ireland. But she feared her son would end up like him. She hoped, though, he would soon settle down with Kizzy and start a family, and show an interest in the horses again. His born talent could make money, but his dealings with the O'Connells dragged him down the wrong road. Her heart ached when she saw him sneaking around, late at night, up to no good. It was hard enough when Joey, her husband of twenty years, got locked away for armed robbery. The kids, all under ten, were stranded with her on a site in Ireland with no way of earning money. The horse business took off again in Kent so she moved out to the London campsite, where she knew a few folk. When she needed to she would travel down to the county to buy and sell her horses. She still went over to Ireland every month to see Joey, and dreamt of the day he would be home and curled up in her bed again. It was funny because, although the London site was gypsy only, she was Irish and they were Romany. It took a while before they understood her accent because the O'Connells were mixed. Johnnie's grandmother, Rose, was a strong-willed Romany. She married Mikey O'Connell, an Irish tinker and a quiet, placid man who had four sons, but they lived the Romany way.

Kizzy stood watching Ocean in the distance until a tiny voice called her name. "Kizzy, girl, where you been at, you look poggered?" A real Irish accent. It was Shirley, one of Ocean's sisters.

Kizzy's blue eye makeup had smudged into her cheeks, giving the impression of her having two black eyes.

Shirley had a Celtic complexion, with her light skin, freckles and green eyes. At thirteen, she looked up to Kizzy because she acted and dressed like a twenty-year-old.

"What you doing out so late, Shirley girl?"

"I was watching out of the window and I saw ya there." She held Kizzy's hand and walked with her back to her van.

"Come in, Mam's still up, she'll make you a cup of tea." Shirley, a sweet girl, could tell something had happened, and she wanted to sit in on the gossip. They didn't have a TV in the trailer, so a good chat was their entertainment. Kizzy was nervous. She would have to tell Ocean she had ruined the plan so, tired, sore, and stinking of vomit, she tried to escape.

"I'm gonna go to me own trailer tonight. I'll see ya muvver tomorrow." She hoped to sneak away and leave all the grief until the next day, to give herself time to figure out how she would tell Ocean.

"Ocean! Kizzy's back. Looks like she's been mullered!" shouted Shirley, very loudly, so more lights came on around the site.

"Shut ya fucking mooi, Shirley girl." Too late, though, the damage was done.

He and four other men ran towards her. Some of the travellers opened their caravan doors, all wanting to get a look at the commotion, which set the sleepy dogs off barking. Once awake, they were off in unison. The campsite sprung to life. Ocean stopped in his tracks and looked her up and down. He saw the mark on her cheek, the makeup all over her face, the vomit down her clothes, and the fear in her eyes.

A crowd gathered and Kizzy hung her head in shame, and then she heard Ocean ranting.

"I swear, on me muvver's life, I'll muller whoever's done this to you. Just give me their name!" Ocean shouted, louder than he needed, to let everyone hear he was a hard man, protecting his own. Some smirked, others smiled, proud of him anyway, defending his girl. It shocked even Kizzy, he was publicly announcing her as his girl – a serious acknowledgement. So, from now on, whatever Kizzy did or didn't do, would go back to Ocean and not her Uncle Johnnie. It was the gypsy way.

She looked up and into Ocean's eyes, hoping he meant it. She was ready to cause a storm; an Oscar-winning performance.

"It was the Vincents. They tried to cut me fingers off!" she lied through her back teeth, and once she started she couldn't stop. She loved how he threatened to kill to protect her, proud to be his girl. The ahhs from the audience spurred her on to give more. "They held me head down, and was gonna slice me tongue off, but I kicked that Fred Vincent hard in the bollocks. I swear, if I didn't fight back, they would have cut me up into little pieces!"

Ocean put his arms around her, proud his woman was a fighter, and she revelled in the euphoria. She was too caught up in the moment to admit she had let the cat out of the bag.

"Get the chavi a drink. Poor thing's had the shock of her life!" Kizzy was led to the fire and sat next to fat Billy. The gypsies gathered: men, woman and children. On went the pots, out came the sausages, and they sat ready for a story and grub. She went over the details again and again, exaggerating every version until they visualised her being stripped naked with torturous instruments poked over her body. The women gasped and the men planned to wage war on the Vincents.

Kizzy was now the Queen bee, perched on a stool, sitting higher than anyone else. Any more idolising and she would have been wearing a crown. The younger girls admired her. She looked classy despite her smudged makeup. The fire lit up her face and her thick mass of black hair fell about her perfect frame.

Some of the older women were sceptical but, if their men were taken in by it, then far be it from them to open their mouths and upset the apple cart.

"They will never get away with this. Cowards, is what I say! Taking our dear little harmless Kizzy, a tiny chavi, and torturing her like that," declared Billy O'Connell. He hated the Vincents and had a deep, burning desire to have them all killed. After all, Sam had left him for dead all those years ago in that prison cell. That attack gave him epilepsy and deafened his left ear, so he would do anything to see the Vincents dead.

The travellers sat talking until the early hours. It was the best evening they'd enjoyed in a long time. Kizzy's story led on to another tale of violence and torture. By the time they'd called it a night, there had been more tortures and brutality amongst the gypsies than in the Second World War. The young men wanted in on the action, and it was that kind of bravado that fired them up, and made them eager for war.

But not one of them asked why they beat her, or why they threatened to cut out her tongue, until Farley crawled onto the site.

Most of the woman and children had gone back to their beds. The old folk had returned to the trailers for a warm cup of milk or cocoa, leaving the youngsters to continue fighting the world. Kizzy was still perched on her stool, enjoying the attention. Ocean was getting half-cut when Farley's dog, Duke, an old Lurcher, started barking. Billy looked over and saw Farley a short distance away, dragging his leg.

"Oh, Christ, look!" shouted Billy.

The men turned to see the blood-stained Farley and rushed to help him. Two men put their bodies under each arm, took the weight, and guided him to the fireside. Carefully, they placed him on a deckchair and waited, with baited breath, for Farley to tell them what had happened. Billy knew Farley had been on the club door and guessed this was the Vincents' work.

"Who fucking did this, boy?" Billy asked, speaking calmly and gently to his youngest brother.

Farley didn't say a word. He turned his head slowly – to face Kizzy – and nodded. A coldness in his action changed the atmosphere. Kizzy could sense her new-found respect being ripped from under her.

"What's going on?" shouted Ocean, who felt uncomfortable with the way Farley glared at his girlfriend with hate in his eyes.

"Ask her, Ocean. Ask your slut," replied Farley.

Kizzy, rooted to the stool, was unable to speak.

"Well?" he turned and glared.

"Ocean, I swear on me uncle's life, they were gonna muller me. They had that fucking knife in me mouth!" she cried.

He looked back at Farley to see what he had to say.

"You stupid, little prat, they wouldn't fucking cut you!"

With all the aches and bruising, he still managed to jump from his seat and grab Kizzy around the neck. "I took a beating, 'cos of you. I lost me poxy job, 'cos of you!" All the time he bellowed, he shook her by the throat. "You ain't no decent O'Connell, you're just like your stinking slut of a mother. We should have drowned you at birth, you fucking grass!"

Billy struggled to get out of his chair. His belly was so big it hung well over his trousers. As soon as he was up, he pulled Farley off Kizzy. Ocean didn't attempt to intervene. As far as he was concerned, she had made a mockery of him. He had declared his relationship with a wrong 'un, a no-good grass.

Farley tried to catch his breath, as Kizzy went to run off, but Ocean grabbed her.

"Oh, no, you fucking don't. I wanna hear this." He threw her to the floor, demonstrating his allegiance with the O'Connells and not Kizzy. He desperately wanted to be part of the big boys' club. Standing his ground, and therefore showing his honour, was one way of doing it.

"Well, what's she gone and done?" Ocean asked brazenly.

Farley was surprised that Ocean, a fifteen-year-old boy, was acting like a man, but he went along with him.

"She's told the Vincents that we set them up for a police raid and we are gonna get them closed down." There was a gasp and then silence. Everyone stared at Kizzy as Ocean kicked cold ash into her face.

"I didn't, I swear on me muvver's life, I didn't." She wasn't only pleading for her life, but also for the respect she had earned only moments ago. However, Farley bore the black and blue marks and they would not believe her now.

Ocean turned to face Farley. "I'm sorry, mate."

He nodded, aware it wasn't Ocean's doing.

As he walked away, Kizzy jumped to her feet and chased after him. She tried to plead for forgiveness but Ocean was too ashamed. As she touched his big, strong shoulders, he flipped. Spinning around, he slapped her hard enough to knock her to the floor. The onlookers cheered. He threw back his shoulders as he strode towards his caravan alone.

Kizzy lay on the floor sobbing, waiting for everyone to go inside before she could pass the fire to go home. She didn't make it. She slept on the cold, dew-covered grass, only to be woken two hours later by Jimmy Docherty, a three-year-old gypsy boy, urinating on her hair. She jumped to her feet and slapped the child hard, unaware that Jimmy's mother, Kitty Docherty, had witnessed it. From nowhere, she came and belted Kizzy clean across the mouth.

"Don't you ever touch my little chavi again!" she shouted in a strong Irish accent.

Kizzy realised that some of the other women were watching. Kitty, a scary gypsy, could beat the crap out of men if need be, so she said nothing and walked away. Those women helped raise her, but now they shunned her.

The damp gripped her bones as she walked towards her caravan. The shivering was relentless – a mixture of fear, tiredness and wet clothes.

*

Johnnie had been staying with Cedric, one of his brothers, at a camp site in Kent. Cedric, the oldest living O'Connell, a wise old man who kept himself to himself, was dying of lung cancer but refused to go to a hospice. He thought everyone would write him off if he was out of sight, so he swallowed lots of pain killers and took to his bed inside his van. It wouldn't be long before he finally popped his clogs. So Johnnie visited as much as he could and sometimes stayed over.

He received a phone call from Merlin, an old friend, to update him on the Kizzy incident, He had no idea of the extent of the trouble or even how his niece was involved. He cut the visit short and headed back to London.

Johnnie knew his nephew, Billy, held a deep grudge against Sam. He had manipulated the lads on the site to work with him in getting the clubs shut down. Billy hadn't planned it alone, as he didn't have the brains. His idea of revenge was to take a shooter and blow them away.

Nigel Napper and his brother, Kenneth, South London boys, had several clubs, including one on the Old Kent Road. Like the Vincents, they wanted to run the nightclub scene but, unlike the Vincents, they hadn't done too well. One club closed down after three warnings and two raids. In allowing the gypsies to come in, with their flash cars and wads of cash, they thought they were onto a winner, but they could not have been more wrong. The bouncers left. More stilled water and pop were sold than spirits. Their Irish tinker clientele were dealing, and the nightclubs became more of a rave, with kids dancing, half-stoned, for hours to shit music. Two hundred crates of champagne were stolen, and there was bloodshed most nights. So when the clubs got raided, the police found two guns, twenty-three knives, and enough cocaine to block up six toilets. But the Nappers still blamed the Vincents for their downfall.

However, the Vincents' success was down to hard work, trusting no one, having the hardest bouncers, and being well-known Faces. It was rare, these days, for any of the brothers to get their hands dirty. They clicked their fingers and a heavy would be there, putting the boot in, which made them even more dangerous.

Kenneth got the phone call on Sunday morning. "I'm sorry, mate, but the stupid little slag wasn't up to the job. She grassed!" said Billy, who wasn't afraid of the Nappers but gutted he might not have their support.

"What do you mean, she grassed? She was only supposed to strip. How the fuck can she sing like a canary when she's only meant to take her fucking clothes off and swing around the pole?" Kenneth was fuming. He had just sat down to eat a good fry up, cooked by his wife Celia, when his blood pressure went through the roof. His face turned bright red and the veins in his neck popped out.

"Calm down, dear," said Celia, who dressed as though she still lived in the sixties, with her bleached blonde beehive and pencil skirt.

"Don't fucking tell me to calm down, woman!" he screamed.

"So, what do you propose we do now?" He tapped his foot like a madman.

Billy held the phone to his right ear because the left one was deaf. "Leave it with me, I'll come up with something."

"What is it with you lot? Can't you fucking get anything right?" Kenneth slammed down the phone.

Billy sat in his caravan, staring into space. The Vincents weren't getting away with beating his brother, Farley. Slower these days, and a hell of a lot fatter, he didn't have the strength or the nerve to do much himself. But he still saw himself as a Face.

*

Johnnie returned early that morning. A fit man for his age, he didn't care for his fat nephew Billy. Even though his father was in a bad way, he couldn't get his lard arse off a chair and see the old man. Cedric O'Connell didn't mind as much as he would have, when his youngest boy, Farley, didn't visit him. He had never really taken to Billy, who would quite often pick on Farley. Even as a boy he found him a bully, always picking on the younger kids. Farley was different. He was the baby, and full of life, having lots to say and boundless energy, but Cedric was also blind to the fact that the endless chatter was one effect of the cocaine. Cedric had four sons in all: Billy, the eldest, Tommy, Zaac and Farley.

The O'Connells were a large family, mainly men. Cedric and his wife lived at the Kent site with Tommy and Zaac whilst Billy and Farley stayed in London.

Johnnie was so close to Cedric that it broke his heart to see his brother dying. So, when he returned to the campsite, early that morning, he wasn't too impressed with Farley, or Billy for that matter. "No good selfish cunts," he mumbled under his breath.

The air was chilly and the dew remained for a while. The women were up and out and about, clucking like chickens about the night's events, whilst the small children ran around barefoot and half-naked, poking at the remains of the camp fire. But the dogs were unusually quiet. Johnnie parked his lorry next to his caravan. He had a neat plot, had concreted the base, and had even made enough room for his truck. Anyone caught leaving any rubbish by his bit would get a good hiding. He stepped out of the cab and noticed the women gawking. Nosey bitches. They were waiting for a scene but he wasn't going to give them one. Kizzy lay sleeping in her bed, so she didn't hear the lorry pull up.

He took his boots off at the door and went inside. There was silence, except for the loud ticking from his grandmother's clock. Everything looked as it should, with the lace curtains hanging perfectly, the cushions placed strategically around the tiny sofas, and the clean pots stacked regimentally on the shelf. He smiled. Kizzy always kept a good, clean van. It was too small to make a mess; it was the gypsy way. Never would the inside of the van house an ounce of dirt. The brass horseshoes on the walls were polished and gleaming. The china Shire horses, with the old wooden caravans, were positioned neatly in the windows, and there was a bright white crochet tablecloth with a small vase of roses in the centre of the table.

He put the kettle on and waited for her to appear. He wasn't going to rant and rave at her and he didn't really care about the stupid plan. Johnnie was of the old kind – a scrap metal man with a history of vicious bare knuckle fights, and he hated anything to do with drugs. Gypsies were not businessmen. That wasn't their way. Most couldn't read or write for the simple reason that they didn't need to. As for Kizzy dancing for her money, well, it was tradition a long time ago, back in his father's day, for the young girls to dance in the taverns for a few quid. He knew Kizzy was stripping for money but, as long as she wasn't tapping him for dosh, he didn't mind.

She heard the whistle of the kettle and sat herself up. She had only slept for an hour, and her body ached, but it was the humiliation which hurt the most. The thought of the night's events made her want to run away – and never come back! How could she ever face anyone again? Now she was probably in for a grilling from Johnnie. So, numb and devoid of pride, she got out of her bed, still wearing the jumper and jeans she had on the night before and still covered in dirt and ash.

"Want tea?" asked Johnnie without looking her way.

"Yes, please," she whispered, as she slid her legs under the tiny table with the white tablecloth.

He placed a rose-patterned, china tea cup under her nose and sat himself down opposite her.

"Looks like you need a good wash, girl."

Kizzy looked up at him, with moist eyes and a sad countenance. She appreciated his kindness and his loyalty and generosity of spirit. Although a man of few words and certainly not a person to give her a hug when she felt down as she did now, he was doing the next best thing, by making her a cup of tea. He looked out for her and she was grateful for that. No one else wanted her.

She wondered whether her life was predestined to follow a murky path of deceit or whether there was something out there which she could aspire to. She now realised, very starkly, she didn't really belong in this world: she really was a square peg in a round hole, dragged up by the whole site.

Kizzy looked into her teacup and a big tear fell from her cheek. Her thoughts, somewhat disconnected, drifted to other times and places.

The women looked out for her, but she wasn't tucked up in bed by a mother's loving arms, or told a story by a caring dad. She enjoyed staying in the other caravans when Johnnie was away. She liked sitting up in a big double bed with the other children, having warm milk and playing eye spy; only, none of them could spell, so they made it all up.

She used to go fruit picking with the women and kids. The gypsies looked out for each other, so Kizzy just fitted in. She never went short of food. One of the mums would have something on the table for her. Although her clothes were all hand-me-downs, that didn't matter – as long as she had warm clobber in the winter. Johnnie handed over money for her new boots or shoes. She had learned to thieve at a young age. It was the way it had been since the farming work had dried up. The other kids looked like gypsies but Kizzy had a cleaner, English rose appearance. When the shopkeepers weren't watching her, she took from under their noses. As she grew into her teens, she stole whatever she needed: makeup, clothes, and jewellery, and even spoke like a gorger too, if she had to.

Unlike most of the children, Kizzy was sent to school – the best form of babysitting, so Johnnie didn't have to look out for her during the day. She eventually got expelled for fighting and, from thirteen, didn't bother returning. The kids had picked on her for being different so, as soon as she had taken enough, she battered them. They hadn't realised she could fight like a boy and better than most of them!

A small gang of girls, four in total, had teased her in the classroom for having a fresh rose in her plait. Kizzy hadn't noticed, when Kathleen Docherty braided her hair, she had pushed a beautiful, red rose in the centre and added a crystal clip. Kathleen thought she looked stunning. To any gypsy she did but, to any gorger in their teens, she looked stupid. It wasn't fashionable unless you were five years old. Kizzy sat at her desk, unaware the flower was in her hair, or that the girls were taking the piss. As they left the classroom and entered the canteen, the bully in the gang, a girl called Amy, noticed the older boys there and showed off. "Gypsy Rosie Lea, make us some tea," she laughed, and the other girls joined in.

Kizzy placed the tray of food on a table, picked up a cup of orange and, walking over to Amy, poured the contents over her head. In anger and humiliation, Amy lunged forward and pushed Kizzy. A crowd immediately gathered, chanting 'fight'. Kizzy pulled Amy by the hair and dragged her around like a rag doll, before finally punching her to the floor. The other girls jumped in and tried to wrestle her to the ground. But, in a frenzy, she punched and kicked, until two girls fled, nursing their wounds.

Amy, meanwhile, got to her feet and hit Kizzy in the side of the head. For a second, everyone held their breath, including Amy, who stared into the eyes of a deranged teenager. She went to run but Kizzy had other ideas. She grabbed her arm, pulled her fist back and punched Amy full-force on the nose and again on the chin.

As Amy fell backwards, Kizzy gripped her throat and sank her teeth into Amy's cheek. Her legs buckled, and the flesh tore away as her weight pulled her down. The crowd screamed in horror at the sight of the deep wound with blood oozing from her face. Kizzy ran from the school – and back to the only world she knew.

*

As she had reached fourteen, her appearance had changed. Her hair now black, and her eyes darkened, she resembled the O'Connells. Her body became womanly, with large breasts and hips. Her father still refused to believe she was his, but it made no difference to Johnnie.

Kizzy felt safe in her uncle's presence.

"So, Kizzy, gonna tell me what happened, then?" He sipped his tea, his voice calm and soft.

She needed to get the story out in the open and done with.

"Uncle Johnnie, I swear on me life I had no choice. They really did have a knife to me fingers. If I'd kept me mouth shut they would have cut them off!" She paused as she waited for a reaction.

"Who put you up to this in the first place?" He talked slowly, like a policeman.

"Billy asked Ocean to ask me if I could help them. I had to use the fake ID they gave me to get a job there. They wanted me to be dancing on the pole when the club got raided." She was surprised he didn't already know all of this.

"Go on, girl, then what happened?"

"I was on the pole, dancing, when the manager, a fucking horrible tall bitch, tells me to get upstairs. When I went into the office, they were there – all three Vincent brothers. They got my hand, and threatened to chop me fingers off if I didn't tell them what I was doing there. I had to fess up," she sobbed. "I swear, I would have been cut to pieces. If I knew they were gonna treat me like that, I would never have promised to help Ocean." The tears streamed. It was the first time Johnnie had ever seen her cry. He touched her hand.

"Listen, my girl, I'll be having a word with Ocean, and that cunt, Billy!" He looked at her dirty face. "Go and get yourself cleaned up. You can spend some time with your Aunty Violet down in Kent."

Kizzy was relieved. She didn't have to run away and she had a place to go which she would like. Violet was all right. She had stayed there when Johnnie served time in prison.

"Can I ever come home, Uncle Johnnie?" she asked.

"You were born a free spirit, Kizzy, so that I can't answer, but this is your home. If you want to come back then do it." He stood up and held out his arms for her to fall into. She was surprised he had offered her any form of physical affection. So she held on to him, as if her future depended on it.

It did not take long for Kizzy to clean herself up, remove her makeup, put some modest clothes on and pack her bags. She was glad to be leaving the site and the humiliation behind, but she would miss Ocean and it deeply hurt her. Johnnie opened the passenger's door of the truck for her and she hopped in. The women watched, knowing Kizzy was being sent away. Kathleen Docherty had a soft spot for her and rushed over to the lorry before it drove away.

"'Ere, Kizzy girl, take this with ya, it's me lucky chain." She pulled a heavy gold belcher from her neck and, like a garland, placed it over Kizzy's head. Kathleen turned to look at the other women, glaring scornfully at her.

"Oh, for gawd's sake, she is still our Kizzy!" she shouted.

She leaned down and kissed Kathleen on the cheek. "I'll be back one day."

Kathleen had loved the girl as if she was her own, and her eyes welled up.

"Look after yaself, Kizzy girl."

The drive down to Kent silent, but that's how it always was. Johnnie had never been a man of many words, only important ones.

They entered the site, which was very much bigger than the London one. Before they reached the caravan, Johnnie stopped the truck.

Kizzy looked his way and smiled with such a sad expression. Johnnie bit his lip to stop showing his emotions.

"Listen, Kizzy girl, I've not done good by you. I know I should have handed you over to the authorities, and I feel bad that I didn't let you go to a good home. I know I let you run wild. Truth is, I thought I could do it, but I guess I was wrong..." He pulled out a handkerchief and blew his nose. Kizzy didn't know what to say. "I did love ya, though, girl, in me own way. Loved you more than me boys. I wish I could go back in time, put it all right, give you more attention, like I should have... I've been a rotten uncle, ain't I, Kiz?"

Kizzy swallowed back the tears. "Yeah, Johnnie, you have been a rotten uncle..." she paused, to see his head nodding and what looked like a tear escaping his eye, "but ya been the best farver."

He turned to face her with his head tilted to the side.

"I know you found it hard, but you did your best. I only ever had you though, no one else wanted us. Me own fucking muvver left me in that tyre, behind the van would you believe, before she scarpered."

Johnnie was wide-eyed.

"They never kept it a secret. The old girls reminded me whenever I got under their feet. So to me, Johnnie, you were always me dad. I just wished I could have called you that. I might have felt like I belonged."

Bite as hard as he might on his bottom lip, those tears still rolled down his face.

They clung to each other and sobbed. "You always was and always will be my daughter, my baby girl."

"You watch, Dad. I will make you so proud of me!"

He rubbed her back. "I am prouder than I ever could be. You're stronger than me boys, kinder, and a good person, so don't you ever forget that I loves ya, always 'ave and always will."

Violet's caravan was the same as it had always been. She didn't like too much change and kept herself to herself. She was the O'Connell sister and grew up with four brothers, Johnnie, Cedric, Henry and Albi. No questions asked, Kizzy was to be living with her and that's how it was.

*

Johnnie drove back to London with a lump in his throat – and hate in his heart for Billy. The poor kid had been slyly manipulated into doing a grown woman's job. That was how he saw it and, since he brought Kizzy up, he would be the one to take fat boy, Billy, down. Nephew or not, he shouldn't have used her.

The lorry wasn't parked neatly on the drive; instead, it was abandoned on the path. As he marched to Billy's caravan, the women gathered to watch the sideshow. Johnnie almost ripped the door from its hinges.

"Billy, get out here now, you fucking fat bastard!" he screamed at the top of his voice, attracting more onlookers.

Dossing in his string vest, black trousers and braces, Billy was about to tuck into his bacon sandwich when Johnnie came ranting. He tried to jump up, but didn't have a chance to, as the door was flung open.

"What the hell's going on, mush?"

Billy looked fatter than ever, with his big jelly belly hanging over his belt, and his round face wobbling as he spoke.

"Ya fecking used my Kizzy girl like a whore just to get at fecking Sam Vincent!" His Irish accent was back. Johnnie, in his sixties, had the physique of a man in his thirties. He gripped his fists to the side of him as Billy eyed him up and down.

"Ya used ya own family, ya nothing but a bully, always have been, always will be, ya big, fat pig!"

Billy stood in the doorway, not knowing whether to jump down and beat Johnnie or tell him to fuck off. Before he had a chance to do either, there was a voice in the background.

Farley had heard the shouting and pushed his way through the crowd.

"She ain't fucking family anyway. Kizzy is just a whore, she ain't an O'Connell!" he spat.

In a fit of anger, Johnnie spun around and gave Farley a right hook to the chest. As he doubled over, Johnnie punched him again, this time on the chin, and he fell to the ground in shock.

"Ya call her a whore 'cos she dances for a bit of dosh. But why does she? I'll tell ya why, 'cos you nasty little bastards don't help. Not a fucking penny have you ever given that girl. Then, you expected her to help you two slimy gits get your fucking hands on a nightclub!"

Billy jumped down from the caravan and tried to throw a punch but, before it could land anywhere near him, Johnnie clouted him hard on the chin, and he too fell to the floor.

"Kizzy never asked for nothing off of any of ya. Kept herself to herself, she did. Whether by blood or not, she is an O'Connell, 'cos I fecking well brought her up. That means you should respect her as mine. Got it!" He was shouting loudly enough for all to hear.

The women looked at the floor in embarrassment and the men shook their heads at Billy and Farley.

"Well, I don't have to respect her, or you," said Farley. As he got to his feet, an earlier toot boosted his confidence again. The beating from yesterday was numbed by the drugs.

"Nah you don't, eh? You fucking will do!" replied Johnnie, as he pulled a huge spanner from down his trousers and whacked it across Farley's back, to the horror of the ever-increasing crowd of onlookers. He crashed the spanner again, this time on Farley's shoulder. Billy tried to crawl away, afraid of getting the same clump. The crowd cringed at the sound of breaking bones. Farley pleaded for Johnnie to stop. He did, but only to lift the spanner above his head and, with an almighty force, hit Billy in the chest, managing to break three ribs.

Johnnie was enraged and hurting because he realised in his heart that Kizzy was gone for good – all down to his nephews.

"You ain't no family of mine. I know what you did to my Kizzy girl. Ya killed her fucking dog when she was six years old, you hit her, and she still went choring for ya. All she ever fucking wanted was to fit in, be part of a family. And you, ya cunt, knew it. Ya fecking used and abused that girl and she messed up your plan. You silly fat bastard, you couldn't take down the Vincents if you had a whole fucking army!"

Ocean snuck away from the crowd, afraid that Johnnie would catch sight of him and do the same to him. Eventually, one of the old gypsies took Johnnie's arm, leaving the two brothers a crumpled mess. Farley's agonising pain didn't stop his cocaine-fuelled temper.

"You wait till Levi gets here. He will put you right!"

Johnnie held the spanner above his head again and demanded to know what he was talking about.

"Ah, yeah, see, wanna know now, don't ya? Well, it was all Levi's idea. Yeah, Levi, your precious son!"

He walked away in disgust. No one said a word. Johnnie, being an elder and blood relative, had the right to do what he did.

He thought about his son, and how he was never around these days, always having business to take care of. Levi had got himself a little flat near Roman Road. It was a nice pad with all modern conveniences. Johnnie never asked any questions as to how he could have afforded it, but he had a good idea. The boy hardly spoke sense anymore – sniffing and chewing the inside of his mouth. He was convinced it was drugs.

Farley and Billy brushed themselves down and slouched off into Billy's caravan to nurse their wounds. The crowd dispersed and gathered in various caravans to talk over the events. Johnnie guessed there would be gossip but he really didn't care. He had always held his head high and he knew in his heart that the site folk still looked up to him, even though he was getting on a bit. He saw the fear and respect in their eyes when he pulverised his two nephews.

Levi was tucked up in his bed, with an old Tom from King's Cross, when he got the phone call from Billy.

"Ya best come to the site and put your old man right. The silly old codger's gone fucking mental with a spanner and near-on murdered me and Farley. He thinks it's us that put Kizzy up to the pole dancing. I tell ya, bruv, he's fucking lost it!"

Levi slapped the prostitute on her bare backside and flicked his thumb, telling her to get dressed and go. He had business to attend to. Well, that's how he put it. Really, his business meant a quick chat with anyone who would listen to his bullshit, but this, on the other hand, was family business.

The cocaine dealing was a doddle – easy money. Most of the gypsy boys were hooked, which increased the demand. They only wanted to deal with their own kind. Levi had it sewn up. He had a parcel sent from the Albanians to Dover. It was then taken to Euston by black taxi every Friday and he stored it in his spare wheel. He was clever enough not to drive around in a flash BMW. Instead he used a dark blue Audi which looked respectable and not likely to get a tug off the Old Bill. The pikeys were queuing up for it by Friday night and it was sold out by Sunday morning. He dabbled himself and cut some of it with rat poison and baking soda so it didn't eat into his profits.

The prostitute put her clothes on and then she stared at Levi, curling her lip in disgust.

"What you gawping at?"

"Your fucking nose. It's caved in and bleeding."

Levi didn't feel the blood pouring from his nose, as his face was numb from the line he had snorted.

He dashed to the mirror and laughed. Sure enough, his nose looked like the end had dropped. When he tilted his head back he could see why, as the middle piece of skin had gone and was dripping claret everywhere. At first he thought he resembled a boxer but then reality set in. The cocaine had burnt the inside of his nose so badly it had collapsed. The effects of the drugs wore off more quickly than normal and Levi felt sick. He never had been a looker but now his own reflection repulsed him. Two teeth missing at the back, brown rings around his eyes, sunken cheek bones and, to top it all, his nose should belong to a turtle.

"Shall I take this fifty?" shouted the girl, finishing dressing in the bedroom.

Levi was gutted. He didn't give a shit if she nicked all the money. He was staring into the mirror and grieving over his train wreck of a face.

Tinkerbell, the prostitute, pinched two fifties and scarpered, leaving Levi to pull himself together. He looked at the bag of cocaine in the bathroom cabinet and contemplated having another line just to take away the shock of his crumpling nose. He then concluded it would make matters worse and so rolled a fat joint instead. The phone rang again and this time it was Johnnie. "Levi, boy, get your arse over here now, mush, no excuses!"

He didn't argue. The one person he feared was his father. They had been kids when their dear, old mother died. Johnnie was firm. When they got out of line he beat them with a stick but when they were good he treated them with kindness. There were no in-betweens. They had to work hard in all weathers, even as young as ten, and didn't go to school. Kizzy was the exception, but she was the baby and he couldn't take care of her then.

His day had gone from bad to worse and now he was stoned.

*

Johnnie was visited by Merlin, and another old friend, Zeb. They had grown-up together – and they would often sit talking over the old times, especially any unrest in the camp.

"I can't have all this trouble on the site. Me fecking nephews and my boy Levi are messing with the big club owners. Whatever are they thinking? I don't know anymore. If they were out choring I wouldn't mind, but this is a dangerous game. I'll tell ya something. I know the old man Vincent. He's a decent enough fella. For years, I took me scrap there. He always gave me a good price, no questions asked like, but that was a front and, let me tell you, his sons are clever." Johnnie opened a can of beer and chucked one each to his visitors. "I remember his boys when they were teenagers, and they had more savvy than men in their forties. If our boys bring the Vincents to the site…" he paused, "that will be the day I up and leave. Those Vincents… you just don't fuck with them!"

Zeb nodded slowly and Merlin shook his head but both men agreed.

"I tell you, Johnnie, it's drugs that's changed those boys. Made 'em greedy," asserted Zeb, who had been keeping an eye on the lads.

"It's like my Davey Boy. Always got red eyes and it's not drink. But I can't tell him. It ain't like the old days when you did as you were told. It's all fucking changed. Even the malts are getting a bit big for their boots!" squeaked Merlin.

Johnnie laughed for the first time. "'Ere don't give me that. Your Lou has always fucking kept you in check."

Merlin looked at both the men and grinned as his cheeks flushed red.

"Yeah, cheeky fucking mare she is." He said it with affection.

They changed the subject from the Vincents and the boys and reminisced over the old times.

*

Contemplating their next move with more anger now, although it was their Uncle Johnnie who had given them both a good hiding, it was the Vincents who Billy detested and he vowed to take revenge one day.

Farley, however, had already taken two batterings in the space of a few hours and thought maybe he should take it easy. Besides, he needed to get ready for another punch up. Noah, down in Kent, had made a public threat to muller Farley and so it was a fight that would happen, either now or in the future, but it remained on the cards.

When Levi arrived at the site, he drove past his father's plot and straight to Billy's van to get the low down on what had happened at the club.

Billy's van was bigger than Johnnie's but not as clean and tidy. Levi was still stoned when he tried to untie his boots before entering the caravan and he lost his balance and fell.

Billy and Farley laughed for the first time that day. But they soon stopped when Farley yelped like a dog at the pain from his cracked collar bone.

"Cor blimey, mush, dick at the hooter," said Billy, deadly serious.

Farley screwed up his eyes to get a better look.

After he plonked himself on the sofa, Levi concocted a story of how he'd got bashed by two drug dealers and how they had come off worse.

Billy wasn't as clever these days, and with Farley's short-sightedness, they were both sucked into the bullshit. Levi was ashamed to admit – even to his family – that his coke habit had caused his nose to collapse.

"Looks like me old man gave you two a right poggering," Levi laughed. Funny to think that, as old as his father was, he still had it in him to fight. Knowing his dad had a reputation, he had grown up to be proud he was the son of Johnnie O'Connell, a prize boxer in his younger days.

"Yeah, all 'cos of fucking Kizzy girl, the dirty chavi," replied Billy.

Levi was sobering up. The effects of the skunk had now worn off.

"Look, boys, Kizzy is family, and well you know it. The chavi, she is a dead ringer for any O'Connell, well, except you, Billy, ya fat cunt." He laughed and so did Farley.

Billy wasn't amused. "What do you mean I'm not an O'Connell? Are ya saying me muvver's a slag?" His voice raised a pitch in temper.

"Easy, bruv, I was just joking with ya," said Levi, who wanted to have a dig. Out of all the O'Connells, Billy was the fat bully who only teenagers looked up to – listening to the bullshit that poured from his mouth, his tales of prison life, and the endless fights he'd had. Levi was sucked in when he was young, and knew no different, but once he was wrapped up with the London gorgers he soon discovered that bashing people didn't always get you what you wanted. Manipulation, coercion and planning did. However, the previous beatings from Billy, as he was growing up, still haunted him, and he wouldn't push the fat boy too far.

"So, as I was saying, I can see me dad's point. After all, she is our family. You wanted in on the deal with me and the Nappers, right? You were supposed to take care of the underage dancing, drinking, gambling, find some clever little chavis. I didn't mean use your own fucking family, divvy!"

Billy sat staring at Levi with pure hatred in his eyes.

"But, Levi, she ain't even your sister!" he spat back with venom.

"No she ain't me sister, but she is me cousin, and blood is blood. Whatever is a matter with ya, boy? Fuck me, what is it with you two, always denying Kizzy. Makes me wonder if you wanted a bit of her arse for ya selves!" He nervously laughed, trying to take the edge off his 'near to the truth' statement.

Billy took umbrage. "What, you saying, cunt face? I'm into incense?"

Levi laughed. "Incest, you fick fucker!" He giggled like a kid. "Well, if you don't believe she's related, it ain't incest, is it?"

Farley, ignoring their pettiness, wanted to get down to business. "So what do we do now?" he asked, changing the subject.

Levi knew that if he wanted a stake in any club he needed to keep the Napper brothers happy.

"I will see Kenneth, and decide what needs to be done, even if it means taking those fucking Vincents out, one by one."

Billy jumped up. "Right, I'm ready when you are, cuz."

"Sit down, you ain't going anywhere. From now on, I'll be the one doing all the talking. Don't even answer the phone to the Nappers. You will only fuck things up!"

Farley remained quiet, hoping that Levi would take him along, but with a quick 'see ya later' he was gone.

"Cousin or not, that Levi is too big for his boots, cocky cunt."

"Leave it out, Bill, you hate everyone!" said Farley, gripping his painful shoulder. Bill's weight only added to the pain from his broken ribs and the agony, which swept over his face, was proof of this. The two brothers stopped arguing and tried to rest their injuries.

*

Levi went to see his father and as he entered the caravan Zeb and Merlin left. It was only right. Family business needed to be taken care of.

"All right, boy?" said Johnnie, who was now a little jolly from the two cans of beer. He wasn't a drinker. He never really had been. Only after his wife had died had he taken to the whisky, and that had only lasted a month.

He soon realised it didn't get him anywhere and so he stopped and threw himself into work.

"I've been to see Billy and Farley. Ya gave 'em a right good hiding then, Dad?"

Levi tested the water; he was not sure what else to say.

"Yep, and I'll give you the fucking same, boy, if you don't tell me what you were up to getting our Kizzy involved in a scam like that."

He didn't expect to be explaining his plan to his father, but he wasn't about to go telling lies to him now. Johnnie was a clever man and could find out for himself.

"And before you begin…" Johnnie sat dead opposite Levi and stared, "don't think about lying or leaving anything out, 'cos if ya do…" He raised his eyebrows, making Levi shudder.

Levi confessed everything, except the fact he was the one responsible for the cocaine and ecstasy. He told how they intended to get the Vincents' clubs closed down and ensure the Nappers' clubs were up and running, but in his name, and reclaim all the business that went to *Dan's Palace*.

Johnnie threw his head back and laughed.

"You must think I walk around with my head up my fucking arse."

Levi felt belittled. "I don't know what you're laughing at, Farver, but you watch. I will have the Nappers' clubs up and running just like the Vincents', only even better. I am taking this personally. The Vincents opened the *Palace* on me doorstep and now all my punters are going there!" He sat back on his seat.

"Your punters, what do you mean your punters? You never owned any fucking club!" shouted Johnnie, annoyed at his son's immaturity.

"The Nappers' club was owned by the Napper brothers but I ran it. I had a right tidy earner going until it got closed down. All down to the Vincents, so I'm taking it back." Levi shuffled nervously, uncomfortable with his father's expression.

Johnnie looked at his son with disgust. "Yeah, boy, I know what ya mean… ya divvy cunt! I raised you lot to be smart, go and earn a few bob, but you are one thick bastard!" He nodded his head, almost pacing his move, just as he would before a fight. Levi's eyes widened. He could tell his father was ready to clobber him. "Those Vincents own clubs, the gym, the boxing club and how? 'Cos, you prick, they are fucking businessmen. As for the Nappers' clubs closing down, that's 'cos they had no-good wankers like you running yer dirty dealings!"

"Dad, what's your fucking problem?"

Johnnie lunged forward and grabbed his son by the hair. He dragged him from around the table and pushed his face into the art deco mirror above the tiny fireplace.

"Take a good look at your ugly face. Your nose is fucked, ya fucking teeth missing, 'cos of drugs, and you wanna do this to kids? Sell them shit in a nightclub? Make them all look like you?" he shouted at the top of his voice, then threw Levi to the ground, kicking him hard in the chest.

"You stay away from 'ere. Stay away from me and don't you ever go near Kizzy. You're not my son!"

Levi felt a deep pain to be disowned by his father, as he really admired him. To be shunned shook him to the core. He got to his feet and went to walk away but his father's big, strong arm stopped him.

"And before you go, I think you had better know this much. If you want to mess with the Vincents, be prepared for the consequences. It was believed that they removed the McManners' family in the dead of night for fucking with their family. So, boy, fuck with them and they won't just dance on your top lip; they'll have ya buried, along with ya divvy cousins!"

Levi left the caravan that day with more than enough to think about. His world had just caved in, like his nose, and it was all because of cocaine. But those words his father had said, that the McManners were taken away in the dead of night, would play on his mind. He had remembered what happened about ten years ago, when the McManners' scrap yards just closed down and the old man, Mick, and three of his sons, just disappeared. No one was ever pulled in for questioning, and by the end of the week their disappearance was old chip paper.

When Levi sat alone on his huge, leather corner sofa, facing his flat screen TV, he realised he had everything money could buy. He had the perfect pad, all the gadgets and gizmos, but it felt cold and lonely. He had lived a gypsy life and now he was in a flat alone with dead silence unless the TV was on. No one knocking on your caravan door selling knocked off gear. None of the gossip. He had always dreamt of having a luxury apartment which was warm and comfortable, with a big living room and a bedroom with lots of cupboard space. But all of this came at a price, and that was loneliness. The gorgers he mixed with were not his mates but only dealers or druggies. No one came for a beer, just to score dope. Now even his father didn't want to know him. He thought carefully about pursuing the Vincents' empire. There was something in the way his father had spoken about them which gave him the shivers. The Vincents had that locktight affiliation with each other. He had watched them in the boxing club, not knowing they owned it, and he was conscious then that the brothers were close-knit. They didn't converse with the other lads unless they had to. If they had done away with the McManners, then they were a dangerous lot and he would be forced to reconsider his plan. Maybe he should lie low. It might be prudent for the time being not to have any connection with the Nappers or the Vincents. He was out of his league and he should back right off until the time was right and then, maybe in a few years, he would revisit the whole idea. Besides, he had very little backup. Billy was as good as a chocolate teapot and the rest of them were either too young or too thick. He was, however, stupid enough not to realise you don't get that far in the club business if you're a soft touch.

He poured the contents of the cocaine onto a mirror and with a flat razor blade made three lines and snorted them, one after the other. Then he sat back and waited for the hit. It was there in a second. He sweated and the perception of euphoria swept over his body. The issue with the flat nose and his failure to close down the clubs disappeared. One day…

Chapter Eight

On Sunday morning, Sam was up early, cooking breakfast, when Ruby appeared. She looked as a teenager should, dressed in jeans, a sweatshirt, and with no makeup.

"Good morning, my angel, and how are you this morning?"

Ruby smiled. "Yep, I'm fine…" She paused. "Dad, I'm off to visit my mum." She bit her bottom lip, waiting for a shouting match.

Sam stared at the bacon frying in the pan, trying to control his emotions. He wanted to say 'you are not going' but he guessed that if he did she would go anyway. Then there would be an atmosphere when she returned. Not only that, he was afraid of losing her forever.

"What time will you be back? Only, you have school tomorrow and after your exclusion for the week you don't want to piss them off."

He tried to keep his voice on an even keel.

"About six o'clock."

Ruby did not put on her expensive designer labels or even attempt to make herself up. She remembered how her mother looked and it made her self-conscious of her own clothes and accessories.

The weather wasn't so dismal today. As she arrived on the estate, the sun lit up the greyness and highlighted the colourful graffiti. She hoped her mother would be home, as she hadn't made any specific arrangements to meet her.

Just as she went to knock on the door, it opened, and out came the man from the café. He acknowledged Ruby and she smiled back. She assumed he was collecting the money Jesse owed.

He left the door ajar for Ruby to walk in and although it was her own mother's flat, she still felt like an intruder.

"Mum, it's me, Ruby!" she shouted.

No answer. She must be in the toilet. As she entered the living room, she made out two people curled up on the floor with old blankets wrapped around them. On the table was a tall glass ornament with protruding pipes. Ruby had seen these before in Egypt whilst on holiday with her Aunt Francesca, who used to smoke flavoured tobacco. Unbeknown to her, however, they were for drugs. As she went to leave, one of the people unravelled themselves. It was Jacob, the black guy with the green eyes who she'd met last week.

"'Ello, Princess," he said, as he sat upright.

Ruby blushed. She didn't expect to see him again, and she felt scruffy with no makeup and just plain jeans and a top.

111

"Oh, hiya, I was looking for me mum," she whispered.

Jacob jumped up and stretched his arms. "She is still asleep, on a late one last night."

Ruby frowned, puzzled by what she had seen this morning. If she was still in bed, why did the café man just leave her flat? Out of her comfort zone, she shuffled from foot to foot.

"Hey, let me make you a nice cup of tea!" offered Jacob, who beamed from ear to ear.

She remembered the last cup made in her mother's kitchen and thought better of it.

"No, it's all right. I might have a walk and come back when she wakes up," said Ruby.

Jacob would not let Ruby slip through his hands again. Unable to get her off his mind, he didn't like the way she pulled the same face as Jesse when she was angry, but he still fancied her.

"Listen, babes, I've got to run an errand for me Aunty Gloria. How about you come along?"

Ruby liked his lively personality and cheeky smile. She followed him.

Jacob knocked on the door at the end of the block, which was so different from her mother's place. It was painted bright red and had a big black polished knocker. On either side were two plant pots, and the window sills sparkled in brilliant white. As Gloria opened the door, the distinctive perfume of lavender and roses hit Ruby. She remembered the smell but had associated it with her mother.

She stared at Ruby for ages. Jacob looked at Ruby and then back at his aunt.

"Well, Aunty, you going to let us in? Oh yeah, this is —"

Before he could finish, Gloria jumped in. "Ruby!"

Ruby smiled and nodded.

"Oh, look at you, all grown up and beautiful." Her big, caramel arms reached out and enveloped her. The familiar sensation reminded Ruby of her childhood. The warm embrace, the soft voice, and the love which Gloria had given her all those years ago, now came back to her and made her feel so comfortable. She hugged her back.

"Come in, come in!" urged Gloria, so excited.

She led them into the living room. It hadn't changed in ten years, and Ruby recognised the flowered curtains, the coloured cushions, the rugs on the floor, and the lamp in the corner. Knitting needles and balls of wool lay on the table, and in the corner by the large dresser was the sewing machine. Ruby recalled the soft humming sound but had associated it with her mother. Deep in her memory, she must have got the flats confused. She remembered the smells, the warmth, and the big arms that enveloped her and also recalled the chocolate milkshakes and soft, cosy bed.

As she sat on the sofa and gazed around, a tear sprang from her eyes. "Did I live here?" asked Ruby.

Gloria was unsure what to say, so she threw a glance at her nephew. He shrugged, clueless.

"You used to come and visit with me, child. When your mother had problems, you stayed a while." Gloria's accent was as Jamaican as ever.

Ruby's head was awash with mixed emotions. Maybe Jack was right and her memory was skewed. Jesse seemed kind enough. She was certainly not the frightening monster her brother had made her out to be.

Before her world came crashing down, Gloria asked, "How have ya been then, and how is Jack?" She sat on the edge of her special chair, which had long legs so she didn't have to struggle to get up and down. The arthritis had worsened over the years.

"Jack is okay. He is into his boxing. He is Kent Champion for Under Eighteens." Gloria noticed how Ruby's face lit up when she spoke of her brother.

*

Jesse dragged herself out of bed to ponce a cigarette from the other man who had stayed the night before, getting stoned.

"'Ere, chuck us a fag!" she said, in her croaky old lady's voice.

The man pushed the blanket away from his face. "Jacob took 'em, and he went to his aunt's with your daughter."

She froze, rooted to the spot. "What did you say?"

"Jacob's gone to Gloria's with your girl." He sat up straight, mumbling under his breath. "Poor fucking kid."

Jesse panicked. She had visions of Gloria slating her and telling her daughter the truth, or exaggerating it.

She threw on her tracksuit bottoms and an old t-shirt, slid her dirty feet into a pair of flip flops, and dashed out of the house to Gloria's. She almost smashed the door in with her erratic banging.

Gloria opened the door and, without an invitation, Jesse stormed in to find Ruby sitting comfortably next to Jacob.

"'Ello, my babe. Sorry, I was asleep, you should have woken me!" she said, out of breath.

Ruby jumped up, ashamed at her mother's appearance. She had matted hair, her T-shirt had a massive stain on the front, and she smelt rotten.

Immersed in the familiarity and reluctant to leave, Ruby hugged Gloria once more – to the distaste of Jesse, who glared at her with her face screwed up. Caught in the middle, with three women who had different agendas, Jacob could almost taste the tension. He waited for them to depart and stayed behind, interested to discover how his aunt knew Ruby.

"I looked out for the poor little mites, her and her brother. I don't like to run a woman down, and I believe it takes a village to bring up a child…"

Jacob was confused by her comment, but listened. "But she was cruel to those two children, and I never imagined I would see the day when they would return to find her. All I can think is they were too young to remember, but I do, and I will never forget the pain and suffering she caused them. If she didn't go to prison then, I would have called the social services meself."

"But, Aunty, if she was so young, how did she remember you?"

Gloria shrugged her shoulders.

"Maybe, child, the brain remembers only the good things, and blots out the bad. You see, Jacob, I took them in when they got shut outside in the rain. I put shoes on their feet when they had blisters and gave them food when they were hungry, but, most of all, I showed them love. I prayed for a miracle for those two little children, and God answered my prayers. I heard they went to live with their father in a nice home and, your uncle will tell ya, I slept like a baby, knowing they were safe. Watch out for that child. She has no place 'ere, not with Jesse, the sorry state of a so-called woman."

Jacob looked up to his aunty. She was a good person and he had no qualms helping her with the odd errand or carrying her shopping.

*

Ruby returned to her mother's flat, only to find the cold ugliness of her home amplified.

"So, how are you feeling now, Mum?" she asked.

Jesse remembered she needed to keep up the pretence. "Oh, ya know, plodding on, taking me pain killers."

"Have you seen the doctor again?"

"Yeah, he reckons there's a surgeon in the States who can do me op for four grand." She looked at Ruby's face for a reaction. Ruby didn't answer. Four thousand pounds was a lot but if it saved her mother's life, surely her dad would give it to her.

"If I get you the money, will you have the operation?"

Jesse was on a high; her act had worked and she would reel her in and bleed her dry.

"For you, my darling, I'd have me head chopped off and sewn back on again."

She put her arm around Ruby's shoulders and led her into the kitchen.

"I'll find a way to get the cash, Mum."

Jesse kicked herself. Four thousand. She should have made it five. "But that's just for the operation, and I don't have a grand for the flights and the stay in the hospital."

Ruby nodded. "Well, then, I'll try to get five. I'm sure to be able to con it, one way or another." She wanted to give the impression she was fighting for her mother and on her side.

"My babe, you are a lovely girl. You have turned out to be a diamond, but I can't ask you to do that for me." Jesse put her head in her hands and tried to cry. She managed a single tear. "I wasn't there for you growing up. God knows, I wanted to be, the nights I sat up crying, hoping that your dad loved you the way I did." Jesse stopped for a second and looked for a reaction. But Ruby was embarrassed, not used to the tears and drama. The only tears she experienced were hers – when she didn't get her own way.

"Look, Mum, I'll do my best. There's shit loads of stuff at home I can sell. My jewellery – I never wear it anyway."

Jesse couldn't believe her daughter owned at least five grand's worth of jewellery. If she had that amount in gems, what else did she have? She grinned to herself as she imagined the pounds rolling in. If she moved in, Sam would see to it that they lived in a decent place. He'd make sure his precious little kid wanted for nothing. She had the power to manipulate Ruby to scam her old man. This was it – the long awaited payback. Then her thoughts switched to Francesca, that fucking evil dangerous cow, and those warnings. Jesse decided better of it and to keep Ruby in her back pocket but skim off what she could, without involving the Vincents.

She offered Ruby a chair opposite her in the tiny, bare kitchen. Ruby gazed around at the minimalist design. There were no doors on the cupboards and only one ring on the cooker with an iron grate to cook on. There was, however, a new toaster and kettle – an expensive, sixties diner style. The red and chrome seemed so out of place in the run-down, dirty, hovel.

Jesse could see the disgust written all over Ruby's face.

"I got burgled. They pinched everything, even wrecked me home, ripped the doors off me cupboards, took me china, even nicked me sofas, and I cancelled me insurance just the week before." Convinced by her own lies, she shed another tear.

From the living room, a gruff voice shouted, "Any chance of a cuppa, Jess? Me mouth's like the bottom of a fucking parrot's cage!" Solly, a local lad, one of Jacob's mates, who had just sat up through the night smoking skunk and listening to weird music, was still in the living room.

Jesse had forgotten about him. She frantically jumped to her feet and dragged him out and onto the street.

"Shut up, Solly. I've got me daughter over for dinner. Now, do one, will ya?"

"What, you gonna fucking cook a roast? The only thing you can cook is yaself." He laughed as he walked away, but she slammed the door shut so Ruby couldn't hear.

Ruby felt sorry for her mother. What thieving bastards to rob off a woman with cancer. No wonder she looked such a mess.

"Did they take your clothes too, Mum?" Ruby was so into fashion, the be all and end all, that the worst thing they could pinch would be her clothes.

Jesse nodded furiously, although she took that comment as an insult. Cheeky mare – she wanted to lean across and slap her one.

"I tell ya what, Mum. I've got loads of clothes I haven't even worn yet. If you want them, I can bring them next time I visit."

Jesse tried to work out if she could get any money for the clothes or if she should say they wouldn't fit. Ruby might offer her the money instead.

"Do you think they are my size? I have lost so much weight. It's the cancer, ya see, it does that."

Ruby looked away. It made her feel sick – the notion that cancer could eat you away, like a living parasite, gnawing through the flesh.

"Do you fancy going shopping? I've got my bank card," suggested Ruby, feeling so sorry for her mother with all her problems.

Jesse's eyes widened. "You have a bank card at your age?"

Ruby nodded. "Yeah, all my mates have," she replied, unaware of the differences between the girls who went to a private school and those who went to a normal comprehensive.

Ruby hung around with the Sevenoaks kids and, yes, they smoked dope and had a few fights, but they were spoilt, rich kids. They came from professional parents: most of them were doctors, lawyers or judges. Ruby's father was classed as a businessman, but she knew the difference. She regularly visited the London gym with her brother and boxed, and she was a good fighter who could land a punch like a man. So, street fights in her own neighbourhood gave her respect. That's how she fitted in, because the other pupils' hobbies and conversations included horse riding, clay-pigeon shooting and ballet. So Ruby steered towards the wayward kids who, in her mind, were more interesting.

Jesse, itching to find out how much she had tucked away in that bank account, said, "Listen, Ruby, I couldn't take your last few quid, it wouldn't be right. Just because the thieves nicked me stuff, it ain't up to you to get me out of this mess."

"Mum, I've got more than a few quid. I had around nine hundred pounds last time I looked, might be more." Ruby, being so open and honest, threw Jesse.

"Good God, girl, that's so much money!"

Ruby smiled. She didn't need it and it would be great to help her mother out, especially now her mother might not live for long.

"I can go to the cash machine now and draw out four hundred, if you like?"

Jesse imagined the drugs she could buy with that money. She heard that there was good quality cocaine around. The thought sent her on a high.

"Well, if you're sure, my babes. Then, as soon as I get meself sorted, I'll pay you back. I promise."

Ruby felt proud of herself.

Jesse guessed that their relationship would be short-lived. After all, what could she offer her daughter except freedom to smoke pot in her home and have a drink? Nothing, really.

"He's not a bad lad, that Jacob. You'll not go wrong with him," said Jesse.

Ruby was astounded. If her father thought for one second she was entertaining a man in his twenties, who smoked dope and didn't work for a living, then he would go mental. She liked the understanding side of her mother and she did have a soft spot for Jacob, who was older and more confident. He looked at her in a special way – unlike her teenage friends, with their stupid, childish grins and slobbery snogs. Her mates would be so jealous.

"He is nice. I like his green eyes," giggled Ruby.

Jesse was onto a winning streak and knew she had to keep her daughter's interest. All the time she came to visit, the money would follow. They talked for hours about the things Ruby did not dare talk to her father about. Jacob knocked at the door, hoping Ruby was still around and to retrieve his blow tucked behind the sofa.

Jesse was full of smiles, which was a rarity. "Come in, Ruby's in the kitchen!" Jesse acted as if he and Ruby were already a couple.

"And you ran off with my fags," she said, whilst maintaining her smile. Jacob pulled out the packet and offered Ruby one. She looked at her mother, who just smiled and graciously took one. It felt strange at first, smoking in front of her, but then as all three puffed away it became the most natural thing in the world. Jacob had a plastic bag containing six cans of special brew. He handed them out and, like an old hand, Ruby took one and joined in the drinking. They laughed and joked. Jacob set about impressing Ruby with his antics and Jesse encouraged him. "Go on, Jacob, tell Rubes how you had the Ol' Bill running over the estate looking for you. Cor, it was funny. We was watching out of our windows!"

Exaggerated tales of skulduggery impressed Ruby, as her eyes widened, and Jacob played up to it.

He went to the living room and retrieved his puff. "Ya don't mind if I roll a spliff, do ya?" He looked at Ruby, who glanced at her mother. Besides, it wasn't her house. Jesse smiled. "You go ahead, boy. I could do with a puff meself, I'm in that much pain at times." She made a pathetic attempt to appear downtrodden. He rolled his eyes; this was yet another load of bullshit spewing from her mouth.

He didn't care that she was a pathological liar who sold drugs – and her arse. His interest was a free house for a late night pipe session and a good-looking daughter who was easy pickings.

He sucked deeply on the joint and coughed, passing to Jesse, who dragged heavily. Ruby took the fat spliff herself and puffed on it but the effects were far stronger than the silly bit of weed she shared with her mates in Knole Park on a Friday night. She coughed and felt light-headed. Jesse laughed. Her teeth looked blacker than ever and the green in Jacob's eyes shone like emeralds.

"'Ere, look at that. My daughter loves puff, she does." She slapped Jacob on the arm and giggled.

Ruby compared this life to her own. She concluded her mother had more respect for her by treating her like an adult. Her dad and the rest of the family made sure she knew she was the baby who was never allowed to act her age – never included in their drinking sessions or privy to their conversations.

They spent the afternoon smoking dope, drinking and talking shit – but, at fifteen, Ruby thought she was having fun. When six o'clock came, she walked to the station accompanied by Jacob, who insisted on ensuring she was safe. Ten minutes before the train arrived, Ruby stood face-to-face with him, hoping he would kiss her before she left.

"Text me when you get home so I know you're okay."

She stared into his eyes and nodded, thrilled he was so interested in her.

He tilted his head to the side and, with half a smile, he whispered, "You have a pretty face and a beautiful smile."

Ruby tingled with excitement. He leaned forward and kissed her. This was a grown-up kiss – not like her stupid boyfriends, slobbering over her. He knew exactly what to do.

"Will I see you again, Ruby gem?" His voice was charming and she fell for it. She wanted to act cool and say maybe but she couldn't help herself. He had her hooked.

"Yeah, I'll come over in the week, if you want."

He nodded as the train pulled in. He kissed her once more and said, "Call me."

Delighted she had a new, grown-up boyfriend and a good relationship with her mother, she felt less like a child. She could smoke and drink and at least Jesse treated her as an equal. She was so immersed in the day's events, Ruby almost missed her stop.

Jesse counted the twenties which her daughter had drawn out of the cash machine. Four hundred pounds! She would have a fucking ball with that money. She would get as high as a kite.

*

When Ruby arrived home, she went straight to the bathroom and had a long soak.

"Are you all right up there, Rubes?" shouted her father, who had hoped she might first have come into the living room to say hello.

"Yeah, I'm fine. I'll be down after my bath!" she exclaimed.

She needed to get rid of the smell of smoke and drink. If her father suspected either then he'd stop her going over there again. She was still stoned, but the alcohol gave her false confidence. When she had put her nightclothes on and entered the living room, Sam saw right away that she had been up to something.

Slowly, he walked over, grabbed her chin, and pointed her face to the light.

"What are you doing, Dad?" Ruby hadn't realised that cleaning her teeth didn't get rid of the smell of alcohol and getting so stoned left your eyes bloodshot.

"Tell me, Ruby, where have you been, and what have you taken?" He didn't shout at her but he looked very concerned.

Jack marched into the room when he heard his father. He glared at his sister.

"See, what did I tell you? That fucking mother of yours has given you drugs, hasn't she?" he shouted, but Sam waved his arms to stop him.

Ruby needed to think quickly, but the puff made it more difficult.

"I didn't see Mum. She wasn't in."

Sam and Jack looked at each other.

"So, where have you been then?" questioned her father.

"Just out with me mates, and I admit I drank half a can of Fosters." She turned around and headed back to her room before they began any more interrogation. From now on, she decided to keep her visits a secret.

She scoured her bedroom for anything of value. Her jewellery box held obscene amounts of expensive bits – from diamond rings to Tiffany necklaces.

Her handbags were designer quality – not fake shit – worth at least a grand. She could get a taxi, load it up, and head to her mother's after school on Wednesday. That would be the best time as Jack would be at the gym and her father would be working at the club. She planned it all out. She would rescue her mum by giving her the cash she needed for her operation.

The day's experiences had once again left Ruby with so much to consider. She looked around her bedroom and convinced herself that it was claustrophobic. Her father smothered her and she should be treated more like a young adult than a five-year-old. Jacob had regarded her as a grown-up and so had her mother. She soon forgot Gloria, the flowered curtains, and the smell of lavender. It might have been warm and fluffy, but her mum's flat offered her freedom.

She dozed off to sleep, dreaming of Jacob, and woke up thinking of him, and that's how it was – until the next visit.

*

Monday afternoon, the Vincents held a meeting at the club to sort, out once and for all, the pikey situation.

They had sent out their own men to find out what the hell was going on and they hoped they would soon be provided with some evidence of skulduggery.

Dan sat rocking on his leather, high-back chair while the others perched on the sofas.

"Looks like it was a put-up job. Those fucking travellers were organised by none other than the low-life Napper brothers!" said Dan, with a big grin on his face. They laughed, shaking their heads.

"Well, that will have me quaking in me fucking daisy roots," chuckled Fred.

"For fuck's sake, what's the matter with them? As if they think they could get away with that," growled Sam.

"So, it turns out that Kenneth Napper, the stupid bastard, blames us for his club going down the pan. Now, it seems to me, and correct me if I'm wrong, it got closed down because of drugs, guns and no sign of rock n roll." They all laughed.

"And now, the fucking muppets want to get us nicked for the same thing and then have the cheek to reopen Nappers under a new name… should call it Nappies, 'cos they are so full of shit."

Fred wobbled off the chair, laughing.

"I'm going to hit them right where it hurts!" said Dan. His brothers sat on the edge of their chairs, waiting to hear the proposal.

"I am gonna buy the old warehouse in the Old Kent Road, next to the old Nappers' building, and open it as *Vincents' Palace*, just to piss them off." There was an all-around thumbs up. The Nappers' clubs had lost their licence and were left with a building and no business. They had the money to set up under another name but their customers were now filling the trendy *Palaces*. The Nappers needed to get the *Palaces* out of the picture. The Vincents had a reputation for running a clean joint and there would be no problem getting their hands on the warehouse. Until it was up and ready for opening, no one should know who the new owner was. The Vincent empire was growing and so was the size of their man power.

"Can we afford to open another *Palace*?" asked Sam.

"I should cocoa. Have you looked at the last two months' profits? With the clubs selling out every opening night, and selling vast amounts of champagne, we could afford all the clubs in the Old Kent Road."

He opened one of the better labels of champagne and poured each brother a drink. "Cheers! Let the fun begin!"

"I don't know about you guys, but I am fucking proud that we made good money from a clean club. All right, so the punters might have a bit of Charlie on 'em, but it ain't no fucking rave." The boys looked at Sam, who hated drugs with a passion. He smiled and nodded.

Fred jumped up. "Well, I still think they need a fucking visit with me mate, the iron cosh." Always ready for a ruck and now thirty-seven, he still bounced around like a teenager. Sam pretended to spar with him. They were like two kids. "Leave off, you two, I don't want any bloodshed. Buying the building on their manor will hurt them more. Besides, fucking 'ell, they are old 'as beens!" said Dan, who was too old for the fighting game himself.

"Yeah, but you need to make a statement – or you'll have another mob doing the fucking same. Nah, I say we give them a beating, teach them a lesson in respect," stated Fred, punching the air.

"You'd better get down the gym, Mr Blobby," laughed Sam, who whacked his little brother around the face for not moving out of the way in time.

"No one's gonna get their hands dirty. Johnnie and his brother can give the Nappers a pasting, if that's what you want, Fred. 'Cos I'm sure Johnnie has been itching to bash the old bastard. By all accounts, Kenneth loves to give his missus a slap now and then!"

*

Kenneth's wife, Celia, had taken enough abuse off her husband, but refused to leave due to the lavish lifestyle she had – the holidays to their Spanish villa, the shopping sprees on Oxford Street, and her luxury home, complete with shag pile carpets and corner bath units. Kenneth was a bully who shouted and hollered every time he laid eyes on her and, if he'd had too much gin, got handy too. The years had taught her to say little, keep a clean house, have a dinner on the table for him and, other than that, keep out of the way. Nigel, Kenneth's brother, married Celia's sister, Maureen, and that was also a reason for Celia to stick around. She loved to spend time with Mo, as she was commonly known.

John, the bouncer at the club, a long-time doorman for the Vincents, was secretly knocking off Celia. It was a little indiscretion not even Mo knew about, but their pillow talk had inevitably landed on Dan's ears. Any news like this was a power tool and the deliverer would be held in high esteem as far as the Vincents were concerned. If push came to shove, the best side to be on was theirs.

Fred agreed to stay away and let the Lees do the dirty work.

Kenneth and Nigel were worried now that the pikeys had cocked up the plan. They took a big risk getting the travellers involved, and should have known that if you put a gypsy under enough pressure he will save himself – even if that means grassing. That's what happened so, right now, the Nappers would not stick around to find out the consequences.

Kenneth was packing his suitcase and had told Nigel to do the same. The phone rang and he shouted to his wife, "I'm in Spain, if anyone asks!" His face was tight and she knew he was in a blind panic.

Celia was on edge herself. She had said too much to Johnnie but he had always been a good listener and she loved him. Maybe she had always wanted it to fall on the Vincents' ears.

She answered the phone to her sister, who was furious that Nigel was packing and going off to Spain without her.

"Fucking selfish bastard, he is. Thinks he can fuck off to Spain, and leave me 'ere on me own!"

"Maureen, just let the boys go, and we can join them later," replied Celia, who hoped her husband would soon leave. He was getting more uptight by the minute and she would be in the firing line. She needed to get Mo off the phone so she could help her husband on his way. If he had any idea she had been earwigging on his conversations and blabbing to Johnnie, then she was a dead woman.

Celia had married Kenneth because she had fallen in love with the villain. Both brothers had a reputation as hard men in their younger days. Two major bank jobs later they had money and were sensible enough to make more by investing in the clubs. But they got greedy, which was the start of their downfall. Celia led Kenneth to believe she couldn't have children but the plain truth was she wanted none. Maureen, however, had a son, but he was far from the apple of his father's eye when he turned out to be 'bent as a nine bob note', as Nigel would say. As soon as he was of age, he moved to Brighton to run a coffee shop. So the four of them were in each other's pockets, but that suited them. When the men didn't come home some nights, the girls had each other. They knew, only too well, what their husbands were up to. It was part of the lifestyle. The clubs, in the early days, were not far off a knocking shop. A few Bacardis and the promise of a new dress and the men had their fun for the night. But each went home to his wife and his respectable four bedroom detached house with the double garage and the small pool in the back garden.

Some nights, Celia sneaked out to see Johnnie. She used the same old story, 'off to bingo'. That story lasted for ten years. Kenneth never questioned her. He never believed, for one minute, his Celia would have it away with a big bruising bouncer like Johnnie Lee. She had always been shy in the bedroom – nightdress on, and the lights off. He didn't mind, though. If he wanted a freak in the bed, he paid for it. His little Celia was a tiny woman with sharp features and pretty heart-shaped lips, fashionable in the sixties. He loved her in his own way, but he had no clue what she was up to.

*

Johnnie had met Celia when he went to her house to meet Kenneth about a debt which had to be paid. Kenneth owed a lot of money because he kept losing at poker. It was rare for a doorman, like Johnnie, to knock on the door of a club owner but, as far as he was concerned, he worked for the Vincents and this was a different business. It was his own business. Celia was nursing a black eye at the time. Kenneth had lost the BMW, twenty grand, and his gold Rolex to the doorman and was therefore not in the best mood. When he rolled in at four in the morning, demanding a sausage sandwich, he was raging. Celia, still half asleep, cooked him a bacon one.

She placed the sandwich in front of him, along with a cup of coffee, and smiled, hoping to go back to bed.

After one bite, he realised the sausage was bacon, picked up the plate and aimed it at her. She ducked and it smashed his prize possession, a Royal Doulton china racehorse, which had pride of place on the mantelpiece.

"Now, look what you have made me do, you useless fucking scarecrow!"

Celia shook all over. She knew he'd strike her but before she could get away he grabbed her by the beehive and thumped her in the face. His chunky gold ring caught her hard on the cheekbone. She screamed in pain and anger, loud enough for the noise to carry outside, so he let go of her and stormed off upstairs. She didn't go back to bed; the shock was too fierce and she couldn't have slept with the pain.

Kenneth got himself up and out the door by eight o'clock, not even bothering to say sorry – but then, he never did.

When Johnnie knocked, around nine o'clock, Celia was still in her satin nightdress. She looked like the bride of Frankenstein, with her hair sticking out all over the place and a purple ring circling her eye.

Johnnie, dressed in a navy blue Crombie coat, combed his hair back and splashed on expensive aftershave, ready to take what was owed. Celia got a shock as she opened the door. She had expected it to be Kenneth, since he had a habit of forgetting his keys and sure enough they were there on the table.

He tilted his head. "Hello, you must be Celia."

She liked the sound of his voice and nodded.

"May I come in? I think your husband is expecting me."

Celia, still upset over the fight that night, hadn't listened to what Kenneth had said.

"Well, you had better come in then."

Politely, Johnnie wiped his feet and took a seat in the living room.

"Can I make you a drink? Coffee? Tea?" She tried to straighten her hair and hide her face.

Johnnie walked with her to the kitchen and asked how she got the shiner. He hated to see women abused and he assumed Kenneth had done it. He had listened to the Nappers' conversations during the poker games, slagging off women with no regards for them whatsoever. Johnnie was different. Strongly influenced by his mum's strict moral code, he treated ladies as the fairer sex. Every Sunday, he popped in with flowers and the newspapers and shared a pot of tea.

Out of the blue, and so unlike her, Celia put her head in her hands and sobbed. Immediately, he went to her, placing his great, big arm around her shoulder. "Now then, girl, how about I make you a cuppa tea?" There was a small table and chairs in the kitchen where, most mornings, Celia read her newspaper. Johnnie guided her over to the table and sat her down before going to make them both some tea. Celia felt so comfortable considering there was a huge man – a stranger, in fact – in her kitchen, making them both a brew, even though she didn't know him from Adam. But she liked the way he wiped the kitchen sides down when he'd finished pouring the tea. It was quite a picture: a big, burly bloke with a tea-cloth in his hand. "There you go, girl, get your laughing gear around that." He winked.

Celia giggled, much to Johnnie's delight.

"I'm sorry, I didn't mean to cry. You must think I'm a right silly old tart."

"Hey, it's all right. I have big shoulders and you are not old or a tart. Silly, maybe."

Celia looked Johnnie up and down, not slyly, but for him to see she was having a good gawp. He laughed.

"You look rather big all over," she said, and then, before she'd had time to think, they were on their feet and kissing. She had not had any real affection from a man in years, and this six-foot-six monster of a fella, with a gentle nature, stood there in her kitchen, making her a cup of tea.

He kissed her with passion. He was huge and, as he ran his hands over her satin nightdress, her legs wobbled.

"Will Kenneth be home soon?" whispered Johnnie.

"I don't know, but he has left his door keys here so I'll have to open the door to let him in," she replied, insinuating that they could go further than a snog. With no more words spoken, he picked her up and carried her to the sofa. As he removed his coat and unzipped his trousers, she felt a sense of revenge – she was a rebel with a cause. Her inhibitions went out of the window as she dived on top of him and rode him like a cowgirl. The pain in her face had gone and she tingled all over. Johnnie was captivated by Celia. To him she was a little pixie with a need for passion and he wanted more of her. He liked her tiny body and her gentleness which turned to rough, brutal passion when she got excited. Under the messy hair and black eye he could see a little diamond and, for the first time in his life, he was attracted to a woman not for her big tits. In fact, Celia didn't have big tits. He liked her because she was sweet and clean. Without the fucked-up hair and shiner, she was a looker.

When they'd finished, Celia looked at the floor, utterly embarrassed. Never had she acted so brazenly, so out of character, and she felt ashamed until Johnnie helped her to her feet and told her she was special. She smiled graciously but concluded she had just been a quick lay.

Before he walked away, he handed her a card with his number on it.

"Right, my little nymph, call me. I'd love to see you again." He kissed her and left.

That was the start of their ten-year love affair.

*

The phone rang again. This time it was Nigel. "Put Ken on, we have a fucking problem!" Nigel was panicking.

Celia didn't question him. She just handed the phone to Ken.

"The Vincents know it's us. My mate Steve, from the boxing club, has just called. Word's gone around that we have been after getting the club closed. Why you trusted Levi and Billy, you must have been mad. I could have told you they'd fuck it up. Grasses, the fucking lot of 'em!"

Kenneth ran his fingers through his hair and beads of sweat appeared on his top lip.

"Look, just get in the car and get over here. We will go straight to the airport, stay in a hotel there overnight, and fly off in the morning. I know those fucking Vincent cunts won't let that one go."

Nigel was the quieter of the two brothers and always went along with Kenneth. Celia had listened to the conversation and was relieved that this information hadn't come from her. The phone rang again and Celia picked it up. "Get out of the house, babe!" It was Johnnie. Her heart was in her mouth.

"Who was that?" shouted Kenneth as he tried to shove the last pair of jeans into his suitcase.

"Double glazing sales. Ken, I've run out of fags. Do you need any for your journey whilst I get myself some from the garage?"

Kenneth was not listening to her as usual and didn't even notice her disappear.

*

His brother's car pulled into the drive as he dragged his luggage down the stairs. He could hear the motor running. When he opened the front door, it wasn't his brother he saw first but four meat-heads. On the drive lay a crumpled body, covered in blood, with deep wounds to his head. He gasped when he realised who the bloody mess was. Holding his arms in front of his face, he pleaded for his life. Johnnie was first through the door with the crowbar, aiming to take a few chunks out of old Kenneth Napper's head. He hated the vile man with a passion. All those bruises Celia had suffered. He would make sure he'd never be fit enough to hurt her ever again. The first thump was the bar hitting Kenneth's shoulder. Kenneth felt it crack as he put his hands up to protect himself. Johnnie raised the bar again and smashed it across Napper's knuckles. The blood sprayed and made a nasty mess of the cream carpets.

Kenneth pleaded for his life whilst the others watched, laughing.

Johnnie had no intention of killing the brothers, but he was going to leave them in a fucking sorry state. The claw on the crow on the bar tore at Kenneth's face but his hands were so badly broken he couldn't hold them up to protect himself. The final hit was a hard crack to the shin, sending shivers up the spines of the other bouncers. They heard the bone break and the scream which came from the back of Kenneth's throat.

"Now then, boys, no more silly ideas regarding the clubs, 'cos if I hear even a fucking whisper you have been up to no good, I will have to finish you off!" threatened Johnnie, who was towering over Kenneth. The victim looked as though he had just been in a car crash. The other men picked up Nigel and dropped him inside the house before they shut the door and left.

Celia had parked her car just across the road and waited for the men to leave.

She lit up a cigarette and calmly smoked it before she went in.

Shocked by the mess on the carpet, and the blood up the walls, she should have screamed in horror or ran to her husband's side, but she didn't.

Kenneth was trying to drag himself to the phone whilst Nigel lay unconscious. Celia silently walked over to her mobile and called an ambulance. She helped her husband to the couch but left Nigel on the floor, sickened by the blood stains on the carpet and now on the light beige furniture. Her husband was in agony and not fully aware that his wife was behaving strangely. The phone rang again. It was Johnnie. "Are you all right? I'm sorry about the mess," he said calmly.

"That's all right, babe." She hung up and turned to her husband, who could now focus better.

"Who was that?" he whispered, trying to get his breath. Like a robot, she replied. "Just a double glazing salesman."

Kenneth stared at his wife and he realised at that moment she knew.

The paramedics arrived. They strapped Nigel onto a stretcher and rushed him inside the ambulance. One paramedic suggested calling the police but Kenneth said no – they had fallen off the roof. It was no one's fault. Celia remained seated whilst the second lot of paramedics helped Kenneth into a wheelchair. The tears on his face were nothing compared to the broken bones hidden under his clothes. Through the agonising pain, he still focused on his wife and the eerie feeling which now gripped him. Did she set this up?

"Mrs Napper, would you like to sit in with your husband or follow in the car?" asked the paramedic.

Kenneth glared at his wife as she shook her head.

As soon as they were gone, she poured carpet cleaner over the hallway and up the stairs. She scrubbed away with an old-fashioned scrubbing brush. She tried to think about the times when Kenneth had made her happy – but the problem was, he hadn't! It was so sad, she could only think of one time, and that was when he'd proposed in front of everyone with a big, flash diamond ring. He was half-cut, of course. He announced to the club she was the love of his life and he would make an honest woman of her. A tear rolled down her face. Later, she discovered her ex-boyfriend had come back into town and had made enquiries about where she was. As soon as Kenneth had got wind, he beat the boy up, and then he'd proposed himself. That story came out when he'd had too much to drink, laughing in front of a room full of their friends. Celia, gutted that their engagement was merely bravado, had left the party in floods of tears and ended up on antidepressants for the next twenty years. Popping pills saw her through the heartache and his long-term affair with a stupid, blonde tart which had kept him out all hours. Not that she'd really cared about that, it was the constant abuse that had left a bitter taste in her mouth. If he had treated her kindly, by buying her special presents like the gold heart necklace he'd given to his mistress, she wouldn't have minded so much. She'd sussed it out early on, as he never threw away the receipts for the five-star hotel rooms, the little souvenir spa days, or the fur coats and diamonds. Okay, so now she lived in the big house, drove a nice car, and had holidays abroad, but when she thought about it, there had never been any special gifts for her. She'd never owned a diamond. Even the engagement ring he'd bought was a chunk of cubic zirconia. It was all for show. She recalled the sense of euphoria at the size of it when he'd planted the ring on her finger, to the gasps and cheers of the crowd. But when she'd had the ring made smaller, and the jeweller informed her that it was not a diamond at all, her heart had sunk. She soon gathered he was full of shit. However, she still went ahead with the wedding, thinking he would change, only to find, twenty years on, he was still a horrible wanker.

The blood didn't want to leave the shag pile, no matter how hard she scrubbed. Celia thought about all the happy times she'd had with Johnnie and, of course, there were plenty. She threw away the scrubbing brush and stared around the room. This, for a life of fucking misery and, to think, she had thought deep down she must always have loved him and he must have loved her. Now, seeing him lying there, she just could not feel anything for this sorry state of a husband of hers. Even with the pain etched all over his face, she still couldn't raise any feelings of warmth and love for him.

In fact, she had no feelings for him whatsoever. Half her life she had been stealing moments to be with her lover. To his credit, he'd put up with it for ten years and now, looking around the house and its luxuries, she realised she should have sacrificed it all to have had ten happy years. She would not waste another day.

Pulling the loft ladder from the hatch, she retrieved her set of suitcases and spent a few hours packing, ensuring she only took what was hers. The phone was ringing, and she guessed it was Kenneth, but she couldn't be bothered to answer it. She had always rushed to be by his side, to help out when he needed her, dragging herself out of bed when he rolled in, in the early hours of the morning, just to make him a cup of tea or a sandwich. But not this time.

The jewellery box on the dressing table held only costume pieces from high street shops and two gem rings which were her mother's. She peered inside. The emptiness of the old wooden box upset her and the tears trickled down her face. Johnnie had bought her gifts. But she could never keep them at her home just in case Kenneth found them. Her life with Kenneth was as empty and fake as that old jewellery box. Her heart ached, not for Kenneth, but herself. She looked down at her deformed finger, where he had battered her so badly one night, stamping all over her body. It was all because she couldn't give him a child. She remembered it so well. Fifteen years ago, he came home in a stinking mood and glared at her, demanding to know why she couldn't get pregnant. She'd had enough and told him to fuck off and make one with his tart if he wanted one so badly. That was the worst thing she could have said because he ran at her, gripping her face in his hands and lifting her in the air, screaming like a man possessed. He said, "If she had my kid, I would leave you right now, you ugly cunt. Don't ever talk to me like that again. I wish her child was mine, then I wouldn't have to put up with your fucking moaning and constant sulking." With that he threw her to the ground and literally stamped all over her, crushing two fingers and her ankle. The bruises took months to go but the mental scars stayed forever. So, when Johnnie came into her life, she never felt guilty, not once. It was funny, because after that beating Kenneth stopped seeing the skinny blonde bird. She guessed the girl must have moved on or dumped him.

She dialled Johnnie's number from her secret mobile phone.

"'Ello, babes, are you okay?" His voice was so gentle when he spoke to her.

"Johnnie, I've packed me bags and I'm leaving him. Can you come and get me?"

Johnnie's heart pounded. He had loved this woman for years. Now, finally, he could have her all to himself.

"I'm on my way, babes."

He spun his car around and headed to her house. They bundled the luggage in the boot, looking up and down the street, ensuring the neighbours weren't curtain twitching, and left.

Johnnie's flat was small but tidy. It had two bedrooms, a kitchen and a fair sized lounge. Celia had been there twice a week for ten years but had never stayed late or overnight. She plonked the smaller suitcases down and Johnnie carried the bigger ones into the spare room.

"Why did you put them in the spare room?" she asked, hoping he knew she wanted to move in permanently.

He laughed. "Oh, don't you worry, my babes. You will be sleeping with me, but my wardrobes would collapse with the amount of clothes you have in those cases. I'm gonna build a nice big wardrobe in there and you can use that as a dressing room."

She watched in admiration as he pointed to the walls, describing where he would hang a long mirror and build a dressing table under the window and the huge wardrobes, floor to ceiling, across the far wall. Celia loved him even more. Her Kenneth would never have been so thoughtful. She thought about Kenneth, and his selfish ways, and smiled lovingly at Johnnie. He treated her like a princess. He wanted to make her happy and started by offering to cook a special curry, make chocolate covered profiteroles, and finish with a warm Irish coffee. Celia thought she had died and gone to heaven. Her big fella could cook too. There was no end to her future happiness.

"I need to have a meeting with the boss and then I'll be home. You make yourself comfortable and I'll be back shortly." He gave her a long, loving kiss before he left.

*

Dan was sorting out the accounts when Johnnie knocked.

"So what's the verdict, Johnnie, me old son?"

He grinned from ear to ear. "Well, guv, they ain't dead. Almost, but not quite."

129

"So, that should put the fucking word out. I tell you something, Johnnie. I worked hard for these clubs, I never conned no fucker, and it makes me mad when dirty has-beens, like the Nappers, want a piece of what's mine." He shook his head. "I have always been a fair man. I never opened a club on anyone's doorstep. I made sure I catered for a different customer, for fuck's sake. As if my punters would have gone to his shit-pit anyway. They took a right fucking liberty!"

"I don't wanna tell you how to run your own business, but it's my guess that the Nappers were planning more than underage pole dancing. Let's be honest, they wouldn't close you down for that alone, would they?"

Dan frowned. "I think, mate, that was just the start of it. See, they weren't man enough to pay me a visit, 'ave a chat. I would have told them where they were going wrong, even offered to help, but no, the sly cunts resorted to underhand dealings. Well, they cocked up big time. Let's hope that's the end of it."

"Yeah, well, I was gonna suggest that the boys do pat-down searches. Men only, of course," said Johnnie, stretching his neck, wary of speaking freely.

"You're Head of Security, mate, you call that one, but I think you're right. The Ol' Bill would shut this gaff if they found firearms. It's what finished off the Nappers."

Dan gave him a cheeky grin and handed him a packet.

"What's this?" he frowned.

"Five grand."

"Why?" asked Johnnie.

"It's about time I looked after those who look after me. You and ya brother have worked with me for fucking years now, and I can trust you, so it's a little Christmas bonus."

Johnnie couldn't believe his luck. His bird moving in, a five grand bonus, and his boss telling him he trusted him.

Chapter Nine

Kenneth and Nigel spent a week in the hospital, Ken with concussion and Nigel in a neck brace. Once they were well enough, they had to answer questions put to them by the police. This was just a formality. They fell through the garage roof and sustained their injuries that way.

When Kenneth returned to an empty house, the blood was gone. There was not even a pink stain. He called for his wife, but he knew in his heart she'd already left. She should have been up the hospital every day as a dutiful wife or, at least, answered one of the hundred calls he made to the house. It wasn't the terrifying picture of the crow bar coming towards him which gave him nightmares, but the vision of Celia's expression as she lied to him. She knew his attack was planned. The weeks lying sick in a hospital bed left him with nothing to do except think. He concluded who was on the other end of the phone and they would pay with their life.

Grant Smith had been a thug most of his adult life and was now bang in trouble. He owed dealers money left, right and centre, and if he wasn't careful he was going to get a shooter put in his back. In his desperate need to make a load of cash, he bought a dodgy bag of cocaine, heavily cut with lactose, and sold it to the local Rasta by the name of Neville. Grant was handed fifteen grand – a good start to paying off his debts. Neville sold it on to the Yardies. But the deal went sour due to the lack of coke in the lump. Neville went searching for Grant and his so-called friends, especially all their regular haunts, and put the word out he was after him – offering a tasty reward.

Kenneth, who was lying in his hospital bed, got wind of Grant's predicament and offered to help solve his problems, but for one small favour.

Johnnie, in his element, booked a three week Caribbean cruise for Celia and himself. He held the tickets in his hand and marched towards his flat with a smile on his face and a spring in his step. Celia sat with her feet up, sipping a cup of tea whilst watching Richard and Judy. She was excited that they were off on holiday. She had never been to anywhere exotic before, only the Costa del Sol with Kenneth. Now, she was going to have the time of her life with the man she truly loved.

The air was chilly and as usual Johnnie threw on his big Crombie as he walked back to his beloved Celia. He was a smart-looking man, in his trademark suit and Italian leather shoes. He was known in the community because he was a Face and built like a brick shit-house. When he walked along the road, everyone noticed.

Johnnie saw a car pull up with blacked-out windows. He tried to see who was driving. But all he saw was the end of a gun as the bullet hit him clean through the chest. Before anyone could take a number plate, the car drove off. The incident happened outside the betting shop and two men, who heard the tyres screeching, ran outside to see what the commotion was all about. They knew Johnnie, and tried to help him, but he lay there with half the contents of his insides exposed. Terry, the shop manager, went as white as a sheet and threw up. The rest of the punters came for a gawp before the paramedics moved them on. No way could he be saved. The police arrived and taped off the area. He was still clutching the holiday tickets as the blood poured away from his body and down the drain.

As the day went on, Celia assumed he had gone to work. She couldn't even call him on his mobile because he had left it at home. The evening was long and she paced the floor. As the digital clock flashed four thirty a.m. her mood turned to anger. She could not believe he was just another Kenneth – out all hours, shagging other women. After calming herself with a brandy, she got dressed, wrapped herself up in a fur coat, slipped her feet into a pair of red stilettos, and marched off up to the club. She was unsure what she would do when she arrived there, but she couldn't stand and stare out of the window any longer.

Outside, the cold air hit her and she contemplated going back inside. A taxi was passing and she hailed it down.

"*Dan's Palace*, please!"

The driver looked her up and down and then said, "Darling, the club closed hours ago!"

"Errm… don't matter, take me there anyway."

He was right. The club appeared to be in darkness, even the offices upstairs, but she thought she could just make out a light on.

She banged on the dense door, but the noise dissipated into nothing. Michael, another doorman, who worked with Johnnie but wasn't a close friend, appeared from the side. He looked Celia up and down and half smiled with a sad expression.

"I'm sorry, love, we are closed now. Club shuts at two o'clock." He spoke politely. She wasn't an old brass touting for business.

"I was looking for Johnnie Lee. He is a doorman here!"

Michael's eyes widened. He had no idea who she was but it was obvious she didn't know that Johnnie had been shot and now lay on a slab at the mortuary.

He put an arm around her shoulder and walked her silently inside the club.

Celia guessed then, by the sadness in his eyes, that something terrible had occurred.

"Where's my Johnnie?" There was a lump in her throat and her mind raced. She thought he had been in an accident, maybe aggro in the club, or worse.

"Mr Vincent's in his office. Let's go in there, shall we?" His voice was gentle. They climbed the stairs together and by the time they reached the top Celia shook all over and her legs felt as though they would give way.

Michael opened the door for her to walk in. The room was filled with blue smoke and men, some seated, some standing, all smartly dressed. Dan sat at his desk, his tie undone and his sleeves rolled up; Sam stared out of the window, still in his suit, and Fred was talking to two of the bouncers. Dan looked at Celia and guessed immediately who she was. He stood up and walked over to her. "Come in, my love. Here, sit down. I can't tell you how sorry I am!" He had been crying and she could see that.

Celia's heart was in her mouth and, in a blind panic, she shouted, "What's happened to my Johnnie?"

Dan had assumed she knew. "Oh, my God, has no one told you?" He was horrified.

"Fred, get..."

"It's Celia," she said harshly.

"Yes, I know, babe. Get Celia a drink." He took a deep breath. The room fell silent as they watched Dan hand Celia the news. The scream could be heard in the next street and she crumpled in her chair. Joe, the best person to deal with this situation, went to her side, and with a big meaty arm he held her.

Dan waited for her to collect herself before he spoke. "He was a good man and I will make it my business to find the person responsible for his death and make sure they will never live to tell the tale."

Instantly, Celia responded. "It was my husband!"

"Are you sure, babe?" Dan replied, aware she was married to Kenneth Napper.

She nodded. "Yes, I am dead sure. I should never have left him. I should have kept things as they were, then my Johnnie would still be here," she sobbed.

There was a silence as the men in the room gathered their thoughts.

Celia knocked back the brandy and the fuzzy feeling went. She could now focus. From the clear description he had given her, Dan was just how Johnnie had described him. As for the others, she could have named them all. He had spoken about them with real affection, as if they were family, and right now, with him dead, she was glad to be in their company.

After an hour or so the doormen left and the Vincents gathered around.

"Celia, he adored you, and so I need to know what you want us to do," said Dan, who held his hands together as if he was about to pray.

Fred was fidgeting again.

"I say we take him out and be done with him!"

"Shut up, Fred, this is Celia's call. He was her bloke and Ken is her husband."

Fred had never been told to shut up before, but then again Dan was close to Johnnie. They had worked together for years.

"Sorry, love, he is right, what do you want us to do?" asked Fred.

Celia looked around the room to see the brothers staring at her. Their eyes all the same, they were, as Johnnie had said, babe magnets.

"I loved Johnnie more than life itself. He was a good man, and he was good to me. All we wanted was a bit of happiness in our own little way and Kenneth has taken it away from me. He made me miserable when I was with him, and he has made me devastated now I'm not." She took a deep breath.

"I have no children. I have no future now, so leave Kenneth to me. I'm gonna take care of him. Even if it means I spend the rest of my life inside, it will be worth it."

The men looked on in amazement. There sat this tiny-framed, middle-aged woman with a sixties beehive, looking like the church flower arranger, dressed in a black fur coat and red shoes, ready to knock off Kenneth Napper.

Dan reached for her hand across the table.

"You need not get your hands dirty. Give us the okay, and he will be dead and cemented under the new M20 bridge!"

"No, I know what I'm doing, Mr Vincent. I've fucking been planning it for the last fifteen years, I just didn't know it. I know Kenneth didn't shoot him, so he must have paid someone. So, you take care of the low life that shot him. I'll deal with Kenneth. It will be my pleasure."

Fred chuckled but the rest stayed quiet.

Dan drove Celia back to Johnnie's flat to let her grieve in peace. He offered to help with the arrangements. He would pay all the costs of the funeral and the insurance money would go to her.

Fred and Sam remained behind, waiting for his return to plan their next move.

"I don't know, Sam, there's something more to all this. First, we've got the fucking pikeys, trying to close us down, then we have the Nappers on the rampage, blowing away the doorman. What's gonna happen next?"

Sam nodded in agreement. "And Jack reckons it's quiet down the gyms. The travellers have kept away."

Fred bit the inside of his lip. "We had better be one step ahead of them all. Sam, do yourself a favour. Make sure when Jack goes training, he takes one of the boys as security. That Michael's a big fella, he likes to train, he can go with him."

Sam frowned. "Fucking 'ell, Fred, do you really think things will get that bad?"

Fred paused. "Sam, I don't know. It might all be nothing and just blow over, especially when the Nappers are out of the picture, but I feel uneasy so it's best we watch Jack's back."

Sam nodded furiously. "Yeah, for sure."

Dan pulled up outside Johnnie's flat and offered to go inside with Celia, just in case.

"I'll be fine, Mr Vincent," she whispered.

"Please, call me Dan."

She nodded.

"Look, Celia, you said you will sort your husband but it won't be necessary. I'll have him dealt with. You won't need to worry."

Celia looked up at the flat in darkness and a lump lodged in her throat. Her man, who had brought so much joy in her life, was gone, and that darkness was to be a permanent fixture in her future. But, right now, she had no future, no real friends, and no children.

"No, love, I need to do this," she replied, still staring at the dark windows.

Dan turned sideways in his car seat to face her. "Celia, how do you plan to do this?" he asked, intrigued by her calm and determined manner.

She unexpectedly laughed out loud.

"Do you know what, Dan? For fucking years, before I met Johnnie, I used to collect bees, hold them in a jam jar under the sink, and Kenneth would say, 'Why are you keeping those killers?' and I'd reply, 'So they don't sting you…'" She laughed again. "I didn't have the nerve back then."

He had no idea what she was talking about.

"One sting from a bee, just one, would kill Kenneth, if he didn't have that special injection pen."

Dan smiled. "Wrong time of the year, though, for bees…"

Celia slowly turned to face him. "And that's a fucking shame. If I could get my hands on a bee, I would ram it down his throat. I'd watch his tongue swell up, his throat constrict and his body convulse, until his ugly eyes popped out of their sockets."

Dan believed then she had been planning his death for many years.

As she sat in the quiet darkness, she prayed for Johnnie's safe-passing into the gates of heaven. The bed was cold, but his smell, still lingering on the pillow, gave her comfort. She wasn't sure if she had slept at all. She was so racked with grief her mind entered a dream state to escape reality. As the sun came up, she climbed out of bed, with every muscle in her body aching and the lump in her throat still there. She stared in the mirror at her eyes, swollen from the endless crying.

Her hatred for her husband increased by the minute. The only thing that kept her sane was devising the plan to kill him.

She had to take it seriously and do away with the bastard once and for all. The years of keeping a jar of bees in amongst the cleaning products under the sink was her way of having one over on her husband. If he clumped or humiliated her she'd hold the jar and grin. However, she had never taken it further than just a fantasy.

The house keys were still in her bag. The serious injuries which Kenneth had sustained still wouldn't be healed by now. Broken ribs, fingers, leg, and those deep lacerations, meant at least six weeks before he was up and about, without taking into account his age.

She hadn't contacted her sister since the day she left and didn't want to. The weeks spent away had given her time to reflect on her life. Maureen had been a good sister in that she was female company to talk to but, as for real problems – such as her own husband bashing her – Maureen didn't want to know because it upset her perfect, naive little life. Their lifestyle was the same. Maureen enjoyed it, happy with her four bedroom detached house with the swimming pool and the villa in Spain, because her husband wasn't so handy with his fists. As long as she had company for her trips to the pub, the odd meal and the holidays on the Costa del Sol, she didn't care if Celia was black and blue and totally miserable.

*

Celia drove Johnnie's car and parked it up the road from her house. She sat for the whole day, monitoring who came and went. Maureen arrived with a casserole dish and then along came the district nurse. Celia clocked the routine.

She was still there at midnight, just waiting. The ground floor lights were off, with only the bedroom light on. That was a first – Kenneth in bed before two a.m. She carefully turned the key, so as not to make a noise. Luckily, he hadn't thought to change the locks. The kitchen looked a mess. Maureen was a sloppy bitch but she didn't care; it wasn't her home anyway. She heard him snoring so loudly. Her Johnnie never snored. As she climbed the stairs, aware of every creaking floorboard, she smiled. The irritating grunting sound told her he was still asleep. The bedroom door was open and she could make out his silhouette from the moon that shone in through the bay window. He lay on his back with his mouth wide open. She almost laughed. He was such an ugly bastard.

She tiptoed over to his bedside to see the large bottle of sleeping pills on the cabinet. Beside it was an opened bottle of whisky, an ashtray with half a smoked cigarette, and one of his flash square lighters with a nude woman engraved on it. She stared at his round, swollen face. The gruesome wound, it appeared, had now become infected. She smiled, gripping the carving knife which she had spent hours sharpening. He stopped snoring so abruptly she snapped out of her trance. She held the blade to his neck, ready to slice from ear to ear. Suddenly, he grabbed her wrist and opened his eyes. His fingers were not healed but he still had the strength to clench her tight. She gasped in horror as his corpse-like face glared back at her. She tried to tug free. However, he continued to hold on to her, pulling her close to him. His breath reeked of anaesthetic and sour milk. She wasn't afraid. She was too racked with grief to feel fear. As she pulled her face away, she smirked. His grip loosened as he watched the demonic expression on his wife's face. He had neither the strength nor the will power to fight. He knew he was going to die. Suddenly, her plan changed. She didn't want him to have a quick death. She took hold of the whisky bottle, poured it over the bed and onto the floor, and then she flicked the lid off the lighter. His eyes widened when he realised his demise was to be by a naked flame. In desperation, he tried to move up the bed.

"Please, Ce, please, don't do this." His voice was meek and desperate. She held his life in her hands, enjoying his frantic pleas. "Tell me who shot Johnnie?" she demanded.

"Wait, wait, I'll tell you, just don't this!" he begged in despair.

Raising her eyebrow, she shouted, "Go on, Kenneth, who pulled the fucking trigger?"

"Grant Smith! It was Grant Smith!" he cried.

She looked at the local newspaper lying by his side and laughed, wondering what tomorrow's headline would be. She ignited the old Zippo lighter, allowing it to fall onto the whisky-soaked newspaper, and stepped back. She wanted to see her husband one last time, in agonising pain, and then she would be able to keep that image in her mind to console herself.

She didn't run out of the house right away, as she was too concerned he would survive. His screams were high-pitched but short. The sedatives had made him drowsy and the broken bones made him weak. She felt the heat from outside the door. The hissing and crackling began to subside. She was annoyed. He was supposed to burn to death. She would have to go back and slit his throat this time. The flames had died down when she opened the door. They hadn't managed to set fire to the plastered walls or the bedside cabinets – only the bed. She was surprised to discover that only the bed clothes and his pyjamas had caught alight, but it had been enough to kill him. The smell of cooking flesh made her gag. The fire had obviously taken a hold of the newspaper and the sheets and then contained itself within the bed. But, importantly, the fire alarm didn't go off and the windows didn't smash.

She closed the door and casually walked down the stairs, out of the house, and into the cold night air. It was so quiet and peaceful. She slowly clambered into Johnnie's car and looked up at the house. It appeared exactly the same. No one would have known. They were probably all tucked up in their beds asleep. She searched her handbag for her phone, which she had left on the passenger seat, and dialled Dan's number.

"Grant Smith shot my Johnnie!" She wasn't ready for a conversation so she switched off the phone. The only person she wanted to talk to was Johnnie.

"There you go, Johnnie, you can deal with him up there."

Celia drove back to the flat, where she had deliberately left the lights and heating on. She assumed the pain of losing her man would go once she had avenged his killer – but it was still there. Only her anger subsided.

It took only a day before the news spread. Maureen had been the one who had found him dead. The sight of his half-burnt body, and contorted expression, had left her disturbed and in need of sedatives for post-traumatic stress disorder. Nigel was present when the coroner made his report. He had concluded that Kenneth died because of a massive heart attack brought on by the accidental fire. The whisky, the cigarette, and his limited use of his hands had in all probability led to the bed catching alight.

Once Dan heard the gossip, he rushed to Johnnie's flat to see Celia.

She opened the door, expecting to see the police, but was relieved it was Dan.

She smiled. "Come in, love."

"I heard that Kenneth died. They believe it was a heart attack. The silly old cunt set himself alight, pissed or something."

She laughed. "Word got around then?"

"Yeah, thanks for the tip off. That Grant Smith is one 'orrible piece of work."

"Is he..." Celia had to know, but was unsure if she could ask.

"Dead? Oh yeah. Well and fucking truly dead. Word has it he was messing with some hard core drug dealers. They found his body shoved in the boot of his car. The whole thing was burnt out. No need for a cremation now, eh?" He sniggered.

Celia smiled and nodded.

"How are you doing, anyway?" Dan asked.

She looked down. "To tell ya the truth, I am lost, lonely and, if I polish this flat one more time, there will be no paint left." They sat and had a large glass of brandy together.

"You're the first person I have actually spoken with. I need to keep busy, find something to take my mind off it all."

Dan gazed around the room. It was immaculate.

"Celia, you can always work with us. I need people around me I can trust. Any good at accounts?"

She smiled. "You know what, I gave up me little book keeping job when I married that wanker."

138

He was surprised at how together she seemed but, then, Johnnie had remarked on what a tough cookie she was, underneath her fragile exterior.

"When you're ready, give me a call or come to the club, and see if it's what you fancy."

Celia looked up and half-smiled. "It's been a long while, so I'm a bit rusty."

"It's fine, you take your time." He looked around the flat and for a second he sensed how lonely she must be.

"I tell you what. If you fancy getting out of here more often, I could always do with more staff behind the bar."

She laughed, genuinely, for the first time since Johnnie's death. "Johnnie told me how you only have the prettiest of girls in your club. I think I'm past me sell by date."

"Nothing wrong with the way you look, babes. I need a more mature woman behind the jump to keep an eye on the youngsters. I've got Cassie, who is the manager, but she could do with a hand, I'm sure."

Celia was beaming. She loved glitz and glamour and had envied Johnnie when he used to tell her of the dressed-up women, drinking champagne and dancing the night away. She had visualised it and only wished she was twenty years younger, but now she had the chance to be part of it. Her heart still ached and she was desperate to have something which would take her mind off her grief.

"I would love to, Dan. It would make me feel closer to Johnnie."

He gave her a hug. "Come along tonight and I will introduce you to everyone, but, remember, if you are not up to it, don't worry."

Celia felt half human again. She had, at last, a reason to get up in the morning, and she was grateful.

Chapter Ten

Ruby had managed to pawn a vast amount of designer jewellery and raise three thousand pounds. Her father had no idea – and he wouldn't know – what she'd had in the first place. She sold her handbags and raided her savings account and, all told, she had four and a half grand in cash.

Money had never been an issue. She had everything she wanted and more. This gift could save her mother's life. Now she could honour her promise and make such a huge difference to the woman who gave birth to her.

She looked forward to seeing Jacob again, especially after their secret meeting on Wednesday. Not even her mother knew about that.

Today, she was going to look extra special. She visualised Jesse's face when she handed her the money. She would be ecstatic.

Her father was still in bed, Saturday morning, when Ruby got up. She scribbled a note saying she would be home late. Sam, who was used to Ruby going off with her mates and coming back late, thought nothing of it.

The wind bit into her cheeks, her eyes watered, and she cursed. It had taken her an hour to fix her makeup. But she was too near the station to turn back. People on the train looked her up and down, which unnerved her, and she gripped tightly the handbag containing the four and a half grand.

As she walked past the park she saw two small children playing. They were roughly three and four years old. She was surprised to see them alone but, the times she had been on the estate, she concluded it was just a way of life.

Jesse had been expecting Ruby and made sure she was up, washed and dressed. Any punters hanging around were pushed out of the door pretty sharply. She borrowed the neighbour's vacuum cleaner and gave the flat a clean. She also bought new cups, cushions, a second hand rug, and put bright, pink curtains up at the window. She had to get new bits as well, because otherwise Ruby would smell a rat. Giving her some credit, her daughter couldn't be that stupid – could she?

The biggest change which Ruby noticed was the fragrance. It was apples and cinnamon.

Jesse looked and smelled clean, her hair was tied back and she had makeup on. Ruby was surprised to see how different Jesse appeared.

"Come in, babes, look at you, all posh and pretty," said Jesse, who actually wanted to say 'come in, and leave me the money, then fuck off again', but she had to play the game.

Ruby was pleased to find her mother had made such an effort and even agreed to have a cup of coffee, once she had spotted the cups.

She sat opposite her at the small table in the kitchen, "How have you been then, Mum? You look better." Her voice was sweet and cheery.

Jesse forgot for a second. "Oh yeah, well I had a rough week, ya know, with the pain, but I'm much better for seeing you, my babe."

Ruby was thinking of a good time to hand over the money, but she couldn't contain herself. "Mum, you can go to America now!" She grinned from ear to ear. "I got you the cash!"

Trying to control her excitement, devoid of integrity, she blurted out, "How much?" to the surprise of Ruby, who hadn't expected that type of reaction.

"Four thousand five hundred pounds." She dragged the words out.

"Oh my God, four and a half grand!" screeched Jesse.

Ruby was nodding.

"Christ, girl, where did you stuff all that?" Jesse asked, staring at Ruby's handbag.

Then, she realised she was focusing on the money too much.

"That's so generous of you but, really, babe, I can't take that off you," she said, knowing full well that if Ruby had gone to those lengths to bring it here, she certainly wouldn't take it back.

"Mum, it's fine, it's yours! It's the least I can do."

"Well, if you are sure, my darling, and you know, it will save my life!"

Jesse couldn't believe her eyes when she saw the cash in Ruby's handbag. She had never seen so much money in one lump sum. She shook with excitement. Once the money was in her hands, she wanted shot of Ruby. Her mental shopping list consisted of crack cocaine, skunk, and a few bottles of Jack Daniels to help her sleep at night. No more selling a few grams here and there to spotty teenagers to make ends meet, and no more quick fucks for a score. She was going to milk it, like taking candy from a baby. Inside, she was laughing. Perhaps she should have gone into acting.

Ruby didn't want to stick around either as she wanted to see Jacob again.

"So, Mum, have you seen much of Jacob?" asked Ruby nonchalantly.

Jesse, still counting the stack of notes, replied. "Nah, not really, his girlfriend probably kept him in," she laughed. "As soon as she lets him out, he don't go home for days. Spends it here, sometimes."

Ruby never knew he had a girlfriend. Her heart sank and she slumped back into the chair. "So he lives with her then, does he?"

Jesse looked up and grinned. "Oh, Ruby, sounds like you have a little crush there."

Ruby didn't answer. She sipped her coffee.

After realising what she had said, Jesse backtracked. If she could get her hands on over four grand in just a week, then more would follow. Jesse was determined she would be on the receiving end of all that money, but it would take more than a rekindled mother-daughter relationship. She had been young once, and an interest in boys always came first.

"Actually, babe, I remember Jacob split with his bird a while ago, and I do believe he has a soft spot for you. I heard him telling his mates he thought you were real eye candy."

Ruby smiled. Her world lit up and she was dying to see him again.

"Here, babe, want a fag?" offered Jesse.

Ruby took it and puffed away like an old hand.

There was a knock at the door and hastily Jesse answered it. Ruby heard muffled voices and then the door closed. Just as Jesse went to resume drinking her coffee and puffing on her cigarette, the doorbell rang again. This time she headed for her bedroom and came back with a bag, handing it to the men outside. Ruby didn't question it.

The final knock was Jacob, who swanned in, stoned. He kissed Ruby on the cheek and almost fell onto the chair. His jeans hung around his arse and he looked unusually scruffy.

"Hello, my little princess," he said, to Ruby's elation.

She nodded – acting cool.

He rolled a fat joint and lit the end, turning it around to look at it as he blew a smoke ring. Jesse grabbed it from him and sucked away.

"Cor, Jacs, this is good shit!" she said.

Ruby wanted to laugh. It was like listening to her mates.

Jacob passed the joint to Ruby, who in turn had a good drag but, unlike the other two, she instantly felt stoned. The spliff contained skunk, a very strong weed which, unless you were used to it, would blow your head off. Jesse laughed as her daughter slid off the chair onto the floor. Jacob, distinctly unimpressed with Ruby's mum, quickly scooped her up, carried her to the living room and laid her onto the sofa.

"'Ere, Jacs, don't let her throw up on me floor, for fuck's sake!"

"All right, Jesse, she won't be sick. She will come around in a minute," he shouted back, but Ruby had heard everything.

"'Ello, Princess, had a bit too much of me special weed?" laughed Jacob.

Ruby was shaken and looked into the eyes of her mother, who was laughing. She jumped up and headed for the toilet to empty the contents of her stomach, which was even more embarrassing.

"I said she was gonna be sick. Lucky she woke up," stated Jesse.

"Yeah, she might have choked," replied Jacob, thinking of her health.

"No, I mean she could have chucked up all over me couch."

Jacob glared at Jesse; he soon realised she had no feelings for Ruby at all. It was just as his Aunt Gloria had said.

Ruby stayed in the bathroom for a few minutes, trying to tidy herself up. She opened the cabinet with the cracked mirror, hoping to find toothpaste or a baby wipe to freshen up, but found only syringes and needles. Humiliated by the whole experience, though, she didn't take much notice of the cabinet's contents. After washing her face and sloshing water around her mouth, she reappeared, to see Jesse and Jacob still puffing away on a joint.

Jacob threw her a vodka pop. "'Ere, princess, drink this, and you will feel better." She did as he said and sure enough she livened up. He patted the seat next to him and she slid over, while watching for a reaction from her mother. Jesse had no interest in her daughter's antics and acted as if she was any of Jacobs's girlfriends. He leaned over the side of the sofa and then he pulled up a bag. Inside, were a few more bottles of alcohol pops. "These are for you."

Ruby smiled. "Thank you," she whispered sweetly.

"I'm fucking starved. Anyone fancy fish and chips?" asked Jesse.

Ruby nodded. "Can I have chips please, Mum?"

Jesse shuddered. Her own daughter, so far removed from her, with her overly polite ways.

Jacob offered to collect them but Jesse insisted she would go.

As soon as she was out of the door, Jacob climbed on top of Ruby, kissing her. She responded with just as much passion. It wasn't the first kiss. The Wednesday before, they had secretly met and had spent an afternoon snogging for hours. Tonight though, Jacob wanted more. He had laid out ten quid on a few drinks. In his world that meant a shag.

Jesse had been gone over an hour but Ruby hadn't noticed the time – too engrossed in Jacob's hands roaming all over her body and feeling his tongue searching inside her mouth. She knew he was going too far when his fingers crept under her clothes, gripping her breasts, but she liked him a lot. Most girls her age had moved beyond the kissing stage anyway.

As the door opened, Jacob jumped up and tidied himself, whilst Ruby tucked her shirt in her trousers and sat upright. The strong smell of chips filled the air, inducing the hunger pangs. Jesse plonked the chip bags onto the kitchen table and searched the drawers for knives and forks. She found two forks but only one knife, and all three needed to be washed up.

"I can eat mine with my fingers, don't worry about me," piped up Ruby, who could see there was a serious lack of cutlery. Jacob opened his wrapper and began munching straight away. Jesse looked preoccupied and just ignored her daughter. They all sat around the table, enjoying the fat, greasy chips, drenched in vinegar and covered in salt, sharing a saucer of tomato sauce to dip. Ruby smiled. Her home scene would have been so different. She visualised the scene: matching plates, on a highly polished table, with napkins and a condiment set.

Jesse was working out a way to send her daughter home without being too obvious, but the more she watched her, the more apparent it became that Ruby was besotted with Jacob. If he stayed around, then so would she. Jesse greedily shoved three fat chips into her mouth and ate with her mouth open, smacking her lips. Ruby was amazed at the lack of table manners. If she had dared to eat like that her dad would have removed her food. But, still, she oddly enjoyed the company. Her relationship with her mother was growing into a friendship.

Jacob kept looking over at Ruby, smiling. He wanted to keep the flame still burning to ensure his much-earned shag. The only problem was where.

"So, Jesse, what are you up to this afternoon?" Jacob asked, trying to sound casual, but it didn't fool Jesse. She looked up from her tomato dip and smirked.

"Oh yeah, I have to pop out, get some shopping," she lied, instantly relieved she had an excuse to leave the house and score some serious drugs.

Jacob grinned from ear to ear. He had smoked his weed, filled his belly, and now was ready for his afters. Ruby was still eating her chips, trying not to look messy when she ate; it was a teenage thing, embarrassed to eat in front of her so-called boyfriend.

"So, will you two be all right if I'm gone for an hour or so? Only, I must get a few household bits before the shops close."

Ruby wasn't listening. All she heard was her mother saying she was going out. It gave her time to be alone with Jacob and listen to more romantic words being whispered in her ears.

Jesse grabbed her bag and slipped off out, still munching on a chip. The door slammed. Jacob slid his arms underneath Ruby and carried her into the bedroom.

"Jacob, we can't go in here. What if Mum comes back?"

This was a clear message to him that she knew he was going to have sex with her. But Ruby didn't mean that at all. She thought they'd enjoy more snogging and maybe touching – but that was all.

He laid her gently on the bed. The foul odour from the filthy sheets soured the mood, so she hoped her perfume sweetened the air. Jacob didn't seem bothered. He lay on top of her and kissed her with a passion she had never experienced before. His mouth was hard, pressing against hers. His hands rummaged around under her blouse but Ruby was disappointed that the seductive compliments had vanished.

She pushed her face away to catch her breath – and then it dawned on her – he was going too fast.

"I'm sorry, my sweet thing, it's just, you are so beautiful. I can't seem to stop kissing you. I could eat you, you smell so good." His voice was soft and she fell for it. Her body relaxed and she allowed him to touch her breasts and open her blouse to see. He buried his head between her bosoms, kissing and licking her smooth, young skin whilst he undid her buttons, trying to tug away her jeans.

As much as she was enjoying the kissing and kind words, her nerves got the better of her again so, when he ripped off her bottoms, she said, "No, not yet," hoping he'd stop.

His kisses were rough on her neck, he was sucking so hard on her breast it was making her wince, and his hands were everywhere before she could stop him.

"Please, Jacob, no." Her voice was a mere whisper. He ignored her.

She attempted to grab his wrists but he was far too fast. He threw her jeans and silk knickers onto the floor. Now, she was in a panic. Barely a stitch on her, she tried to get up but he was on top of her – his hands pawing every curve of her body.

"Please, Jacob, not yet!" Her voice grew louder, but he wasn't listening. She searched his eyes: they looked wild, his pupils wide and scary.

"Jacob, no!" she screamed, as he touched between her legs. She was struggling – he thought she was playing games. With one hand he undid his belt and trousers, whilst holding her down with the other.

Her heart pounded. What had she got herself into? Surely, he wasn't going to have sex with her? She was still a virgin – she was only fifteen, for fuck's sake. Ruby just wasn't ready – it shouldn't be like this. Suddenly, she realised she had to stop this right now and, with all the strength she could muster, she slid from underneath him and turned over to get off the bed.

Jacob, though, in his stoned state, had other ideas: he saw the perfect, round backside and, within a split second, he was on her again. This time, his urge was too great. With one swift movement, he parted her legs and forced himself in.

Ruby screamed at the top of her voice: the pain was excruciating. But Jacob wasn't listening to her as he was thrusting hard and fast. He had been looking forward to having sex with her. Her ample breasts and clean, soft skin got him so aroused he gripped her hips tightly, lifting her up to force his cock deeper inside, pummelling like a hammer drill. He had hoped that it would have lasted a little longer but the tightness made him come quicker. For Ruby, however, it seemed like hours of pain.

As he pulled away and looked down at Ruby, with her head buried in the pillow, he saw the tears.

"Hey, what you crying for, sugar?"

His voice was somewhere in the distance. Was he really so heartless, did he not hear her screams, sense her dread, or did he just not give a shit? Slowly, she turned back over and grabbed the grubby sheets to cover her exposed body.

Jacob loved her naive shyness and tried to tease her, but her stiff expression remained.

"Fuck off me, Jacob!" Her anxiety had now turned to anger.

"Oh, Ruby, I love it when you're cross," he laughed as he bent down to kiss her again.

Her knee came up and met with his chest, just enough to wind him slightly. She scrambled to her feet and grabbed her clothes whilst Jacob lay there, clutching his ribs.

Before she zipped up her jeans, he was off the bed and holding her.

"Hey, my girly, what's the matter?" His tone was so calm and sweet, as if he was talking to a five-year-old. Ruby looked into his eyes in disbelief. Was he really unaware he had just raped her, or was he playing one sick game?

"Why? Why did you do that to me?" Her voice was on the verge of sounding hysterical.

He exaggerated his frown, "What do you mean, babe...? You wanted it, didn't you?" He inclined his head to the side.

Was she imagining it all? She knew she had asked him to stop, but had she been clear enough? "I screamed, Jacob... I fucking screamed!"

"Ruby, we were naked in the fucking bed! What did you think we were doing? Playing fucking monopoly?"

Ruby, shamefully, avoided eye contact, realising she had been a fool. She knew, then, she had let him go too far and whatever way she looked at it, she should never have been in the bed, naked with him.

"Baby, if I had known you didn't want to do it, I would never have touched you. I thought you wanted it as much as me because you said you was worried about your mum coming back. If we were not getting up to anything, why would you be so concerned?" He ran his hand down her cheek. "I wished I had never met you and then I couldn't have hurt you. I'm so sorry, angel." His voice was a whisper as he turned away. Like Jesse, he was a good actor. All that was on his mind was the fear of Ruby screaming rape to the police. That was all he needed, another setback.

Ruby sat down on the bed and sobbed. She felt a fool, acting the grown-up and, when it came to it, she had bottled it and Jacob had got the wrong message.

He pulled his jeans on and slipped the sweatshirt over his head.

"I'm sorry, Jacob, I didn't mean for this to happen." Her emotions were mixed. If she let him walk away, he might go forever.

Jacob grinned to himself – yet another silly slapper.

He sat next to her and put his arm around her shoulders. "Now then, why was you so upset? I didn't hurt you, did I?"

Ruby was still sore and bruised but shook her head, afraid he would see her as a kid. "No, Jacob, you didn't hurt me. I wasn't ready, that's all."

He picked her up and sat her on his lap like a child.

"Next time, I will take longer getting you in the mood and then it will be easier. Tell me how you prefer it and we can do it your way."

Ruby's eyes widened. He must have thought she had done it before. She couldn't admit to him that she was a virgin, shit no. He would think she was a silly schoolgirl. She smiled and nodded.

*

Jesse was gone for hours, getting out of her tree on cocaine samples.

Jacob had his own business to attend to so he walked Ruby to the station and went home to his girlfriend.

The journey back was the longest ever. All Ruby wanted was a hot bath and to feel the comfort of her warm, soft bed, which smelled of summer jasmine.

The train stopped at every station and seemed to linger for ages. She couldn't get the incident out of her head: the disgusting, grey sheets that smelled of sweat and piss, the wallpaper peeling off the walls, the pain, and the awful way she had lost her virginity. Was it supposed to be like that – her face pushed into a pillow, and that horrendous pain which was so repetitive? A hot tear rolled aimlessly down her cheek. He was so rough. Was it like that with men? After all, compared to her, he was a grown man. She went over the event in her mind and decided that if she had been honest with him from the beginning he might have treated her differently. He would have been slower, more gentle and kind. He thought she had done it before and so of course he would be rough. She had seen a porno film and that was just how they did it. She was playing in the grown-ups' world now. She could leave that world behind and go back to being Daddy's little girl, safe in her big house, going to her posh school and playing hockey. But the idea seemed to suffocate her and so she decided to continue being a part of two worlds.

Chapter Eleven

Ruby sat in the bath, contemplating her future. The house was empty when she arrived home which, in light of how she was feeling, was just as well. Try as she might, she could not get the incident out of her head. It was so humiliating – not how she had imagined her first time would be. And the pain, well, it just wasn't supposed to be like that at all, was it?

Jacob was happy. He sat down to a good warm meal with his girlfriend and pretended the whole fiasco hadn't happened. And he thought how lucky he had been she had not cried rape.

He did have a twinge of guilt, thinking that the way she had reacted she may well have been a virgin, but he soon consoled himself with the fact she had seriously led him on.

"This steak's delicious, babe!"

Noreen, his on-off girlfriend for the past three years, smiled sarcastically.

"No, I mean it, this tastes fantastic."

She stared for a while and then said, "I take it you have been on the pipe again and have a serious case of the munchies because, my darling, this ain't fucking steak – it's liver, you prick."

Noreen jumped up from the table, snatched her plate and threw it in the sink.

He grabbed her arm as she walked by and spun her around to sit on his lap, and then he gave her a really long, passionate kiss. She softened instantly.

"All I can say, babe, is the liver tasted so good I thought it was steak."

Noreen nodded, knowing only too well he was sucking up to her.

"If you think you can get around me that way, you are very much mistaken."

He smiled and rubbed his hands over her tiny bump. It was time he settled down and prepared himself for fatherhood. There was to be no more messing with silly little lovesick teenagers.

Ruby was feeling sick with the thoughts flying around her head. She wanted to talk to someone about it, but who could she go to? Her father would go ballistic and kill Jacob. Jack would probably do the same. There was Aunt Francesca… She stopped to think. No, she couldn't go to her, not now, not after she had been so horrible to her. Another wave of sickness crept over her – a deep gut-wrenching feeling of guilt. How could she have been so cruel to the one woman, apart from her nan, who she loved so much?

Jesse, her mother, would understand. She would be the perfect person to converse with. Besides, she wouldn't judge her. She could talk to her mum about anything – even smoke a joint in front of her. Ruby was now under the illusion her mum would have the answers to this grown-up world she had unexpectedly become a part of.

The next day, she got up ready for school in her green and tartan uniform, white tights, and with her hair tied back in a ponytail. She felt a comfort in being a child for a while.

Sam was sipping tea and Jack was reading the newspaper.

"'Ello, Rubes, fancy a cuppa, babe?" smiled her dad.

Ruby, unsettled, shook her head.

"What's up, love, you look pale and tired?"

"Nothing, Dad." She rolled her eyes.

Sam put his cup down and grabbed his car keys. "I'll run you to school today. You look like you still need to wake up."

She didn't argue. Instead, she decided just to go with the flow, try to get the school day over and done with, and then head to her mother's.

The inside of the car still had that smell of new leather. Ruby took a deep breath.

"Dad, I'm going to Sophie's after school, so I will be home late." She needed to divert her father away from any notion she was sneaking over to Jesse's. It was so much easier to keep it a secret.

"Oh, Rubes, I was hoping you'd be home early. Only, your aunt's coming around for tea, and my guess is she will let you have the watch."

Ruby looked at the floor. She felt guilty for lying and disgusted with herself for wanting to see her mother more than her aunt. Not that she disliked Francesca but she preferred the laid-back acceptance of her mother's home more, and she really needed to talk about Jacob and the whole sex thing. Besides all that, she wouldn't know what to say to Francesca to make up for all the heartless words which had come out of her mouth. The vision of her sad face was still on her mind. She had never before witnessed her aunt look so hurt. She would make up for it one day.

"Dad, I need to get my science assignment done. Tell Aunt Sisco I'm sorry for the other week and I will see her soon," she said, knowing that a second-hand apology was far from acceptable.

Sam sighed, but he was pleased his daughter was now bucking up her ideas and taking school a lot more seriously.

"All right, babe," he replied.

The school was like a hive, with children buzzing around everywhere. Sam smiled as he watched the smart-looking children walk into the main gates. It was so different from the school he went to, where the uniform was a scruffy black blazer and grey trousers. The children at Ruby's school even walked smartly: they carried bundles of books, violins, flutes and hockey sticks. A far cry from what he carried as a kid – a few oven-baked conkers, a homemade pea shooter and muddy football boots slung over his shoulder.

Ruby was met by two girls her age. They seemed excited to see her, as if she had a secret to tell. Sam, pleased his daughter was popular, smiled. Ruby wasn't a model student, far from it. She was, however, intriguing in the eyes of the other kids; her father was a well-known nightclub owner and her brother an up-and-coming and extremely handsome boxer. She was trendy. Naturally, the children were drawn to her.

Ruby had bragged to her friends about her grown-up boyfriend and they wanted to hear more. He sounded cool, too, but today Ruby didn't want to talk about him. She needed to get her head straight.

"So, did you meet Jacob this weekend, Ruby?" asked Lauren, dying to know more about the older guy she was dating.

"Well, no, I didn't. I thought we should have a break. He was getting too intense," she lied, hoping they would drop the topic.

Lauren was wide-eyed and curious. She loved to hear the tales of naughtiness but was clearly too well behaved to do any of it herself.

The first lesson was English with Mrs Russell. She was an extremely strict teacher and hard on any child who showed any form of rebellion. So, as soon as Ruby entered the classroom, her eyes made a beeline for this most recalcitrant of pupils. She made Ruby sit at the front of the class and kept a very close eye on her. Not that Ruby was bothered today. She was in a world of her own.

"For goodness sake, Ruby, will you pay attention? I have asked you all to look at page forty-three of *Hamlet*, and you haven't even opened your book…"

Ruby tutted, and slowly lifted her bag onto her lap to find the book, but soon realised she had left the damn thing at home.

"Ruby, will you please have your book on the table and open to page forty-three?" screamed Mrs Russell. Her high-pitched exaggeration of the words echoed in Ruby's head.

"Mrs Russell, I need to go to Nurse. I feel ill," said Ruby, knowing full well her missing book would give her detention. This was the last thing she wanted.

The teacher glared at her. "You look absolutely fine to me. Now, please, get your book on the desk!"

"Miss, I am ill, I have to go!" complained Ruby, who, by now, was ready to lose it.

"Well, what's wrong with you then?"

Ruby stood up in defiance. "I am having a heavy period, all right?"

The class sniggered at Ruby's cheek and Mrs Russell threw down the whiteboard pen in anger.

"How dare you speak that way! Now sit back down, this instant!"

Ruby picked up her bag and swung it over her shoulder. "I keep telling you I feel ill and need to go to the medical room, but you ain't listening to me! You want to know what's wrong and I told you. Now, I'm going, before I chuck up all over the floor and really piss you off!"

"Get out of my class and go to the headmistress' office. I shall see you there at the end of break. I will not have my class disrupted!"

Ruby headed off, but with absolutely no intention of going to the headmistress. Instead, she went straight to the estate and the comfort of her mother. The school was just a short walk away from the station so she ran along the road, keeping an eye on passing cars, making sure her father wouldn't spot her.

She reached her mother's house at ten thirty and hoped she was in. She remembered her mother saying she would visit the doctor's this week in order to make arrangements for her overseas operation. Ruby shivered as she gingerly knocked. Aware she was in her school uniform, she didn't want to bump into Jacob.

No answer. She knocked again but there was still no answer.

With a cool breeze in the air, she wished she had worn her jacket. She decided to see if Gloria was in and perhaps wait there until her mother returned. But, when she knocked at Gloria's, she found no answer either. She thought maybe Jesse had popped to the local shops – a small parade just around the corner.

It was a strange set up. The café, off licence and small grocers were underneath a tall block of flats surrounded by other blocks. It made it appear quite daunting, due to the lack of light in that area and the amount of graffiti and towering, steel dustbins.

Ruby stood for a while, contemplating going into the café alone. She noticed four girls, including one with a pram, standing outside the grocer's. One girl, a very tall Jamaican woman, looked over and glared. Instantly, Ruby recognised her from a week ago. Jacob had walked Ruby to the station to say goodbye. They had been in the middle of a long kiss when this woman tapped him on the shoulder and asked who Ruby was. He shifted around uncomfortably and replied, "Jesse's daughter." Ruby had hoped, at the time, he would have introduced her as his girlfriend. The girl was unusual in her appearance. She had a very long weave in her hair, pulled back so far, her forehead went as far as her crown, and her eyes were slanted. Ruby had admired her looks. She thought that maybe she was a catwalk model like Naomi Campbell.

Ruby caught the woman staring back and waved to her quite innocently. The tall Jamaican leaned towards the other Jamaican, a very pretty-looking girl who resembled a tomboy and dressed in a tracksuit and trainers, whispering in her ear. Ruby sensed unease about the situation and thought it best to spin on her heels and head towards her mother's. As she turned, she heard a voice call after her. "Oi, I wanna fucking word with you!" Noreen shouted.

Ruby panicked. Normally, she would have confronted her aggressor, back in Sevenoaks. But not here. And certainly not four black girls who sounded as though they wanted a piece of her. She ran down the street, the cold air burning her lungs, aware of footsteps chasing her.

When she reached her mother's door she banged hard, hoping that Jesse would open it and she could be safe inside. But there was no answer. She spun around to face her pursuer and was shocked to find all four girls there. Even the girl with the pram had arrived. Ruby, in a panic, backed into a corner, with the girls surrounding her so she had no way of getting away. Her legs were like jelly and her heart hammered. She could fight when it was fair, one on one, but not four. This was new territory for her: not only a rough estate but four angry-looking black women. Looking more closely, she saw that they *were* women, not kids.

"Think you can fuck wiv me fella then, you silly little slut!" screamed Noreen in Ruby's face. Ruby felt like a cornered rat, with no way of escape.

She shook her head. "No, I don't know what you're on about."

"Don't fucking lie to me, you fucking whore!" spat Noreen, who had just been informed by her best friend, Denise, the tall woman.

"I saw you with Jacob at the station, remember," shouted Denise, who now looked menacing.

Ruby's eyes widened. This couldn't get any worse. Jacob, who had used and abused her, was also this woman's boyfriend.

"She's Jesse's daughter," said Denise, smirking.

"Oh yeah, don't surprise me. The mother's a two-bit fucking brass. Like mother, like fucking daughter. I'll smash her head an' all! The smack-head cunt!"

Noreen, angry that Jacob had been seeing a schoolgirl – and a very pretty one at that – behind her back, with a quick move, punched Ruby in the side of the head. Ruby was completely stunned and rooted to the spot. Her brain just could not take in what was happening to her. The next thing she knew was a second punch landing considerably harder than the first. Her lips took the full force because her head had nowhere to go as she was up against the wall. The pain wasn't bad – she just felt numb. The voices in the background goaded Noreen on and the chanting sent a chill of fear through Ruby. The only way out was to fight back. Her eyes glared and her nostrils flared. All the hard work in the gym would be needed to get out of this in one piece. She grabbed Noreen by her weave and yanked as hard as she could to pull her to the floor. With a quick jolt of her knee, she crunched the cartilage in Noreen's nose, and with a clenched fist she punched her in the face. Noreen fell away, utterly shocked that this kid had lashed back. Denise watched in horror as Ruby kicked Noreen with a mighty impact to her

152

stomach. She gasped, knowing Noreen was pregnant. Instantly, like a cat on a hot tin roof, she steamed in, pounding Ruby on the top of her head. In a frenzy, she snatched Ruby's hair and launched her face into the brick wall. One of the other girls, Shelley, who didn't really have a hard reputation herself, decided she would also put the boot in. As soon as Denise and Noreen stepped away from the crumbling mess, Shelley took a step back and ran up with a forceful fly kick to Ruby's chest, sending her to her knees. When Noreen got her breath back from being winded, she grabbed Ruby by the hair and bit into her cheek – so savagely, the blood instantly appeared. With a final blow, she punched Ruby's eye socket, crushing it – and knocked her clean out. Before the four of them walked away, each one gave a cowardly and excruciating dig to the ribs.

"That will teach you to fuck with my man," said Noreen, in-between gasps of breath.

Jesse remained inside the flat, listening to the fight and waiting for the commotion to end before she opened the door. She had been asleep when Ruby banged hard the first time and also pretty pissed off her daughter had come over again. She was pleased with the money and thrilled with the drugs she'd bought, but she didn't want the whole parent thing. Now, though, she had Ruby bringing trouble to her doorstep and she was having none of it. She was well aware of those girls' reputations, especially Denise. No way was she going to cross her path. The girl was known all over the estate for bullying. She was from a big Somalian family. Most of them had been moved to Woolwich but she and three of her brothers had been offered a move, and they were not happy about it. Consequently, the slightest provocation could spark their anger, as it was obviously doing now. Noreen, she knew, could also ruck: she had given Jacob a couple of black eyes; and the other girl, a lesbian by the name of Shelley, was Denise's sidekick. The three of them together were lethal and Jesse always took a wide berth, even avoiding eye contact.

Most of the neighbours stayed inside when there was any trouble. It was just not worth the aggravation, either getting hurt yourself or having to spend hours down the cop shop writing a statement. Jesse didn't want attention drawn to her. It always meant the police could pop around and get nosey. Worse than them were Denise's three brothers, as they didn't have any morals or boundaries. They would hold a knife to your throat for a pound coin and slit it for a tenner.

She stood in her dirty night dress, with a fag in the corner of her mouth, and looked down at the bloodied and bruised girl. Even Jesse gasped at the state she was in. She winced at the gruesome mark on her cheek. The teeth marks were indented in the very swollen pillow of her face. Her eyes were mere slits and her lips were split open. The blood oozed from other places – her ears and her nose. Jesse was afraid that Ruby might be dead. After all, she had seen no one beaten up so badly. She didn't know what to do. Should she call an ambulance? That would mean police as well. She couldn't call Ruby's father. He would hold her accountable and no doubt have her buried.

Ruby tried to lift her head, to Jesse's relief. Not that she cared for Ruby, but it meant no police sniffing around.

"All right, my girl, let's get you inside," urged Jesse, as she peered up and down the street, making sure no one was looking. She slid her arms under Ruby's and dragged her into the flat backwards, quickly pulling her into the living room and onto the couch. She hurried back to the door, slamming it shut. Ruby was still unconscious when Jesse placed her on the sofa, but she was reassured, by her moans and groans, that she wasn't dead.

Nursing was never one of Jesse's ambitions and so this would be a real challenge. She stared at the state of her daughter for a while and wasn't sure how she felt. It was sad, she had no sense of love for her child and, really, the person sorting this shit out should be Sam, but she hated him more than anyone – well, except his sister, of course. If she sent Ruby home in this state, it would cause mayhem.

Jesse got a saucepan, the one with the burnt handle, and some warm water. She had just bought toilet paper, so that would do to clean her up.

As she tried to wipe the blood away from the gaping hole in her cheek, Ruby came to, but the gruesome wound made Jesse want to vomit. She let Ruby flop back on the sofa, rushed to the toilet, and heaved.

The pain and soreness were unbearable. Her head was pounding and Ruby felt sick. It was the first sign of concussion. She emptied the contents of her stomach onto the living room carpet. Not knowing where she was or what had happened, she closed her eyes and hoped the pain would disappear.

Jesse took deep breaths and braved the sight again, making a feeble attempt to wipe the blood with the tissue.

"Ruby, can you hear me?" whispered Jesse, who was trying not to look at the blood and the open wound which had somehow, in the space of five minutes, appeared to have doubled in size. She screwed her face up in disgust when she viewed the sick all over her carpet.

"Um," replied Ruby.

Jesse couldn't cope. It was simply too much to deal with. Quietly, she walked to the kitchen, where she rolled a fat joint and lit the end, puffing furiously. As the sense of relaxation hit her, she decided that the best thing for Ruby was to have a good sleep – she would feel so much better in the morning. She had sleeping tablets lying around somewhere but the effects of the skunk were causing a massive memory blank. So she wandered from room to room, looking for something and then forgetting what she was searching for. Then, suddenly, there they were, on her bedside table. She grabbed them, fumbled with the cap, and emptied the contents onto her sweaty palm. Two strong sleeping tablets should do the trick.

She hurried back to Ruby; she was still moaning and groaning, not yet fully conscious.

"'Ere, girl, try to swallow these. You will feel so much better."

Ruby had no idea who was speaking to her. She thought maybe she was in hospital and so, slowly, she opened her mouth as much as she could, but she was struggling to do so because of the pain.

Jesse winced when she saw the bite marks peel open even more. She pushed the two pills inside Ruby's mouth. She watched her daughter try to swallow and realised she needed a sip of water to wash those big bastards down. She filled an old cup with no handle and tried to dribble some water into Ruby's mouth. It spilled down the sides but enough went in to ease the tablets down her throat. She knelt on the floor and watched with curiosity as her daughter gradually stopped moaning and her head drooped to the side as she fell into a deep sleep. She returned to the kitchen, where she had left the joint. Relighting it, she sat on the chair and drifted off into another world. It was still early and she thought that once Ruby had woken up she could probably call her a taxi and send her home. Perhaps she would even go with her, to show that she was the caring, dutiful mother who had come to Ruby's rescue when she was viciously attacked by a mob. But, then again, Sam might not see it that way.

Once the swelling had gone down and the wound had healed up, she wouldn't appear so bad. She would just have to get Ruby to call her dad and say she was staying for a while.

The skunk was not helping her at all. What she really needed to help her think straight was a good line of Charlie. She fumbled underneath her bed until she found a soft bag containing her secret stash of cocaine. She opened it very carefully over a mirror on the floor and cut two lines. After rolling up a five pound note, she snorted one after the other and instantly sprang to life, clear-headed and ready to get to work.

She grabbed her blanket off the bed and headed back to the living room to cover Ruby. She stared for a while, not comfortable with how Ruby looked – her head was at an odd angle and white foam was bubbling from her mouth.

"Ruby, wake up!" Jesse was really panicking now.

She opened her eyes but closed them again.

"Ruby, can you hear me?" said Jesse.

"Yeah…" Her voice was slow and almost a whisper. But at least she was alive, thought Jesse. The tablets were obviously working. She wiped the foam away from her face and felt her forehead to see if she had a temperature, but even if she did Jesse wouldn't have a clue what that meant or what to do. Leaving Ruby covered and warm, Jesse decided to go to the pharmacist to get some bandages and antiseptic cream.

She pulled on her jeans, tucked her night dress inside, and threw on an old, baggy sweat shirt. She slammed the door shut and headed off, with the intention to do the right thing.

Ruby lay unconscious now. Her heart rate was slow, three of her ribs were broken, her kidney was damaged, and her brain had a small bleed. The air was cold and the heating in the flat had run out. The blanket gradually slid away from Ruby and her body temperature, which had been steadily falling, had now reached a dangerously low level.

Jesse crossed over the main road to the other half of the estate where less people lived, a part which was even more run down, but the pharmacist was still open. After she bought witch hazel, a few plasters, and some ibuprofen, she headed back.

"Hello, darling, and how are you doing? I haven't seen you for a while," called a deep, gruff Scottish voice.

She turned to face Barry, her old dealer. He was still as big as ever, with an enormous beer belly and a long, snowy white beard. He looked like an ageing Hells Angel.

Jesse nodded. "All right, Barry."

He waddled over and put his meaty arm around her shoulders.

"I've missed you."

Jesse knew exactly what he meant and she wasn't interested. Those days of sexual favours for a couple of joints were over. Now she had a serious amount of money she could buy her own drugs.

"Yeah, yeah, look, Barry, I'm in a rush, mate. Maybe next time, eh?"

He laughed. "So, Jesse, you wouldn't want to try my latest gear then? Only, I wanted my regulars back. I'll tell you this. There's never been a finer powder in these parts since 1988."

Coming down off her Charlie, she could do with another line, and if old Barry was serving up clean shit she would be interested, especially now she had the cash flow.

Jesse looked at the bag she got from the chemist. She decided that it would be best for Ruby to sleep before she applied any witch hazel and plasters. She had left her warm and comfortable and guessed the tablets would knock her out for at least four hours.

"Oh, go on then, I'll have a taste."

Barry knew she had come into some money. She hadn't been exactly quiet about buying decent shit.

His flat was in the heart of the estate. He had bars up at the window and ten chains which crossed his front door. Jesse entered, eager to try the top class cocaine as he'd promised.

Ruby held on to life by the skin of her teeth. It was dark when she slowly opened her eyes and she had no idea where she was, or even who she was.

Her face was burning and her head hurt beyond belief. Tentatively, she lifted her hand to feel her cheek and was surprised to find it so bloated. The air was like icicles, stabbing her body. She was shivering uncontrollably and yet her face was on fire. Trying to sit up to see where she was, she was gripped by an immense pain in her ribs and quickly she lay back down.

She closed her eyes and was back in the world of sleep.

*

Jack was thrilled to see his aunt again. She was always good for conversation, showing so much interest in his life. Sam was dishing up the roast chicken when she knocked at the door.

At thirty-seven years old, Francesca was still every bit a beautiful woman. Her figure would make most women green-eyed and the thick black waves, which bounced on her shoulders, shone like ravens' wings.

She entered, hugging her nephew as if she hadn't seen him for a year, yet it had only been a few weeks. Not having any children of her own, she loved Jack and Ruby as if they were her own and they knew it.

"Where's Ruby?" asked Francesca, as she looked over Jack's shoulder.

Sam heard her and called out, "All right, sis. Ruby's over at Sophie's doing her science homework and she said she would catch up with you later."

Francesca's heart sank. She had been so looking forward to seeing her niece and getting their relationship back on track. She hated that the last time she saw Ruby there had been an awful row. She thought maybe she would hang around and wait for her to return.

The roast chicken was slowly being devoured by the three, in between chatting. However, when Sam told his sister that Ruby had been to visit Jesse, Francesca nearly choked on her wine.

"Why would she do that?"

"She was probably just curious, but don't worry, she hasn't been again," Sam replied quickly.

"Yeah, she must have seen the old slag for what she is!" mumbled Jack.

"Are you sure she hasn't been back... What did she say about it?" Francesca was angry. She had done everything in her power to keep her niece and nephew away from Jesse and now, out of the blue, Ruby was doing just as she liked.

"She didn't say anything, actually. To be quite honest, I think she was embarrassed by the whole episode and hasn't spoken another word about it since," said Sam.

Francesca looked at Jack. After all, he would be the one Ruby would confide in.

"No, she ain't said a word."

There was a bang at the door.

"Oh, for fuck's sake, if Ruby forgets her key one more time!" shouted Sam as he walked to the hallway.

Francesca was quite pleased, thinking that Ruby had come home, but was rudely awoken when a thin, blond girl entered the room, stood with her head down, looking as though she was in serious trouble.

Sam was in a panic, his eyes wide, as he ran his hands through his hair.

"Ruby left school early today. She never even went to Sophie's," said Sam, pointing to the frightened child.

Jack jumped up from his seat. "Sophie, where did Ruby say she was going?" Sophie shrugged her shoulders.

"But, didn't you plan to do homework together?" yelled Sam.

Sophie went white – she was not used to being shouted at.

"I'm sorry, Mr Vincent. Ruby mentioned nothing about homework. She came to English, asked to leave, argued with the teacher, and went. I just popped over to give Ruby her assignment," she replied.

"I'm sorry for shouting, love, but obviously I am worried."

Sophie nodded and smiled.

Sam pulled out his mobile phone and dialled Ruby's number. It rang for ages.

Francesca asked Sophie to contact all of Ruby's mates to see if she was at any of their houses. Sam kept redialling and Jack paced the floor, trying to work out where she would go.

"Sophie, is Ruby seeing anyone?" asked Jack.

They stared at her expression, looking for clues.

"Well?" demanded Sam.

Sophie knew about Jacob, but if she told on Ruby then she would receive a good hiding. Right now, however, she was more afraid of Ruby's family.

"Someone called Jacob, and he is twenty-four." The words spilled out so fast that all eyes glared at Sophie as if she were responsible.

Sam grabbed his jacket and car keys. "Right then, love, you come with me, and show me where he lives!" He clutched her arm.

"Mr Vincent, I don't know where he lives. I'm sorry, I really don't know."

Sam demanded that Sophie tell him everything.

"Mr Vincent, I don't know any more than that!"

"Give the girl a break, Sam." At this point, Francesca was up from her seat and walking towards Sophie. "Now, sweetheart, you have been really helpful, so just one last question. Do you know when Ruby began seeing

Jacob, and where they met?" She was a professional at drawing answers out of people – after all, she had been a top barrister for years.

Sophie sat down on the settee and counted on her fingers. "It was three weeks ago, and in a place called, err…" She paused, trying to remember the name. "Kiddiewell, no Kidmore, something like that."

"Kidbrooke!" shouted Jack.

She nodded and the three looked at each other, knowing full well where she had been going.

Sophie left for home, worn out. The three jumped into Sam's car. The drive wasn't too long, since the rush hour was over, and it was dark.

Sam's intention was to kick Jesse's door in and demand she tell him where this Jacob lived, because, as far as he was concerned, she was responsible. Jack was so angry he couldn't speak. He knew his father would knock at his mother's door and he was just as anxious about that. His little sister was now dating a grown man, and from the Kidbrooke estate of all the shit-holes.

Francesca didn't know what she would do if Jesse had been part of the reason that Ruby was seeing a man of twenty-four. Her throat tightened like she was being strangled. She hated Jesse with a vengeance and would happily send her to her grave.

As they drove into the estate, Jack felt sick. He recalled it so well – especially the park, where he was sent to look after his little sister, even when it was freezing cold, so his mother could have her friends over. He had a clear recollection of a time when it was bitterly cold and their mother had entertained her so-called mates. She had handed them a packet of crisps each and sent them outside to play. Ruby wore a summer dress and cardigan. They skipped around the swings. The night drew in and the temperature dropped to a point at which Ruby was shaking uncontrollably. He banged on the door and shouted through the letterbox to be let back in, but all he heard was a dull, thudding sound of reggae music. Gloria was not in either and it wasn't so much the cold he agonised over but the terror of the dark, the howling noises and the fear in his sister's eyes as she stared up at him for help and he could do nothing. He learned that day how to survive. He grabbed Ruby's hand and they ran along the road, tugging at every car door. Finally, one sprang open and in they jumped. The owner had left one of those thick tartan car blankets and his jacket, along with a bar of chocolate and a bottle of fizzy drink. He remembered the tears trickling down her cheeks as he rubbed her blue legs to warm her up, and then, burping loudly from the pop, making her giggle. They dozed off, huddled together. When the owner returned, they were lucky he wasn't a kiddie fiddler. They showed him where they lived and he almost smashed the door down. Jesse answered, surprised to see a man standing there holding the hands of her two kids. She made out they had run off and her husband was out looking for them. Jack gripped the man's hand tight, praying he would do something to make sure she didn't hurt them. He looked down at the two children and then back at Jesse. "If I ever see these kids out at night again, I'm gonna report ya, got it?" Jesse was nodding with fear in her eyes. Jack never knew who the man was, but from then on Jesse always had them inside before it was dark.

Francesca shuddered as they turned into the estate. She remembered it from when she had paid Jesse to stay away from the kids.

Sam screeched up outside the house and left the car door open. He leapt forward and banged on her door. Jack got out too. Francesca stayed seated in the car, waiting.

There was no answer. Jack peered through the letterbox but it was dark inside.

"She ain't 'ere." He threw his hands in the air. "Finding some fucking bloke called Jacob is like looking for a needle in a haystack."

Francesca then stepped out of her car.

"Knock on the neighbours' doors. See if they know where Jesse has gone."

Jack tried to peer through the letterbox again, using his key ring torch. He saw straight into the living room and could make out a person, lying on the settee.

"There's someone in there, Dad!" Francesca grabbed the torch and looked herself.

"Yeah, he's right."

Sam looked up and down the block. "It's probably Jesse, the fucking lazy whore." Within a second he had kicked the door so hard that it came straight off its hinges. Francesca stood outside, keeping an eye, whilst Jack and Sam stormed into the flat. Jack tried to turn on the lights. But the electric meter had run out so he continued to follow his father into the cold, smelly living room.

"Cor, fucking 'ell, it stinks like someone's died in 'ere," laughed Sam.

When he got to the settee and peered down at the crumpled heap, he jumped back in fright at the state of the woman's face. It looked like something out of the night of the living dead, swollen and bloody.

Jack peered down, not recognising his little sister. Then, as realisation hit him, he screamed, "Oh, no, Ruby!" He fell to his knees. Sam was already paralysed in disbelief as his sister ran into the room. Her heart was pounding. Please don't let her be dead. A scream like that would mean only one thing. Sam was shaking with shock and Francesca pulled Jack away to get a better look. She grabbed Ruby's limp arm, fumbling for a pulse. "Come on, baby, stay with us." She felt her niece move only very faintly, but she was certainly alive.

"Sam, help me get her in the car." She could see Ruby was barely breathing.

Sam went into automatic pilot, scooped up his daughter, and hurried her to the back seat of his Jag. The interior light was already on and the full extent of her injuries could be seen. So bad was the state of her face, Sam swooned for a second. Jack steadied him and then, when he recovered, pulled him away and clambered in.

"Oh, my God! Ruby, please be all right, please be all right. Wake up, Rubes." The tears streamed uncontrollably and his voice was erratic. Gripped with fear that she could die, just as she nearly did all those years ago when they ate the dope cakes, the same emotions of dread and helplessness came back to him. Ruby came to, but barely alive, and then sank deep into a coma.

Sam called an ambulance. He didn't know how bad she was and precious wasted minutes could cost Ruby her life.

"Ruby baby, it's Dad here, speak to me! You're gonna be all right." The tears poured down his face.

Jack was as white as a sheet. He couldn't believe he was witnessing the gruesome sight of his sister's face. She lay there, limp and very cold.

Francesca shut the doors and put the heating on full. "Let's get her warm." She took off her fur coat and placed it over Ruby but still there was no sign of recovery. Her breathing was shallow and her lips – what was left of them – were blue.

The neighbours had ignored the commotion. They assumed it was another drugs raid until they saw the ambulance arrive. Then they guessed Jesse had taken an overdose and no one really cared. Except Gloria. She heard the screams and struggled to get to her feet. After searching for her dressing gown, she waddled along the hallway and out into the street. The Jag was parked outside Jesse's and she could make out the smartly dressed man and woman. Then, as Jack clambered back out of the car, she realised who they were. The scream! Suddenly, she had an awful feeling of dread. Ruby! Without a second thought she rushed over to the car, much to the surprise of Sam and Francesca. They had absolutely no idea who this woman was. "What's happened?" Her soft Jamaican accent had an air of panic.

Jack's tear-stained face looked with utmost compassion at Gloria and instinctively he put out his arms to hold her. She cradled him as she had done all those years ago. "Ahh, me little Jackie, calm yourself, what's happened?" She felt his shoulders move with the sobs.

He stepped aside as Gloria peered into the car. Neither Sam nor Francesca stopped her.

"Jesus!" She stared for a while and then ran her hands through Ruby's hair. "Aunty Gloria's here now. Can you hear me? I know, try to open your eyes for me, or squeeze my hand."

There was nothing. "Have you called an ambulance?" she said to the three faces, who were watching her every move. Sam nodded. He was too distraught to speak.

Gloria pulled herself back out of the car. "My God, that poor child... she is very sick..." She stopped when they heard the sirens. "Oh, thank you, Jesus!" she whispered.

Francesca held onto Jack, who was in such a mess, rocking backwards and forwards as if he was in agony himself. She tried to stay in control and not lose it. But, inside, her head was a burning, raging emotion of hate and fear. She understood more than anyone what her family would be going through. The paramedics wasted no time in getting Ruby onto the stretcher and into the ambulance. Francesca, in her professional manner, spoke with them, giving as much information as she could. Sam was too shaken to string a sentence together. Gloria held on to Jack. The two of them, now clinging to each other, had formed a very close emotional bond when he had been a small boy. After all, hadn't she been his rock and saviour in the past? He felt safe again. That comfort, from her soft skin and sweet perfume, somehow had a deep, calming effect.

"She's gonna be all right, just you see," she whispered.

She kissed him on the forehead and said goodbye, not wanting to be in the way, and then crept back to her flat. She had never wished bad on anyone, but at that moment she wished Jesse dead.

Sam jumped in the ambulance with Ruby whilst Jack and Francesca followed in Sam's car.

"What's happened to her, Sisco?" whispered Jack, just like a little boy.

"I don't know, but I will find out, and whoever is responsible will wish they'd never lived!" Francesca was staring ahead as if she were in a trance. Her words were slow and deliberate. Jack knew then she meant business. He had heard bits of conversations between his uncles. Francesca was the dangerous Vincent; she was the one you really didn't want to cross. But to him she was an angel. He thought back to Gloria. Another woman he had loved.

"Jack, who was that lady?"

There was silence for a few seconds, and then he said, "Another angel."

Chapter Twelve

Francesca detested hospitals. They brought back memories of her ordeal twelve years ago. It was like history was repeating itself. She, too, had been cruelly attacked and left for dead by someone she had loved. She ended up unconscious, with her face ripped to ribbons. The evil monster was her late husband, who, after years of abuse, had tried to kill her.

Right now she was feeling so angry. Her niece was looking, just as she had, battered and bruised. Yet, she had been in her mid-twenties when she was attacked; this shouldn't be happening to Ruby, who was a young teenager. She had dealt with her physical scars. The mental ones, however, she still had problems with. To this day she suffered bouts of nightmares, but she hoped that Ruby would pull through and tried not to think if this could have any long-term effects. It didn't enter her head that her niece was close to death. That thought was too far removed. Her brain just could not process it.

The crash team were on standby as Ruby's heartbeat began to diminish. They gave her shots to speed it up and rapidly transported her to be scanned.

The doctors had to prise Sam away from Ruby to get to work on her very fragile body. The scan showed the damage to her brain. The medical team bleeped the neurosurgeon to operate immediately to stop the bleeding.

Francesca hugged her brother as he sobbed. Jack stared out of the waiting room window, praying to God to save his sister.

Reluctantly, Francesca called her mother and father. Her heart was breaking when she heard her mother's voice on the end of the phone. She could picture her sweet face crumpling when she gave her the news. She still recalled her mother's expression of torment and the horror that day when her nurse had removed the bandages from her own butchered face. The memory would stay with her – for the rest of her life.

Francesca decided not to tell her the full extent of poor Ruby's injuries.

Mary, her mother, took comfort in the calmness in Francesca's voice and so didn't go into a blind panic. She called each of her sons and suggested they make their way to the hospital. Bill, still a handsome man, every bit the Vincent father, with his tanned skin and what was once a thick head of black waves – now grey – took control. Their family had been through enough heartache to last a lifetime. Now, however, they were together and they would face any problem as a whole family.

Mary was proud of her kids and loved her grandchildren even more.

Unlike Francesca, Mary was a mothering woman. She would bake cakes, make jam, and buy thermal underwear for the colder weather – not for herself, of course, but for her children, who were now grown up. She had helped to bring up Ruby and Jack from when they were little and now she spent most days watching over little Alfie so that Joe's girlfriend, Belinda, could keep her hairdressing job. The house seemed too quiet when they grew up and left. After all, Mary and Bill had raised five kids all told.

The uncles arrived one by one at the hospital. Dan and Sam cried and Fred was hopping mad. Typical of Fred, his pain was always shown by aggression. Someone had to be blamed and someone was up for a good hiding.

Fred pulled Jack aside.

"Right, boy, who the fuck did it, any clues?" Fred was still in his suit, minus his tie, but ready for a serious round of violence with whoever had laid their hands on Ruby.

"Fred, all I know is, she has been seeing a bloke called Jacob and, when we went to find out where he lived, that's when we found our Rubes…" He couldn't speak anymore. The tears flowed and that drew attention from everyone. They knew how close he was to his sister.

"Come 'ere, me boy," Mary held her arms out to her grandson and hugged him until he stopped crying.

"She's a fighter, our Ruby. If ever there was a fighter, she is it. I know this for a fact, so just you wait and see. She will be up and out of here as soon as you can blink."

"Thanks, Nan," whispered Jack.

Francesca was so glad her mother hadn't seen the state of Ruby, as she might not have been so confident. But then she thought of her own ordeal, and how she had survived, and Mary was right – Ruby was definitely a strong girl.

Joe was the last to arrive and before he even saw anyone he was crying.

Francesca hugged him. He was still treated as the baby.

"How is she doing?" he asked, between snivels.

"We are just waiting now for the doctor to let us know," she replied.

The Vincents sat in the waiting room for four hours, until finally a doctor appeared.

"Okay, she is out of the woods. I have stopped the bleeding and I think she will make a full recovery. However, any blow to the head can cause other problems, so let's take each day as it comes," announced Dr O'Neal, holding his hand up to show his crossed fingers.

Jack was the first to speak. "What about her face? Do you think it's gonna scar?" He looked around, hoping he hadn't asked the wrong question. That would bother Ruby the most. She was so fussy about her appearance.

Dr O'Neal smiled at the boy. "The bruising and puffiness look far worse than they are. We have put a stitch in her cheek and one in her lip. Once the swelling subsides, she will have a few minor scars but otherwise there is nothing to worry about."

As he went to walk away, he noticed the amount of people there. "Oh, yes, I have to tell you that Ruby has been through one hell of an ordeal, with three broken ribs and a ruptured kidney. She will be in hospital for at least two weeks and I suggest you visit two at a time." He smiled, showing his brilliant, white teeth to match his bright, white hair.

All the Vincents nodded in unison as if they were being spoken to by the headmaster. The relief was enormous. Sam could breathe properly and Jack could smile.

"Sam, you don't think her mother did that, do you?" asked Fred.

He shook his head. "I can't see how, unless she beat our Ruby with a bat or a cosh."

"Well, I think we need to pay her a visit and fucking find out," fretted Fred.

"All in good time. If anyone's gonna sort her out, it's me," replied Sam.

Jack jumped in. "No, you won't. That woman tried to ruin our lives when we were little and she ain't gonna do it now we are older. I will be the one to sort her out."

It was the first time the men had ever seen Jack answer them back, but they admired him for his gumption and pride.

Minutes later, the doctor reappeared. "Two of you can have a quick visit. She is coming round." He smiled again. "Oh, one question, were you aware that Ruby had taken sleeping tablets? Only, we found traces in her blood."

Sam frowned and shook his head.

Jack and Sam went in, gingerly. In the middle of the white room was a bed and machines, with wires and tubes everywhere. Ruby looked like a sleeping angel. Although her face was swollen, and her head was wrapped in enormous bandages, they could still make out it was her because the nurses had cleaned up her face. Slowly, her eyes flickered open.

Jack held her hand. "'Ello, Rubes, it's me, Jack. I'm right here, look, holding your hand." His lips quivered and he tried to bite down to stop the tears.

Ruby squeezed to let him know she could hear.

Sam said, "I'm here too, my baby. In fact, we are all here. It's just they could only let two of us in." His words trailed off as he fought back the lump in his throat. It hurt him to see the state of her.

"Listen, baby, you have to tell me who did it. Was it Jesse?" whispered Sam.

Ruby heard her father's voice but she didn't even know why she was in hospital.

The doctor came in and asked them to let Ruby rest. They agreed and walked with the doctor to the visiting room.

"Doc, can you tell me what has happened to her?" asked Sam.

Dr O'Neal was hazarding a guess. "I would say, from those injuries, and they are multiple blows, she has been attacked. Possibly by more than one person. You see, she has contusions all over her head, a bite mark to the cheek, and injuries to the stomach, the back and the face. Now, when a person is attacked, they typically follow a bruising pattern, but she is covered, which suggests multiple persons were involved."

Sam was feeling sick, imagining his daughter being beaten so badly.

The men agreed not to do anything until Ruby regained complete consciousness and could tell them what had happened. Jack had unfinished business of his own to deal with. After all, even if it wasn't Jesse who had hurt Ruby, why was she left alone in a dark, cold, smelly flat, dying?

*

Jesse eventually arrived home. She was completely stoned. Finding her door off its hinges and two policemen standing outside, she panicked and turned to run, but the police officer was far quicker than the wobbly Jesse, who could just about tell the time of day.

"Bollocks!" she said.

"Well, well! Look who we have here. Going somewhere, were you?" asked the copper, who was now gripping Jesse's skinny arm.

"Nah," she replied. Her heart was in her mouth. She felt the pulse in her neck pounding. The door was kicked in. It could only mean one thing: the police had carried out a drugs raid. She would go back to prison. No way could she get out of this one. There was a grand's worth of cocaine under her bed and three grand in cash. She was bang to rights. With a charge of intent to supply, she was looking at a seven year stretch at least.

They took her inside the police car and pushed her back on the seat. She wasn't cuffed but, considering the way they restrained her, she may as well have been.

"What are you arresting me for?" croaked Jesse.

The police officer sitting next to her, Officer Conners, turned his face away because her breath was so disgusting. "Who said you were under arrest? I just want to ask you a few questions."

Even though she was stoned, Jesse assumed they hadn't found her gear because her rights would have been read by now. It must be to do with Ruby.

"Well, if you ain't fucking arresting me, let go of me arms and let me out of this stinking pig car," shouted Jesse.

"Shut it, or I will find a good reason to arrest you. I'm sure you have a bit of personal – marijuana, cocaine, amphetamines?" said Conners.

"So, shall we continue?" snapped PC Manners, the other copper in the car.

Jesse chewed the inside of her mouth and nodded in disgust, but she was relieved they had no grounds, so far, to arrest her.

"Right then, Jesse. When was the last time you saw your daughter, Ruby Vincent?"

She shrugged her shoulders, needing to think this through. Not knowing what was going on, she replied with a question.

"Why, what's happened to her?"

"Ruby was found alone, in your flat, needing medical attention."

Jesse was silent for a minute. Then, she wiped the snot running from her nose with the back of her hand and smeared it down her jeans.

"How bad is she?" She tried to sound concerned.

"Just answer the question. When was the last time you saw her?" growled Conners.

The effects of the drugs were wearing off and Jesse was thinking straight. It's amazing what fear can do to your adrenaline levels.

"Well, this afternoon, when she came to visit, I needed to go shopping and so she stayed in the flat."

The officer presumed she would lie. She was a person who found it easier to bullshit than speak the truth.

"Who attacked Ruby?" shouted Conners, frustrated with Jesse's cocky attitude.

"I don't know. I didn't know she had even been attacked."

"So, how does a teenage girl end up in your flat, hanging on to dear life? You go off shopping until eleven o'clock at night, come back off your face, and know nothing?" he screamed.

Jesse sat motionless, staring into space.

"Right, tell me from the beginning. What time did Ruby arrive at your home?" asked Conners, calmly.

"Ruby came to see me about two o'clock, maybe three. She often pops over. I needed to do some shopping. See a few people. I came home, and I find you two standing there, with me door down the fucking hallway."

He wanted to punch Jesse's lights out. A nasty piece of work, she didn't deserve to be a mother.

"Who knows her around here? Who had a grudge against her?"

Jesse went to say Jacob but thought better of it. After all, she could end up looking like Ruby and she needed no more grief.

"No one, officer. She pops over sometimes to see me then goes home again… look, she has only seen me four or five times in the last ten years."

Conners was now confused and he scratched his beard. "So why did you say she often pops over?"

Jesse rolled her eyes. "Because she has only just got in touch with me after all these years…" She thought for a second. "Who found her?"

"Her father did and, if he hadn't rushed her to hospital, she would be fucking dead. So got it now, 'ave ya? Attempted murder!"

Jesse grinned. She was going to cause real grief to the Vincents now. She could fuck them up – just as they had fucked her up.

"Well, there you go, officers, there's your culprit. Sam Vincent. He is the bastard who did that to her. My Ruby came to visit me because he was beating her. She hated him, wanted to move in with me, she did." She smirked at the police.

Conners knew Sam Vincent due to the fact he had been the one to carry out routine checks on the clubs, along with DI James. Unbeknown to Jesse, the two coppers had been well-informed of the whole incident of how Ruby was found.

"Nice try, Jesse, but that's not washing with me," laughed officer Conners. "Sam wasn't alone when he had to kick your door down to rescue his daughter. He was with his sister and son. Oh, and by the way, I have another witness, but I probably won't need her." He smirked. "So, any other clues how your own daughter got herself inside your flat, smashed to pieces?" asked PC Manners with a sarcastic tone.

Jesse shrugged. "Sorry, officer, you've got me there. It's as much a mystery to me as it is to you." She shuffled about in the back seat, itching to get out of the car. "So, if there's nothing else, I need to take a piss."

The two officers let her go, shaking their heads in disgust.

"It puzzles me, mate, how the fucking hell Sam Vincent, one of the *Palace* owners, could look twice at a trollop like her."

PC Manners didn't know the Vincents but was aware they owned the chain of nightclubs and kept their business fairly clean. There was always the mystery of the McManners, an Irish family who disappeared off the face of the earth one night, and there was a whisper that it was the Vincents. It wasn't investigated, owing to the fact that no one cared enough. The McManners had terrorised many a villain and had untold enemies, so if the Vincents had been responsible, then good luck to them.

As the police drove away, Jesse hurried into the bedroom and searched frantically for the cocaine and the money. It was still there. "Thank fuck!" she said out loud and rolled herself a joint.

*

Three weeks later, Ruby was back at home. Her recovery was quick, seeing as she was such a determined girl. Her memory slowly returned but she kept the true facts a secret until she decided what she should do.

The scars on her face were not as bad as they first looked. In fact, her lips were almost the same. The teeth marks in her cheeks were superficial wounds and so the scarring would eventually fade. The whole family were concerned about how this attack could affect her in the long-term. Would she be traumatised once she started to recall the incident? What they didn't realise was that Ruby recalled everything: who did it to her, why it happened, and how her mother had dragged her into the flat. It was odd because, as she had lay there, going in and out of consciousness, it was the rancid stench which made her aware she was in her mother's flat. Frightened and in pain, she also remembered the smell on the hand that shoved the tablets down her throat. It was afterwards, when there was silence, and the cold crept in, that she knew where she was, and – although she was confused – the polluted odour painted a clearer picture.

It was so obvious what had happened. Her own mother had refused to let her in until the fight was over and then she'd just dragged her inside, hoping she'd fall asleep and die.

Ruby wanted to cry every time she thought about it. How could Jesse be so damn cruel? She could have died, and her own mother was nowhere to be seen.

Jack described how they had found her lifeless body, confirming how evil their mother was. But none of what Jack had said was new to Ruby. She had to find out for herself and she would do that all right. She had a very good idea of what Jesse was like. She just wished she hadn't had to go through such horrendous suffering to discover it.

Ruby didn't mention the money she had given her, or the times she had spent with her smoking pot and drinking alcohol.

It was a hard lesson to learn but, when it came to it, the one sure thing in her life was her family. They loved her unconditionally and it was they who had saved her, not her selfish, neglectful mother.

Gloria had taken it upon herself to pay Ruby a visit in the hospital. Knowing her father was a dangerous man, she sneaked in when visiting hours were over. She had always loved Ruby and Jack and was heartbroken when the police told her she had nearly died.

Ruby was wide awake and sitting upright when Gloria entered. She handed her a modest bunch of flowers and gave her the biggest hug. Ruby was warmed by Gloria's visit. She learned so much that afternoon.

Ruby now had a very clear picture of her mother's character and how she lived her life. She now understood that Jesse didn't have a brain tumour and she'd never wanted to be a mother. In fact, Gloria spilled the beans about everything and hoped Ruby stayed well away and continued her life with her loving family.

Ruby was grateful to Gloria for so many things. But, by far the most important of these was Gloria allowing her to hear and learn the truth. That's all she wanted to know at this point in her life. Mistakes had been made, she knew that, but there was no point in dwelling on these. Hindsight was a wonderful thing! She loved to feel her big, caramel arms engulf her. It was the same feeling of security as when she was a child. That's why she had thought her mother was such a nice person – it was actually Gloria she had remembered mothering her. After all, she had only been three years old at the time.

Gloria was older now and grey strands peppered her hair. She struggled to get to her feet after sitting so long. But before she left she gave Ruby another word of warning.

"Listen to me, child, our Jacob may seem a good boy, and at times he is, but mix with the boys where you come from, good boys, ya know. Boys with a future!" Her Jamaican accent was as strong as ever. She winked and left.

Unlike Jack, Ruby didn't want to go in and beat the crap out of Jesse. She wanted to bide her time and devise a plan which would pay her back for the hurt and suffering she had caused. It was there, staring her in the face. Her mother hadn't cared at all if she'd lived or died, unlike her father, who would kill to protect his children, and so she knew that, no matter what, her family cared and cared a lot.

*

Francesca waited three days before she returned to the estate, giving Jesse a false sense of security. This time, she wasn't alone. She had Dominic and Beano with her. Beano was one of Mauricio's men. He lived in London but was always on hand if they needed insider information. He was like a hunter – a Red Indian tracker. With his nose to the ground, he could sniff out anyone and anything.

At two o'clock in the morning a punter left Jesse's. Before he had a chance to close the door behind him, Beano had put his foot in the way. "Cheers, mate," the man nodded, "all yours, what's left of the bitch." He laughed.

Francesca stepped out of the car and walked past Beano. He remained in the hallway whilst she casually strolled into the bedroom, flicking the light switch on and removing her gloves. Jesse sat bolt upright and trembled. "What's going on, what you doing here?" Her voice was childlike.

Francesca smirked. "Oh, Jesse, I think you know damn well why I am here."

Jesse, wide-eyed and dry-mouthed, tried desperately to think of how to get out of this nightmare. The last words Francesca had said to her were still there, as clear as day. "Look, I swear I didn't hurt Ruby. I'd never hurt her. She came to me, I never went looking…"

"Shut the fuck up. I detest your voice and your ugly face. I want you dead…" Francesca pulled out her gun and pointed it at Jesse's head. "Bang!" she shouted, as Jesse threw herself into a ball, quaking uncontrollably and urinating over the bed.

Francesca grinned. "But it's like this. My niece is in hospital, in a very bad way, and I know you don't have the balls to fight, and wouldn't dare touch a hair on that child's head, because I do believe you took my threat seriously. You see, Jesse, I have this ability to see right through weak, pathetic creatures like yourself. Cowards in every way, no use to society, like leeches…"

"Please don't shoot me!" Jesse clasped her head, expecting any second to be shot.

"Shoot you? Oh no, I would never let you get away that easily. Besides, right now, I want answers!"

Jesse stopped shaking and listened. So what did she want? Perhaps she wasn't going to get skinned alive. She sat up again and cocked her head to the side.

"Yeah, o' course. I swear I never touched her, I never would…"

Francesca stepped towards the bed. In a flash, and gripping the gun, she whacked Jesse across the nose, cracking the bridge and spraying blood up the wall. Jesse gripped her face and yelled in pain but remained frozen in shock. What was to come next was worse than death.

"Oh, don't piss yourself. I haven't come here to kill you – this time. I want to know who the fuck put my Ruby in hospital?"

Jesse sighed. "It was Denise Ade Abdu… or something, a tall black bird, lives above the café with Shelley Cartwright, she's a short, stocky girl, and Noreen Fenton... they did it!"

"Yeah, and how are you so sure?" Francesca's lips were white and her eyes menacing. She waved the weapon under Jesse's nose. "Tell me, or I might change my mind and blow your fucking head off."

Jesse pushed herself further up the bed and winced at the thought. "Ruby told me…" The gun was cold and hard as it was shoved into her neck.

"How the fuck did Ruby tell you? You'd better tell me the truth, because if I get a whiff you're lying —"

"No, please believe me. I came home, found her on the floor outside. I got her inside and she said it was them. On me life. I tried to help. I ain't got a phone, see, so I laid Ruby on the couch and ran up the road to call an ambulance. By the time I found one that worked, and got back 'ere, she was gone. All I saw was them driving off. I thought it was the ambulance I called!"

Francesca shook her head, knowing Jesse was lying, but she couldn't kill her – not here, not now – but she could wait.

"Mention me to a single soul and... well, you know what, don't you?"

Jesse nodded and as Francesca left she smiled to herself, having left out the little nugget of information regarding Denise's nutty brothers. For sure they would come looking for her, and Francesca's days would be over, and she could then spit on her grave: one less Vincent.

Francesca nodded to Beano as he held the door open for her. They drove away, leaving the depressing emptiness of the estate.

"So what do you know about a Denise Ade Abdu..."

He grinned. "Do you mean Denise Ade Abdulla?"

"If she lives above the café then, yes, I do."

Beano nodded. "Yep, she does. Nasty fucking bunch, her and her sly brothers. Proper evil lot. The Ol' Bill stay clear. They run the manor."

"Does she stay in their company all the time?" She lit up a cigarette and opened the window. Beano raised his eyebrows. "Nah, she's a fanny muncher. Lives with her bird, Shelley."

Francesca chuckled. "You amaze me, Beano. How the fuck do you know everyone?"

He lowered his gaze. "All those years ago, when you asked me to keep an eye on Jesse, I made it my business to know who's who. That's why Mauricio pays me well. I'm good at my job. I leave no stone unturned. Get my drift?"

"Good. Find out if she ever leaves the estate. I wanna word with her!" She winked.

"Actually, I don't have to find out. She visits the gym up the road, every Wednesday, her and Shelley. I know that because I pump me own muscles on a regular basis."

Francesca rolled her eyes.

"I might be five foot two and a fag paper but, underneath this shirt, I'm all rock hard. Anyway, they go to the same gym."

Francesca threw her cigarette out of the window and faced Beano. "I need you to bring her and Shelley to me."

He bit down on his lip. "Far be it from me to tell you what to do but, whatever you have planned, please make sure you have backup 'cos that Denise is dangerous. A right hard bitch. Guaranteed, she'll have a blade on her."

Francesca smiled. "Thank you, Beano, but I don't get my hands too dirty. I have certain people to do that for me." He chuckled, forgetting for a moment who she was. "I just thought you should know."

*

The set up was simple. Beano drove to the bus stop on the Wednesday evening, asking if the girls wanted a lift to the gym. As they stepped inside the blacked out Mercedes jeep, they got a rude awakening. Two meatheads grabbed them. The girls struggled like feral cats but stopped once the shooters were shoved in their mouths. Denise looked from one to the other and then at Shelley, who appeared terrified.

"Move an inch, and you're a dead woman!" said the bigger of the two men. He pulled back the gun.

"What the fuck is all this about, and who the fuck are you?" Denise was acting her cocky self.

"I'm nobody, and you will know, soon enough, what it's all about. I strongly recommend you sit still and shut the fuck up!"

The rest of the journey was in silence. The girls glanced at each other, knowing they were in severe shit. This was no two-bit gang. The men were serious heavies. They were driving a flash, new car and their shooters were held like professionals. Denise racked her brains, trying to think who was behind it, and concluded it was something to do with her brothers. They had pissed the wrong person off this time. She prayed to God they were just being used as threats and there was no real intent to harm them. It didn't even cross her mind that it was over the schoolgirl, Jesse's daughter.

They were now on the motorway, heading out of London. The sky was black and heavy. Looks like rain, thought Shelley, too shocked to actually consider she was a dead woman walking. She stared as the fields went by, imagining she was on a journey to the seaside. Suddenly, Denise spoke up. "Are you sure you have got the right people, only I don't owe any fucker money, and haven't pissed anyone off. Is this some kinda prank?"

The bigger man leaned forward and, in a low gruff voice, replied, "Does this fucking tool look like a joke to you?" He flicked the end of her nose with the gun at which she stared, wide-eyed and frozen.

She realised they hadn't blindfolded her. There would be no return. Her legs began to shake and she made a humming sound. Shelley turned to face Denise and saw the look of terror in her eyes. She had never before witnessed her girlfriend so petrified. Denise had always been in control: she was the one who would shit people up. This wasn't supposed be happening.

The car veered off along a country lane. Nothing for miles but fields and a wooded area. Finally, in the dark, Denise could make out what looked like a scouts' hut. The road was unmade and overgrown. She tried to plan her escape. Her long legs and fit physique could easily out-run the two meatheads. Two cars were parked outside. Her knees were almost knocking together and her teeth bit a hole in her lip. All the lights were off and it was hard to see what was what. The smaller man clenched Shelley's arm and ripped her from the seat. "Try anything stupid and you're a dead girl!" Shelley didn't struggle. There was no point. She watched as Denise stepped out with the gun to her head.

They were marched into the scouts' hut and thrown on the floor. Suddenly the lights came on and standing there were two other men and a woman. Denise glared at each one, hoping for a clue, but she recognised none of them. The woman stared as the others circled. Beano locked the door.

"Get up!" ordered Francesca. "I want to see what you're all about!"

Denise jumped to her feet, tilting her head back in defiance. "And who are you?" She tried to suss out who the formidable woman was. She had never come across a woman who appeared so composed. She could be an actress out of a spy film, standing there in her long black coat, leather gloves, impeccably made up. A woman she would have wanted to aspire to, but far out of her league.

"Me, I am your worst nightmare. You see, I have an issue. It's to do with a thing called a moral compass. In my world, you can act as hard as you like but, if you live by the sword, you die by the sword."

Denise cocked her head to the side. "Look, I think there's been a big misunderstanding. Ya see, I don't know you. I've done you no harm, so what's the crack?"

A voice behind her made her jump. "Oh, but you have hurt her, and me. In fact, you ugly cunt, you have upset me whole fucking family!" Fred was jumping around, working himself up. He had taken one look at the tall woman and imagined Ruby terrified by the size of her. She was easily twenty-five years old, whilst Ruby was a baby at fifteen.

Denise spun around to see Fred, glaring with so much hatred across his face – those eyes and the woman's, so much alike. She glanced back at Francesca's and sighed. Her heart sank and she knew then she was kissing her arse goodbye. She now saw the family resemblance – the schoolgirl, with the same steely-blue, distinctive coloured eyes. Shelley remained on the floor, too shit-scared to move.

"I don't know what you're on about, lady, but I ain't done nothing to you, or your family. I'm afraid you got the wrong person." She tried to stay calm, and firm, and act innocently.

"See, when I say die by the sword, our little girl wasn't in that circle of violence. A fucking fifteen-year-old school kid. Now, if you had been a teenager, and had a one-on-one fight, you wouldn't be here today. You see, I play fair, don't I, Fred?"

"Oh yeah, sis, we were brought up that way." He leaned into Denise's ear and screamed, "Unlike scumbags like you!"

Denise didn't move. She went over in her mind how she was going to escape. Her knife was tucked inside her boot; one quick move and she could slice the leery bloke's throat. As if Francesca read her mind, she shouted, "Frisk the bitch, check her boots!"

Fred jumped back as the men ran their hands all over her body, finally retrieving the blade. Denise was powerless. All she had left was words. She had to talk her way out of it.

"So, tell me, Denise, whatever possessed you to beat a kid half to death?"

There was silence, except the trickling sound as Shelley wet herself. She had seen the table with tools on and watched enough torturous slasher films for this to scare the living shit out of her. To her shock and horror, Denise pointed to Shelley. "I didn't beat the kid, she did. I admit I was there, but I swear to God I didn't lay me hands on her. It was me that pulled her off."

Francesca looked at Fred and smirked. He smiled back and nodded.

"Okay, thank you for that piece of information." Francesca's voice was calm but demonic.

Denise couldn't look at Shelley but relaxed her shoulders. She was out of the woods and hopefully they would let her go. Shelley was feeling faint and sick. She had put the boot in a few times but it was Denise who had smashed the girl's face in.

Francesca walked over to the table and picked up a torque wrench. She walked towards Denise. The sound of guns being cocked unnerved Denise. She scoured the room and realised they were aimed at her.

"Now then, this moral compass I was talking about. Right now, it's pointing at you. I have a problem with bullies and, it's my reckoning, you should too – so here's the thing. When I pass you this wrench, I want you to teach the bully a lesson. Our little girl, see, she didn't have a weapon and, as far as I can tell, your girlfriend, Shelley, hurt her so bad she might as well have been beaten with a tool. So, fair's fair. You take this wrench, and you put an end to it."

Denise stared at the heavy metal object and then back at Francesca.

"Don't think of bashing me. They are shit-hot hit men, so you will be dead in two seconds!"

Denise took the iron tool from her hand and looked at Shelley, who was shaking her head. "Please, Deni, don't, please. I love you, don't do this!"

She gave Shelley that sorrowful look which spoke a thousand words. The wrench came up above her head and, using all her strength, she crushed the tool onto Shelley's skull. Instantly, she was dead. No one could survive that. Francesca calculated the force and imagined Ruby suffering the same impact from Denise. Francesca's chest tightened and, in an instant rage, she snatched a hammer and, as Denise stared down at her girlfriend in total disbelief and regret, swung it, striking Denise at the nape of the neck. Immediately, she fell to her knees and went into convulsions. She raised the hammer again and Fred tried to take it from her. "No, sis!"

Francesca stopped, still clutching the tool. "Listen, Fred, that moral compass, well it goes like this. Women don't beat kids and men don't beat women. So, it's my job to see to it she never bullies another child again. She should never have touched our Ruby."

Fred stepped away and smiled. He wasn't going to argue. He only went along to make sure she was safe. As always, he wanted to be by her side. It was just the way things were. He was the closest to Francesca – so close he knew she was up to something and wouldn't let up until she told him her plan.

The hammer came crashing down and the blood and liquid oozed from the crack across her skull. She, too, was dead.

"All right, boys, let's get this fucking mess cleaned up," said Fred.

The hut was left scrubbed and polished – cleaner than when they arrived.

Halling Lakes was out of bounds: no fishing, no diving, but an ideal dumping ground. It was the old cement works – a huge chalk pit. It had deep edges and it was a long way to the bottom. Any disturbance and the lake's crystal blue colour turned a milky white. The bottom of the lake, originally a resting place for old cranes and equipment used to excavate the chalk, was now a disused site. The bodies were wrapped in a cloth bag, weighed down, and eased gently into the water. It was a while before the area became murky, so they guessed it was a few hundred metres deep.

Fred and Francesca sat in the back of the car whilst Dominic drove them home. She wiped the blood splatters from her coat and a spot on her face. Her brother grinned. "Are you going to tell Sam?"

She lit up a cigarette. "No, I think they are best left out of it. I don't like to load their minds with nonsense. They are overburdened with enough shit."

"Sis, don't it bother you? I mean, you don't even flinch, like it's nothing to you, smashing someone's head or blowing them away."

Francesca rubbed his hand. "Oh, my dear brother, I hope to God you never feel the way I do. There are two ways my emotions work. I either love you or hate you. My family, my friends, even my security, I would do anything for. But piss me off, and it takes a lot, I have this hate, so deep, that removing the shit out of existence is like emptying my dinner plate into the bin. Some bits might flick off and land on me, but I take a wet wipe and clean it away. I have no forgiveness in my heart; they hurt our baby. I couldn't rest until I knew they were dead... wrong, maybe, but that's how I see it!"

Fred nodded. He knew he could never feel like her. He hadn't been through the pain she had – but he would always be by her side.

Chapter Thirteen

Christmas was on its way and the buzz of happy shoppers filled the air. Francesca loved New York shopping at this time of year. There was a real, friendly atmosphere.

Ruby had been staying for two weeks with Francesca and her husband, Sergio Luciani. Her injuries had healed, she was almost a hundred per cent better, but the family still fussed and made sure she wasn't anxious or stressed. Francesca's home was like a castle, with maids and a butler. It wasn't exactly to Sergio's taste – after all he was recognised in the world of casinos as he came from a well-known Italian family – but he loved Francesca so much he gave her whatever she wanted, even if the house was somewhat unconventional.

Ruby was as close to the Lucianis as her own family. Roberto was a powerful man in the States but she treated him as another grandfather. Too big to jump on his knee, she still had a huge hug for him. He was the father to Mauricio and a father figure to Sergio. Sergio was actually his nephew but tragically his parents were murdered and so Roberto had raised him. When Ruby met her aunt for the first time she was three years old. She remembered her Uncle Sergio and his family. They were so kind and loving. Being so young, she suddenly had lots of loving uncles. To her, there was no difference; there was just one big, happy family.

After three hours of retail therapy, Ruby came over faint.

"Sisco, I don't feel too good," she said sheepishly.

Francesca looked at her niece's face and could see that she was tired. They stopped in a burger bar and rested.

"You sit there." She helped her niece to a comfortable-looking chair and carefully unloaded the bags. The waitress took their order.

As soon as Ruby's colour returned to her cheeks and she was relaxed, sipping a massive hot chocolate, with cream and chocolate flakes, Francesca popped the question.

"Ruby, do you want to live here with me and Sergio?"

Ruby nearly choked. "What?"

"I have spoken with your dad and, if you would like a break from England and the whole incident, you can stay with me."

Ruby stared into her drink and watched the flakes melt.

"Sisco, I love coming here, and staying with you and Uncle Sergio, but if you think you need to keep me away from Jesse, then you're wrong."

Francesca raised her eyebrows. That wasn't what she had meant.

"Look, Ruby, your father and I didn't dream for one minute you'd want to go back to that nasty piece of work!" She lifted Ruby's chin. "We just thought about a fresh start. It might help you to get over the whole ordeal."

Ruby grinned and her eyes lit up. Francesca noticed how sweet she looked when she smiled. She wished she did it more often.

"I appreciate how you care for me, but I am fine, and the attack – well, to be honest, I don't remember it. Only waking up in hospital. So it doesn't bother me. As for Jesse, I know where I stand, and that's as far away from her as possible." She stirred her chocolate and looked out of the window to watch the shoppers hurrying along the street.

Ruby wanted to get back to England in time for Christmas, to give Jesse her Christmas present.

"'Ere, Sisco, can I have me watch now? You promised!" Ruby was genuinely smiling now.

Francesca laughed. "Well, do you think you deserve it, madam?"

"Yeah, fucking 'ell, Sisco, don't you, then!"

Francesca tapped her on the nose. "Not if you keep swearing like that."

Ruby rolled her eyes in jest.

The change of scenery, as well as being thoroughly spoilt by everyone, helped to get Ruby back to be fighting fit. Francesca treated her to a very expensive make-over, to cover her tiny, pink scar, and bought every product they used. It gave Ruby confidence and instantly turned her into the cocky teenager she was before.

Dominic picked them up and drove them home. They had to squeeze in between the endless number of shopping bags. Ruby kept looking at her made-up face in the mirror and Francesca sat admiringly. She was pleased she could help Ruby. She knew only too well how it felt to lose your face. Ruby only had a tiny scar but to a teenager it would seem like the end of her life. The beautician had not only hidden the scars but enhanced her steely-blue eyes.

Sergio was there at the door to greet them.

"Hello, my two beauties, and how much money does Uncle Sergio have left in his bank?"

His Italian accent was still as strong as ever.

Ruby laughed. "Not much, mate. I tried my best to clean it out, but still didn't manage it. Better luck next time, eh?" She swanned past him, smiling.

Francesca kissed her husband gently on the lips. He never appeared to age. His tanned, toned body, and thick, black hair, swept back, gave her goose bumps even to this day. He was just as smitten with her.

Ruby stood in front of the grand mirror and gazed at her face again.

As Sergio passed her, he whispered in her ear. "If you crack my mirrors, you can pay for them."

"Sergio!" she shouted as she slapped his arm.

"I tease you, little Belle."

Ruby wanted to cry when she looked at her aunt and uncle. How could she have ever thought her mother was as loving and caring as her family? Unexpectedly, she ran over to her aunt and hugged her, and then Sergio.

Francesca didn't say a word. She knew it was Ruby's way of saying 'I appreciate you'.

Every Christmas, the two families, the Lucianis and the Vincents, made arrangements to go to Francesca's house in Kent. It had been a tradition for ten years. The one day they would be together, come what may. The only person who grumbled was Joe's girlfriend, Belinda, who insisted on having Christmas with her mother, so she was invited too. The house was more than big enough, with plenty of bedrooms to sleep the two families and more. Mary and Bill went along a week before Christmas to make sure the house was warm and everything was in place. Of course, that was just an excuse to get away from London and have a few days of romance themselves. The gardener always turned the heating on and ordered the huge tree, the turkey, goose and pheasants. Mary busied herself cooking the puddings, cakes and trimming, whilst Bill appreciated the country walks and soaking up the clean air. In the evening they sat alone in front of the roaring fire on the thick rugs, enjoying a glass of red wine from the cellar before the mad rush.

Francesca flew back with Ruby, accompanied by Dominic, who was now the official bag carrier. Besides, there wasn't any real need for a security guard in England. It was different in the States, since the Lucianis were a very wealthy family, and so Dominic's job was to look after Francesca.

Sam was at the airport to meet them and, as Ruby walked through the arrivals, he instantly saw the difference in her. She had a huge grin and colour in her cheeks. She ran over to him with her arms outstretched. Sam was choked up. It had been years since she had shown so much affection.

"'Ello, my angel." He gave her a big hug.

Her grip was tight and he then realized, she had her strength back.

"Look at you, you look… well… really pretty… and the scars have gone." He held her away so he could get a better view.

"No, Dad, Sisco bought me proper makeup to hide them." She grinned.

Sam was glad to have his sister over for Christmas and was looking forward to the family being together.

Ruby was so happy to be back in her own home with her dad and brother. Not that she didn't enjoy staying with her aunt; it was always a treat.

Jack had the Christmas lights twinkling on the tree and the fire alight in the living room, just so it would be cozy and, more to the point, homely. He had heard that Sam had suggested Ruby stayed with Francesca but deep inside Jack prayed she'd say no.

As Ruby stepped indoors, she felt relaxed. She loved the smell of leather sofas and the pine from the Christmas tree. The fire made its crackling sounds and she sat heavily on the puffy settee.

"Cor, that flight from the States, it's a bloody long one." She was glowing.

"So, Rubes, feeling better now then?" asked Jack, wearing a big smile.

"Yeah, I do, even me face has healed up."

"So, have you decided to stay, or do you think you might go back with Sisco?" Jack couldn't help himself. He could only settle once he knew what his sister wanted to do. He looked at Francesca, who winked.

"Well, it's like this. I have no one to argue with over there. They are too nice... but here, I've got you when I need a good ruck," she laughed.

When Francesca left, and Sam went to work, Jack sat opposite Ruby and stared for a while.

"What's up, bro?" she asked, peering over her *Hello* magazine.

"You know what happened that day, don't you, Ruby?"

She bit the inside of her lip and nodded.

"Do you want to tell me?" he asked calmly.

"Jack..." She stopped for a second, trying to control her quivering lip. "Jack, I thought I knew Jesse. She seemed nice but it was an act."

A tear rolled down her cheek. He wanted to cuddle her and tell her it was all right but the need to know the truth was greater.

"What happened, Rubes?"

"I'd been seeing our mum for a few weeks. I lied because you and Dad would have gone off your heads, so I kept it a secret."

Jack nodded, listening intently.

As she revealed the whole story, including the episode with Jacob, the tears fell effortlessly, but Jack didn't console her, not until she had told him everything. Then, he sat beside her and held her for ages, until her sobs subsided. He was now an angry man. He had never felt so bitter in his life and wouldn't rest until Jacob and Jesse were seriously fucked up.

As he went to get up from the sofa, Ruby grabbed his arm. "Jack, I don't want you to do anything, that's one reason I didn't tell you." He wasn't listening.

"Jack, listen to me. I want them hurt in the worst way possible. Going in there, throwing punches, means nothing to these people. Trust me, I know them!"

He sat back, intrigued as to what she had in mind.

"I intend to get them for this, but not in the way you think. You have to trust me. I know I'm younger than you, and you all feel you need to protect me, but I have to do this alone or it won't work."

Jack was in a temper. "So you think you're going back there, to a place where you were fucking left for dead, and it won't happen again?" He was shouting now.

"I wished I had never told you now. I thought you would understand, and let me do this my way." Ruby jumped to her feet in a fit of rage. "Why do you, Dad and Fred reckon you have the right to take revenge? It didn't fucking happen to you, or Dad, or any other fucker, for that matter. It happened to me!" Ruby was screaming and poking herself in the chest, "It was fucking me... do you understand? I was the one attacked. It was me who nearly died, not fucking you!"

Jack grabbed his sister and hugged her again. "We know, we know. I just want to protect you though, Rubes." His voice was gentle and soothing. "All my life, I've tried to make up for the times I was too young, too helpless, and too small, to stop her hurting you. I couldn't fight back, Rubes, only hide you, wipe your tears, and cuddle you at night. I can't get that out of my head. It probably ain't normal, but most kids don't go through what we did."

Ruby calmed herself and sat back down on the sofa.

"Jack, if I don't seek retribution, the hate I have will eat me away... I want closure. Please, Jack, I have to do this. If I need your help, I will ask you."

He stared at his sister and realised she had grown up over the last few weeks. Reluctantly, he nodded. "On one condition, though. I have to know when you're planning on doing this, just in case."

She agreed and then headed to bed. The day had been long and tiring.

Before she walked up the stairs, she looked back at Jack. "Tell me I'm not anything like our mother!"

He smiled. "You are nothing like her. You're a Vincent, Ruby, and don't you ever forget it!"

She spent the night twisting and turning, and with thoughts of revenge flowing through her mind, but these were halted by the fear of prison. When the morning arrived, and the aroma of bacon wafted up the stairs, she felt fresh and at peace. She had battled with her demons and won. Her plan was devised and her head clear.

She would not waste time. Out of her suitcase she pulled a teddy bear. It was a big, expensive-looking teddy which sat upright, holding a heart. The heart had a pouch for a note or anything else. The teddy was in fact a nightdress case and the back could be unzipped and nightclothes carefully stored away. Ruby smiled. "Perfect," she whispered to herself.

Jack emerged with a big smile. "Breakfast is served, madam." He bowed, mimicking a butler. "That's a nice teddy."

She nodded. "Cute, ain't he?"

Ruby, although trying to keep an eye on her figure, thoroughly enjoyed her fry up and wiped her plate clean with her bread and butter.

Sam laughed. "Well, they might have the best burgers in the States, but they can't cook a breakfast like your old man, eh?"

She waited for her dad to go out before she talked to Jack. Sam had the banking to sort out, and they were interviewing more staff, so he would be out of the house for some time.

Jack was loading the dishwasher when she walked up behind him.

"Cor blimey, Rubes, you made me fucking jump!"

"Jack…" There was a long pause. "Jack, I need your help."

He nodded. "Go on."

"I need a gun."

Jack's eyes widened. "No way, Ruby, you ain't gonna shoot her. You will get life inside!"

She laughed. "No, I'm not going to kill anyone."

"So why a gun?"

Ruby took a deep breath. "I just need one. Look, please trust me. I promise you, it's not for shooting anyone. I don't even need the bullets."

He looked into Ruby's eyes. He could usually tell when she was lying. He concluded she was being honest.

"Dad has one in his drawer in his room."

"Will he notice it's gone?" Her voice sounded so sweet and innocent.

Jack shook his head. "He has probably forgotten it's there."

They crept into their father's bedroom. It was the grandest in the house, with a bath you needed to step into and a walk-in wardrobe, and as big as a three bedroomed semi.

The drawer in the bedside cabinet housed the gun. As Jack slid it open, they could see there – under magazines, broken watches, and love letters – was the monster. Ruby grabbed it and shut the drawer.

"Rubes, you promise me it's not to shoot anyone?"

She rolled her eyes. "Fuck off, I'm not that angry. Yeah, all right, I hate their guts. But want them dead? No… worse than that!"

"So why the gun?"

"Jack, just trust me."

He nodded.

Ruby wiped the prints off the gun, wrapped it in a new pair of pyjama bottoms, placed it inside the teddy, and sewed up the seam to hide the zip. She held it away from her and admired her piece of work.

No one could guess there was any weapon inside the toy. It was soft and padded enough to fool anyone, especially her mother. In a pouch, hidden at the back of her wardrobe, was a small bag full of marijuana. She rubbed the contents over the teddy.

That was the easy bit. The hardest part was yet to come – seeing Jesse again.

She took a cab over to the estate. That was Jack's idea. "From now on, Rubes, you make sure you get cabs, so you are safe. How long do you think you will be?"

Ruby hugged her brother. "A good few hours, but I will keep my mobile on, and you can call me anytime… Jack, if my phone is off, then I'm in trouble."

He took a deep breath. "Ruby, let me come with you."

She shook her head. "Not this time."

The cab pulled up outside the cash machine and Ruby withdrew five hundred pounds.

She shoved it in her bag and told the cab driver to go to the Kidbrooke estate.

It was a cold, wet day and the estate looked gloomier than ever.

"Here, stop just here!" said Ruby.

"Are you sure, love? This is not a place a nice young lady like you should hang around in."

"Yes, it's fine, thank you."

Ruby admired Jesse's new properly fitted front door, courtesy of the council.

She thought she would be nervous but she wasn't. She felt very strong and in control: she had a plan.

Holding the bear proudly in front of her, she knocked firmly.

Jesse usually shouted 'who's there', but this time she opened the door. Her face said it all: guilt, shock and fear.

There was silence for a few seconds.

"Well 'ello, Mum, ain't you going to let me in?"

Jesse didn't see a young teenager full of eagerness and admiration as she had done before. Now, she was staring into the eyes of a woman.

"Yes, of course I am, my baby… come in, come in."

Ruby walked confidently past Jesse, who nervously glanced outside for fear of a posse.

"Here, Mum, I got you a present, just to say thank you." She handed the teddy to Jesse, who was looking very uncomfortable at this stage.

"What did I do to deserve this, then, babes?" Her face displayed an enduring smile.

"Looking after me, the way you did, until the ambulance arrived. If it wasn't for you, Mum, I could have died."

Jesse tilted her head to the side. "What do you mean, love?" she said rather hesitantly. She was worried that this was a plot, but totally confused as to where Ruby was leading her.

"Well, finding me in that state and then calling the paramedics," Ruby replied.

Jesse was nodding and listening to the story her daughter was spinning. Her fear had gone and she was content that Ruby saw her as some kind of hero.

"I am so lucky to have you in my life, Mum. The doctor reckons, if you hadn't called the ambulance when you did, I would not be here now."

Jesse tried to fathom out why Ruby thought she had called for help when really she went to the chemist and had a smoke with her mate. But she would not argue. Ruby was back and that meant money. She still had the huge drug stash in the bedroom, and a grand left, but that would not last too long.

"So, Mum, when are you off to America for your operation?" asked Ruby as she made her way into the living room.

Jesse's eyes widened. She had forgotten that little lie; she felt totally off guard and vulnerable. There was something very different about Ruby and she couldn't put her finger on it.

"Oh, yeah, well there has been a minor delay. My surgeon is away on holiday, so it will be next week."

Ruby tried to contain herself – the lying bitch. She looked around the filthy room and guessed that the money was spent on drugs.

"Seen much of Jacob, only I was hoping he'd call… I miss him, Mum."

She was acting sad, but inside she was boiling – with every bone in her body she hated them.

Jesse smiled. She must have completely blanked out the whole incident.

"Jacob should pop around later. He owes me money." Jesse bit her lip and watched the smile creep across Ruby's face.

"Do you think he missed me?" It was hard work keeping up the pretence. Jesse nodded.

Ruby detested Jacob. The man she had fallen for was nothing but a heartless user. He didn't even visit her in hospital.

Before long, Jesse was talking the same old shit and Ruby was pretending to be interested.

"'Ere, Mum, fancy a drink? Vodka?"

Jesse's eyes lit up. "Oh, yeah."

Ruby opened her bag and pulled out a fifty. "Mum, they won't serve me. Will you get it?"

Jesse leapt from her seat and, in a flash, snatched the note. "Yeah, we will have a celebration: you, me and Jacob." Her face was screwed up from the stupid expression of excitement. A month ago, Ruby thought it cute. Not now, though. Now, she found her deplorable.

"Mum, I'll wait here. I get tired too quick these days."

Jesse was out the door before Ruby even had a chance to say 'I'll have a Bacardi Breezer'.

It was her chance to have a good nose around. Ruby laughed out loud when she finally came across the stash hidden in her pillow case. Very original, she thought. The rancid stench of the room would put any sniffer dog off the scent. As for original ideas, well, the pillow case was the most ridiculous. The other one contained the money. Jesse was so predictable that the plan would be executed like a dream.

It puzzled Ruby how on earth she got away with keeping a large amount of powder in her bedroom and even a set of scales under her bed. If the police raided her flat now she would be bang to rights. There was enough cocaine to get her five years. The scales increased that to possibly seven with an intent to-supply charge. The addition of a gun would lock her up for a long time.

As she sat on the settee, going over the past few visits with Jesse, the penny finally dropped. Her mother was a prostitute: the man from the café and the other men who were at the door were all punters. Her house was never searched, even though Ruby's attack was the scene of the crime. She concluded that Jesse was shagging the coppers.

Well, she won't get away with it. Not this time, smiled Ruby.

She expected her mother to be a while and was surprised when there was a knock so soon after she had left. She naturally assumed Jesse had forgotten her key or, better still, had come back to ask what she would like from the shop. No, thought Ruby, that was stupid. From now on she would not be disillusioned by her. As far as she was concerned, Jesse was the devil herself.

Ruby got up and opened it, without a concern for who else might be on the other side of the door.

Her eyes widened when she saw Jacob standing there. He was leaning on the doorframe, puffing on a spliff, and holding a bag of beers. He obviously didn't expect to see her ever again, and so he also looked shocked and uncomfortable.

Ruby's plan nearly went out of the window. She had an overwhelming urge to grab a kitchen knife and run it through his chest. She took a deep breath, smiled and invited him inside. Without a word, he entered and made his way to the living room, as he frantically racked his brains to think how he should handle the situation. He had known that Noreen and her mates had given Ruby a kicking. Yet Ruby had kicked his girlfriend so hard in the stomach she had lost the baby.

His heart was beating so fast and never in his life had he felt so much mixed emotion. Noreen had really suffered. The baby was further on than they'd both thought because at the time she didn't show. If no one had told him she was pregnant, he wouldn't have guessed. It wasn't until the doctor said the baby couldn't be saved he realised how much he had been genuinely looking forward to being a father. She had cried every day for two weeks and blamed him for sneaking around with the schoolgirl.

Then he looked at Ruby and could see the faint scar on her face and felt guilt for luring her, by no means deliberately, into his clutches to end up nearly dead.

It was his Aunt Gloria who told him of her serious condition – the life threatening damage caused to her body. She also insisted he stay away from Ruby. Little did he know she would return.

"How are you now, Ruby?" asked Jacob, in a very sober voice. He had never spoken like that before. He had always laughed and joked.

He perched on the settee and she sat in the armchair. "Yeah, I'm good." She smiled.

"Aunt Gloria said you couldn't remember what happened." It was almost a question.

She shook her head. "No, all I know is I was beaten up and left for dead... apparently!"

Jacob's palms were sweaty. "So, you have no idea who attacked you?" He had to know if there were going to be any repercussions.

"Nah. Have you heard anything, Jacob?"

He shook his head. "All a bit of a mystery."

Ruby was fuming. She had tried anxiously to keep a lid on it, aware she had bitten her lip and could sense her nostrils flaring.

"Fancy a coffee?"

He pulled out a beer. "Nah, babes, I'll have this. Want one?" He wanted to sound jolly and upbeat but his heart was still pounding. He had visions of Ruby killing his baby. It was amazing how a small joint of skunk can make your illusions appear so real. Others might call it paranoia.

Jesse was back in ten minutes with three bottles of vodka, cigarettes and plain crisps. She had spent the whole fifty.

She stopped dead in her tracks when she saw Jacob.

"Poor Ruby can't remember a damn thing, eh... can you, babe?" Jesse thought she was being clever, getting in before he said anything that would get them both locked up or worse.

"Yeah, she was just saying," he replied.

"And the doctor says if it weren't for me calling the ambulance when I did, well, she would be dead now."

Jacob raised his eyebrows, aware that it was Jesse's father who had kicked the door in and found Ruby. Why was Ruby saying it was her mother who was the saviour?

He gulped back his beer and put it all down to rumours. Perhaps Jesse did call an ambulance but had to use the phone box and, by the time she got home, the ambulance, along with Ruby's dad, had been and gone. He finished another can of beer and followed that with a large vodka and coke.

He gazed at Ruby. She was so sweet: her tiny dimples, even her little, pink scar looked cute. She could sense him looking her over. That was how it had been in the beginning, but unlike then she felt sickened by his glances.

Chapter Fourteen

As Jesse and Jacob slept soundly, armed police surrounded the flat and after a knock, which was ignored, kicked the door down and rushed in. Jacob, the first to wake up, nearly wet himself when he saw the police standing in front of him, wearing armoured flack-jackets and holding guns. His eyes widened and instantly he put his hands up.

"Fucking 'ell, man. Don't shoot, I ain't done nuffin!"

Being woken up from such a deep sleep had put Jesse in a foul mood.

"What the fuck is all the noise?" she croaked, and was still half asleep when a copper crashed into her room. He grabbed her arm and pulled her to her feet.

"Put your hands behind your back!"

"Get the fuck off me. What the hell's going on?" She tried to struggle but the clink of the cuffs stopped her in her tracks. The officer marched her into the living room. Instantly, she came to her senses and scanned the room. She clocked Jacob, handcuffed, and a policeman carrying out a body search. He grinned as he pulled a clear bag containing white powder from Jacob's pocket.

Jesse laughed out loud. What a result! That's what you get for pinching someone else's gear. She now believed she was in the clear. They couldn't nick her if the drugs were on him.

Jacob turned a deathly grey and his legs buckled. His words were a desperate plea. "I swear, I don't know where it come from!"

He turned to look at Jesse, who smiled. He had the cocaine so she was scot-free.

Amber, the sniffer dog, darted all over the place. She hadn't found the powder on Jacob. She was searching for something else. Jesse then realised there was something more serious going on. The flat was now full of police. At that moment the dog stopped and sat down next to the fluffy toy. The room went quiet as everyone looked at the stuffed bear.

Sergeant Hoskins put a pair of gloves on and picked up the teddy. As he turned it around, he could see the back gaping open and, clearly visible, the gun.

Gently he retrieved it, holding the tip between two fingers, and slid it inside a clear bag.

Jesse shook. It was a nightmare. She tried hard to focus and comprehend the situation but everything seemed to move in slow motion. One minute, she was having a drink with Jacob and… the penny dropped: the teddy, the deep sleep, and her cocaine in Jacob's pocket. Ruby, the conniving bitch, had set them up. Just like her Aunt Francesca, all those years ago, now her own daughter had done the same to her.

"That gun belongs to my daughter, Ruby! That's hers, check it for fingerprints. You'll see, it's not mine, she planted it there." Her voice was desperate.

The police made way for Detective Inspector James, a portly man, with a red face. He liked his drink.

"Well, well, if it ain't Jesse Vincent... Oh, sorry, you're not a Vincent, are you?"

Jesse frowned. She had never seen him before but somehow he knew her. He looked around the room and smelled the air.

He took off his black leather gloves and unbuttoned his long trench coat.

"Are we all done, boys?"

The sergeant nodded. "Yes, sir, we found a bag of powder in the bedroom, a set of scales, narcotics on him, and a gun concealed in a teddy."

DI James smirked.

"Take him away and leave her with me."

The police left the flat. Jacob, who was cuffed and in a bit of a state of undress, with his tracksuit bottoms falling down, was put into the meat wagon.

Jesse sat down, with her hands securely tied behind her back.

DI James pulled the front of his trousers up before he sat down. Heavier these days, he needed to adjust his clothes. His big belly hung over his belt and his collar looked like it was choking him. He hated wearing suits but it was expected now he was a DI.

He smiled at Jesse, enjoying her expression of fear and anger.

"So, it looks as if we've got you bang to rights, eh?"

He pulled out a cigarette and tapped it on the box before he lit it with his new engraved silver lighter.

"Listen, detective, that gun is not mine, I promise you that. I might have the odd toot and puff but, fuck me, do you really think I have a need for a shooter? And where the hell would I get the money for all that gear? Come on, mate, give us a break," said Jesse.

The DI took a deep drag on his fag and slowly let the smoke fall from his mouth. He nodded.

"Yeah..." He looked around the room again. "Mmm, you don't look like a big-time dealer."

Jesse smiled. He was on her side – but her newfound confidence was short-lived.

"See, now you have to believe me. It was Ruby Vincent who planted all this stuff. I didn't even know the gun was here... or the drugs!"

He took another long draw on the cigarette and blew the smoke into her face.

"So, if you saw your daughter, as you say, plant the gear, why didn't you stop her? I mean, what sort of mother lets her child run around with a fucking shooter, and a bag of Class A? Try again, Jesse, but without the bull shit."

He laughed a loud chortle, which made him cough.

Jesse was angry. "I didn't fucking see her plant it. I just know she did. Must have drugged me or something!"

"Now, Jesse, why would your daughter want to do a thing like that?" His voice was full of sarcasm.

She avoided eye contact in humiliation. "'Cos I fucking left her in the flat when she got beat up, and I didn't stay with her... but that still ain't a good enough reason to set me up."

James stood up. "Well, I know what you did, Jesse – a proper cunt stunt, wouldn't you say?"

She looked up and noticed the hatred in the DI's eyes.

"I was the one who put Sam Vincent in prison years ago and I remember it like it was yesterday. You scarpered and let that man serve time for you and his nippers. Ya see, those Vincents have morals like meself, so we understand each other, but you, Jesse Right, have none. In actual fact, you have to be the vilest woman I have had the displeasure of meeting."

Jesse's jaw dropped. She remembered it too.

"I have heard a lot about you over the years and, what sickened me the most was you leaving your own flesh and blood to die here, in this rotten, stinking flat. So, Jesse, if she set you up... well, shit happens. Oh yeah, and mark my words, I will see that you go down for a very long time. Now, Jesse Right, I am arresting you on suspicion of intent to supply Class A drugs and possession of a firearm. You have the right to remain silent..."

She trembled, knowing full well she had no hope. The DI yanked her from the chair and practically dragged her to the car, with no compassion and no respect for the woman.

*

Ruby was back home within a few hours and sitting at the dining table in front of Jack, much to his relief. She spilled the beans, leaving nothing out.

"Oh, Jack, I hope they don't arrest me."

He laughed. "No, they won't do that. The police won't think for one minute that you – a fifteen-year-old girl – would plant drugs and a gun. I wish I could have seen her face when they arrested her."

Ruby, relieved and excited by the whole event, said, "You should have seen her when I knocked her out with those sleeping tablets. She looked gross. That is one ugly bitch. What Dad saw in her, I can't imagine."

"By all accounts, she used to be a right looker," Jack frowned. "So, when you called the Ol' Bill, what did you tell them about the gun?"

She smiled cheekily. "That bit was easy. I said that, when the crowd of girls were kicking me and punching me, all I could see was Jesse watching and, as soon as they ran off, she dragged me inside and forced me to take some tablets. When I refused, she held a gun to my head."

Jack nearly choked. "Fuck me, Rubes, she will get a serious prison sentence for that one!"

"So fucking what, she might as well have done it. Fucking 'ell, Jack, I didn't even know what time of day it was when she shoved those tablets down my throat. I don't know what she or anyone else did to me after that."

He jumped up from the chair. "What do you mean 'or anyone else'?"

Ruby looked up at her brother. "Jack, our so-called mother has no scruples. She sells herself, and she might have even sold me for all I know."

Jack tried to hold back the tears of anger. His stomach churned with the thought of anyone touching his sister when she lay there dying.

"You don't really think that, though, do you?"

Ruby bit the inside of her lip and shrugged her shoulders. "After the sleeping tablets kicked in, I only remember waking up with you and Dad in the room."

He paced the floor in a temper.

"We will have to tell Dad, because you're gonna have to testify in court... this ain't the end of it."

Ruby smiled. "Actually, Jack, it is. Once Jesse gets locked away, along with that rat Jacob, I will be free to have a life!"

Jack sat back down and thought about it all. His sister was absolutely right.

*

Sam was full of mixed emotions. He had come home from work to hear his daughter and son reel off the day's events.

At first he was livid and screamed at them. "You are so damned stupid! What the hell were you doing, letting your sister go over to that fucking estate with my gun... what are you, the fucking Kray twins?"

Ruby defended Jack, as always. "Dad, he didn't know I was going."

Sam poured himself a brandy and knocked it back. He slid off his tie and ran his fingers through his hair.

"Ruby, you have just played a very dangerous game. How the hell are we going to get out of this one? I'm gonna have to say it was me!"

Jack and Ruby looked at each other.

"But, Dad, they won't think for a minute it was me. Besides, the gun has her prints on it."

"And how the fuck did you manage that?" His voice got louder.

"Calm down, Dad!" shouted Jack.

"Calm down, are you fucking serious?"

"Dad, listen, when Jesse was asleep, I wrapped her hands around the handle, and then placed it in the bear. My prints ain't on it. I wore gloves."

There was silence as Sam gulped back another brandy. He looked at his little girl – well, not so little now, is she, he thought to himself. In fact, he was staring at the double of his sister. Ruby was indeed a woman. Maybe he should give her more credit.

He sat down on the sofa and loosened his top button.

"Ruby, where is the teddy?" he asked calmly.

"At Jesse's. I put the gun inside it."

Sam thought for a while and sighed. "If they find the gun in the teddy, they could trace where it came from, and that will lead it back to you."

Ruby smiled. "Dad, I told the police that I was on my way to visit Jesse. When I reached the front door, I suddenly got flashbacks of what happened, so I ran as fast as I could to the cop shop to make a statement, just in case my memory went again."

"Did you mention the teddy?"

Ruby smiled again. "No, I didn't but, if they question it, then I will tell them it was a present for her and, as soon as I had those visions of the attack, I dropped it on the doorstep and ran."

Sam calmed down. His children were stupid to have taken on a set-up like this but, if the worst came to the worst, then they always had Francesca – the top dog lawyer.

The three sat in deep thought when the doorbell rang. Each looked at the other.

Sam got up to answer it.

DI James admired the house, its big oak door and grand drive. He smiled to himself, remembering the day he had arrested Sam Vincent. Sam had had a fairly modest home then, but life since his time in prison had been good, along with his finances.

Sam thought he recognised the man standing before him.

"Hello, Mr. Vincent, I'm Detective Inspector James. Do you mind if I have a word? It's about your daughter, Ruby."

Sam looked him up and down and then he remembered him. He was a good cop. He had tried to help Sam then. He just hoped he was on his side this time.

"Yes, please come in."

James gazed around at the plush hallway and wished he had a home like this one. The sitting room was large. A huge marble fireplace and chunky cream leather sofas dominated the room. Every ornament and piece of furniture looked classy.

Ruby slouched on the chair, a typical teenager, with a copy of *Heat* magazine and nail varnish next to her. Jack, in his tracksuit, sat on the sofa playing with his mobile.

James stopped and stared. "You must be Jack."

Jack looked and smiled.

"Mr Vincent, I don't know if you remember me..." Before he could continue, Sam interrupted him, "Call me Sam. Yes, of course I do, and I wish I had listened to you all those years ago. You were good to me, so I don't forget a friendly face."

Sam poured the pair of them a brandy and invited him to sit down.

Jack thought it best to leave the room, since this didn't concern him.

"We have arrested Jesse, and her sidekick, Jacob, for supply of Class A drugs and possession of a firearm, thanks to your daughter."

Sam nodded.

"Sam... I want you to be aware that she has accused Ruby of planting the gun and the drugs."

"What?" spat Sam.

James looked at Ruby. "You didn't, did you?"

Ruby shook her head.

"Good. Now, I know you did visit with your mother on occasions, so there will be your fingerprints dotted about, but can you assure me they are not on the gun, or the drug packets we found in her flat? I need to be sure before I request forensics." He paused. "Look, what concerns me is that Jesse is demanding that fingerprint tests are done. Why would she be screaming for testing if she had touched the gun?" His voice was calm and genuine.

Sam guessed James was on his side.

Ruby gave her most innocent expression. "I don't know why but she held a gun to my face and made me swallow those pills."

DI James laughed. "Well, then, she must have been so out of her head on drugs she forgot that little matter. Never mind, if you're sure her prints are on that weapon then we have her."

Sam stared at his daughter.

"They must be," she smiled.

DI James finished his drink and thanked Sam. "It was nice to meet you again."

Sam nodded and watched as DI James walked up the path.

James sat in his car, smoking a cigarette and looking at the wonderful surroundings. It was perfect for a young family to grow up in. He knew Ruby had planted the gun, maybe not the drugs, but she was too calm and her statement had already been written in her head. He smiled to himself. Who would have thought it? A fifteen-year-old schoolgirl gets revenge on her mother by sending her back to prison.

The DI had been haunted by the thought of a kid being left for dead in that vile flat and kept asleep by tablets. He imagined his own daughter, Lindsey, lying there helpless. She had been only fifteen when she'd died. They had found her body, half decomposed, in a derelict flat. She had choked on her own vomit and lay undiscovered for weeks. A tear fell unexpectedly onto his fat cheek. He had never cried for her; he was too consumed by hate. He lit another cigarette with the one he was just about to put out. He coped by burying himself in his job and climbing the ladder fast. They never found who gave his daughter the drugs, or who was with her the night she passed away.

Jesse would go to prison, of that he was sure.

Ruby had no remorse for what she did to Jesse. The hurt went deeper than anyone could have imagined. For years she had believed her mother – deep down – was a good person.

Now she could rest, knowing her family hadn't lied to her. Jack had told the truth all along. She really was a spiteful, selfish druggie.

*

The court case was over in a day. Jesse had gone before the magistrates, who had then sent the case straight to the Crown Court.

Francesca was Ruby's lawyer and therefore nothing would go wrong. The Vincent family and friends filled the gallery. Jack sat eagerly in the front row. It would be the first time in twelve years he had laid eyes on his mother. But he also wanted Ruby to know he was there rooting for her.

Mary, Sam's mother, gripped Sam's hand. "It's gonna be all right, son, she will get what she deserves."

Fred and Dan sat together. They still couldn't get over the whole thing and whenever Fred thought about it, he grinned. "She's just like our Francesca, a lot of balls, that girl."

Dan grinned. "Well, she's a Vincent, I expect no less."

The men were dressed impeccably in dark suits and crisp white shirts. The court was ordered to rise and the judge sworn in. After the formalities the clerk brought Jesse up from the cells. There was silence in the courtroom as everyone stared intently.

She looked pathetic. She wore a flowery, summer dress in black with tiny, red roses on it. It was two sizes too big, but it was better than the prison clothes. Most of the inmates had friends and family to send them a suit and shoes but Jesse had no one, well, not now. Her hair was greasy but she had made the effort and tied it back.

Ruby couldn't look at her mother. She knew it would put her off. Instead she pretended she was in a school play.

The short period on remand had taken its toll on Jesse. Her frail frame and gaunt features didn't detract from the look of spite on her face.

Francesca looked directly into Jesse's dark eyes and smiled. It was the same smile she had given her the last time she had sent her to prison.

Jesse shivered. She tried to stare at Ruby, who looked the other way. Then she turned to see who was seated in the gallery. Did she have any friends at all?

Her eyes widened when she saw so many steel-blue eyes staring at her. She saw the very handsome young man and knew he was her son. He was crying and tears were rolling down his cheeks. Her heart pounded and for the first time she felt sad – a real deep heartache. She looked back at Ruby and realised that Jack wasn't crying for her but for his sister, as he had always done, even as a little boy.

She had loved him, not as much as she should have, but she did love him. Ruby was the child who had ruined her looks and when she was born Jesse had felt her own life was never the same. But, if she had just had Jack then her future would have been different. They would have bonded better and she might not have taken drugs. She gazed at her son and saw his grandfather place an arm around his shoulder as Jack leaned into him. Her loathing for the Vincents turned her fragile expression to one of angry spite. The jury didn't miss a trick. They clocked the vicious glares from Jesse to Ruby and Jesse's glances at the emotional boy in the gallery. They had it sussed. The girl, the boy, the barrister, and all the smart onlookers, were family. The accused: a druggie. There was a story there, already, before the case was even in motion.

"Ahh! Look at her, don't she look just lovely?" purred Mary, as Ruby was led into the witness box.

Ruby was even taking on some of Francesca's expressions and in the last six months Ruby had laughed and smiled more than ever, which made her look more like her aunt.

"'Ere, Sam, there's no way our Rubes can get done for anything?" questioned Joe, under his breath.

"No, apparently, they have to present all the evidence before the trial, and our Dolly said it's an open and shut case," whispered Sam, who was sitting on the edge of his seat, resting his tense arms on his knees.

Bill, Jack's grandfather, the head of the Vincent family, hugged Jack. They had always been close; me and my shadow, Bill used to say.

"She's just like your Aunt Dolly. Look at her. She's so confident." He always referred to her as Dolly. She was his baby, the apple of his eye. He loved his sons and grandchildren, but he doted over Francesca. The years she'd had to live away from him, for her own protection, grieved him. Nothing would get back that precious time.

Francesca had coached Ruby on how to behave and what to say and she, too, was proud of her niece for listening and doing as she was told.

The defence lawyer was a scrawny-looking man. His hair was thinning, brushed to the side and, as he leaned on the bench, you could see his suit was too small. The trousers were swinging around his ankles and the seam in the backside was stretched. His jacket was shiny, from ironing, and his white shirt had that grey tint to it. Francesca imagined him coming home from work and taking his clothes off, before putting them in the washing machine, all together, ready for Monday morning. She looked down at his feet. The laces were odd – one black, one brown. Surely a man with his sort of money would buy a decent suit and a new pair of shoes? Her notion was: a slovenly appearance – a careless defence.

DI James was also there, watching the proceedings, but as a witness for the prosecution. He glanced up at the gallery, amazed by how many Vincents there were, and then he smiled. Jesse would probably be safer behind bars than facing that mob. He had heard the stories about the Vincents but had never seen them all together. They were a handsome-looking family, but there was something about their cool exterior. They were more dangerous than a gun-wielding maniac on speed. He had met them individually, when the clubs had needed a new licence, but he hadn't met Francesca, the sister. He was surprised by how sophisticated she was. He could tell they were related but there was more to her. She was the black widow spider. The stories of how the mad Irishman and his sons were murdered may have been just rumours, and over the years exaggerated, but if they were true then he knew she was the one behind it.

Francesca asked Ruby to give her account of the whole event, from the minute she got up that morning to the second she regained consciousness in the hospital.

Ruby's acting was as good as any Oscar-winning performance. Anyone listening would have needed a serious box of tissues. Even the grown men in the gallery were welling up, and they already knew the facts.

Jesse just kept rolling her eyes and shaking her head. She hated her daughter more than ever.

Jack, as tough as he was, still let the tears roll. Watching his wretch of a mother and her nasty expression brought back painful memories of how they were really treated. He pictured her slapping Ruby time and time again. He remembered her pushing Ruby outside in the snow, with no shoes on, because she had wet the bed. He also recalled Ruby begging her mother through the letterbox to let her in. He took a nasty clump that day for sneaking her inside.

When Ruby was cross-examined she answered the questions just as Francesca had said. And when she felt uncomfortable, she replied 'I don't remember', and that was sufficient, since her head trauma would have cáused some areas of her memory to go blank, which was backed up by the doctor's report.

When Jesse was in the witness stand she had no medical report and couldn't claim any memory loss.

Having listened to Ruby's account, Jesse was fuming and, with no prior coaching, she continually messed up.

Mr Hall, the barrister for Fen, the scruffy solicitor, was just as careless as he was. After all, this was a legal aid client with no hope. He had taken an instant dislike to Jesse the minute he'd met her.

Jacob was the last to take the stand and as he appeared in the dock the Vincents glared at him. When he looked up at the gallery his insides felt as if they would fall out. The Vincents were menacing. He'd had no clue that little Ruby came from such a dangerous family. That was, until he got a visit.

He was on remand in Brixton Prison when an older man, big guy, bald head, slurred speech, assumed to be a boxer, approached him.

He was Tom Malice by name and also by nature: a nasty piece of work. He had worked with the Vincents on the doors at the *Palaces*, but one night he'd left work early because he was feeling sick. Joe, being the softy he was, had let him go. Tom, a loyal doorman for the Vincents, headed home to find his missus in bed with an old friend. He killed the pair of them with his bare hands. No one messed with him. He was a nutter before the incident but he had loved his wife and so the whole affair had sent him screwy. Joe and Sam had promised to look out for his kids, who were two boys in their late teens. Sam got them working down the gym and helping out around the clubs, giving them money and their father peace of mind.

Tom marched Jacob into his cell and told him, matter-of-factly, that, come what may, he was to say that the drugs found on him were his and he had never met Ruby, never seen her and didn't even know what she looked like.

Jacob was shitting himself. He was playing a big boys' game now. Not the same as acting the big man on the estate with all the sixteen-year-olds looking up to him.

Tom grabbed Jacob's shoulder and squeezed it hard, forcing him to sit on the bed.

"If you don't, you will die, and not a nice death either. They will cut off your scrawny little limbs, one at a time, watch you bleed, and then set you on fire. How about that?" His laugh was deep and haunting.

Jacob didn't hesitate. He agreed there and then.

And, true to his word, he denied all Jesse had said about Ruby.

A question which concerned the jury was why Jesse would hold a gun to Ruby's head and make her take sleeping tablets. But Francesca covered every doubt that would form in their minds. She made the jury aware that

Ruby had pawned all her expensive belongings, and made cash withdrawals, to cover the cost of her mother's fake operation. Bank statements were produced to prove the withdrawals. They also showed there was a lot more money in the account. Pawn tickets, and the photographs of Ruby's brutalized face, were handed around. She knew exactly how to win their hearts and guarantee a guilty plea. She left no stone unturned.

"So, members of the jury, I put it to you: Jesse holding a gun to Ruby's head to make her take the sleeping tablets was to give her time to use the cash machines and withdraw the rest of the money. And, being a naive teenager, Ruby assumed she had lost the card. What Jesse didn't realise, though, was that the four-digit number, written in her purse, was her locker combination and not her card number. Jesse was only after Ruby's money. We know this from the lie she told her daughter. Since she is a well-known drug abuser, the need for money was paramount."

Bill and Mary had never seen their daughter in action. They sat in awe and pride.

It was looking good. Jack stopped crying and sat, gripped, on the edge of his seat. Ruby was nervous now; she bit her nails while staring at the floor. Fen, the barrister, was itching to get the case wrapped up and head home. He had argued with his boyfriend that very morning and was afraid he might go back to an empty house, so his eye was not on the ball.

Jesse's argument was that Ruby had planted the drugs and the gun herself but the fact that Jacob denied seeing Ruby established Jesse as a liar.

Jesse was fraught with worry and anger. The case was not going in her favour and that was obvious to any sane man.

She tried to get her daughter's attention, by glaring hard at her head, but Ruby refused to look her way.

Jack stared at Jacob, hating every bone in his body. He was also annoyed with his sister for even liking a dodgy character like him. But he acted rationally, and kept his hands firmly gripping his seat, just in case one broke free and ran a finger diagonally along his neck – indicating to Jacob that he was a dead man. The jury was, after all, keeping one eye on the proceedings and the other on the gallery. The Vincents had all been warned, especially Fred. Francesca had held a family meeting telling all the inside stuff, including how to present yourself and why. Jurors can be swayed by the family's reactions in the court room, so they were to act like upstanding members of society.

*

The jury was out for an hour and then gave their verdict. Guilty!

Jesse was raging and, as she was carried down the stairs and back into the cells, she shouted, "I wish you had died, Ruby. You ain't my daughter, anyway. You're too ugly to be mine!"

All eyes were now on Ruby, who sat looking at the floor. As she raised her head to face the gallery, she smiled. It wasn't a pretty, girly smile, but a satisfied smirk that said it all... I got her back!

Chapter Fifteen

Four years later

The *Palaces* were a huge success and Dan decided it was time to invest in another club.

The old warehouse was still up for sale, just off the Old Kent Road, far enough away from the estates to pass off as a venue. He had already made enquiries with his mate at the planning office and practically started the wheels in motion. He called a meeting with the family.

Fred was the first to arrive at the building, followed by Dan.

"Cor blimey, this will be a job and a half!" said Fred as he gazed around at the dull, bleak exterior.

"It's perfect. Have a butcher's inside. It's huge," replied Dan, who could see the potential.

The other brothers arrived with their sister.

"Think of it this way. We already provide the nightclubs. I was thinking something along the lines of the Circus Tavern. Ya know what I mean. Shows and stuff."

Sam looked around. "I dunno, mate, Circus Tavern has had its day."

"Dan, why don't we open another *Palace*, just for weekends, with a comedy show and high class performances?" suggested Fred.

Francesca walked around the huge square space and then laughed. "This will be fabulous, trendy, very American... well, it could be."

The brothers nodded enthusiastically.

Joe, not knowing what to say because he could never visualise the finished project, piped up with, "What ya gonna call it?"

It wasn't a silly question. Dan paused and smiled at them all.

"It's going to be called *Ruby's Palace!*"

Sam's eyes lit up. "Dan, you know our Ruby, she's gonna love that, a club named after her."

Dan shook his head. "No, Sam, not only named after her. We can build this into a big moneymaking joint, fresh and fun, and run by Jack and Ruby. So, bruv, our Rubes will have her own *Palace*."

"Fucking 'ell, Dan, are you sure you want to do this for my kids? This is generous."

"Look, the *Palaces* are a family-run concern. We have always split the profits equally. Let's face it, we have more than enough money to keep us happy. It will go to the kids anyway."

"Do you think they are ready, though?" questioned Sam, who, nevertheless, was chuffed by the whole idea.

Dan shrugged his shoulders. "Were we ready when we first bought the *Purple Club?*"

Fred laughed. "Cor, those were the days, eh? All those women, you would have thought it was a game to us. But we made enough money, even through the odd screw up."

Francesca wasn't part of the club scene back when the first one was opened, so she couldn't reminisce. But she could see why their businesses were so successful.

"All the time the kids will have the family behind them, like you guys had each other, so it doesn't matter if they struggle. We will help them."

The boys looked at their sister with pride. They still felt gutted when they thought of her making her own way in life, alone, when they all had each other.

"Jack is a hard worker, and such a sensible lad, and our Ruby, well, she has taken to working *Dan's Palace* like a duck to water and, give her credit where credit's due, she listens now, no more cocky lip," said Dan.

Ruby's attitude had been noticed by the whole family. Her overnight change, since Jesse had been put away, was a good one. She stopped the cheek and snarls and now she was helpful and polite.

School wasn't really her thing so she didn't stay on. Instead, she learned the ropes in the *Palaces*, much to the relief of her family. Sam put it down to the glamour. Ruby was in her element, dressing up, looking glamorous, and being part of the team.

*

The O'Connells stayed clear of the clubs and dealt their cocaine in the surrounding pubs. They still held a grudge and planned to get their feet back in the door one way or another. They bided their time for an opportune moment.

Johnnie O'Connell returned from work, nursing a deep gash which ran from his shoulder to his wrist. A nasty, jagged sheet of metal had slipped from his open back truck and ran down his arms. He screamed in fear, rather than pain, as he saw the shirt rip away along with his flesh.

Luckily, Merlin was with Johnnie and got him in the truck and down to A&E to get a tetanus shot and sixty-five stitches. The wound was sore so he took himself off home to rest with two cans of Stella for company. As he lay there sipping his beer, the new mobile he'd acquired vibrated in his back pocket, accompanied by a silly birdie tune which he didn't know how to remove.

He struggled to retrieve the phone. Luckily, the ring tone lasted long enough for him to get to his feet and answer it.

"Hello, Uncle Johnnie."

"Well, hello, my babe, and how are you?" he said, pleased to hear his niece's voice.

"I've got some bad news. Violet passed away this morning..." She paused. "Are ya still there?"

"Yeah, I just didn't think she would go so soon. Are you all right though, Kizzy?"

"I will be. She needed to go though, Johnnie. She couldn't take the pain anymore."

"Kizzy, you've been a good girl, looking after her the way you have."

"Well, she looked after me for four years, I owed her that much."

"Yeah, but we all know that you did a fair, good job. So what will you do now, my babe?"

"I've got me own van and me horses, forty-one in all, so I guess I'll keep the money rolling in. It's what she would have wanted." Her voice was soft now. She had grown into a gentle and good-looking woman with her long, black hair down her back and a natural, warming smile.

The men down in Kent, gypsy men, all liked her. She was a perfect catch with her own caravan, a field full of shires and cobs, and also not short of a few bob. But Kizzy was bitten so badly at only sixteen by Ocean that she never wanted to experience hurt like it again. She had loved him with all her heart. When she had to live with her aunt she thought her world had collapsed. It was Violet who helped rebuild her self-esteem. She taught her to ride horses and break them in. She appreciated that Kizzy was wild and recognised her ability to be brave. So, she made her ride bareback on a horse to teach her to understand the beasts as an extension of her own body. She laughed with delight and it was her understanding of horses which gave her the knowledge she needed to be successful. She bred them, trained them, and sold them for a good profit. Violet also was a little fierce in her day, but losing her husband calmed her down. She was a good role model for her niece, upholding the gypsy ways, yet she groomed Kizzy to be independent.

The death of Violet would bring the gypsies together. It was tradition.

News of her passing went around the camp within minutes. The women were in and out of each other's caravans, spreading the gossip and adding their own take on things. The men gathered at Johnnie's and gave their condolences.

Billy and Farley pretended to be gutted but really they hadn't seen their aunt in ages because she was so angry over their treatment of Kizzy. So they stayed away. But, to remain in with the rest of the family, they kept up the pretence of caring.

The funeral was to be held in Kent. Years before, when Violet's grandfather had died, they cremated him in his own caravan, along with his possessions. Nowadays, councils refused to allow that so they had to go to a church or crematorium and be buried with the odd personal trinket. The other traditions still followed: keeping the body at home until the wake and covering all mirrors in the van. Although it was more for superstitious reasons, Kizzy took comfort in following some of the gypsy ways.

Violet kept a pot with three grand which she had saved for her funeral. She had already planned it and informed Kizzy of her wishes. She wanted four white horses to pull the carriage but Kizzy went one step further. She used her own white shires. These were dressed grander than any funeral director could have managed. They each had feathered plumes, flowing from their heads, and she covered the tackle with the horse brasses which Violet had collected over the years. Every detail was a symbol of her aunt's life, and the gypsies watched as Kizzy groomed and polished her animals in preparation. Word went around that, in returning her good name, Kizzy had done her aunt proud. Long gone was the shame of a fifteen-year-old wild child sent to live with the queen of the gypsies. Now she was the queen herself, she held her head high and moved with grace and composure.

The travellers arrived in their hundreds from far and wide. Kizzy led the procession, walking ahead of the horses so they would behave. She wanted the crowds to know they were hers. It was good for business and her aunt would have liked that.

Kizzy looked smart in her black, satin suit and with her hair pulled away from her face and just her Creole loop earrings visible. She wore a shimmer of lipstick and a thin coat of mascara. She knew, come the burial, her tears would flow and she'd look a dreadful sight.

She could hear her aunt's words, 'Hold ya head up, gal, be proud.'

Kizzy was honoured. She led the mourners of the queen herself and everyone looked on with respect. The memory of that day she had left London – the spiteful and even hateful look in those women's eyes – still haunted her. But now she saw them there in the crowds, looking on in admiration.

Ocean arrived with his mother and two sisters. She insisted he paid his last respects. She feared her son was losing his roots. He had less time these days for the gypsy ways. He was getting into more trouble with the O'Connells, especially Levi 'no nose' O'Connell. She guessed they were peddling drugs, but he was the only man in the van and she needed him there.

Moira heard of Kizzy's success and hoped that Ocean would get back with her, just as he had been in the past. But he was a player. He was forever shagging one bird or another. 'It's those Irish eyes of yours, which get you into trouble and out of it,' she would say, and she was right.

Ocean was on his mobile phone when the horses approached him. The crowd lined the street and were all watching Kizzy. He suddenly put the phone away as he gawped in amazement. No way could that be his Kizzy. 'His Kizzy', he called her now.

She sensed his gaze and turned her head to steal a glimpse. All the eyes which stared didn't bother her, except those of Ocean. Her heart was pounding as she fought back the tears. Her one and only love was there in the crowd. She thought she had gotten over him. After taking a deep breath, she concentrated on the road ahead.

Meanwhile, Ocean was still mesmerised by her every move. She had grown up differently, from a sexy, wild teenager, to a serene, sophisticated woman. He remembered how easy it was to get her in the sack and he would put on the charm and do it again. He watched her arse sway gracefully from side to side as she led her horses to the church. But he wasn't the only one looking on in surprise. Billy, Levi and Farley stood ogling with no shame. Farley wished she wasn't a cousin; he wanted her for himself.

Kizzy stopped the horses by the church as the pall bearers, including Farley, Levi and her Uncle Johnnie, carried the coffin inside.

Each man nodded at Kizzy as a mark of respect. She didn't smile back. Her face remained still and cold. Johnnie winked and smiled at Kizzy, who responded by kissing him on the cheek. She remembered who was good to her and who wasn't.

The wake took place in a huge converted barn owned by a wealthy land owner, a traveller himself. The ceremony was short but the speeches were long. Kizzy didn't give a speech, as she had said her goodbyes and played her part.

She walked her horses back to the fields, unbridled, fed them treats and headed to the wake. The air was cool, not cold, but it was still a perfect summer evening. She could hear the noise from the road. People had gathered, drinking and talking. The country lane leading to the barn smelled sweet from the honeysuckle along the side of the road. It was the smell which started Kizzy crying. Her tears fell without warning and she wept for ages. Honeysuckle was Violet's favourite flower and she often sent Kizzy to pick fresh blooms for the caravan.

Violet was the nearest to a mother she had ever known and, although she hadn't always grown up with her, the last few years had been good. They shared a lot in common – acceptance was one thing, and trust was another. It didn't matter what she had done; as far as Violet was concerned the past was the past. She was family and, besides it all, the kid had practically dragged herself up, although she was aware that Johnnie had tried his best.

The sound of the wake was getting louder as the travellers were getting more inebriated. Kizzy thought it best to head back to the caravan and stay away from the crowd. She was fragile. She had been trying to hold it together for so long just so she could perfect all the arrangements. But it was hard and now, as the tears fell, she sensed a heavy weight lift from her shoulders.

There was the sound of footsteps behind her and her name being whispered. She knew the accent – the tone of his voice – and her stomach churned. She wiped her eyes and stopped in her tracks.

"Kizzy, gal!" called Ocean.

She tried desperately to be calm and controlled as she turned to face the one man who had held her heart all those years ago. He could make her knees go to jelly, her emotions swell and crash, like the ocean waves on a winter's day.

"Hello, Ocean!" She remained still and expressionless.

He stopped dead and gave her the half smile she used to love. She still didn't move. Her stare was cold but inside her heart was bursting. She could see the child and the man and yet, despite everything she had told herself over the last four years, she knew now she still loved him.

Ocean was in awe of her. She had grown into a woman. His memory of her was a pretty teenager with a cocky attitude, showing off and acting the slag. She used to hop around, flick her hair and chew gum. Not now, though. Now, she looked tame, just like her horses. She had been broken in. She wasn't wild anymore.

"You look odjus!" said Ocean, using a gypsy term for beautiful.

Kizzy tilted her head in shame and embarrassment. She shouldn't receive compliments on the day of her aunt's funeral and he shouldn't be giving them. But she liked them. There were many other men in Kent who called her beautiful, but it meant nothing until now.

Ocean's confidence faltered. She seemed too cool and maybe too good for him. He had heard the rumours of how Kizzy could take a wild grey and ride like the wind and how she would fearlessly break the horse in.

He couldn't imagine Kizzy being anything other than the scatty teenager who didn't know one end of a horse from the other.

"So those greys, they are yours then?"

Kizzy smiled with pride. "Yeah, they are mine."

Even her voice was different. He could still recognise the faint travellers' accent but she spoke more slowly and sharply.

"You did Violet proud then."

Kizzy nodded. "She wanted white horses. It was the least I could do."

There was a silence for what seemed ages.

"I miss you, Kizzy. You were my gal and always will be."

Kizzy was on the verge of bursting into tears. If only he had told her that all those years ago. If only he had freed her from the pain of believing she was so ugly and unworthy. That day she left London was the day she had left her spirit behind. What people thought was a grown woman was really a teenager who had burst all her bubbles. She wasn't sophisticated or graceful, she was empty and sad. There was no mystery as to why she was at one with the horses. It was the mere fact that she had lost her faith in people.

Ocean stepped closer to her. He wanted to feel her, hold her and kiss her face. Her eyes widened as he held both her arms. She stiffened.

"You are my Kizzy, always have been, always will be." She looked into his eyes – those eyes she dreamt of, cried over and missed. Her body relaxed as he gently touched her face and slowly kissed her lips. No man had come close in four years.

To the surprise of Ocean, who had never experienced rejection, she pulled away and walked back to her aunt's caravan.

His heart sank as he watched her because with that kiss he fell in love. She really was his and he would make it happen. It was only right and proper. He had taken her virginity and now she would be his wife.

He returned to the wake and joined the others for a beer.

Levi, Farley and Billy huddled together, up to scheming again, and any bit of action Ocean wanted in on. The drug scene was making good money – perhaps not as much as it could, if they had access to the clubs, but the Vincents ran a tight joint and there was no way in.

"It's like fucking popcorn. The *Palaces* are popping up all over the place," said Billy, through his wheezy voice. He was fatter than ever, red-faced and ready to have a heart attack at any moment.

"Yeah, I heard *Ruby's Palace* is doing well, now a younger crowd gets in there," said Farley.

"I would love to get in there. All those fucking hot shot kids, making a lotta lolly in the city. Love the ole Charlie," replied Levi.

Having just heard the end of the conversation, Ocean only heard them mention *Ruby's Palace*. "Yeah, a young girl runs that one. My age, ain't she?" said Ocean.

The boys laughed.

"Trust you, Ocean. Fuck me, he can't keep it in his pants for five minutes. I suppose you've had her too, ain't ya," said Levi, who was nodding like an old pervert, wanting to know more.

"Nah, mush, I don't wanna get me face poggered by the Vincents. It's their fucking daughter or niece, or whatever. Imagine that, their princess of the palace, being shagged by an Irish tinker."

They all laughed for a while. Then there was silence. "You may have just answered our little dilemma," giggled Billy.

Ocean looked at the men, who were smiling with contentment.

"No way can I shag her! Fucking hell, I don't even know what she looks like!"

Billy laughed. "A few pints, boy, and you won't even care."

"Bollocks, if those Vincents got hold of me, I would be lucky to survive. I've heard they torture you first."

"Gawd, mush, you have watched too many *Godfather* films," replied Bill.

So the plan was set up. They would take the gypsy out of Ocean and turn him into a gorger.

"The dealer boots have to go," said Levi, as he knocked back another Stella.

"All the gold as well, especially the earring," pointed Farley.

"You're gonna have to get your locks chopped and styled, like those London toffs," laughed Billy.

Ocean jolted in shock. "Fuck off, I ain't cutting me hair off, that's what all the malts love."

"All right, keep your hair on," said Billy, who thought the comment was hilarious and ended up nearly having an asthma attack. The travellers, who were standing next to the O'Connells, glared in disgust. It was, after all, a wake, not a wedding.

Ocean nodded and almost agreed to the idea but all the while his thoughts kept drifting back to Kizzy.

The night was drawing in and Kizzy changed her clothes. She put a loose, black dress on and a lowered, heeled shoe. It was only right she said hello to some of her relatives. Just before she left the caravan, she uncovered the mirrors and placed the small vase of honeysuckle on the table.

The air was still cool and the walk to the barn was peaceful. She didn't know what to make of the whole Ocean incident. Did she still love him? Or was it a ghost sensation from the past? She never wanted to experience hurt like that again.

As she entered the barn, heads turned and she received smiles instead of snubs. Johnnie was the first to go over to her.

"'Ello, my gal." He kissed her on the cheek and led her over to the makeshift bar area. "Me gal will have a brandy."

There was a buzzing sound as conversations switched to her arrival.

Two wealthy landowners, Ethan Brown and Thomas Barnes, came over to meet Kizzy, acknowledging her achievements in her horse sales. All the while, Ocean had his eye on her. She was up in the ranks. Not even the O'Connells did business with them. They were out of their league, yet little Kizzy was there like lady of the fucking manor. Ocean wanted her on his arm to proudly show her off.

Ethan Brown kept over six hundred horses and land all over the Home Counties. Thomas Barnes owned farmland in Ireland and also some in Kent.

They bought from Kizzy and had been more than pleased with their goods. Thomas complimented her on how obedient the mares were. She had done well and he wanted to work with her on a full-time basis. His understanding of the animals wasn't as good as hers, but his knowledge of business was. But Kizzy wasn't ready for that. She was happy to buy and sell at her own pace.

Ocean watched as Brown and Barnes shook hands with her and left. She got respect from men who wouldn't even give him the time of day. He continued to stare as the mourners paid their respects. How she gracefully brushed cheeks, even how she sipped her brandy, was a cut above every other woman in the room.

Kizzy turned away from the bar and peered around, content she had given her aunt a good send off. Violet had given her the money for the burial but Kizzy used her own savings to hire the lavish barn, which looked a picture. There were rows of tables filled with food: a hog roast, crusty rolls and crates of their favourite shellfish. She also put cash behind the bar for drinks. Johnnie made sure everyone knew that this big feast was compliments of Kizzy. It put her up on a pedestal where she belonged. She caught Ocean gazing at her and she smiled kindly.

His heart leapt to his mouth. She had looked his way. She wasn't looking for anyone else. Ocean was eager to get more of her. She was hypnotic to him and he was hooked on her like the cocaine he often snorted. When it was gone the cold emptiness took over his body and when he had it the hit was great and the euphoria overwhelming.

He went to get a drink from the bar, heading in her direction.

"Kiz, wanna top up, baby gal?" he said, offering to take her glass, but she shook her head.

"No, I'm not a real drinker. Just the one, to drink to her passing, is all."

Ocean nodded, surprised at her cool demeanor.

"Err… I am sorry, Kizzy, truly sorry." He lowered his gaze in shame.

She knew what he was apologising for. "No need, Ocean, I was young and foolish and the move to Kent did me a huge favour." She was confident and absorbed the attention she was getting from him. It was new, unlike when she was fifteen and he had treated her as a shagging toy.

"Yeah, but I felt bad after all that… Kiz, I missed ya, ask me muvver." His voice almost begged to be believed.

"Well, we both survived, didn't we?" Her tone was sarcastic and he sensed it. He learned that day his charm and bullshit didn't wash with her. She could see right through him. He needed to be honest and caring. Fuck: that was going to be difficult, he thought.

Kizzy walked on to say hello to friends of Violet as she left Ocean standing awkwardly alone.

Billy and Farley were watching him, laughing. They called him back to take the piss.

"Blanked you, did she?" laughed Billy.

"Nah, she wants more of me, mate, you watch," said Ocean.

"Forget Kiz, just concentrate on how you are gonna get your hands on that Ruby," said Levi.

Ocean rolled his eyes. "Levi, you are joking about this Ruby malt, ain't ya?"

Levi smiled, showing two missing front teeth. He looked ugly now. With his nose flat and a gaping hole, he gave the impression of a car crash victim and he told many wild stories to that effect.

Farley had the more serious look on his face. "Listen, boy, we need to get in that club. For fuck's sake, it's on our own doorstep, and those fuckers are rubbing our noses in it… no offence."

Levi nearly choked. "Are you ever gonna let up about me fucking hooter, or what?"

"Sorry, bruv," replied Farley, who was more interested in getting the plan right and convincing Ocean to go along with it.

"Osh, we all know you can have any old malt. I would do it meself but you are younger, and the birds do love ya."

He smiled, sucking up the compliments, and eventually agreed.

"So what do you want me to do?" he asked, as he turned his head away from Kizzy.

After four rounds of Stella, followed by a few brandies, the boys pretty much had the plan in place.

Kizzy had gone around to most of the mourners and thanked them for coming. Some of the conversation pertained to her business and so she increased her list of customers and potential sales. She didn't feel ashamed of networking at the wake, as she knew her aunt would have done the same. 'Business is business, never look away from an opportunity,' she would say.

Parading her white horses had worked as planned, and a few of the wealthier travellers had offered her a lot of money to buy them and check out the others in the field.

The sadness had lifted a little and Kizzy had found her spirit again. The mourners had given her a great deal of respect, and she held her head up high, and Ocean – well, he didn't know which way to turn. He was still the handsome man and she loved how he had touched her cheek and kissed her lips. It wasn't like before, when he rudely fumbled to get his oats. But she was wary, as one slip of her guard and she would be in his clutches and sobbing into the latest *Mills and Boon* book.

The mourners slipped away, saying their goodbyes. Kizzy then realised that it was her place to stay to the end and wish everyone a safe journey. Even Johnnie left, his arm still very painful, as he needed to go to sleep. "Ahh, my gal, you did Vi proud, and me. Come and visit soon."

"I will, Dad. Of course, you can always come and visit here, stay a while, rest your bones." She smiled.

A lump gripped his throat. She had called him dad again. She didn't always but she liked to, just now and then, to remind him she loved him.

Billy, Farley and Levi left, still talking over the plans they had drunkenly put together.

Ocean's mother and sisters had gone earlier that evening. They weren't the type to drink too much and overstay their welcome.

The last stragglers departed and Kizzy made her way down the moonlit lane, going over the night's events.

"Kizzy gal."

She turned to see the silhouette of Ocean; his perfectly shaped body and fair waves were set against the moonlight. She felt excited but also afraid. She wanted to be in control. But knowing he could melt her heart so quickly sent her into a silent panic.

"Oh, hello there."

"Let me walk you home. It's dark. Anything could happen to you," he said as he skipped by her side. Not waiting for an answer, he just walked beside her.

"Beautiful evening!"

Kizzy knew he was trying to be romantic.

"Um," she said.

"You're beautiful!" he stated.

Kizzy blushed. She hadn't felt attractive in years. But she was.

"You are the most gorgeous woman I have ever seen." His voice was so serious.

She felt a lump in her throat and knew she would have to fight hard to stop those big, fat, juicy tears from rolling.

"I never stopped loving you," he said, with so much conviction. Well, so it seemed to her. But he was just older and cleverer in his manipulation. He thought she was stunning and right now he loved her, but all those years ago he didn't. She was pretty then and he could shag her at a moment's notice. All he wanted back then was recognition and respect from the other men, and throwing Kizzy to the floor had given him that. That night, when he had gone to bed, he felt a twinge of guilt. When they had sent Kizzy away, he soon realised she was the one person who respected him and he missed her attention.

"If you never stopped loving me, then why didn't you come for me? Why did you leave me for four years?"

There was a silence as they faced each other. He looked into her eyes and could see the hurt. It was the same expression she'd had when he had thrown her to the floor and kicked the dust in her face. She had longed for him to come and get her but instead he went off, shagging all and sundry. With a lump in his throat, and an overwhelming sense of guilt and shame, he lowered his eyes.

Kizzy tried to hold back the tears but couldn't. As she saw the water fill his eyes and glisten from the light of the moon, she sobbed in his arms.

"I'm so sorry, Kiz." Ocean's voice cracked as he cried. He didn't know if it was the drink or the fact he really had let the best thing in his life go. When the tears eventually stopped, he put his arm around her shoulders and walked her to her home.

They sat in her gleaming new caravan, sipping coffee and talking. He didn't attempt to get her into bed. She wasn't a shagging toy anymore. She was a woman who deserved so much more. He stayed that night – but in Violet's van, not wanting chins to wag in the morning. He never wanted to hurt Kizzy again.

She got up early to see to her horses, feeling better. With her black wellies and her flowing white muslin dress, she headed across the field. Her long hair was left loose; tying it back so tightly gave her a headache.

Ocean watched her from the caravan. He couldn't take his eyes off her as he gazed in awe at her smooth, tanned skin and those black locks blowing in the wind. It didn't take long to catch up with her in the field.

"Good morning!"

Kizzy was startled. "Oh, hello, Ocean."

She looked even more beautiful as the morning sun reflected on her fresh, clear complexion.

"Can I help you?" he asked, standing rather awkwardly, with his hands in his back pockets and his white shirt open.

Kizzy couldn't help but look at his chest. She loved the pictures in the magazines of the boys with their shirts undone. He could have been a model. There was a magnetic sexual tension between the two of them. It was something which Ocean had never experienced before but she had. She had felt it when she was fifteen, every time he had looked her way. Now he had it; he wanted her to kiss him, to love him, to be his. She wanted the same but she wouldn't be so easy, not now, not this time.

"Yeah, I need to check them over."

"What are you checking them for?" he asked.

"I check my horses every morning and every night, for anything – ticks, sores. I have to make sure they are in good condition."

He knew then she was no ordinary girl: she had a passion in life and a connection to these horses. He watched in amazement as they gracefully walked over to her and allowed her to check them over. She didn't have to call them, they came to her. He looked at Kizzy and watched her movements. They were as elegant as her beasts and what he noticed even more was the bond between the animals and her. Then, he realised, when she was shunned from the site, it was the horses which gave her respect and unconditional love.

"Kizzy…" He took her arm and said, "I am sorry for what I did to you, and maybe, truthfully, I didn't love you properly then, but I love you now."

She smiled. He was being honest because, deep down, she had known all along.

"Kiz, I'm gonna go home out of respect. I have wanted no one as much as I want you right now."

"It was good to see you again, Ocean, and thank you for being so truthful. I knew you didn't love me, and it was my fault for hurting so bad all those years."

Her soft words pulled at his heart strings.

"Goodbye, my Kizzy gal."

They stared at each other before he touched her cheek and gently brushed her lips. Her heart pounded. She thought he would feel the drumming next to his bare chest. She wanted him to hold her tight, as if he would never let go. Her hand reached up and stroked the soft waves at the back of his head and she felt him quiver. She was in control. He kissed her, this time with passion.

"Oh God, Kizzy, I want you so bad, I can't stop looking at you. I'm sorry, I need you." He sounded out of breath. His emotions were so high she had literally taken the wind out of him.

This time she kissed him with a womanly force, with a passion which had festered for four years. A kiss that had waited to be planted on Ocean's lips for so long.

He pulled away and stared at her. "Kizzy, be my gal. I love you!"

She drew him back and kissed him again, running her hands up his neck and down his tight chest.

He laid her on the floor and touched her face. "Do you want me, Kizzy? Because I can wait until you are ready."

She smiled and slipped his shirt over his shoulder and gazed at his golden waves, tumbling down his neck. His piercing eyes were drawing her in and now her body was aching for him.

He looked down at her breasts, just visible through the muslin. Slowly, he removed her dress. Even her figure had changed from the little girl she once was. Unable to get enough of her, he touched and kissed every inch of her womanly body.

They lay in the grass as the warm summer sun blanketed their skin. Kizzy wondered, now he had got his way, if she would ever see him again, but she wasn't afraid anymore. If he didn't come back, then she would move on. If he did, then it would be on her terms. Ocean didn't want to leave. He wanted her to be with him, in his arms, forever.

Chapter Sixteen

The latest *Palace* was quick to fill. Dan and Sam had upped the marketing and even the radio stations were advertising the clubs. But, as for the new *Palace*, they waited until the day of the opening to reveal the name. Before the doors opened, the family arrived in limousines. Even Bill and Mary had dressed to impress and had come along just to see the look of joy on their grandchildren's faces. Jack and Ruby had no idea. Now they were of age, they assumed they could join in the celebratory launch. The warehouse style building was completely overhauled. The outside was painted in a light grey, with a purple awning protruding from the door. On either side were thick silver ropes with a red carpet which ran along the centre. Spotlights shone from the floor to illuminate the club and two shone directly at the sign, which was not turned on. A doorman came out with a tray of glasses and Dan did the honours of popping the champagne. The family gathered as Dan gave a small speech. "As a family we work together, we stick together, and we look after our own. So, it gives me great pleasure to welcome Jack and Ruby to their own *Palace*."

Ruby gasped. "What!"

Jack's eyes widened. "Are you serious?"

Sam placed an arm around his son's shoulders. "Yes, boy. You two now have your own club."

Bill, Mary and Francesca were wiping their tears whilst Ruby gazed in shock. Suddenly, the lights came on and there, across the top of the building, was the illuminated sign: *Ruby's Palace.*

Jack grabbed his sister and they jumped up and down, hugging each other in excitement. Both were crying.

Ruby had always hoped one day to manage a nightclub, but never in her wildest dreams imagined owning one at such a young age.

"Oh my God, it actually says *Ruby's Palace*," she squealed.

Fred laughed. "Well, on paper, it's Jack and Ruby's Palace, but we thought, as a name, *Ruby's Palace* has a certain ring to it."

"I love it!" exclaimed Jack, winking at his sister.

It wasn't long before they could run the club without the help of their father and uncles. Growing up in the business and helping out at the *Palaces,* Ruby picked up all the do's and don'ts to make her club just as successful as those run by her family. She was tough when it came to hiring and firing, being perfectly capable of standing up for herself. Jack let his sister take charge. She was a good manager with a no nonsense approach. She enjoyed the bossy position but never complained when Dan or Sam popped in to check everything was in order. She respected them and was grateful they had given her the opportunity.

Jack was Head of Security and he enjoyed his role. Few people took a chance with him. A big lump now at twenty-two, he had the cute Vincent look, similar to his Uncle Fred but built like his father, tall and solid.

The queues to get in on a Saturday night stretched far down the road, and it took longer with Jack on the door, due to the young women flirting with him. Unlike his uncles, he was shy when it came to the ladies and not inclined to bed a new girl every night.

Ruby hadn't dated very many men either. Her love was the club and she had little time for affairs. She needed to run her ship and keep it afloat to show her family she could do it. Not that they judged her, but she felt duty bound.

Ruby's Palace had been open a good six months and the money rolled in. The scene was young: over twenty ones only. Jack had sourced the best DJ. In fact, he went to Ibiza to find him, so the club hit the ground running.

One night, Ruby arrived late, which was unusual for her. Normally she'd be the first to open up.

"My fucking car has cut out again. I'm sending that bastard to its grave," she snapped, as Jack opened the door to let her inside.

"Run out of juice again, has it?" he laughed.

"Well that's what the AA man said. Quite frankly, it should have a light come on when it's low, to give me warning!"

"Rubes, when the little hand rests on empty, that should tell you it needs fucking filling up," snapped Jack.

"I don't like the car anyway; it just isn't me."

Jack rolled his eyes, aware his sister was after a new BMW and she would no doubt get one.

She strutted in front of him, dressed in a figure-hugging silver satin dress, puffing on a Marlborough Light.

"Rubes, you need to quit the fags. It will fuck you up."

"Jack, listening to your whinging will fuck me up," she snapped.

He shook his head. His sister acted so sharp sometimes but he loved her nevertheless, and was also very proud of her.

"Ruby…"

"What now?" she replied, standing with her hands on her hips.

He giggled. "You have still got your nightdress on."

Taking a deep breath, she sighed. "Jack, you are so pathetic. If that's meant to be funny then you need to go back to joke school."

She headed for the bar, smiling. She loved her brother really and she liked the way he looked out for her. But she wouldn't be her if she didn't give him stick.

Like her Uncle Dan, she made a thorough overall inspection before the doors opened, checking all the staff were tidy and alert, the tables clean, and the shelves filled to capacity with every possible drink. She did the same every Saturday night. She gazed around the huge dance floor and beamed with pride. Unlike *Dan's Palace*, with separate sections for pole dancing and gambling, *Ruby's Palace* was large but simple. There were no VIP lounges; instead, American diner style seats and tables lined the walls. It was for the younger clientele to have fun and spend money. There were no dolly birds touting champagne and no cheap alcopops either. She hired two cocktail waiters who were part of the entertainment – juggling the shakers and drawing in the crowds.

Jack had two men on the door and three other bouncers on the floor. The dress code was no jeans. The men were searched and the women had to open their handbags. As punters came rolling in, a man in his early twenties walked over to Ruby who was behind the bar. "'Ello, sexy, get us six Bacardi and cokes." He winked and glanced back at his mates huddled around the table. They looked over, sticking their thumbs up. He obviously thought she was one of the bar staff and they had placed a silly bet on who could get her into bed.

"Sadie, would you serve this gentleman?" said Ruby to the new girl, who grinned and stood in front of the man.

"'Ere, love, what's wrong with you getting my drink. Aren't I good enough?"

"Listen, darling, my job ain't to serve," she curtly replied as she went to walk into the back room.

Sadie leaned across and whispered, "She is Ruby Vincent and she owns the *Palace*. You don't want to get on the wrong side of her."

"Oh yeah, bit of a taskmaster, is she?"

Sadie giggled, taken with the guy's sexy wink. She leaned closer and said, "Yeah, a right bitch by all accounts. It's my first night, so I'm just going to smile sweetly and keep out of her way."

The young man nodded, carefully balancing the glasses as he headed back to his mates.

Ruby was in earshot. She stopped at the gangway before entering the office and heard Sadie's comment. Without causing a scene, she waited for the punter to carry his drinks away before she approached her. "So I'm a bitch, am I?" She stood with her hands on her hips and a snarl on her face.

"Oh, sorry! Nah, I was only joking." Sadie flushed crimson with embarrassment.

"Right little bitch by all accounts, eh? So tell me, by whose accounts were you referring to?"

"I'm sorry, Ruby, I was just flirting. I meant nothing by it – no one at all." Sadie needed to keep her job. They were paying top dollar and she could only work nights to juggle the babysitting arrangements. "I am sorry, really. I heard Jack call you it earlier, that's all."

"Well, there is only one person in this entire club who gets away with calling me a bitch, and that's him. I can't have people wrapped around me who have no fucking respect, so best you grab your coat and do one."

Sadie's eyes welled up. She so desperately needed the money. "Look, please forgive me. It will never happen again. I really need this job, my boys… well, we are in a mess."

Ruby's face softened. "Your boys?"

"Yeah, me ol' man pissed off, took our savings, and I have to work evenings, cos that's the only time me neighbour can babysit or I'd be potless."

"So how old are your boys?" asked Ruby, in a gentler tone.

"One and two, babies they are. Truth is, I did get a bit cocky out there. I ain't been out to a nightclub before, so I guess I got carried away. I don't think you're a bitch. Everyone seems to love it here so, if I gave you the impression the staff were talking about you behind your back, ignore me, 'cos it ain't true." A tear escaped and she wiped her nose.

"All right, Sadie, those girls over there need serving. Come and see me at the end of your shift."

Sadie smiled and hoped she was forgiven.

Ruby was checking an outstanding order when she heard a commotion in the club. As she headed for the dance floor, she could see some bouncers trying to separate two bleached blondes fighting hammer and tongs over some sleazy guy.

"Bar them. Make sure you take them down the road away from me club," said Ruby.

Jimmy and Jeff nodded, as they continued to grip tightly the skinny, wriggling women.

"I ain't going nowhere. Me ol' man's 'ere somewhere!" spat the bigger of the two.

Ruby went to within an inch of the woman's nose and whispered, "If you don't go quietly, I will make sure you won't have a mouth left to say another word, got it?"

The women saw more bouncers approaching and decided to leave of their own accord.

Ruby relaxed her shoulders and looked around, hoping that the atmosphere would resume and the punters would go back to enjoying themselves. The music was turned up a notch and girls got up to dance. Ruby sensed a man staring at her. As she turned her head, he smiled a half smile which just showed his very white teeth. There was something about him, and the way he tilted his face and bit his lip, which grabbed her attention. As she headed for the office he disappeared and her curiosity got the better of her. He was a real good-looking fella. She hadn't seen him in the club before but, then, there were new people arriving all the time. He was special. With a glint in his eyes he stood confidently, showing he had a decent body too. She tried to stop thinking about him but as soon as she reached the bar a soft, sexy voice spoke. She guessed it belonged to the mystery man.

"May I have a brandy and coke please?" He had a tiny hint of an Irish accent.

Ruby turned to face him and unexpectedly blushed.

Without thinking, she served him his drink. All the while he stared and smiled. She handed him the glass and, with the light from the bar, she could see clearly his bronze complexion and was awestruck by his brilliant green eyes. He winked and gave her his half smile. Ruby felt awkward. Usually she brimmed with self-confidence. Her cheeks glowed and she was lost for words.

"Hello, my name is Ocean." He held his hand out to shake hers.

"I'm Ruby." She shook his hand, almost trembling.

"You're not *the* Ruby of *Ruby's Palace* now, are you?" he asked, still holding her hand.

Coyly, she nodded.

"Well, Miss Ruby Palace, it's lovely to meet you." He winked again and walked away.

She was still staring when he looked over his shoulder.

She took a deep breath and poured herself a brandy and then asked the barmaids if they knew who he was, but none of them did.

The night dragged on and, every so often, Ruby scanned the club to find her mystery man. She felt disappointed when he wasn't in sight. Then, just before she prepared for last orders, he appeared again to order another brandy. This time, Ruby was more confident.

"So, Ocean, is this your first visit here?" she asked.

"Yeah, I think you have done a good job. It is a great achievement for someone so young," he replied, trying hard not to let his gypsy accent show.

"Thank you very much," she replied.

"Not at all, I admire a person such as yourself."

Ruby enjoyed his soft Irish brogue and felt complimented. She had become used to the way men spoke about her looks, but somehow Ocean was different.

"So, Miss Palace, what do you do in your spare time? If, of course, you have any?"

Ruby was caught off-guard and had to think. The truth was, she shopped or worked.

"Well, not a lot really. I have been too busy getting this club up and running," she replied.

"Would you have time for the pictures?" He cocked his head to the side and smiled.

Ruby tingled inside. "Maybe I could find time."

"Do you think you could find time on, say, Tuesday night?" asked Ocean.

Ruby smiled from ear to ear. "I think I could find myself free on Tuesday night, say seven o'clock, here, outside my club."

"It's a date," said Ocean, who knocked back his brandy and left.

Ruby was bemused by the whole event. He didn't hang around, he didn't kiss her, or even ask for her phone number. However, she did appreciate his obvious good looks and air of mystery.

The evening came to a close and the doormen waited for Ruby and Jack to close up. It was a necessary precaution – to ensure they were safely in the cars. Sadie was standing by the office, praying it wasn't her first and last shift.

"Oh, yes, sorry, Sadie, to keep you waiting. Here, take this." Ruby handed her an envelope.

"Am I fired then?" she asked, assuming it was her wages for the night. Usually, the staff were paid monthly.

Jack glanced at Ruby with a frown. He didn't interfere with the bar staffing issues. She laughed. "No, that is to show you I am not a bitch. See you Saturday."

Jack laughed. "Fuck me, sis. You have to bribe people to believe that now, do ya?"

Once outside the club, Sadie ripped open the envelope to find one hundred pounds in cash. She decided, there and then, she would make sure she never let Ruby down and would go the extra mile.

*

Ocean arrived back at the site to see the eager Farley and Levi. Billy had taken to his bed with a chest infection.

"Well?" enquired Levi, throwing Ocean a can of beer.

He grinned. "Putty in my hand!"

"Did you give her one?" asked Levi, rubbing his hands together.

"What's with you, mush, can't you get any sex these days? Is it your flat nose?" Ocean was annoyed with Levi. He always saw him as a pervert and right now he felt guilty for almost cheating on Kizzy. Come Tuesday evening he would be cheating, but the only girl Ocean wanted was down in Kent.

"Fuck off, Osh, my nose ain't that bad." Levi got up to look in the mirror.

"Well! What happened?" asked Farley.

"I'm taking her out Tuesday night!" His voice was flat.

"Yeah… so what's the problem, Oshi boy?"

"Noffin. I just don't fancy her, that's all."

"Do you want in on the deal, or what?" shouted Farley out of frustration. Ocean nodded.

"Well, fucking learn to fancy her. Win the malt over and get us in that club!"

Ocean chewed the inside of his mouth. He wanted in on the action, but his head told him to stay clear of Ruby if he was to keep Kizzy.

He left the caravan and headed home. Marching up the hill, he thought of Kizzy and instantly ached to be in her bed but he had to be patient and give her time.

Behind him he heard the roar of Levi's BMW, the latest model. He turned to see the bright red monster tear off into the night. He chewed the inside of his mouth again, which was something he always did when deep in contemplation. The car, the trendy flat, the respect, would all be his, if he managed to get Ruby in the sack and keep up the pretence. He deliberated over Kizzy. She would never know. Not if he was clever. She lived down in Kent with her horses as she wasn't brave enough to visit the London site. Her safety net was her caravan.

He concluded that to get anywhere in life he had to take risks, and the benefits were his and Kizzy's to share.

He thought about Ruby. She wasn't like his Kizzy. But she was still a nice-looking woman and it wouldn't be so hard to lead her on and show her a good time.

The Nappers' club in the Old Kent Road was snapped up by the Vincents but under a different name. It had been turned into a club called *Little Palace* and was being managed very well by Celia, Napper's widow. 'Ironic,' laughed Celia when Dan handed her the keys. She had worked hard and proven to them she was more than capable of running it. He knew she wouldn't stand any nonsense. Her aim was to execute a clean and profitable business and show any of Kenneth's friends she wasn't fucking around. The pikeys tried a few times to get in but she wasn't having any of it. It was Billy O'Connell and Ocean who made the first attempt. They had arrived, suited and booted, and the naive bouncer let them in. Celia had been doing the paperwork that evening and didn't notice them peddling their gear. They were premature with their new-found confidence in supplying drugs to the punters in *Little Palace*. The fact that no one had noticed was not a good reason to go in the following week with a serious amount of cocaine stashed in their jackets. There were plenty of buyers, as everyone fancied a toot, and the first night was rocking. They had punters asking if they would be serving next week. Ocean had sold his car and set aside the money on cocaine, eager to be a big shot dealer. Potentially, this was a huge earner and theirs for the taking.

The following Friday they arrived, as they had the week before, only this time with enough gear not to run dry. Some of the regulars made a beeline for them, which caught Celia's attention. She was at the bar and instantly clocked them. The sovereign ring on fat Billy's little finger gave them away. He had tried hard to get it off but he was so fat these days that only the fire brigade could have removed it. She remembered Johnnie telling her about the travellers and their drug scams, and she would not have a hedge mumper crossing her *Palace*.

Jason, Johnnie's brother, was head doorman and he was the one who threw them out bodily. But not before Celia gave them a good look over.

"Come near me club again, and I'll make sure you wished you had been born a porker, not a fucking pikey." Her face looked tight and spiteful with anger.

Jason looked out for Celia. Always by her side, he knew that's what Johnnie would have wanted.

He got two other bouncers to give Ocean and Farley a slap and, while they had hold of them, Jason frisked their pockets and pulled out a good thirty grams of coke. They opened the packets, to the dismay of the wide-eyed pikeys, and let the wind blow the powder into the night.

It was the half smile of satisfaction on Celia's face which Ocean would not forget. That bag of cocaine was his and there she was, a midget of a woman, grinning at his misfortune. He walked away with a black eye, a debt of two grand, and hatred towards the Vincents.

*

Dan's Palace still brought in the most money, but when Dan looked at Ruby's books his eyes lit up. The takings were increasing each week and the youngsters were spending more than the rich old boys. Dan held business meetings every Tuesday. Ruby loved to be part of that. At long last she was being treated as an adult and respected for her handling of the club.

Jack also went along, but Ruby put forward the new ideas and updates.

"I want to have a foam night once a month!" she said excitedly.

"Rubes, foam nights went out in the eighties, it won't work!" laughed Fred, who loved his niece but liked to reel her back in every so often.

"Well, Uncle Fred, you're so wrong. I have asked my punters if they like that sort of thing, and they love the idea. Come the summer, I want my customers dancing in the wet, sexing it up, and downing the vodka. Jack's well up for it." She giggled and the rest joined in.

"That shut you up, you old timer!" laughed Sam, who was proud of his kids and their success. Aware of his son's protective nature, he knew only too well that Ruby couldn't manage the club completely on her own and was content in the knowledge that Jack always had Ruby's back, no matter what.

The profits from each club were put into the pot and divided equally amongst the Vincents. It was the fairest way and everyone agreed to it. Ruby reserved herself the BMW she was after and had the cheek to call it a company car. Jack had tried to purchase a number plate with 'princess' on it, just for a laugh, but anything similar was already gone. So he bought a plaque which fixed to the rear window and read, 'Keep back, Princess on board'.

Ruby accepted it, all in good faith, ready to be stuck on.

The new car was available for her to collect on Monday, and she was brimming over with excitement. Jack drove her to the garage and she very excitedly took her princess plaque with her. A brand new BMW sports car, in midnight blue, was there on the forecourt, awaiting the princess's arrival.

"Fucking 'ell, Rubes, you had better retake your test. That is one mean machine. Are you sure you can handle that?"

Ruby was simply glowing. Her new baby was there, ready for the taking.

The salesman was a good-looking young man, dressed in a blue pinstripe suit and a hairstyle which suited a Calvin Klein model. The diamond stud in his ear and Rolex watch said, 'I'm successful and flash'. So typical. He eyed Ruby up and down and liked what he saw, but assumed she was daddy's princess and this was a twenty-first birthday present.

He dangled the keys in front of her face and grinned. "Shall we take her for a spin before you go it alone, just to make sure you are one hundred per cent happy."

"Oh, don't worry, any problems and it's coming straight back here." She smiled sweetly, but her tone said, 'Don't fuck with me'.

Sean, the salesman, was intrigued. Usually he was good at summing up girls by the way they looked, but he guessed he was wrong this time.

"So, Ruby, the car, is it a birthday present or —" Before he could continue, Jack jumped in.

"No, mate, my sister bought it for herself." Jack stood by Ruby's side and looked the salesman over.

Sean felt his neck get hot and hoped he hadn't offended his customer, as the sale had been done over the phone. Ruby had seen the car in the showroom and decided there and then she wanted it so she'd made the arrangements. Sean, of course, assumed daddy was footing the bill.

Out of embarrassment, he said, "So, you have a good job then!" and then nearly kicked himself afterwards.

Ruby felt sorry for him and smiled politely.

"I run *Ruby's Palace* in the East End. Here, take my card and pay us a visit one night."

Sean gracefully took the card, realising he was facing a woman further up the ladder than himself, and felt foolish.

As they left, Ruby gave Jack a dig in the ribs. "You are wicked sometimes!"

He frowned. "Ruby, he was chatting you up."

"So?" she spat.

"Well, sis, don't get sucked in by any old Tom, Dick or Harry. You have got status. You want someone on your level."

Ruby took a deep breath. "Jack, you need someone... anyone, on your level or not!"

He rolled his eyes and waited for the princess to get settled in her new set of wheels before he left.

Ruby itched to get going. She secretly wanted this beauty before her meeting with the mystery man to impress him – as if owning a nightclub wasn't enough. Before Tuesday approached, she paid her hairdresser a visit and had a spray tan followed by a manicure. There was something about Ocean: maybe it was the lack of words, or just facial expressions, which made her want more. She was intrigued by his obscurity and charmed by his looks. She hoped, by looking her best and driving a flash car, she would secure his attention.

*

Tuesday night arrived, and both Jack and Sam sensed Ruby was going on a date. She spent far longer than usual getting ready and the strong perfume could be detected down in the wine cellar.

Jack called up the stairs, "Rubes, your hairspray has anaesthetised me tonsils!"

Ruby carried on adding more, ignoring her brother.

Eventually she emerged, looking too sexy for Sam's liking.

"Ruby, you can't be fucking serious, your boobs look like they are balancing on that... whatever that is," snapped Sam.

"Dad, it's called a corset and they are not balancing. These puppies are well and truly strapped in!" laughed Ruby.

She looked down at her outfit – the black sequined top and tight jeans. She glanced then at her brother. "Well, Jack, how do I look?"

He smiled. "Like you're carrying two bald puppies." They both laughed.

If her brother noticed the glamour side to her, then certainly Ocean should. That was her intention.

The summer evening was perfect for Ruby to put down the soft top on her convertible and head off into the sunset. She hoped he'd be there waiting, just so she could pull up looking the part. The sun was setting and everywhere had a warm, bright orange glow.

As she pulled up outside the club, there, not twenty feet away, stood Ocean, leaning against a smart red BMW. Ruby's heart began to pummel. He put her in mind of James Dean with his leather jacket, jeans, those blonde locks, and the way he tilted his head and lowered his gaze.

She waved as she locked the door. He walked slowly towards her with that half smile which made Ruby melt.

He kissed her on the cheek and led her to his car, well, Levi's car. The wheels and the flat were part of the bargain. Ocean could use it all as long as he reeled in the Vincent girl.

"So, Ocean, where are we going?" Ruby mistakenly assumed he was loaded. The BMW he drove was top of the range, and the leather jacket had a Prada tag sewn on the side.

"I thought maybe a light meal, perhaps Italian." He tried hard to sound posh but was struggling. A traveller all his life, with a real tinker accent, he would indeed find it hard. His lack of words gave Ruby the impression he was a man of importance – perhaps a wealthy stockbroker.

"So, tell me, Ocean, what do you do for a living?" she asked, as they sat in the romantic bay of the *Lugini* restaurant.

He smiled. Knowing that question might crop up, he had the answer planned.

"My business is in race horses. I buy, sell and breed."

Ruby raised her eyebrows. It sounded exciting. She took it all in. He was rich, interesting and extremely handsome.

"And what do you do, Miss Palace?" he asked.

Ruby frowned. She had told him she ran *Ruby's Palace*.

"You know what I do," she laughed.

Ocean looked over his menu. "But I thought you were joking."

Ruby was foolishly pleased. He was with her for herself and not for who she was. So she believed.

They spent the evening talking and smiling whilst Ruby yearned for him to kiss her or say something more complimentary. As the evening came to a close, Ocean drove her back to her car and stepped out to say goodnight.

"Ruby, I have had a wonderful evening, and I would like to do it again sometime." He was acting the perfect gentleman, much to Ruby's disappointment. All she wanted right now was a passionate kiss and the promise of more. She was so immersed in his sexy green eyes she would have fucked his brains out in the back of the car.

"Yes, Ocean, I have too, and I would love to meet again. How about tomorrow night?" She was being forward but she couldn't help herself. He was so gorgeous.

He almost gasped. Tomorrow was too soon. He had made plans to be with Kizzy and nothing and no one would get in the way.

"How about Thursday, only Wednesday I won't be home until late? I am off to Birmingham for the day."

Ruby wanted to suggest she spent the day with him but she knew that was far too serious and no doubt would scare him off.

She nodded gracefully and suggested they should meet at the same time.

Just before he left, he gently kissed her on the lips and pinched her cheek. Ruby didn't know whether she felt like a woman or a child. Her dad pinched her cheeks. She stood, bewildered, as he drove away. It was odd. Did he fancy her or not? She would soon find out on Thursday. She watched him drive away into the distance and suddenly believed in love at first sight. Convinced she had fallen head over heels, she was going to reel him in. By hook or by crook, he would be hers.

Ocean shuddered, pleased with his performance, but also keen to get away. He thought of Kizzy: she was his, with her natural, dark-haired beauty, her round, childlike eyes, but her womanly body. There was no comparison. Ruby's hair was neat and groomed but her tan was fake and she wore a ton of makeup. She was pretty but in a fake way, although, if he hadn't met Kizzy again, he may have shagged her in the back of the car there and then, but it was different now. His heart and soul were with Kizzy. Tomorrow night he would take her for a meal, make love to her in her bed, and treat her like a queen. A smile spread across his face.

The need to be rich from drug dealing, to be admired, and to be held high in the travellers' esteem, was becoming less important. His hunger for respect had goaded him for years and spurred him on to take risks, hurt people, and remove some of his natural feelings. He would have mugged a blind old woman if it had meant the others patted him on the back. But things had changed. Kizzy had got to him. His lust for her was overwhelming and yet he believed he needed clout to keep her interested

He gripped the steering wheel and imagined it was his car. The power behind the accelerator, the groaning of the engine, and the smell of new leather seats, gave him the jolt he needed. There was to be no more stalling. He would get on and date Ruby, get her into his bed, and work in the club. He knew she was keen on him and yet the hatred for the Vincents made the scheming palatable. He toyed with the idea of telling Kizzy the plan but decided it was not worth the risk. He would just have to work extra hard to keep her out of the loop.

Kizzy was content for Ocean to visit her. She had no intentions of going to London. It was their little love nest, her caravan and a bit of land. She didn't want to go back to the site which held too many bad memories. It suited him perfectly. What the mind didn't know, the heart couldn't grieve over.

When Thursday evening arrived, Ruby was ready. The music blared from her car as she sped along the Old Kent Road. When she pulled up outside the club, her heart sank. No red BMW. She felt sick and retrieved her mobile phone from her back pocket to see if he had called. There were no missed calls and no text messages. She thought perhaps he had got held up in traffic. After waiting for twenty minutes, she decided to get herself a drink, and what better place than her own club? Luckily, she had the huge bunch of club keys with her and could let herself in. It was just as well she had remembered the alarm code, even though Jack always locked up, or she would have found herself in an embarrassing situation.

The club was eerie with no customers. She turned the bar lights on and poured herself a brandy. The dance floor seemed so much bigger and the lounge sofa looked inviting. She smiled at the large disco balls reflecting any tiny splash of light. She remembered the opening night and how her family had arrived, an hour before opening, with bottles of champagne. Dan had poured everyone a glass and, with beaming faces, they had all toasted the new owners of *Ruby's Palace*. 'Here's to Ruby and Jack.'

The surprise and excitement had been overwhelming. Her months of euphoria had gone just like having the rug ripped from underneath. She knew it was stupid as, after all, she barely knew Ocean, but she wanted him so badly. Never before had she felt so attracted to a man. It was meant to be. He held the key to her future happiness. Now, her life would be perfect: the club, the status and the stunning-looking husband. But what if he blew her out? She shuddered. *No, think positive, Ruby. He will turn up, he will.*

She poured another brandy and sat on a sofa. Suddenly, she became conscious of a noise at the back of the club. It was coming from the office. Ruby jumped up and her first reaction was to see who was there but then instinct took over. She needed to call for help. The best place to hide was behind the DJ's box. She tiptoed over whilst keeping an eye on the back. Once she was hidden, she searched her bag for the phone. As her hands fumbled frantically inside, she could hear footsteps coming towards her. Then she remembered she had left the damn phone in the car.

Her heart was thumping. She needed to take a deep breath, but she wanted to stay as quiet as she could and hope the intruder left. She knew it wasn't Ocean. That odd sensation, like watching a psychological thriller, engulfed her.

As the footsteps came closer she froze, holding her breath, until finally they stopped. As she looked up from her crouched position, there he was, towering over her – a tall man with cropped hair and a cruel grin, holding a monster of a knife.

Ruby didn't recognise him at all and her fear was so great her throat was paralysed. She tried to speak, to tell him to take whatever he wanted, not to hurt her, but nothing would come out. With her heart beating so fast, she thought she would die.

He stared at Ruby for what seemed ages. "Get up!" he demanded. She gingerly rose and as she did so he grabbed her arm roughly and marched her towards the office. Gripped by terror, she was ready to puke. The man looked to be in his sixties. He had two nasty scars on his face and Ruby was petrified he was going to kill her.

Her voice came back. "What do you want?"

He was silent.

"Take whatever, and just go."

He pushed her into the bar. "Take whatever I want? You stupid little girl, this is mine, all the fucking *Palaces* are mine!"

Ruby could hear his words but made no sense of them. His lips were tight with rage and his eyes were red like a wild, rabid dog, foaming around the mouth.

She didn't understand who he was and what he was talking about. But, when he grabbed her again and shoved her violently into the office, she could see the cans of petrol. Fuck, he was going to torch the place.

"Look, please, do whatever you want, but let me go!" Her voice was frantic.

"Shut up!" he screamed. "You are the life for a life. You can burn along with the club. I have waited a long time for this."

Ruby tried to think of a way out of this but she was blinded by panic.

The intruder had grabbed a rope. After throwing Ruby onto the chair, he tried to tie her up. She struggled, but her fear was so great she felt weak and parts of her body could not move. Her right leg was just stiff and her right arm was limp. Her brain injury, years before, had resulted in an odd reaction to fear and stress. Try as she might, her limbs were paralysed and she knew she was going to die in one of the worst ways possible – burned alive.

He looked as though he was a robot – his eyes were strange, as if he was under hypnosis but, in reality, he was a deranged man.

He wrapped the rope round Ruby's body and the chair. The last tug winded her.

Believing he was the only other person in the building, he placed the knife on the side and poured the petrol all over the club: up the walls, along the bar, and then he poured it over Ruby, stinging her eyes. As it ran down her face, she gasped for breath. The rope was so tight across her chest she struggled to breathe. For ages he stood there, just pouring the fuel over her head until the can was empty and she was completely covered in it. The fumes were overpowering. She gagged twice before she eventually threw up. The man smiled, highly satisfied with his night's work and confident he would get his revenge.

He walked around the club, checking he had covered every single inch, and realised that the rest rooms were dry. He wanted it burned to the ground – he was intent on destroying every last bit.

Ruby coughed and spluttered and then, having managed to clear her lungs, she let out a blood-curdling scream for help. The intruder ignored it, however, and continued to pour more petrol, determined to leave nothing to chance or for the girl to survive. No one could hear her anyway. Her desperate cries fell on deaf ears. She was consumed by fear. Eventually, the petrol fumes knocked her out.

Ocean had, as Ruby suspected, got stuck in traffic. Levi had again lent him the car. This time he had taken it for a long spin around the countryside before heading into London, but the traffic had been heavy due to a fire at *Little Palace*.

As Ocean turned the corner, he was relieved to find the blue convertible still there. He guessed she would wait due to her keenness to see him again. But as he drove alongside the car, he could clearly see she wasn't in it. She must have waited inside the club.

The back door was open and, as he stepped inside, the overpowering smell of petrol hit him. Quietly, he sneaked his way towards the office. As he reached the door, he somehow suspected something amiss. His eyes widened and immediately he scanned the room. He saw Ruby was unconscious, doused in petrol, with vomit down her front. He could hear footsteps heading towards him. He crept along the short corridor and hid in a small recess used to hold the cleaning equipment and coats. Ocean registered the sound of only one person. He somehow needed to save Ruby. More importantly in his mind, though, he needed to save the *Palace* – his future bread and butter. The only way to do it was a violent attack but he wasn't a fighter; it just wasn't in his nature. He looked around to see if there were any iron bars or even a shovel. He had to go back out to the car and get the crowbar from the boot. Travellers always carried one. It was like carrying your wallet. You never knew when the opportunity might arise. Not for clubbing anyone, more for opening places itching to be prised open.

Just as he had suspected, there, as bold as brass, was the tool. He hurried back to the club and tiptoed in, clutching the weapon.

Before he reached the office he could hear a chilling voice saying to a now conscious Ruby, "When I strike this match, there will be one less Vincent breathing!"

Sick bastard, thought Ocean. Shaking and sweating, he gripped the bar and crept in and, like swinging a rounders bat, plunged the iron bar deep into the man's head, instantly knocking him to the floor. He raised the bar again but then stopped when he saw the blood making a wide puddle.

Ocean glared in horror at the man's open gruesome wound. Ruby was still in shock. She held her mouth to stop the screams. The man lay there with a sadistic grin on his face and with his eyes wide open, but he was clearly dead. She didn't even feel Ocean untie her. She was staring at the monster who, just seconds ago, had tried to kill her.

Still trembling himself, Ocean helped her to stand up, put his arms around her, and led her outside.

The soft comfort of his body against hers was the medicine she needed to snap out of the petrified trance. As soon as she had calmed down and regained her senses, she called her dad.

Sam and his brothers arrived in minutes, mortified to see the state of Ruby, covered in petrol and clearly still in shock.

Ocean waited by the car as he tried to clear his thoughts. The clump and the blood had disturbed him. He'd had a few beatings in his time, and seen some too, but never taken to these lengths. He didn't know he had it in him.

Sam was fussing over his daughter, getting her to drink some water and trying to wipe the petrol off her face. "Who was he, Rubes, do you know?"

She shook her head and pointed to the club. "He's in there, in the office."

"It's all right, babe, let's get you home and cleaned up. Don't worry about the club. We'll have it cleaned up in no time. Just you take deep breaths and drink this." She was shivering and sipped the water.

Ruby described what happened as Fred went inside to check the man was dead.

It was Dan who spoke with Ocean.

"Look, mate, I don't know you, but we do owe you one. What do you want?" His voice was calm and business-like.

Ocean frowned. "What do you mean?"

"Well, it can be sorted one of two ways. I get this mess cleaned up, and no more said, or we call the Ol' Bill and…" He lit up a cigarette. "We call the Ol' Bill and let them sort it out. I don't know you and, for all I know, you might not need this kinda shit in your life." He shrugged his shoulders, "Your call, bruv!" Dan called him bruv to let him know he knew Ocean was a traveller.

Ocean felt gutted. He had saved one of the Vincents, only to be sussed the very next minute by the head honcho. The drug game was over before it had even started. Unless… He racked his brains to find a way around this. He needed to be on the Vincents' side. Owing him a favour wasn't enough. He wanted to be part of their business.

Meanwhile, Ruby was telling her father how Ocean had saved her life and how wonderful he was.

Fred emerged from the club and called Sam and Dan over to the doorway.

Ruby remained by the car, wiping the petrol from her tear-stained face.

"You ain't going to believe who that is in there, covering the floor in claret. Only that cunt Napper!" said Fred.

Ocean walked over to join the men as the three turned to face him. They would have sent him packing but he had saved their Ruby's life.

"Who have I mullered then?" Ocean brazenly asked.

It was Fred who answered. "Dunno, mate."

Ocean was angry. He had heard so many stories about the Vincents but now he was in a situation which caused him to be part of their plan. It was right what people said about them. They looked alike and they had a certain attitude which, without words, spoke volumes. The way they stood and their confident body language gave them an edge. Ocean felt nervous by their cold approach.

"Look, before I decide what I'm gonna do, I need to know who the fuck I've just clubbed!"

The brothers looked at each other.

"Napper – know him?" asked Dan.

Ocean grinned. "Nah, never heard of him."

Dan knew he was lying and his temper got the better of him. He lunged forward, lifting Ocean off his feet by his neck. "Look, cocky bollocks, don't fuck with me. If I find out you had something to do with this, I'll cut your fucking head off and barbeque it meself!" He let him go.

Ruby ran over, screaming. "Leave him alone. He saved me from being burnt to death!" She put her arm around Ocean's waist.

"I don't know who he is, I swear." Ocean stopped before he gave himself away.

But Dan finished his sentence for him. "On me muvver's life."

Ocean lowered his gaze. He knew they'd guessed he was a gypsy.

Ruby turned to her uncle. "What's all this about?"

"Your boyfriend here is a traveller, a pikey. It's what they call themselves these days."

Ruby looked up at Ocean, who was glaring at Dan. "I don't give a rat's arse if he is a fucking alien. Don't you get it? He saved my fucking life!"

She grabbed Ocean's hand and marched to his car.

Before any of the Vincents could say another word, Ruby jumped into his motor and asked him to drive away. She didn't want her family giving him any more grief. Ocean looked in his rear view mirror and smirked.

Sam shook his head. "For fuck's sake, that girl is so strong willed. She does have a point though, he did save her life!"

"Oh yeah, and how do you know he weren't the instigator? This stinks to me. Something ain't right... I might be wrong. It could be a coincidence: a dead Napper and a gypo on the doorstep," replied Dan.

Ocean loved the feeling of having one over on them. There he was, driving up the road with their precious Ruby in his car – well, Levi's car, leaving a dead body and three Vincents bewildered, so he naively thought.

Chapter Seventeen

Ocean had previously planned for Levi to be out of the flat for the night so he could take Ruby there and pretend it was his abode. He wanted to play the game of the rich horse breeder. Levi had a good tidy up, removing his grotty, smelly bed clothes, and replacing them with clean white sheets. He hated not having a woman and still having to resort to desperate druggies or the odd whore for a shag. He wanted a proper relationship, where the girl cooked and cleaned too. A real gypsy wife.

It was Ruby's idea to go to Ocean's place; she looked a mess and the one pet hate of hers was being dirty.

"Yes, darling, we can go to my flat and, of course, you can get cleaned up. Do you need anything from the shops before we head there?" Ocean was still keeping up the posh accent. He didn't want to put her off at this stage of the game.

"No, just a nice hot bath, soap and shampoo, and a cup of tea." Ruby relaxed in the seat as Ocean drove to Levi's flat. He worried over the state of the place and if there were would even be any tea bags or shampoo there.

He turned the corner off the main road and into a small estate, consisting of new modern flats, each with their own parking space. Ruby was impressed.

Ocean led her to the block, Levi's so-called penthouse suite – the flat at the top – and she was immediately surprised by the clean and tidy layout. The stairs and landings had highly polished oak flooring and the walls gleamed with fresh
white paint.

He opened the front door, hoping that Levi had done as he'd promised. The smell hit him right away and Ocean relaxed. Summer Jasmine air freshener filled the hallway. The cream carpets had been vacuumed and the ashtrays cleaned. He had a mental image of Levi in a pinny, running around with a vacuum in one hand and a duster in the other.

Ruby was pleasantly surprised. "This is lovely," she said as she scanned the living room.

Ocean went to the bathroom to check for shampoo. The bath and toilet gleamed and in the cabinet he found a bottle of shampoo and conditioner. He ran the water and then headed for the kitchen. At this point, he concluded that Levi must have got the cleaners in. Even the stainless steel shone with not a finger mark in sight. Better still, there, in the caddy, were some tea bags.

He put the kettle on and returned to the living room.

"Why don't you get yourself cleaned up and I'll stick your dress in the washing machine." He glared at the remnants of the puke, which now stank to high heaven.

Ruby felt self-conscious again. It was a strange feeling and one she was not used to. He had shown enough interest to take her out again, but he didn't look at her with admiring eyes or even hint at being intimate. She was baffled to say the least, yet intrigued at the same time.

She went to the bathroom, peeled off the dress, and wrapped a towel around her body. Ocean, without looking at her, took the garment. With two fingers holding it away from his clothes, and repulsed by the puke, he ran to the kitchen, throwing it into the washing machine. Ruby quickly climbed into the tub. She scrubbed her hair and skin and then remembered she hadn't any cream, or makeup for that matter. She was completely naked and felt insignificant. She used the comb on the side to untangle the knots and the baby oil to massage into her burning skin. She hadn't realised how sore her face and body were from the petrol until she began to rub in the oil. When she looked in the mirror, she saw her eye makeup was smudged over her cheeks and her skin was pink and blotchy. She tore off more toilet paper and removed the black from her face. Ocean smiled when she finally emerged. His eyes twinkled and he bit his bottom lip.

"What are you smiling at?"

"You look beautiful without that shit on your face."

Ruby felt so much better now.

"Here is a cup of tea." He handed her a mug.

She curled up on the sofa, drank the hot drink and began to unwind. He sat next to her, enjoying the view.

From what he could make out so far, she had a decent body.

"What are you staring at?" She giggled, hoping he would compliment her again.

Instead, he kissed her. She knew then he wanted her and she wasn't going to stop him. He peeled the towel away and looked at her. She was sexy – not as sexy as Kizzy – but she turned him on enough for him to take her to bed.

Ruby was in her element. He finally gave her what she yearned for.

He knew the buttons to press, the right words to say, and exactly how to make her feel like the sexiest woman on the planet. She was hooked and had fallen in love; she immediately wanted to marry him, have his babies and spend the rest of her life with him.

Ocean was, indeed, a good actor, and the more he eased into the role the better he got. By the morning they had planned a future together. They were going to buy more clubs – one for each of their children. They pictured the huge white wedding and the honeymoon in the Maldives and had even thought of names for their babies.

Ocean had no idea where the Maldives were, but if it sounded good to Ruby, then why not?

Ruby was so besotted by him that she hung on to his every word. As she lay on her back, with Ocean propped up on one arm, running his fingers over her body, she thought about what her uncle had said.

"Ocean, how do gypsies get married?"

He stiffened, not quite knowing how to respond.

"It's all right. Like I told my uncle, I don't care... look, it doesn't matter where anyone comes from, it's where you go to that's important."

He smiled. Ruby was so naive. For the first time he felt a twinge of guilt. There he was, caressing the enemy, having just bludgeoned a man to death, and he was now ready to take the Vincents to the cleaners.

Surely it couldn't be this easy, he thought. Then he had a sudden suspicion that maybe *he* was the one being set up.

"So, Ruby, my little flower, how do you honestly feel about me?"

She sat upright in the bed. "What do you mean?" she asked shyly.

"Well, are you serious about us getting married, I mean, really serious, or are you leading me up the garden path?" asked Ocean in a very stark tone.

Ruby felt her heart pounding with excitement. She had only known this man for a few hours and she was deadly serious.

She smiled and nodded, hoping he wouldn't laugh at her.

With that he got down on one knee and asked for her hand in marriage.

"Oh yes, Ocean, I will marry you!"

"Give me time to get you a ring and it will be official, but don't tell your family yet."

"Oh, they are okay really." She tried to laugh it off, not wanting to ruin the atmosphere.

"Not what I've heard. Didn't they kill the McManners in that warehouse fifteen years ago?"

Ruby laughed. "No way, they ain't like that. Yeah, sure, they might give you a good hiding if you piss them off, but kill anyone, no!"

"I think, Princess of the Palace, that you have been overprotected. Your family are more dangerous than that," stated Ocean.

"Well, look at you, clubbing that old geezer, and you're not exactly a gangster are you!" she laughed.

Ocean trembled when he thought about Nigel Napper in that pool of thick black blood. Then he looked at Ruby's face. She was so unperturbed, you would have assumed she was used to seeing guys beaten and dying. He shuddered inside, still watching her laughing and talking. He wasn't listening now. He had to get away from her and see Kizzy: speak with his real accent, use the words he was used to, and feel the softness of Kizzy's skin against his hand. He wanted to listen to the stories of wild horses and future plans of buying acres of green pastures. He wasn't interested in the crap which poured out of Ruby's mouth. Surely she wasn't so protected that she had no idea how dangerous her family were? Her immaturity put him off and he had the urge to leave.

"So, Ruby, do you live far from here?" he asked, trying to stay sweet.

"Err…" Her face changed, gutted at the thought of going home, and even more that he wanted her to go. It was so sudden: one minute he was proposing and the next wanting her out of the way.

"No, it's not too far, Sevenoaks."

Ocean knew it well. "Shall we make a move? Only, I need to get to work."

Ruby, now confused, wasn't going to be fobbed off so easily.

"Ocean, all those things we spoke about…" She paused.

"How dangerous your family are?" he asked.

"No, no, not that… our wedding, were you serious?"

He nodded, but not very convincingly. Ruby, blinded by infatuation, accepted his nod as confirmation.

She slipped her clean dress back on while Ocean pulled on his jeans and took a T-shirt from Levi's wardrobe. One thing about Levi was that he did like expensive clothes, and Ocean enjoyed helping himself. He was going to take full advantage. If the O'Connells wanted him to go along with the plan then he would milk it for as much as he could.

*

The drive to Sevenoaks was quiet. Ocean almost choked when he pulled into Ruby's road. The houses were huge and probably an acre apart. Suddenly, the urge to get his hands on serious money was back, and the only way to get it was to keep up the pretence. When he stopped the car she looked nervously at him. She wasn't sure whether he'd decided to call it a day before it had barely begun. Instead, however, he leaned across and gave her a passionate kiss. "I meant what I said, my Ruby Palace. I do want to marry you!"

Ruby skipped up the drive, so ecstatic that she hadn't given the incident in the club a second thought. To her mind, she had suffered enough heartache over the years, and now she decided that, come what may and regardless of anyone else, she was going to be happy. She was owed that much at least. She had met her one true love, albeit only a few days ago, but that didn't matter. She loved Ocean and no one was going to stand in the way of her relationship.

As she put the key in the lock, the door opened with such force it nearly pulled her arm out of her socket.

Sam dragged her into the living room. "What the fucking hell did you think you were playing at?" he shouted, throwing Ruby onto the sofa. "We have been up all night sorting out your mess!"

Ruby jumped to her feet. "My mess?" she screamed back. "My mess, how do you fucking work that one out? The Nappers are nothing to do with me, and I nearly died. Or did you conveniently forget that part?"

"Well, madam, you didn't seem too bothered when you fucked off with the king of the gypsies!"

Ruby's nostrils flared. "At least he was there to save my life but, for some fucking reason, you don't seem to remember that either!"

Sam took a deep breath. "You should have stayed with your family until all this mess was sorted. For your information, we have saved your pikey's bacon."

Ruby frowned. "What do you mean?" She lowered her tone.

"The body… we got rid of it, so he won't be had up for murder," he replied, looking somewhat shamefaced.

"But he wouldn't have been done for anything anyway!" she said, with her hands on her hip and a cocky tone to her voice.

Sam looked her up and down. For the first time in her life she saw the disappointment on her father's face.

"You amaze me sometimes, Ruby, you really do. I thought you were clever."

She shuffled nervously and her curiosity got the better of her. "So tell me, why would he have been nicked, if he saved my life?"

"He left the scene of a serious crime, he didn't bother to report it, and you didn't hang around to give a statement. The Ol' Bill would have taken one look at the state you were in, and concluded that what happened didn't. You both fucked off and left it for us to clean up. So that makes him guilty, and the least that would have happened would be you remaining in custody until the case came up in court. So, Miss fucking clever clogs, think over that one!"

Ruby went to her room to get changed and dreamt about the wedding plans, totally ignorant of her father's concerns.

*

Dan and Fred arrived at Sam's, looking the worse for wear. *Little Palace* had been burned to the ground and Celia was still missing.

Sam took the boys to the kitchen.

"What a fucking night!" said Fred, exhausted and not a little angry with the night's events.

"That fucking Napper made sure *Little Palace* would not survive. Not a damn thing left, except the four fucking walls," added Dan.

Sam handed them a cup and poured freshly brewed coffee.

"We are insured, ain't we?" asked Sam.

Dan nodded. He looked up at his brother. "Is Ruby back yet?"

"Yes, the fucking madam is in her room."

"Is she all right, though? It must have been a shock for her. Perhaps her going off with that pikey might have been the best thing. Getting away, know what I mean?" suggested Dan, who had worried about the effect all this would have on his niece.

"Oh yeah, she is fine, just the same Ruby. Only like going back five years when she was a cocky teenager!" spat Sam, who was glad she was home safe and sound but livid that the only thing worrying her was her new-found fella.

"I can't imagine it, our Rubes being burnt to death. Well, it ain't gonna happen now. The old fucker's well and truly gone," stated Dan.

Sam wasn't present when they disposed of the body.

"So where did you bury him?" asked Sam casually.

Fred laughed and his eyes lit up. "Well, put it this way. By tonight he will be under the new builds in Hackney Wick. Harry, the concrete pump man, is filling the base of the block as we speak."

Sam smiled. "Shame about *Little Palace*... but Celia can't have gone down in the flames or they would have found a body!"

Dan took a deep breath and sighed. "As long as that nutty bastard didn't take her away to kill her."

Sam frowned. "Nah. Wait a minute. If I remember rightly, he said to Ruby, a life for a life." He scratched his head. "That must mean he would have murdered our Rubes for the sake of his brother Kenneth. The mad prick... I don't know why he thought we killed him. He died of natural causes, by all accounts."

Dan nodded again. "Well, word has it, if Kenneth hadn't been so badly beaten, he could have saved himself from the burning bed. So I guess he blames us, the cranky cunt. Anyway, I hope Celia's all right. I'm fond of the ol' girl. Works fucking hard, she does."

Whilst Ruby's uncles discussed the night's events, Ruby was going over what Ocean had said. At first she thought about the loving words he used. Then, like an electric shock surging through her veins, she remembered how he had described the incident in the warehouse with the McManners, and her body went cold. All those years, her uncles had lied to her. They had led her to believe she imagined it all: her aunt holding that gun – the famous jewelled lighter.

She stared in the mirror and looked at her Vincent face, the face which connected her to her family. She tried to recall that day. Although her memory was hazy, she could picture herself in a warehouse. Her uncles and aunt were there, it was snowing, and she remembered feeling cold, yet safe in her Uncle Joe's arms. It was a weird sensation. She recalled the men covered in blood, tipped back on their seats and tied up with rope. The man who she was so frightened of – the boogie man – sat in front of her aunt with her gun pointing at him.

It wasn't a mad dream, not if Ocean had heard about it.

She hated the secrets her family had. Finding out about her mother was bad enough, but to think that they were real gangsters, shooting people. She shuddered. She was old enough to know the truth and that was exactly what she was going to get.

She heard them talking as she came down the stairs. They stopped the minute she entered the kitchen.

"So what's up now, more secrets!" she spat spitefully.

The men frowned and looked at Sam.

"What's your fucking problem, coming in here speaking to your family like that?" Sam had taken all he could from Ruby right now and was ready to give her a back-handed slap if she carried on.

"I ain't the one with the problem. It seems to me that you lot have enough problems." Before she could carefully select her words, they fell out of her mouth. "Killing the McManners in the warehouse wasn't my vivid imagination, now was it?"

All three men were wide-eyed and dumbstruck.

"I knew it. All those years you have lied to me, led me to believe I was a fucking cuckoo. Well, I know what my family really thinks of me."

Fred jumped to his feet and lurched forward to grab Ruby's arm. "Now, sit your arse on that seat and shut your loud mouth!"

Ruby had never been spoken to like that by any of her uncles and so she instantly did as she was told. "You, young lady, are getting too big for your boots, and you think the world owes you. Well, let me tell you something. You can get the whole McManners' incident out of your head right now. If I hear another fucking word about it then you will kiss *Ruby's Palace* goodbye," growled Dan.

Ruby was near to tears. She had only ever been spoilt by her uncles and now she felt a huge distance between them.

"But I was there! I remember! I still have nightmares!" She tried to win the sympathy vote.

Fred got up to leave. As he passed his niece, he whispered in a slow, menacing voice, "We were protecting you…" He walked away, followed by Dan, who shook his head.

Sam didn't speak until he heard the front door close. Then he gazed in amazement at his cherished daughter. "I don't know you anymore, Ruby… We give you everything you could imagine, even a fucking nightclub, and you're hell-bent on defying us."

There was silence for a while and Sam realised that, for the first time in ages, Ruby was actually listening.

"I do find it hard to forgive you sometimes. I mean, take last night. You just fucked off, leaving us to deal with the mess. It's as if you really do believe we owe you a big favour."

He swirled the remains of his coffee staring into the dregs.

"Ruby, the warehouse…"

She lifted her head, desperate to learn the truth.

"There was an incident."

Ruby jumped from her seat. "I fucking knew it, all those years you lot lied to me. You are what they say you are. Fucking murderers!"

After years of protecting the kids, both Jack and Ruby, living his life to care for them, giving them all they wanted and so much more, it grieved him to hear his daughter's words.

He leapt from his seat, lunged forward, and slapped Ruby around the face so hard she fell to the floor.

"You selfish, nasty piece of work! Those men, in the warehouse, had fucking kidnapped you. They had left you for dead. If it weren't for your own flesh and blood, you would have been buried in a six foot pit now." He grabbed her arm, pulled her to her feet, and shoved her heavily onto the kitchen chair.

"Those fucking men hunted your aunt like a wild animal for all her childhood. Then, my girl, they came for you. With no mercy, they hit you and threw you in a pit. The snow left you blue and hanging onto life. You were three years old. Now tell me we are fucking murderers!"

His chest heaved in and out with anger. Foam had gathered around his mouth and Ruby could see the veins rising in his forehead. "My God, girl, you have no idea how we work as a family, or you choose to ignore it. My sister saved you from a miserable existence; she saved you from the clutches of a madman, putting her life on the line. The fucking McManners terrorised your grandfather, hung your nan from a hook, dragged Fred away at gun point to burn him alive, and you call us murderers? No, my girl, we are not murderers, but we will never ever let another living soul hurt our family again… got it, ave ya? Fucking understand now, do ya?"

"I'm sorry, Dad, I didn't know." She trembled from the words, which were so cold and hard.

"You disgust me, Ruby. The way you go on – as if you have the God damn right to question us, as if you have the right to make demands. You just do as you please, whether it hurts our family or not." He sat back down on the seat and glared at her. "'Ere, every time you get into trouble, we have been there for you, but you choose not to remember that, and now you are a woman you can get on with it. I wash my hands of you!"

With that, he got up and left.

Ruby was numb with shock. Her face stung and her world crumbled.

As she went to her bedroom, thoughts of Ocean came flooding back and she smiled. Everything was going to be all right. She would move out and live with him. Besides, their marriage was only around the corner – well, it was if she had it her way.

*

Fred had driven Ruby's new car back to her house to get her out of the picture. She packed a small suitcase and threw it in the back of the boot as Jack pulled up in a taxi. He had been to Amsterdam with a few of his mates.

"Hiya, sis, where are you off to?" He looked more handsome than ever. The sun had coloured his cheeks and made his blue eyes stand out.

"I'm getting as far away from here as possible. Dad has told me I'm not welcome anymore, and he wants me out of his life." She wanted a good excuse to leave and move in with Ocean and her father had just given it to her. Sam, however, had the bedroom window wide open, heard his daughter and rushed down the stairs to confront the lying mare.

The door was nearly ripped from its hinges.

"Will you ever change, Ruby... I never said that and you damn well know it. I said I've washed my hands of you... I didn't throw you out!"

Ruby shrugged her shoulders and continued loading her car.

It was Jack who grabbed her wrist. "What's wrong with you, sis? Stop all this nonsense and come inside." Jack's voice was soothing but Ruby was determined to go. She wanted to be with Ocean.

"I'm not staying here another day, so let go of me, and I will see you at the *Palace* on Friday night." She looked at her dad, who stood in the driveway. "That's if I still have a club!"

Sam, in a fit of fury, slammed the door shut. He headed for the drinks cabinet to pour himself a stiff brandy before he strangled his daughter.

He was dumbfounded. It was as if she was on drugs. How she could be so nasty towards her family was beyond him. What was the hold this gypsy had on her? He pondered over it for a short while until Jack came in.

"It's all right, Dad, you know our Rubes. She will be back with her tail between her legs." He swung his large holdall onto the sofa.

Sam turned and faced his son, who greeted his father with a huge smile and a twinkle in his eye. Sam's heart melted. If only Ruby was as sweet as her brother. He hugged him. "Jack, I hate to say it, but she is not like us. She is more like her mother, and that really breaks my heart."

Jack gasped. "No way, Dad, she is a Vincent all right, tough as old boots!"

Sam shook his head. "She has no care for the people that love her... no family values, and the one thing you need, to be part of this family, is honour."

Jack laughed. "Dad, shut up. You sound like Uncle Roberto."

"Yeah, well, he is right. If you don't respect your family, then you respect no one."

He tried to laugh it off, but he could see the serious look on his father's face.

"What's this really about?" asked Jack as he plonked himself on the couch.

Sam took a deep breath and began to tell him the whole story regarding the night's events. To Jack's surprise, Sam seemed more concerned Ruby had run off with a gypsy than with all the mess she had left behind at the club.

Jack was wide-eyed. He was shocked to hear his sister had been an inch away from death and that the club nearly burned to the ground. He couldn't understand why his father wasn't worried about her. She must have been traumatised.

"Dad, shouldn't she have gone to the hospital or something?"

Sam frowned. "Your sister ain't five anymore. She's a grown woman, and the way she carried on last night and this morning, well... like you said, she is as tough as old boots."

He poured himself another brandy. He was ready to go to bed, even though it was only ten o'clock in the morning. He didn't have the energy to listen to Jack defending his precious sister.

"Dad, you can't wash your hands of her just because she has pissed you off. She is still your daughter."

Sam slammed his brandy glass on the mantelpiece. "Now, you fucking listen to me, son. One thing you must remember is that family look after each other. The only people who really care are your own flesh and blood. When you and Ruby were little, your aunt and uncles did everything in their power to protect you. They put their liberty on the line." His voice was deep and cracking and he tried to calm his temper.

Jack looked at the floor.

"I know, Dad, I remember it. All the snow, Ruby being snatched, Nan's head gashed open, and I won't forget the mark on Ruby's face when Joe brought her back." He paused to look at his father's shocked expression.

"Dad, I know what they did for us and that's why I will do anything for them, but there were those first few years of just me and Ruby, and I had to protect her then. I was all she had, and that feeling still has a hold over me."

Sam's face softened. He knew his son would never turn his back on Ruby as they had been through too much together.

"Well, son, all I know right now is your sister is seeing a gypsy called Ocean – what a fucking name, eh?"

*

Ruby drove to Levi's flat. She remembered where it was and eagerly she parked her car and headed for the door. There was no answer. She banged for a third time and guessed he had gone to work just as he had said.

As she turned to leave, with her shoulders slumped, she jumped out of her skin. A man with a hole for a nose was standing there.

"Did you want something?" he asked. Ruby shuddered. It churned her stomach, looking at his deformed face.

"Err, no. I mean, yes. I was hoping Ocean, my boyfriend, would be home."

Levi wanted to laugh out loud. He instantly realised who she was. Ocean had dropped his car back at the site and quietly left after thanking him for the use of it. Levi had tried to delve into the goings on in the flat, any juicy sexy bits, but Ocean had made it clear he wasn't going to talk about it. What Levi didn't realise was that Ocean was very ashamed by his deception and betrayal to the woman he loved and so under no circumstances would he divulge what was going on between Ruby and himself.

Ruby could tell from his accent he was a traveller. His clothes were smart yet he still looked dirty. He chewed a toothpick and as he grinned she could see his red gums and remaining, crumbling teeth. His hair was slicked back and he wore the gypsy giveaway – the gold earring.

"Well, I am Ocean's friend and…" He stopped for a moment, not sure what he was supposed to say. "I am the decorator. Ocean gave me a key to look the flat over for a repaint job," said Levi, trying his best to sound like a gorger and not the traveller he was.

Ruby nodded, her face full of disappointment.

Without thinking, he opened his big, fat gob. "You must be Ruby. He has told us about you."

She inclined her head and smiled. "Really?"

Levi nodded. "Reckons you are a real nice girl."

She hoped he would have said something a little more specific, although at least Ocean had mentioned her. She felt uncomfortable with how he eyed her up and down, grinning as if he was undressing her.

"If you see him would you ask him to give me a call?" She was aware of her voice echoing in the corridor.

Levi was still leering and that was enough for Ruby to say her goodbyes.

"Why don't you wait here and I'll give him a ring?" he urged, still ogling.

Ruby debated this for a moment but then agreed. She had decided that remaining here and waiting for Ocean to arrive, even in the presence of the leering eyes of the lecherous Levi, might still be the best option, so agreed.

So she waited uneasily in the living room whilst Levi went into the kitchen to make the call.

As soon as Ocean had left Levi at the site, he headed in his old banger down to Kent to see his true love. Just as he was settling down for an afternoon of romance the phone rang, much to the annoyance of Kizzy, who was enjoying the attention.

"Osh, boy, you need to come to the flat. Ruby is here waiting for you," burst out Levi, almost out of breath.

He looked at Kizzy, hoping to God she didn't hear that. She smiled sweetly.

Unable to ask any questions in front of her, he made an excuse to get to London.

"I'm sorry, my babe, I've got to go. Levi's in a spot of bother, but I promise I'll be back!" apologised Ocean, genuinely gutted.

He drove like a madman. He wanted to punch a bigger hole through Levi's nose. What the hell was Ruby playing at? He was beginning to resent her for taking him away from his Kizzy and that wasn't a good thing at all.

He parked the old Ford Fiesta out of sight and headed up the stairs, jumping two at a time.

Levi had made Ruby as comfortable as possible with a cup of tea. He didn't speak too much because he didn't know what to say.

When Ocean arrived, he smiled at Ruby and marched Levi into the kitchen.

"What the fuck is going on, mate?" he whispered through gritted teeth.

"She was here when I came home, bruv. What should I 'ave done? Look, Osh, do what you have to, but get us in that fucking club, and less of the cocky lip."

With that, he handed Ocean the keys and left.

Ocean poured himself a large glass of water to cool off. He wanted to go in and batter Ruby but it wasn't going to happen. He had to remain calm and keep up the pretence.

"So, my little Ruby Palace, what's all this about?" he said, easing himself next to her on the sofa.

Ruby felt awkward. She wasn't expecting her boyfriend to go off whispering to the man without a nose.

She explained the situation at home, exaggerating the fact her father had thrown her out and she had nowhere to go.

Ocean was now out of his depth. How the hell was he going to continue this game? The flat wasn't his, the car wasn't his, and suddenly he was faced with an obsessed bunny boiler.

"Look, Ruby, you need to go back home and talk with your dad. I'm sure he didn't mean to throw you out."

Ruby's stomach was in knots. This wasn't meant to happen. He was supposed to take her in his arms and tell her everything would be all right. She began to snivel.

"Ocean, you don't understand. My family have disowned me. They want nothing to do with me, and when they say something like that it's no joke… they would kill me if I returned." She was lying through her back teeth, yet the only thing that shot through Ocean's head was the club. If they had really fucked her off, did she still have the rights to the *Palace*?

"There, there, don't worry about it. We will get it sorted out," he said, with a soft, caring voice.

Ruby relaxed. She had misjudged him. He did care after all.

"Does that mean they have taken the *Palace* off you, too?"

She frowned. "No, I own the club, I don't just run it."

Ocean smiled, even better.

"Now then, my little palace, if you are to stay with me, the best thing we can do is get married as soon as possible. Ya see, as a gypsy, I am not allowed to live in sin." He held his breath as he waited for a response.

Ruby turned and flung her arms around his neck. "I knew you would look after me. I know it's only been a short time, but I really feel I love you!"

Ocean cringed. She was so overbearing and the act was getting harder. He tried hard to be kind but she was making him feel sick.

"Right, you stay here, make yourself comfortable, and I will tie up my day's business and be back later." He stood up to leave.

"Shall I come too?" smiled Ruby.

"No!" he almost snapped. "No, let me get sorted out and I can spend time with you tonight."

Ruby kissed him goodbye.

Chapter Eighteen

Billy, Farley and Levi sat around a blazing fire. It was like the old times. Not cold, not dark, just tradition. Some of the other lads were there too and seemed eager to be involved in the conversation. Ocean thought back to being a youngster, when he had wanted to be in on the action. He had looked up to the O'Connells as if they were gods – rulers of the land. They had a reputation on a par with some of the older gypsies from other sites. Their chat was exciting: full of dodgy dealings, scams and robberies, whilst the older men talked about gun crimes and murders. Ocean smiled to himself as he realised now that most of the shit which came out of their mouths was lies or extreme exaggeration. However, he did recognise that some of the stories were true and that's how they managed to drive their 4x4s and own half of Kent.

He strolled over, warmly greeted by the boys.

"How's lover boy then?" laughed Levi.

Ocean shook his head. "She's fucking driving me mad," he replied, taking a can from Farley and sitting on a pile of tyres.

"Worn your cock out, 'as she?" Levi still wanted the grubby details.

"Look, Levi, shut ya mush about Ruby," spat Ocean, still angry and exasperated by Levi's freaky questions.

Farley looked at Billy and frowned. "I guess our Oshi's a bit of a gay boy."

"You lot set this whole fucking plan up. Well, now she wants to get fucking married." He shook his head.

Billy nearly fell off his chair trying to get to his feet. He was so excited, his asthma came on suddenly and he struggled to breathe.

"That's pucker. Wed the malt and you will own half the fucking club!"

There was a silence for a minute as it dawned on the men what Billy had said.

"I can't marry her. I don't even like her," said Ocean.

They laughed at him. Farley jumped in first. "Listen, bruv, you marry the Vincent and that club will be yours. Once you are legally wed, boy, you own half of everything."

They clinked cans as if it was a done deal.

Ocean pondered for a while. In the back of his mind was Kizzy, the love of his life, and right now he was prepared to give up the whole idea to keep her.

He needed to be straight and tell them the truth. "I ain't gonna wed her 'cos I'm marrying my Kizzy."

Billy was now on his feet and larger than ever. "Listen, boy, you can wed Kizzy. Marry that Vincent malt first, get the club, then fuck her off. Imagine the look on her old man's face." He struggled to breathe again. "Cor, boy, this is cushty. I thought you knocking her off would soften her up to let us do our bit of business in the clubs, but fuck me, this is just what we need!"

Ocean took a large gulp of beer and smiled. He could walk away with half: flash cars, his own pad and status. He could have it all. "No one tells my Kizzy then!"

Farley looked at Ocean with a newfound respect. "Osh, I get this is a serious deal for you, and maybe it's best you let Kizzy girl know what you are up to. Tell her you are doing it for you and her." He paused, took another swig of his drink, and then continued. "Besides that, you owe them grief for what they put us through. Even tried to cut off poor Kizzy girl's fingers, they did. So I reckon she will understand. Ya never know, she might even get in on it."

Ocean shook his head. "Nah, she has changed, my gal. Respectable she is, and she breeds horses."

Levi laughed out loud. "She's still one of us, an O'Connell. On the outside she might look hoity, but inside she's a traveller, same as us, and that means, boy, she will have to do as she is told. Don't let ya malt get too big for her boots!"

He was still shaking his head. He knew in his heart Kizzy wasn't like them and it would break her heart if she knew about Ruby.

Farley could see this ending the wrong way. He needed to get his hands on that club. It was an obsession. "Okay, Osh, what we are gonna do is keep Kizzy out of the picture."

Ocean felt relieved and some of the bricks lifted from his shoulders.

"I suppose you need my flat and car for a while," said Levi.

"I need a fucking priest and a church, if I'm gonna get wed." Ocean laughed for the first time.

The night drew near, the fire was topped up, and the beers flowed.

*

Ruby sat alone in the flat. She had unpacked her clothes and placed her toiletries in the bathroom. She wanted to cook a nice meal for when Ocean returned but she had never been taught how. She could bake a cake but that was about it. She went through the channels, watched all the chat shows, and then started on the DVDs. That was, until she discovered a pile of pornographic films. She recoiled and flicked through her magazines.

Ocean came back later in the evening. He had no doubt whatsoever she would be there.

He handed her a bottle of wine and a bag of chips. "Here we go. This is better than a night out."

Ruby sensed he had been drinking and wasn't sure how to handle it.

"Did you get everything sorted?" she asked coyly.

"Yes, babes, I had a stag night. Hopefully, within the next few weeks, we will be married."

Ruby hung on to every word. The doubts she'd had whilst waiting for his return went out of the window.

"Well, let's celebrate!" she squealed.

They clinked the overflowing glasses and downed the wine. But Ruby pulled a look of disgust as the bitter taste hit the back of her throat. She knew cheap plonk and this was utter trash.

Ocean was already too pissed to notice her expression and, more to the point, he didn't like looking at her face anyway. He poured another large glass and eagerly downed it. He knew she would be wanting sex and the only way he could manage it would be if he was half cut. The fact that Ruby was so obsessive, whilst he was so in love with Kizzy, made this situation even more intolerable. Ruby, however, was oblivious to his fake words and insincere actions. She was too eager to believe he really loved her.

It didn't take too long for the O'Connells to organise a wedding. Father O'Leary agreed to carry out the ceremony in three weeks' time, spurred on by a few fifty-pound notes shoved in his back pocket. Well known as a piss head, he had let his church go to rack and ruin. It was only the locals, holding jumble sales and cake competitions, who kept the church roof leak free.

Ruby had gone off alone and purchased the bridal dress. It was the only part of the wedding which she was allowed to plan. The rest was down to Ocean. That's how he wanted it. So he said. She felt guilty her family were not involved in her plans and knew, deep down, what she was doing was wrong. But she had fallen for Ocean hook, line and sinker, and wanted to be married to him, come what may. He was everything she dreamt of in a husband: extremely handsome, no push over, and a successful businessman.

The bridal shop had been ready for her arrival. She had already booked the appointment and the staff were on hand to dress the princess. They had asked how much budget she had before she arrived and when she'd replied 'I don't have a maximum', they had presented her with the most expensive dresses in the shop.

Eagerly, they fussed over her, like a scene out of *Pretty Woman*. Within the hour she had picked out the gown, the tiara and the shoes. The bill was over ten thousand pounds but Ruby didn't flinch. After all, it was her day so, since she would have no family there, she indulged in her fantasy dress and trimmings.

On the eve of the wedding, Ocean decided to leave Ruby to see Kizzy, but was met with a sulky response.

"Ocean, please don't go, I am all alone." Her voice mimicked a small child, irritating him even more.

"It's tradition that we do not spend the night together. You want this to be the perfect marriage, don't you?" He tried hard to keep his tone soft as underneath he was griping.

She nodded furiously.

"Then, Ruby, let's follow the rules, and meet at the church tomorrow as planned." With that he kissed her on the forehead and left.

She heard his car start up and speed away and Ruby experienced the sudden sound of silence. It made her want to see Jack and at least tell him what was going on, but she'd promised Ocean she would not tell a soul – it would be their secret. It had barely been three weeks and already she missed her family. The flat was small and boring compared to her home. Ocean was fairly reserved and worked long hours, or so she thought. Her life had been very different. She had grown up in a family who worked evenings and were mainly around during the day. At some point that would change, as he would be by her side in the club. That much she had established. She remembered his words: 'Imagine it, Ruby, me and you, side by side, running the *Palace*. We can spend so much more time together.' She knew it wouldn't be right away, as she'd have to convince the family, and that certainly wasn't going to be easy. He would have to prove himself first.

She smiled, believing he wanted the same as her, innocently oblivious to his scam.

Trying the dress on for the hundredth time, she felt satisfied and took herself off to bed. She tossed and turned for hours before she eventually drifted off. She had many unpleasant dreams during the night. In one, she dreamt of being stood up at the altar. In another, she had gained two stone overnight so her dress didn't fit, but she awoke to find she was still slim. The seriousness of what she was about to do was pushed to the back of her mind. Nothing, and no one, was going to ruin her day. She tried to convince herself that it was no big deal her family weren't attending: more important was the man she loved saying, 'I do'. They would come around and maybe one day have another wedding, or blessing, but for now she contemplated which lipstick to wear, red or pink.

*

The bells were ringing as Ruby pulled up outside the church. The driver had been paid extra to put a ribbon on the bonnet and wear a suit for the occasion. The bouquet arrived just before she left. Standing in front of the mirror, alone, without her dad or her aunt beside her, she had let a tiny tear run down her cheek.

The driver didn't want to hang around so, as soon as he arrived at the church and walked her to the entrance, he was gone in a flash. The suit he was wearing was his son's, which he had pinched from the wardrobe, and the car was his neighbour's, who had left him the keys to the house whilst they were off on holiday.

The sun was out. It was perfect weather for a wedding. Ruby initially liked the old church because it had a certain rustic charm. The grass was overgrown, the gate hung off its hinges, and there were red roses growing wild amongst the gravestones. Levi stood at the entrance, dressed smartly in what looked like an expensive suit. He smiled at Ruby – quite a genuine smile for a cocaine dealer who was about to lead her, quite literally, up the garden path.

"You look lovely, babe." He meant it, she did. Her dress was simple but stunning, and her tiny tiara twinkled in the sunlight.

The music began to play with a rickety organ bellowing out 'Here comes the bride'. A stunned Ruby would not have chosen that song. It was too outdated now. The inside looked quite dark and pokey, with only a short walk to the altar. Levi held her arm to lead her up the aisle. She cringed. To her relief there stood Ocean, dressed in a navy blue suit, looking so handsome and smiling back at her, giving her encouragement.

It hurt her to have a random man walking her down the aisle when really she should have had her father there, and Jack too. She kept her eyes on Ocean, not wanting to look away for one second. It was as if he had an imaginary string pulling her towards him. Standing next to him was another man; she later discovered he was called Farley, another member of the O'Connell family. Sitting in the front row was a big fat man with red cheeks who, throughout the service, stared with contempt at Ruby. Billy could see she was the daughter of Sam Vincent. She was his double and that made him hate her even more. He never did get over the beating Sam gave him. Just like Farley, he never forgot the hiding he took that night. So the O'Connells had no remorse for what they were doing. Billy smugly thought of Sam's face when he found out his beloved princess had married a pikey – an Irish fucking tinker – and now half the club belonged to him. He wanted to laugh out loud. That would teach those Vincents.

Farley acted as the best man throughout the service, nudging Ocean, and fumbling to find the rings whilst pretending he had lost them. Ruby concentrated on Ocean's face, desperately trying to overlook the fact that the doom and gloom of an empty church and lack of guests was an omen. If she'd had more time, the church would have been decorated with thousands of roses lining the aisle, huge pillar candles, a choir, and a priest who was clean and sober. However, if she had delayed the wedding perhaps Ocean would have changed his mind.

Father O'Leary was drunk, as shown by the fact he was swaying from side to side. Ruby could smell the fags and booze on his breath, but she tried to concentrate on the words which left Ocean's mouth. He took his time and seemed to falter over the vowels, which unnerved her. He looked at Levi and Billy, who were silently cheering him on.

"I do!" he finally said, much to her relief.

Ruby whizzed through her lines, except when she had to repeat all of Ocean's names, which went on forever.

The service was over in a matter of minutes, to the delight of all present except, of course, Ruby. This wasn't her fantasy wedding but he was the man of her dreams. Outside, the wind blew the dust and ancient, faded confetti up and into Ruby's face. Ocean wasn't holding her hand. He was being patted on the back by his mates. No photographer, no bells and no fresh confetti, so she assumed it was the gypsy way.

They left the church and drove to the nearest pub.

Ruby felt ridiculous in her dress, veil and bouquet, but their decision to have a simple, quiet affair was made and lived to the letter.

"A toast!" said Levi, raising his glass. "To Ruby Palace and Ocean."

Everyone raised their glasses and laughed. Ruby didn't get the joke as she thought they were calling her Ruby Palace. Their toasts and well wishes were for Ocean and the clubs. They now had more than a large foot in the door. In fact, they had half of Pikeyville.

"So, Ruby, gal, what's it feel like to be a traveller?" Billy was smug and had a sneer on his face.

She didn't find him funny. She felt as though they were ribbing her but was unsure why. She looked at Ocean for encouragement but he was raising his glass and laughing too.

"So, when ya gonna start making little chavis, then?" asked Levi, who was hunched in his seat, sipping on his champagne.

Before she could answer, he leaned forward, tickled her stomach and laughed. "Knowing our Osh, you may already be in the baby way!"

Ruby grabbed Ocean's leg, hoping he would stop the men being so rude, but he was also laughing.

"We ain't gonna be breeding just yet. Gotta get that club making plenty of money before we start popping 'em out," said Ocean, who appeared to be knocking back the bubbly as if it was apple juice. She noticed his accent had changed and he spoke just like his friends. His words started to ring alarm bells. He talked as if he owned the *Palace*.

"I love the ring, Ocean. Was it your grandmothers?" Ruby could tell it was old and assumed it had a sentimental attachment to it.

Farley roared with laughter. "Well, it belonged to someone's grandmother!" he said between the rapture.

She frowned. "What do you mean?" Her voice was firm now. She'd had enough of the jibes and mockery and Ocean sensed it right away. It was too early in the game to piss her off. "Of course it is, my gal. Had it put away until I found the right woman."

Ruby relaxed. He was a good man, even if his mates were a pain in the backside.

The O'Connells realised they had gone too far and decided to play it Ocean's way.

"Take no notice of us," said Farley. "We are only larking around."

Ruby looked at the three stooges and tried to burst out laughing, but instead she had a sudden urge to cry. This wedding: the best man a pikey, no father to give her away, no bridesmaids, and not a single member of her family there to toast her future happiness. It was a complete shambles. This was looking like a huge mistake – one she would have to live with, like the old saying: 'You made your bed, now lie in it'.

All the excitement, followed by anxiety, had left Ruby at a low point. "Shall we go now, Ocean? I'm a little tired."

Her whining got up Ocean's nose. The drink had been flowing, the laughs were getting louder, and he was having too much fun to leave and end up in a marital bed with a woman he plainly did not fancy.

"Listen, Ruby, I'm gonna have a few more drinks to celebrate… our marriage." He turned his back on her, signifying his distaste for her comment.

She gazed around the pub and realised the grottiness of it. She looked down at her beautiful dress, which may as well have been bought from Oxfam for all the attention anyone gave her. The strong scent from the bouquet was a relief from the vile stench coming from the men's toilets. As the men laughed and talked in a language alien to her, a scruffy, old man came wobbling over to their table. He held a full pint of beer in his hand and swayed. He reminded Ruby of Dopey, out of Snow White and the Seven Dwarfs. Just as he reached the table, he tripped and the contents shot from the glass and completely covered her. She gasped as the beer was so cold, and instantly jumped to her feet, trying desperately to wipe away the brown, wet mess.

The old man, in his paralytic state, tried to apologise. He had only wanted to congratulate them.

Instead of the men getting up to help her, they laughed. They roared uncontrollably, including Ocean, who was red-faced and trying to catch his breath. She ran from the table and headed to the toilets to try to clean the dark stain. The full-length mirror had a crack, giving Ruby the illusion of two dresses. She tried to wash away the marks with wet tissues but, to her dismay and frustration, they crumpled and imbedded into the material. Just as she was about to leave, a young woman came bursting in. She was drunk and giggled at Ruby, "Fancy dress, ain't it?"

She took one more look in the mirror before the tears began to fall. Her world had crashed down around her and she was beside herself with sadness.

The men hadn't noticed Ruby was still missing. An hour passed before Ocean decided to look for his young bride – his future wealth.

She was propped on an old school chair in the ladies' toilets when he walked in.

Her face was swollen from crying and she appeared so sullen he actually felt sorry for her.

"Ruby, what are ya doing?" His voice was gentle as he helped her up from the chair.

"I just want to go home, Ocean," she whispered in a soft and defeated tone.

Ocean panicked. He realised then he had pushed her too far.

"You don't want to go back to your father's, let's go to my flat," he said as he stared into her confused face.

"Ocean… I meant our flat. That is my home now!"

He smiled with relief. "Of course it is, my babe."

His words comforted her and he left the pub with his arms around her shoulders.

Lucky for him, the wedding night was spent with his bride curled in a ball asleep.

Ocean sat in the living room, looking at a blank TV screen, going over the day's events. He didn't know whether he felt sorry for Ruby or if he was suffering from guilt, but whatever it was he couldn't rest. His mind then wandered to Kizzy, as it normally did, and what she would do if she knew. He shuddered and then realised the sense of unease and discomfort was really overwhelming regret. He would have to keep up this pretence and hide this sick secret from his true love. His stomach being in knots sobered him up. All of this to make a better life for Kizzy and him, but what if she got wind of it; how could he explain this? The thoughts rambled around in his head until eventually he fell asleep, still upright on the sofa.

When Friday night arrived, Ocean was nervous and yet excited. He would be walking into the club as part owner with his head held high and whoever got in his way would get fired. He could hear Ruby on the phone. She made excuses not to go into work.

"Jack, I am fine, I promise you, but I am just having a girl's monthly, so if you can get Dad to cover for me, I will be in next week… Yes, Jack, I know it's been a month but I'm okay," was all Ocean heard.

"Ruby!" he called from the living room.

Ruby obediently walked into the lounge to see Ocean looking white and tight-faced.

She turned her head to the side like a confused dog.

"What's up?" she asked.

"I heard you telling Jack you're not going to the club again!"

She nodded.

"Well, are you ashamed of me or something? We are husband and wife now. The sooner you tell them, the better."

Ruby's eyes widened. "Ocean, I'm really not up to it and, besides, we are still on our honeymoon. Why don't we spend time together – just us this weekend?"

His disappointment turned to anger.

"We need to start how we mean to go on. Now then, get your gear on, and let's get to work."

Ruby was flabbergasted. "Ocean, what do you mean, 'let's get to work'?"

Ocean got up from his chair and a sarcastic grin spread across his face.

"As your husband, I will come to work with you. I can't have my beautiful wife looked at by other men, now can I? The sooner they know you are a married woman, the better. I thought we had agreed I should work right alongside you!" He put his arms around her shoulder and kissed her on the forehead.

Ruby knew her father would never have that in a million years. Husband, or not, he was still a gypsy.

"Ocean," her voice was low and sweet, "it's not that simple. My family have to agree to it."

"What?" screeched Ocean. "It's your fucking club, Ruby. Why do you need their permission?"

Ruby frowned. "It's not just my club, it's Jack's too."

Her heart sank. He spoke in such a spiteful manner. It was a side to him she hadn't seen before.

"You never told me he owned it too. You led me to believe it was just yours. It's called *Ruby's Palace*, for fuck's sake!" His mind raced and all he could think about now was how to tell the others that their clever little plan was not very clever after all.

He walked into the kitchen, away from Ruby, to get his thoughts in order, emerging a few moments later. "Ruby, who has the bigger share? Is it you or Jack?" His voice was calm.

Ruby didn't like his questions. The club was none of his business, but she didn't want to upset him.

"I don't know. All I know is the *Palace* was given to Jack and me as a present."

Ocean was irritated by her lack of knowledge and let his guard down. "It doesn't matter, I suppose. I am still part owner, being married to you."

As the words left his tongue, the realisation hit him. And it was too late to take them back.

"I just mean, err... that I can help you become successful as a partner." His feeble excuse for such an outburst didn't wash with Ruby. She suddenly woke up out of a bad dream. Her brain went into gear and she realised Ocean wanted the club, not her. Her heart felt heavy. She looked into the eyes of the first man she really thought she loved and it hurt her like nothing on earth. She searched his face for answers but he stared back, not knowing what to say.

She fled and sat on the bed. Her arms shook and the lump in her throat grew but she refused to cry. She looked around the room. It was suffocating her. The walls closed in and the room darkened; her chest tightened and her breathing became hard. The tingling sensation muddled her thoughts. She dragged herself to her feet but suddenly went crashing to the floor. The loud bang was when she hit her head on the corner of the bed. She lay unconscious for a few minutes. Ocean had left the flat before Ruby had collapsed. There was no one there to see to her when she came to, making her vision of Ocean even more disturbing. She scrambled to her feet, feeling sick and trembling. The room was in focus but her thoughts were still hazy.

She called for her husband but he was gone. Her phone was on the bed and she tried to dial his number. However, it was switched off or he was on the phone talking to someone else.

She saw her car keys on the sofa. In a flash, she snatched them and ran, leaving the flat door open and her belongings behind. She blindly headed to her parked car, hoping her light-headedness left her soon, so she could concentrate on her driving to get home to her dad and Jack. The cool night air was refreshing on her sweaty skin. She sat for a few seconds, drawing in the freshness, before she managed to get herself together and drive the distance home. The radio played an old sixties song and Ruby focused. With the windows down and the music soothing her soul, she eventually made it home safe and sound.

Of course, no one was in, because the busiest night at *Ruby's Palace* was a Friday, and she had given Jack instructions for their father to take her place.

Even though the house was empty, Ruby was comforted. The smell and the warmth enveloped her and her magazines were still on the side and placed neatly. It was strange. Although she had only been away for a month, it was as if her life had moved on ten years. So much had changed in such a short space of time. It had been a real emotional rollercoaster. She was beginning to think she had completely lost the plot by falling in love so quickly, disowning her family, and then marrying a gypsy. She wanted to laugh out loud, but the reflection of her face in the mirror brought her back to reality. She was a Vincent, no mistaking that – and no matter how easy she thought it was to break away from her roots, somehow she always found her way back.

Just as she went to step into a nice hot bath, she heard a knocking on the door. Quickly, she put her dressing gown on. It had been hanging there on the back of the door where she had left it. She hurried down the stairs and, with a deep breath, opened the front door. To her amazement there was Ocean, leaning against the pillar. He looked Ruby up and down without a word. He leaned forward and kissed her gently on the cheek. Frozen to the spot, she never dreamt he would come after her.

"Are you all right, my little Ruby Palace? I was so worried when I came home to find you gone."

Ruby's eyes widened. The reason she had fallen in love so hastily with Ocean was his alluring twinkle. Her stomach knotted up. She wanted to be loved by him, to feel like a newlywed woman, and right now that expression on his face was telling her all those things.

"My Ruby, come home and let us work this out. We are, after all, married now, and we can't be splitting up already."

Ruby stood silently, trying to think of a good reason why she should give him another chance. He had made a complete mockery of their wedding and he had let slip that he wanted part of the club.

He tried to put his arms around her but she remained still, knowing that as soon as she fell into them she would be hooked again and that would be the end of it.

"I'm missing you," he whispered.

His warm breath tickled her ears and a loose curl fell forward and brushed her cheek. A shiver went up her spine.

"Ocean, I thought you married me because you loved me." Her words were soft and fragile. Ocean smiled, a mixture of satisfaction and a hidden laugh.

"I do love you, I love you so very much!" His accent had disappeared and the soft, well-spoken voice returned.

"I don't like it when you're with your friends. You change... you act different... nasty."

Ocean nodded and he didn't argue.

The O'Connells had given him a quick lecture. 'Do whatever it takes to get your hands on that club.' They weren't as worried as him that she had refused to go to work. Ocean had done exactly as they said. He was too close now to throw in the towel. He hadn't expected to find his home empty on his return and so it was fortunate his intuition, or luck of the Irish, had led him to her father's.

"Are you sure you didn't marry me for me money?" Ruby grinned, trying to turn it into a joke but letting him know she was concerned.

Ocean went along with it. "That'll be it. I am after your dosh, your BMW, your club, and your beautiful, sexy body."

She laughed, sucked in again by his charms.

The following week was spent with Ocean joined at the hip to Ruby. He worked hard at showing her how he could be the devoted husband. He wined and dined her, took her to the theatre, and indulged her on a romantic trip up the Thames. By the time Friday had arrived Ruby was hooked again, proud to be Ocean's wife.

Chapter Nineteen

Kizzy

The summer evening was warmer than usual. The horses could be seen in the distance flicking their groomed tails. Kizzy sat on the steps of her caravan, sipping a mug of mint tea and soaking up the warm breeze and the sweet smell of carnations which grew in the pots planted last year by her aunt. They hadn't done too well the last spring but right now they were out in full bloom, a blaze of colours.

Kizzy hoped that Ocean would visit soon. She had grown very fond of him again, and she looked forward to the day they would run off together – running off together was the traditional way of two gypsies being wed. Only, lately he had been behaving strangely, popping over for just an hour and then disappearing again. He hadn't stayed over for a while, due to one reason or another. What puzzled her was the fact that when he did arrive he was always so full of loving words, bunches of flowers and promises of how he would make it all up to her. 'Trust me when I tell you, we will be rich and you can have fields of horses. Just let me do what I have to do,' he would say.

Kizzy wanted to trust him, as he was different now. He showed he loved her and not just to satisfy his sexual appetite – so much more than that. He genuinely admired her and whispered the sweetest, most meaningful words.

From the corner of her eye, Kizzy saw a group of women nattering outside old Mary Anne's caravan. But when Kizzy turned to face them, they quickly looked away.

She usually kept herself to herself and for years now she had kept away from leering eyes and closed her ears to any gossip. Her past had taught her to do that, but they kept looking over towards her and it bothered her. They stood with their big chunky arms folded under their breasts, swaying as if they were rocking babies. Half of the old women had hardly any teeth and one huge smile turned them into Punch out of *Punch and Judy*. Kizzy recognised one of the younger women, Olivia, in her late thirties. By all accounts she had been seeing Billy O'Connell, off and on, over the past year. Not much of a looker herself, she was probably the best malt he could catch.

She had been present all those years ago when Kizzy was sent away from the London site to live with her aunt. She was one of the women who had snubbed Kizzy and was glad to see the back of her. She was jealous then and even more so now. Gypsy women did little with their lives except clean and look after their husbands. Looking at Kizzy, with her beauty and her brains, Olivia beamed with excitement to tell the other women what she had heard. It's amazing what a man will tell you when you're lying in bed and he's itching to have his cock sucked.

Olivia couldn't wait to get back to Kent and spread the news.

"And they fell in love overnight, got married... I mean, proper wed, and she is probably expecting her first chavi," revealed Olivia.

The other women soaked up the gossip and laughed along with her.

"Serves the stuck up cow right!" smirked one of the women, with her head on the side and her finger wagging.

"Look at her, couldn't keep a fella anyhow, loves horses too much, strange girl," said another, and the bitching continued until old Mary Anne jumped up and had her say.

"Now, you lot listen to me. Our Kizzy never did you any harm, now leave her be... and you, Olivia, should be a real malt, and tell her what you know."

No one dared argue with Mary. She was not a woman to mess with. Her sons were prize fighters and adored their mother. They were Romany travellers, as were most of the Kent site, and not a family to be reckoned with – especially her eldest son, Noah. Not many would raise their hand to him.

Olivia's eyes widened. "I can't do that. I promised my Billy boy that I would keep schtum."

Mary took a step forward and nearly stood on Olivia's toes.

Olivia felt the fear envelop her and quickly she stepped back, acknowledging Mary's order. "All right, I'll have a word."

Mary looked Olivia up and down. "You make sure you are kind and gentle, my gal, or you'll have me to answer to..." She took a deep breath before she went on. "I made a solemn promise to our Violet that I would look out for Kizzy, and I ain't about to break my honour for no one!"

Olivia got the message loud and clear and knew she had to be careful. A wrong move and she would have the whole site on her back. No one went against Mary... no one.

Kizzy watched Olivia approach nervously. The years had not been kind to her. Kizzy looked at the deep-set wrinkles from too much sun and the fat around her cheeks. Her front teeth were black and her eyebrows were thick and bushy.

"Kizzy, gal, can I 'ave a word?"

Kizzy nodded and gestured for her to go into the caravan.

Olivia didn't hesitate. The inside was fresh and clean, with not a speck of dust. Jealousy flowed through every vein and she wanted to laugh out loud.

"I just have to tell ya that Ocean..." She paused, looking for a reaction on Kizzy's face.

But she remained still, with one eyebrow raised.

"Ocean has gone and got himself wed, proper wed, to some gorger gal."

Kizzy stared in horror. Was she telling the truth or was this just a sick game?

"I swear it on me father's life!" she went on.

Kizzy nodded slowly and, with the utmost composure, asked, "Who did he marry?"

Olivia, amazed by her calm demeanour, replied, "It's that Vincent gal, the one that owns the club *Ruby's Palace!*"

Again, Kizzy calmly tilted her head in acknowledgement and with that Olivia left. As soon as the door shut, Kizzy's eyes filled and her body shook with pain. The hurt engulfed her and consumed her. This was déjà vu with a vengeance. All she could see in her mind was the scene all those years ago when Ocean had kicked that dirt in her face. But this was far worse. Ocean had seemed different this time. He had seemed so much in love with her and she with him. She sobbed for what seemed like an eternity but was probably only a few minutes. Her feelings and love for Ocean had been thrown back in her face by this two-faced pikey who had had the audacity to fool her – twice.

She tried hard to work out why this was happening to her again. What had she done this time to deserve this cruel treatment; and what about the Vincents, the family, who were the root of the problem? The sad and heart-breaking thoughts went around and around in her head. Then, suddenly, there was a knock on the door. Kizzy had been lying on her bed and must have been crying for ages, because the room was almost in darkness as she went to the door.

Mary Anne stood there, holding two mugs of tea. Kizzy invited her in but decided to have a good look around to see no one else was in sight before she shut the door. However, the spiteful gossiping women had long gone.

She sat down, placing the hot drinks on the honeysuckle-printed coasters which were positioned neatly on the coffee table.

"'Ere, gal, sit with me and drink some tea." Mary felt sadness for Kizzy. She could see her eyes were red and swollen but had admiration for the young woman to act so dignified.

"I know you want to know why, so I asked me boys what's going on up in London!"

She looked up from her tea, eager to hear more.

"I knows your Ocean loves you, Kizzy gal. I might be old, but I ain't blind."

Kizzy laughed between snivels. "Well, I thought he did – I really believed him this time – can't do though, can he? He went and got married."

"Well, that is what I thought, but me boys tell me otherwise."

Kizzy frowned.

"My Zack reckons that it's a scam to get the club. The Vincents owe Ocean and the O'Connells, and they are after what is rightfully theirs!"

She couldn't make sense of what Mary was saying. "How do the Vincents owe them?"

"My Zack boy, believes it goes back years, from when they threatened you, when they beat Billy, Farley and Levi. So they are collecting their dues," she replied.

"But why did my Ocean have to marry her? He was supposed to run off with me!" The tears rolled down her already flushed cheeks.

"I know, my babe, he will, you'll see, he will." Mary held Kizzy's hand.

"But Mary, how can he if he has married her? What woman would marry a man without... well, you know."

Mary turned away, knowing exactly what Kizzy meant and she was right. Ocean, regardless of his intentions, must have had sex with the Vincent girl and that was that.

"I loved him all over again, Mare. He was the only man I ever had and I never stopped loving him. I just learned to live without him. But now it hurts even more, like you couldn't imagine."

Mary moved herself around to sit closer to Kizzy and held her in her arms.

"I know, my babe, I know," she whispered, rocking her as if she were a child.

Mary missed having her daughter. She would have been the same age as Kizzy but drugs had consumed her. She died of an overdose. She hated even the word 'drug' and vowed to beat her sons near to death if they ever even thought about it. Noah was close to his little sister. He loved her cheeky rebel streak and had watched out for her. That was, until he got locked away for a few years. In that time she became addicted to hard core gear and died, leaving Noah racked with guilt and grief. He made a vow to kill the culprit who got her hooked and would never stop searching until he found them.

Soon after Mary left, Kizzy got her thoughts together and decided that this time she would not be the one running away. She would show the O'Connells, her so called family, and Ocean, her supposed boyfriend, that they shouldn't have messed with her, not back then and not now.

Kizzy looked at herself in the mirror and held her head high. She was an independent woman with no need to chase after any mush. No man was going to look after her. She was more than capable of doing that herself. After all, she had grown up without a mother and even though she had been surrounded by men, most of them meant nothing to her and so she had learned to be alone. In fact, she was alone most of her life, in her heart that is. Apart from her uncle, who cared but was most of the time fairly cold, and of course his sister, her Aunt Violet who died, there really wasn't any family as such. No one at the site really gave a shit if Kizzy was there or not.

As the night brought its dark clouds, and the cool air drifted in, Kizzy lay awake with her stomach caving in. Waves of sickness crept over her. Every time she closed her eyes she could see his face. The tiredness exaggerated her mind. She became confused and overwhelmed by her loss. It was as if he had died, yet she visualised him with his curls bouncing off his shoulders, dressed in a smart suit, the colour of his eyes. She saw him in her dreams: toasting his new bride, laughing and swaying to a slow song, their first dance. She saw her parading in a flowing white dress with Ocean looking on in admiration. Then her thoughts would go to that deep, forbidden place, the place which would haunt her on his wedding night. In her mind she sadistically faced the inevitable: her Ocean, making love to Ruby, surrounded by red petals with candles burning and him whispering 'I love you' in her ear.

She grieved for him – for what they'd had and what they had shared. All that remained now were the ghosts of their relationship, tormenting her.

*

As the sun appeared, Kizzy sat up and rubbed her sore limbs, which hadn't rested either. She had tossed and turned, and, with tense muscles, she felt battered. The morning breeze was refreshing. She wanted more than anything to clear away the cobwebs and to remove the pain from her mind. She ruffled her long wavy hair, pulled on a cotton dress, and headed for the horses' field. The dew which covered the grass squelched between her toes.

Kizzy's new horse, Bailey, was by the gate watching her approach. A big cob, one of the biggest in the field, he came from a good breed but had been sold as wild. Not to be ridden though, only for breeding. As Kizzy tickled his nose he quivered his lip. She walked him over to the stool and he stopped just as she told him. She climbed onto him, clutching at his mane. Normally, Kizzy would not have saddled up a young, inexperienced horse, especially this one. However, this morning she felt no fear, her pain was so great that a fall from her horse would not have hurt half as much. Bailey stayed calm as she whispered words of comfort. There was something peaceful about him. Gently, she tapped his sides with her feet and slowly he moved on. The air was fresh, the sky was blue and Kizzy thanked her horse for accommodating her. She took Bailey into a canter and then she galloped, with the wind rushing through her hair.

Two men setting off for work noticed Kizzy riding bareback on the wild horse and called for the others to come and see. Mary Anne heard the commotion and leapt from her caravan to look. A small crowd had gathered and watched in disbelief as Kizzy raced around the field on the back of the wild horse.

"Mary, we had better try to stop her. That horse is a fucker, it ain't been broken in yet, she'll get poggered," said Jimmy Cottle, a middle-aged man, showing genuine concern for Kizzy.

"Well, it looks fairly broken in to me. Never would a beast like that let anyone ride it if it weren't," replied Mary, who was now admiring the guts of the girl.

"Mare, I'm telling you, that cob was sold to her as wild as they come. The old man, Driscoll, who practically gave that horse to Kizzy, says it can't be trained. Says he is good for breeding but can't be ridden!"

Kizzy was oblivious to the gathering crowd. Bailey wasn't, he was showing off. She enjoyed the freedom, the rush of the wind on her face and the exhilarating feeling of galloping at tremendous speed. Bailey did not try to rear up or throw her off. There was a total balance of rhythm.

She was the only one who could handle him but her secret was time, space and consideration. A powerful horse, with a strong personality, it took a person like Kizzy, with a good understanding of horses, to tame him. He ran with grace and speed and was built for it.

"She's just showing off!" grumbled Olivia, still hateful towards Kizzy, but she hadn't noticed who was standing behind her.

Mary Anne tapped Olivia on the shoulder. As soon as she turned around, her face went pale. She hated to get on the wrong side of the older gypsies, especially those who had a lot of clout, and Mary Anne was one of them.

"You wanna shut your mouth, woman!"

The attention turned away from Kizzy and on the two women who were about to fight.

"See that gal up there on her horse? Well, let me tell you, she has got more guts than anyone on this site, and it won't surprise me if, one day, she don't pogger you!"

Olivia bowed her head, as she knew that Mary Anne was right. After all, there was no way anyone would normally get on a wild horse bare back.

"And another thing, don't push her too far. Mark my words, that young Kizzy will only take so much, and the day she turns will be the day you wished you had never been born. I know what I'm talking about. The girl is just as I was at her age," said Mary Anne.

Olivia felt humiliated and silently sneaked away.

The crowd soon realised that there was no accident waiting to happen, as Kizzy had the horse completely under control. A few stayed to watch brave Kizzy but most went back about their business.

"Fearless, that malt!" said Jimmy before he walked off.

Mary nodded.

The horse finally came to a stop down by the bank. Kizzy was exhilarated. Her face glowed pink and she breathed hard to catch her breath. Bailey drank from the stream and Kizzy slid down to join him. She scooped the water and slurped before she washed her face.

He contentedly grazed the buttercup field while she lay contemplating her future. The bees buzzed around and the tiny gnats gathered above Bailey's head. The sun beating down, the smell of the meadow grass, the sound of the water trickling down, the stream so perfect – Kizzy sighed heavily. She wished she had never let Ocean back into her life – her new life, free of greed, insincerity and skulduggery. Maybe she was more like her mother, the gorger, rather than her father, the gypsy. She didn't want to live a life filled with lies. She knew it didn't have to be that way.

She decided there and then that she would do what was right. The O'Connells meant nothing to her, except Uncle Johnnie. Billy, Farley and Levi, on the other hand, gave her nothing but grief. If what she was about to do affected them, well, then tough.

Chapter Twenty

Ruby was nervous to say the least. She was to introduce Ocean to her family as her husband and it was anyone's guess how they would react. Her thoughts flowed from imagining a smooth introduction, whereby her father and brother would shake Ocean's hand and wish them good luck in their marriage, to the other extreme, where they'd go unduly mad and make life unbearable.

She paced the living room floor, very uneasy.

"Ruby, it will be all right. Stand your ground. You're a grown woman! And, for Christ's sake, I saved your life don't forget!"

Ocean was irritated her family had so much control over her. He just wanted to march into the club and throw his weight around.

He and the O'Connells had decided to wait until he had his feet well and truly under the table before they made their move. They had planned their scam down to a tee. Ocean was to take it easy, play the dutiful husband, help out in the bar and on the door, and gradually take over, letting Ruby believe all the changes were her ideas. They had come too far to blow it now.

"Ruby, go and get ready, or we will be late!"

She did as she was told, after she had made a quick call to her brother to let him know she was on her way.

Finally she emerged from the bedroom, dressed in a black satin dress with her hair curled and wearing red shoes to match her glamorous clutch bag. Ocean smiled. She actually looked attractive. She had obviously listened to his suggestions not to wear too much makeup or any fake tan. But she'd never compete with his Kizzy in that department. He sighed at the thought.

"What's up?" she asked.

"You look lovely, Kiz…" He stumbled over his words, realising he had nearly called her Kizzy.

Ruby frowned. Ocean quickly jumped in. "Give us a kiss!" He giggled, to which she responded by throwing her arms around his neck and whispering, "I love you."

*

Jack was in the bathroom getting ready for work, and Sam was still moving his food around on the plate, when the doorbell rang. Sam rushed to answer it, hoping that it was Ruby.

"'Ello, mate." Sam gestured for Fred to come in. "What's up, ain't you supposed to be at the club?"

Fred walked indignantly into the living room. Sam sensed something was wrong.

"Our Ruby's only gone and got herself married to that dirty fucking pikey, Ocean!" announced Fred.

Sam stopped in his tracks. "She can't have!"

Fred flopped on to the sofa and loosened his jacket. "I'm afraid so."

There was silence whilst Sam poured them both a drink. He tried to comprehend what had just been said but he found it too hard to believe.

"One of the boys down the gym told me."

He gulped his drink and quickly tightened his lips, showing his back teeth. The brandy had a bitter taste.

"Yeah, but you know what that lot are like, a fucking bunch of gossiping girls. They've got it wrong."

"Well, that's what I thought, but then I asked Dan's cleaners, those two old pikeys who clean *Dan's Palace*."

Sam nodded. He guessed they were from the site.

"They confirmed it, so I hate to tell ya, mate, but she has married that little shit." Fred loosened his tie and ran his hands through his hair. He took a deep breath. "Does anyone know where she is?"

"Nope, it's like she's disappeared from the face of the earth, and you know those fucking pikeys. It's like finding a needle in a haystack," replied Sam.

Jack descended the stairs, with nothing but a towel round his waist.

"I thought I heard you, Uncle Fred."

He smiled at his nephew, admiring how he kept himself trim and tight.

"What was that about Ruby?" Jack asked.

Sam looked at his bright-eyed son. "I might as well tell ya... Our Ruby has gone off and married that Ocean fella."

Jack screwed his face up. "You're kidding!"

Both men shook their heads.

"Worst of it is, we have no clue where she is!" exclaimed Sam.

"Well, you will tonight. She has just phoned to say she is coming to work and bringing someone she wants us to meet!"

Sam jumped to his feet. "Oh yeah, I wanna meet the bastard all right. I'm gonna fucking kill him!"

"No, you won't, leave him to us. I'll get rid of him, the proper way," suggested Fred, with a sadistic smirk across his mouth.

Jack abruptly interrupted. "Stop it, you two, just listen to yourselves. This is Ruby we're talking about, not a stranger. If you do that we will lose our Rubes for good."

Sam was raging. His face took on a spiteful expression and his knuckles turned white from gripping the glass.

"Shut your mouth, Jack! I ain't having no daughter of mine married to a dirty pikey. All I've done for that girl, and she goes and shits on me..." He paused to catch his breath. "She shits on all of us. Only known the boy for a few weeks, and puts him before her own family."

Jack went up the stairs and Sam sat back onto the sofa. "I adored that kid, she was so sweet, but now all I see is her fucking mother." He turned to face his brother. "I've tried hard to raise her the right way, with proper values, and respect, but she is a selfish cow and sly with it, just like Jesse. I mean, whatever possessed her to up and leave, marry a gypo, and only fucking contact us through a text message every so often to Jack?"

Fred would normally have jumped to Ruby's defence, her being the baby, but this time he couldn't. She had overstepped the mark.

"I have given her everything she has ever wanted. When she is in trouble, the only people to help are her family, and what does she do? She marries a fucking no-good Irish tinker."

Fred hated to see his brother hurting and he tried to change the subject.

"Celia turned up."

"What?" snapped Sam.

"Yeah, I forgot to tell you. She went away for a short break. We think she has hit it off with Johnnie's brother – good luck to her – well, anyway, she is safe and sound. I told her to manage *Ruby's Palace* until Ruby gets back."

Sam flashed a glance at Fred.

"I ain't fucking having Ruby back in her club until she is rid of that pikey, and that's not up for negotiation. I just can't get me head around it, her married to a pikey!"

"Love does funny things to ya, mate. Look at our Dolly, she loved her husband and he tried to kill her. She never really knew him, did she? But she married the cunt!" said Fred.

Sam was silent, gripped by a mixture of emotions. They never talked about Francesca's past. It was too painful for any of them. "Fred, our Ruby is nothing like our sister. I wish she was. She might have fallen in love and all that soppy bollocks, but for fuck's sake, she should have used her brains. It ain't like she's a silly slip of a kid. She's a grown woman!"

Fred didn't even attempt to argue. Sam, as his older brother, was once the quieter one, but lately he had more to say, and harsh words too. Rarely did he put his foot down. Dan usually called the shots and the others followed, unless, of course, Francesca was present. Then all ears would be listening to her. Like a pack, they all comfortably fulfilled a role. Yet, lately, Ruby didn't seem part of it. She was the lone wolf wandering off to start her own pack. Maybe they expected too much from her, secretly wishing she was another Francesca. Fred snapped out of his contemplation when Jack returned dressed in his suit but red-faced. "Dad, I heard that. You can't stop her, it's her club as well."

"Jack, don't stick up for her now, I've had enough of your damn whining. If I say she is not allowed in the place while she is with him, then she ain't stepping foot over the fucking door... got it?" He poked a rude finger in Jack's chest, causing Jack to back away.

"You're gonna push her away for good if you start that shit!" shouted Jack, who was annoyed. He detested being pushed or poked. He had always protected Ruby, but even he wondered why he should. After all, she had betrayed them. He also wished his sister was more like them and had to admit she was different. Rebelling was one thing, and they had laughed in the past at her antics, but going against the family was wrong on every level.

Fred was ready to leave when Sam jumped up. "'Ere, Fred, before you go, make me right." said Sam, with his arms open wide.

Fred hugged Sam and then looked at his nephew, "You're a good boy, and we know you love to look out for your sister, always have and probably always will, but your dad is right. We can't have pikeys in the clubs. It's a strict policy." Fred gave his nephew a sympathetic smile before he left.

"Sit, son, I want to talk to you." Sam's voice was calm so Jack did as he was told.

"Your sister has made her choice. She knew full well we'd never accept a gypsy into the family or the business. They cannot be trusted. If I don't stand my ground now, she will take us all down..." Sam took another gulp of brandy and swirled the ice cubes around the glass. "We have trusted her to run the club, but she is not the only Vincent. There's your future, but not only you, there's little Alfie and Sophie."

Jack frowned. He thought his father was being dramatic. Ruby had only married a gypsy; it wasn't the end of the earth. It didn't surprise him much – Ruby had always had a wild streak in her.

"You don't get it, do you?"

Jack shook his head and replied confidently, "Nope!"

"If your sister gets wrapped up with those muppets then, trust me, they will be in that club and taking over and we won't have a bloody business. The same happened to the Nappers' clubs. And Jack, your uncles and me ain't getting any fucking younger. Ruby, mixed up with those London pikeys, is just stirring up a hornet's nest."

Jack realised his father obviously knew more than he did and decided to take the situation more seriously.

"So, what do we do now then?"

Sam smiled with relief.

"Call your sister and tell her to meet us at the club alone."

He rushed to the phone and dialled her mobile – to no avail.

"She's not answering."

"Bitch!" spat Sam.

Jack bit his bottom lip. He still found it hard not to bite back at a comment like that, even if it came from their father.

"You get yourself off to work and keep your wits about you. I have no idea what will happen tonight."

"For fuck's sake, Dad, she is only bringing him over to meet us, not the complete posse."

"Pikeys are never on their fucking own!"

Jack gave a heavy sigh and left.

Sam called his brother. "Do us a favour, Dan, send a couple of your guys over to the kids' *Palace* to watch the door."

"Calm yourself, mate, you sound wound up. I have already done it. Celia tells me that the travellers tried to get into *Little Palace* a few weeks ago, pushing cocaine, just before it burned to the ground. She is on her way as we speak. She can sniff out a traveller a mile away."

Dan didn't mention Ruby. He decided it best to keep his thoughts to himself. "I wish our Dolly was here. She'd have the answers."

Sam laughed. "I dread to think what she'd make of it. One thing's for sure. She would stop this fiasco in its tracks, one way or another."

"Best not tell her, we'll sort it ourselves. No point in her worrying across the pond."

Jack arrived at the club and was surprised to see so many members of staff. He bit his lip in temper when he saw the two bouncers, the size of Mike Tyson, standing like typical doormen, feet apart with their hands crossed in front of them. They had the radios on – the works. The queuing guests would think they were likely to see a celebrity. Jack nodded at them and they in turn both nodded respectfully back.

Inside the club, Celia was busy checking the bottles and the tills, usually done by Ruby. Jack didn't know whether to laugh or cry. This was his and Ruby's business. They had always managed to keep any little issue under control. Now, it was as if he and Ruby didn't exist.

"'Ello, babe, look at you, you get more handsome every day." Celia had a soft spot for him; he was very much a Vincent, but with a softer nature.

"Hi, Celia, good to see you too. So glad you weren't caught up in the fire." Celia reddened. Jack was so charming and polite. It always got to her.

"Have you seen Ruby? Has she arrived yet?" He looked over Celia's shoulder towards the office.

Celia was uncomfortable. She had been given strict instructions not to let Ruby behind the bar if she turned up with the gypsy.

She shook her head and continued counting the soft drinks.

Jack returned to the door, where the bouncers stepped aside, allowing him to stand in front of them. The queues seemed endless.

*

Sam wandered around Ruby's room. His heart had been ripped out. He thought about his little girl, with the enchanting lisp and beaming smiles, and tears filled his eyes. Why she had to go and marry a man she barely knew, who would never be accepted into the family, was beyond him. He closed her door, left the house, and headed for the club.

*

Jack, now standing in his rightful position, decided to switch off from the situation and just go about his job as if nothing had changed.

A taxi pulled up and Jack's eyes crept over to the woman who stepped out. Too far away for him to see who she was, he half expected his sister. He continued to stare. A gust of warm air blew her thick, dark curls and ruffled her white, flowy dress. She had a grace like Aunt Francesca. The girl joined the queue, looking at the floor, and Jack was surprised to see she was alone. It was rare for women to come to a nightclub without friends or a boyfriend.

At nine o'clock on the dot, Jack nodded to the doormen. "Open her up!"

The crowd became excited. Like Noah's ark, they entered two by two and were searched and released to drink and dance the night away.

A group of girls flirted outrageously with Jack – nothing new there! He laughed it off and sent them in. Jack's interest was with the dark-haired woman who slowly approached.

"Boys, let me check her over."

The doormen grinned.

As she reached the gold rope, which acted as a gate, Jack allowed her through and asked her to step aside.

He could clearly see she was very nervous. "Hey, it's all right. I don't bite, I only want to peek into your bag."

She looked up and smiled. He was so much like his uncles, but not so hard-looking. He was a smoother version, if there was such a thing. Her legs wobbled and for a second she thought she was making a huge mistake.

There was something familiar about her, but he couldn't place her. "Do I know you?" he smiled.

"Maybe." She hoped he wouldn't turf her out as his uncles had done before.

Jack, quite taken by her coyness, stared at her smoky eyes, admiring the complexion of her soft, tanned skin.

Her traveller's accent had gone. She had listened very carefully to her aunt when she'd told her, 'Keep your ways, but don't be loose with your gypsy tongue. It doesn't always do us any favours.'

Kizzy could talk as a gorger more easily than most. Her transformation from child to woman had added a simple charm of sophistication.

She opened her little white and gold clutch bag. Instead of peeking in, he gazed at her and nodded approval.

"It's fine, you may enter." He bowed.

The two doormen nudged each other. It was rare for Jack to flirt with his customers.

Kizzy's spirits were lifted for a moment. There she was, being fussed over by a Vincent, the club owner. She turned her head to the side slightly and blushed.

"Let me buy you your first drink. It's obvious this is your first time here," offered Jack as he led her to the bar.

Kizzy didn't refuse. After all, he was a very attractive man with a kindness about him and she was single now.

"What would you like, err…" He waited for her to tell him her name.

"Oh, yes, may I have a vodka and orange, please?"

He said no more but carried the drinks over to a table. Kizzy, more confident now, sat with her back to the bar, facing Jack.

He had broken a golden rule: never drink with a customer, but he couldn't help himself. He was attracted to the stranger with eyes he had seen before.

"So, what's your name?" he asked.

"Kizzy."

"That's pretty, where's it from? Surely it's not English?" he asked.

She wanted to say 'It's a silly gypsy name which I got lumbered with,' but she took his compliment and replied, "I think it's Spanish."

For a minute, she forgot the reason for her being there, but then good old reality came bouncing back.

"Hey, Kizzy, what's wrong, you look upset?" He stared into her smouldering eyes. His sensitivity made him susceptible to people's moods.

She hadn't planned on this: a drink with Jack, and it all being very nice. She took a deep breath. "I am here because I have a message to give to Ruby."

He leaned his head to the side, a Vincent trait.

"I'm sorry, but I have some bad news for her."

"Go on, sweetheart, what is it?"

"She has married a man called Ocean, and he is a traveller. It was supposed to be a secret." Her voice cracked.

"Tell me something I don't know," he replied.

"Am I the last one to know then?" she almost cried.

"Kizzy, I'm lost here, darling. What's all this got to do with you?" His tone remained soft and sweet but with an air of urgency.

"Sorry, Jack, to be the bearer of bad news, considering you don't even know me. Ocean was supposed to be marrying me." She watched Jack's face. It changed from a sweet expression to anger and his eyebrows began to narrow in the middle.

"So how do you know my name?" he asked.

"Because when I was young, I trained at your family's gym and, this is going to sound totally off the wall, but I was a pole dancer at your uncle's other club when I was fifteen, so I do know who you are." She looked at the floor in embarrassment.

"Hey, we all have a past and, come to think of it, I do remember an incident with a young pole dancer. So that was you then?"

She glanced up to check the expression on Jack's face and was surprised to see a smile.

"So, Kizzy, tell me this. Why did Ocean suddenly, and I mean suddenly, want to marry Ruby? He didn't even know her!"

"The excuse I was given was he wanted to get his hands on the club."

Jack stared for a short while before finishing his drink. He looked around, his mind racing. How was he going to tell his sister and how the hell could he remain calm? He was sick to death of people trying to take advantage of Ruby. Tonight, if that Ocean turned up, he was going to show the man what it was like to go a few rounds with no headgear on with a champion boxer. Ocean was an evil monster and Jack was as bitter as his seething father.

He looked back at Kizzy.

"So I take it you're a…" He didn't want to say traveller.

She nodded shyly. "Well, actually, I am only half a gypsy, and I am partly ashamed of that too."

He grabbed her hand. "Not everyone comes from an ideal family." He was referring to his mother.

"Kizzy, is there any doubt in your mind? Are you sure that Ocean is only after Ruby for the club?"

"I can't be one hundred per cent sure, but that's the rumour."

"Kizzy, why have you come to us? What's in it for you?" he asked.

She was annoyed now. He had assumed that because she was a gypsy – well, part gypsy – she was out for what she could get.

"Jack, I have made a mistake in coming here." She got up to leave. "And, just to let you know, there was nothing in it for me. I don't want Ocean back, or him to hurt anyone. I just thought it was wrong what's going on. Like I said, I'm not all gypsy. We are not all like the O'Connells."

Tears filled her eyes and she stood up gracefully and walked away. Jack was totally blown over. His emotions were all over the place.

"Oi, wait!" he shouted.

Kizzy carried on, weaving through the crowd, with tears streaming down her face.

Eventually he managed to grab her by the arm and swing her around. He saw the cheap mascara smudged over her cheeks and he pulled her into his arms.

"Hey, don't cry. I didn't mean to judge you. I just wanted to understand if there was any more to this mess."

Kizzy didn't pull away, comfortable in his embrace. She had been lonely for such a long time, and not even the odd visit from Ocean had changed that.

He walked her to the back of the club and into the office. It wasn't as big as the office at *Dan's Palace*, which Kizzy had imprinted in her memory, but it still had a Vincent vibe. She wasn't afraid now. Jack had relieved her of her anxiety and she was beginning to trust him. She sat on the leather chair and Jack perched himself on the table.

"Well, girl, when Ocean and Ruby walk in here tonight, they are gonna have a fucking shock, I can tell you."

Kizzy smiled, her black mascara still streaking her cheeks.

He pulled some wipes from the drawer and cleaned her face as if she was a child. She didn't say a word but just looked admiringly into his steel-blue eyes.

"Maybe this time my rebel of a sister will fucking listen this time!"

Kizzy laughed. "Is she a rebel then?"

Jack raised his eyes to the ceiling. "I'm the boxer in the family, but she's the bloody fighter. Always been the same."

As she laughed her face lit up and captivated Jack's attention. He enjoyed her company, finding her charmingly attractive.

The back door slammed shut and, like a gust of wind, Sam marched in, followed by Fred. "Well, Jack, has she turned up yet?" Sam had completely ignored the young woman sitting on the leather chair.

"No, Dad, but there's something you had better know." He nodded at Kizzy.

Sam looked her way but was so wound up about his daughter he didn't recognise who she was. Fred, however, stared for a while and then, like a light coming on, he remembered. "You're that Kizzy girl!"

Her eyes lowered to the floor. She began to shake. Her fear of the Vincents was genuine. She may have exaggerated what they did to her but, nevertheless, she was now frightened for her life. She hadn't realised then that they were only pretending.

Instantly, Jack jumped to her defence. "Kizzy has come here to tell us that Ocean is only after Ruby for the club. He was supposed to be married to her!" He gently rubbed her arm.

Sam looked at Kizzy and then back at his son.

"Is this some kinda joke? You're fucking listening to another pikey. Whatever 'as got into my kids?" exclaimed Sam, throwing his hands in the air.

Kizzy jumped up from her seat, visibly trembling. "Please listen, Mr Vincent, I am not lying. Ocean and my cousins have been after the clubs for years now, and I guess they have stooped to the lowest depths to get there. I will leave you alone. I don't want any trouble, but just be warned, that's all."

Fred was amazed by how Kizzy had changed so much – from a rebellious, mouthy teenager, to a sophisticated young woman with no obvious scruples.

"Hang on a minute, you ain't going nowhere!" snapped Fred.

Jack was outraged and shouted, "Leave it out, she is doing us a favour!"

Fred didn't mean to shout and sound so sharp. "No, sorry, love. I meant, don't go yet. Have a few drinks on us, and I'll call you a cab when you're ready."

Sam's head was so full of shit, he took a deep breath and sighed.

"Well, it just gets fucking better," laughed Sam falsely.

"Right then. When she arrives, pretend all is sweet and take her into the office. I'll drag Ocean outside." Fred was ready to take the gypsy far away and give him the pasting of his life.

Sam nodded, along with Jack, eager for Ocean to have a taste of the Vincents.

"How thick are those London pikeys? He can't really think that our Ruby owns the *Palace*? The fucking idiot. Don't he know you and your sister just run it, and that it's owned by the Vincent empire?" spat Sam.

Jack shrugged his shoulders. "It's probably Rubes showing off that got her into this mess."

Chapter Twenty One

Ruby bit her bottom lip before she announced to Ocean she was going to go to her father's first to break the news there. But he couldn't hide his feelings.

"For fuck's sake, what is it with you? Are you afraid of your own family or ashamed of me?"

Ruby shook her head. "No, no, it's not like that, I just think it's fair, all around, if I tell my dad alone and not at the *Palace*. It makes sense not to cause a scene!"

Ocean sighed. He had gone this far and thought it best to go along with her wishes.

"Okay, Ruby, do it your way. I will meet you there in an hour. I'll be in the car park."

She nodded and set off in her own car.

Ocean tore out of the car park, with smoke billowing from the exhaust, almost blowing up the engine. He dialled Billy's number. One ring, and Billy answered, "Yeah, Oshi, where you at?"

"I am on me way to the club. The malts gone to her farver's to tell him we are wed, and I'm joining her later. Cor, I would love to see his fucking mush when she tells him." He laughed.

Billy laughed more than he should, to the flummoxed Ocean. "What's so funny?"

"Noffin, Osh. You, me boy, will be in for a surprise!"

Ocean ignored Billy's comments which were usually full of shit. He was nervous but knew Ruby wouldn't have her family disrespect him. He had worked too hard brainwashing her; he was very confident she saw things his way. Billy sat back and sadistically smiled at Farley and Levi as he dialled a number. A woman's voice answered. "Where is she?"

"Okay, girl. Ruby is on her way to her farver's. My guess is you will be there before her. Ya know what ya doing?"

A disgruntled voice on the other end replied, "I'm one step ahead of you. I'm already here. The ol' man's gone. Just gonna be me and her!"

Ruby was concerned with getting to her father's house before he left for the club. Luckily, there wasn't too much traffic on the road and she managed to reach there in record time. She pulled into the drive and hoped the reason for her dad's motor not being there was because Jack had borrowed it. The house was in darkness except for the porch light.

Ruby stepped out of her car and hastily marched to the door. As she fumbled in her bag for the key, she heard a rustling sound from the thick bushes which lined the drive. Funny, she thought – normally any action in the front garden, even a fox, would set off the sensor. She found the key and let herself in.

"Dad, are you in?" she shouted, as she headed for the kitchen at the back of the house.

"Jack?"

The front door slammed shut and she realised she had left it open. She was always being told off for not shutting it properly.

"Dad, is that you?" There was no answer. The wind must have blown it shut.

Ruby felt comfortable. She missed her home; the smells, the soft carpets, in fact, all the luxuries.

Climbing the stairs to go to her room, she stopped midway. There was an unusual smell of cheap perfume. She thought maybe Jack had a girlfriend with no taste or, worse, her dad may be dating. The hairs on the back of her neck stood on end. There was something not quite right. The silence seemed threatening. In the depths of quiet, she thought she could hear someone breathing. Ruby froze for a few seconds, trying hard to listen. There was a menacing stillness. She took a deep breath and concluded she was being paranoid.

Her bedroom door was open and gingerly she walked in. The curtains were closed, which was unusual. The smell of cheap perfume was stronger; it was so bad that it almost burnt the insides of her nostrils. The door slammed shut behind her and Ruby jumped. As she turned around, a nauseous feeling swept over her: a foreboding feeling which sent a tingle through her jaw and down her neck, tightening every muscle, constricting her from moving. There, in the shadow, was the outline of a woman.

With a dry mouth she mumbled, "Mum?"

Jesse stepped out of the darkness and stood in front of the door, dressed in black jeans and a black top. Her hair was tied back and she was fatter in the face than Ruby remembered. Her grin revealed a set of white teeth instead of the black and rotting mess they were before.

"That's right, Ruby, it's me."

Both women stared at each other. Ruby noticed the glint of a shiny object partially hidden behind Jesse's back. She tried to think of a way out and all that came to mind was to offer Jesse a cup of tea.

"Can I get you a drink?"

"No, Ruby, I haven't come here for tea." She appeared so different that even her voice had altered.

"It's good to see you, Mum. How have you been?" Why did she ask such a stupid question?

"I've been good, no more drugs, no more drink. In fact, Ruby, I have never felt as clear-headed as I do right now. Amazing, how years in the nick can change your appearance and sober your thoughts." Her voice was hostile and intelligent.

"What are you doing here, anyway?" She tried to sound confident but inside she was petrified.

"I came to give you something you deserve." There was no expression on her face.

"Dad will be back in a minute, and won't be too pleased to find you here." She was almost hysterical.

Jesse rolled her eyes. "Ruby, your dad has gone to work with your precious brother, so don't worry. I'll have you all to myself for hours." She was calm and collected.

"Mum, I need a drink, let me get you one!" She stepped forward towards the door as she kept her eyes on the shiny object.

Jesse laughed and with one great clout across Ruby's face she sent her reeling along the floor.

"You, my girl, ain't going nowhere!"

There was a moment of stillness as Ruby looked up at her mother. Suddenly, as if a veil had been lifted, the concrete blocks which held back those horrific memories crumbled and the truth of the past flooded back. Ruby saw her mother's hand coming towards her. She was three, it was cold, and she was afraid. 'Jack,' she silently cried for her brother, her saviour.

Fear gripped her, but she wasn't afraid of her mother, not now, not at twenty-one, surely not? She was a good fighter, whereas Jesse was a mere waif of a woman and older. But her mind would not escape from the past, when she was a toddler, and her mother was the boogie man.

The room was dark and damp. She was so hungry and her ear was burning from the hard slap which had caught her mouth and those long fingers which had ripped at her tiny earlobes. She bled. She vividly recalled the suffering, the torment and cruelty. The fear which clutched her then was controlling her now. Her courage and confidence were being sucked out of her. Jack had been right. Her mother had abused her, mercilessly beat her, and deprived her of love. No wonder she had never remembered it at all. It was for her own sanity that she had blocked it out. The helplessness was consuming her and, weak with dread, she was powerless to fight back. *Jack, where are you?* He was always there, trying to stop the slaps, stealing food, keeping her warm at night, his hand always gripping hers. She saw him standing in front of her. They cowered from the mother who was towering above them. She was shouting and swearing and clouting them so hard they were sent reeling across the floor.

She had to get a grip. She wasn't three anymore, but the imbedded terror wouldn't leave her.

Jesse grinned. She was empowered by the fear on her daughter's face. That same pathetic expression as when she had been slapped for wetting the bed.

Ruby tried to get to her feet but a sharp, hard kick knocked her back.

"Why?" she screamed at her mum. "Why did you hate me so much?"

There was a long pause as Jesse stared at Ruby. There was a mix of emotions. First, she was elated her daughter was suffering, but then, secondly, she was confused. Why did she hate Ruby, really?

The very first time she had laid eyes on the baby she had felt sadness, not for Ruby but for herself, knowing that the probability of this child being Sam's was high. The blue eyes and mop of black hair instantly took away the doubt and the hope. Her heart sank. She had wanted to throw the baby against the wall, pretend she had died at birth, but she didn't; she had taken the kid home and suffered in silence.

Kenneth knew that there was a chance he was the father and had promised Jesse the world. He would leave his wife, give Jesse partnership in the clubs, and look after her and their daughter, even little Jack. Celia couldn't have children, he thought, and he had wanted what was missing in his life: a child, his child.

She swallowed hard. Kenneth had been the light in her life, the road to a better future. He was older and, while not as good-looking as Sam, she loved the way he loved her, and her only hope was that the child was his. There had been clarity from the beginning. 'If she's mine, I'll marry you; if not, then sling your hook'.

She wasn't his, though; she was her father's daughter all right. She was a Vincent. If only she'd been born with a slight red or even fair tint to her hair. If only her eyes had been brown or green. But they weren't. They were that bright and shiny blue, just like Jack's, like Sam's. In fact, they were the same as every one of the damned Vincents.

Along with the disappointment came the unsightly stretch marks, the crumbling teeth, and the sleepless nights. Of course Ruby was difficult: she was an addict at birth. But was it really Ruby's fault? Jesse didn't care. Her failings and hardship were all down to her daughter, so she anchored her feelings of hate on her.

"You and the Vincents have taken my life away from me and now I have nothing. Your family will know what it's like to feel like I do!"

Ruby was convinced then her own mother wanted to take her life.

She tried again to get to her feet but another hard kick deadened her leg and she fell down again.

"But why, Mum? Why me?"

Jesse laughed: a false, sadistic laugh. "Because you were supposed to be Kenneth Napper's, not a fucking Vincent." There, it was said.

Ruby took a while before the penny dropped but there was nothing she could say.

Another kick came. This time it was to Ruby's stomach. She winced and doubled over. Her bag was tucked up under her and she knew her only hope of rescue was to phone someone.

Ruby's hands scrambled around inside her bag, desperately searching for the mobile. She was hiding her actions. There it was. She snatched it, instantaneously pressing the redial button. The last call she had made was to Jack. With her hand still inside, Jesse kicked again, this time sending the bag and phone flying across the room. However, she hadn't realised that Ruby had just dialled the number and now the phone was lying on the floor and Jack could hear everything.

"Mum! Mum, please stop!" Ruby's voice was high pitched and terrified.

"Please don't kill me, not in my bedroom!" she cried repeatedly, as she prayed her brother had answered the phone and could hear her.

The knife came down and plunged into Ruby's arm. Her swift movement had diverted the blade away from her chest.

Frantically, she rolled under her bed, hoping her mother could not reach her. Jesse fell to her knees and tried fishing under the bed for a limb to drag Ruby out. The pain in Ruby's arm wasn't as bad as it looked. The blood was seeping along the floor but the fear was greater. Ruby was like a caged animal. She snatched Jesse's hand and bit down hard, causing Jesse to scream. But that didn't stop her. She gripped Ruby's ankle and dragged her out. With the other hand she plunged the knife into Ruby's leg.

"Now take that, you fucking little tramp," spat Jesse.

Ruby was struck twice now and felt faint. Her blood was everywhere – thick and warm. The pain was excruciating. Ruby took a deep breath, trying to hold on to reality. She needed help or she would die.

Jesse got to her feet and looked at the red liquid and the pleading look on her daughter's face. The leg wound was more serious. It had severed the main artery and was pumping blood everywhere.

"Thought I wouldn't get you back, did ya? Thought I would forget all the shit you and your family put me through? Oh no, this lady ain't forgetting nothing…" Jesse was breathless, gripped by anger and hate. "I can't wait to see the look on that Francesca's face. Two dead kids, and the precious *Ruby's Palace* run by your widower, and the O'Connell's. Poetic justice, as I see it… and when I'm done with you, I'm coming for Jack!"

Ruby heard those words. They were like a red rag to a bull. She used her last piece of strength to lunge forward and seize Jesse by her legs. Jesse lost her balance and landed heavily on the floor. Her head wrenched back and struck the chunky metal rabbit doorstop. Stunned, she dropped the knife. Ruby snatched the weapon instantly and plunged the blade into Jesse's side, tearing through the muscles which pocketed the ribs. The movement was so quick that Jesse had no time to divert away and save herself.

Ruby just managed to see the last look of devastation on her mother's face before her world became dark and cold.

*

Jack had answered his sister's call, ready to give her a mouthful, when suddenly he realised that this wasn't a normal call at all. The repetitive words, with terror in her voice, made him realise right away she was in danger. He put it on loud speaker and faced his dad. Sam's eyes widened in disbelief.

Kizzy was still in the office and could hear the anguish. Thinking quickly, she pulled from her bag her own mobile and dialled the police and ambulance.

"Jack, what's your address?"

He couldn't speak: he was too transfixed by the screams. Sam grabbed the phone and relayed to the ambulance the address and then the police were put on the line.

"Mr Vincent, please don't move. Stay where you are and keep the line open to your daughter. We need to know exactly what is happening. When we approach the house we will need more information!"

Sam was listening to the police and the desperate cries from his daughter.

"Hurry, smash the fucking door down. Do whatever you have to, but just get her out!"

"Okay, sir, please try to keep calm. Now, how old is your daughter?" came the very calm middle-aged voice of Sergeant Powers.

"Forget the fucking questions. Just get there, hurry up!" Sam was screaming.

"We are on our way. I'm talking to you from the car, sir. I am just a street away from her. Please stay calm."

Jack was sick, with the vomit coming up and out of his mouth and nose. He couldn't handle listening to the torment. He feared the worst. His mother had a knife and Ruby was pleading.

Kizzy pulled the baby wipes from a drawer and helped clean him up.

"I can't stand this. I'm going over there!" cried Sam.

"No, Mr Vincent, you need to hear Ruby. If you take the phone, you might lose signal. Please listen to the sergeant."

Sam looked at Kizzy and knew she was making sense. He nodded.

There was silence, not even a whisper.

"Oh no!" cried Jack, who was convinced Ruby was dead.

"I am gonna kill her, I swear to God. I will murder that cunt with my bare hands." The tears streamed down his angry face.

Kizzy grabbed his arm. "Slow down, Jack, think first, be careful. You don't know what's happened yet."

He stopped in his tracks.

"Kiz, I know you mean well, but I have to go."

She glanced at Sam, who nodded.

With that, Jack and his father were gone. They tore away, nearly crashing into Levi's car, the car which Ocean still happened to have.

"Idiot!" shouted Ocean.

Kizzy searched the office for a phone. Sam had taken hers. There wasn't a landline but she felt awkward hanging around. She wiped her face with a baby wipe and strolled out of the back door. The car park wasn't exactly full, as most customers caught a taxi home. She headed in the direction of the cab rank, hoping one would be early, awaiting a pickup.

There, standing by a car, was Ocean. The moonlight shone against his long curls. There was no mistaking his silhouette. Her heart leapt to her mouth. Instantly, she put her head down and tried to look inconspicuous. But a good-looking woman rarely goes unnoticed. Ocean glanced her way and gasped. That surely could not be his Kizzy, not here.

She took a momentary look and was faced with the intense stare from the man she had once loved so much.

Kizzy carried on walking as if he didn't exist. She wasn't ready to face him. She wanted to get away, to her caravan, her home. She had done what she had set out to do – tell the truth, be kind and hold her head up high. However, she hadn't planned on getting caught up in other Vincent family issues. It was best to keep walking.

She could hear her name being called, Ocean behind her.

"Kizzy, my Kizzy gal, what are you doing here?" His voice was racked with dread and his nerves had made him breathless.

She spun around and made Ocean stop dead in his tracks.

"I have come to do what is right!" She didn't shout or scream.

Ocean stared straight at her, his face lined with shock and guilt.

"What do you mean, my baby?" But he knew what she meant. It was written all over her face.

"You wanted the club, Ocean. Above everything, you had to have the *Palace*. That poor girl, Ruby, lying dead in her bedroom, and you were after her for her money." Kizzy shook her head in shame for him.

"Dead, you say?" Ocean was calm. These weren't the words of a man who had just heard his wife was dead. "Look, my Kizzy, it's only ever been you that I have loved. I did all this for you, for us, for our kids."

She looked on in disgust.

"Kiz, you can have it all." He pointed to the club. "That, there, belongs to me!"

She could not believe he was so cold and selfish.

"Did you not hear me right? Your wife is dead on her bedroom floor and you're talking about owning her club!"

Ocean grabbed Kizzy's arms. "I did it for you. Remember when the Vincents tried to cut you up? I did this for us, for our future. Look, I didn't love her, I just married her for you." His voice was pleading.

Kizzy moved away from his grip.

"You married her for me! How stupid do you sound? So, tell me this, Ocean, did you sleep with her for me too?"

Ocean opened his mouth but nothing came out. How would he answer that one? She seemed more beautiful than he had ever seen her before.

"Look, Kiz, I'm sorry. I made a huge mistake. I never meant to hurt you. I was just planning for our future."

She looked him up and down. "You really don't know me at all, do you?"

Ocean's heart was being ripped from his chest. "Of course I know you. I was the man in your dreams, remember?"

He smiled, hoping she would soften – the way she always did.

"No, Ocean, you are not the man in my dreams. I've moved on." She looked at the club then back at Ocean.

"No, Kiz. Please tell me you still love me; please don't say you've met..." He held his hands behind his head and took a deep breath. "Not a Vincent, please say it's not!"

Kizzy didn't like to lie but he wasn't worth worrying about. She smiled and walked away.

Ocean fell to the floor and sobbed. He didn't want the *Palace*, Ruby or the status. His passion in life was now stepping into a taxi.

Chapter Twenty Two

After the incident at the house, the bloodshed and heartache, the Vincents vowed to take down anyone who even planned to get in their way. Their hate for the O'Connells was so great. They had lured Ruby in and played a sick game, and no one gets away with that, especially a drug dealing travelling family. But it was Jack who had the most anger. He had loved his sister so much he didn't care if his liberty was on the line. He would destroy Ocean.

Johnnie O'Connell had gotten wind his nephews had fucked up and now the Vincents were after them, so he had assumed that the whole site was not safe. Being the bigger man, and the one with the most savvy, he went and paid the old man Bill Vincent a visit. He took a cab. It would have been unwise to take the scrap van. Bill was at home, enjoying his Sunday roast, when there was a bang on the door. Mary, his wife, rolled her eyes. "I bet one of the boys is nursing a hangover – I dunno."

Bill got up from his seat and walked slowly to the hallway. He was still a fair size for an older man.

Johnnie O'Connell stepped back as the door opened and removed his flap cap.

Bill frowned and tried to recall the man's face. Then it hit him. It was the old man O'Connell. He raised his eyebrow.

"Mr Vincent, sorry to disturb you, but can I have a man-to-man talk with you? I don't want no trouble."

Bill looked at the ageing gypsy and, out of respect, invited him in.

Mary made the tea and offered Johnnie a seat.

"So, what can I do for you?" Bill kept his face stern, fully informed of the trouble with the O'Connells. He had as much hate for them as his sons, but guessed that the old man had nothing to do with it. He knew him as a straight, old school traveller, who kept himself to himself and mixed with his own kind.

"I suppose your boys have told ya about me boys' wrongdoings?" He bowed his head in shame.

"Wrongdoings, you say?"

"Yeah, I ain't into their drug dealing shit, told 'em to stop it, but they think they know best... I warned them not to mess with your family, but the bastards ignored me."

"So, Johnnie, why are you here? Cos it's my reckoning my boys won't let this go, not after what happened to our Ruby." He took a deep breath and sucked up his emotions. "Like you, Johnnie, I can't tell my lot what to do."

Johnnie was nodding in agreement. "Don't get me wrong, Mr Vincent, those scumbags deserve all they get, and more. I am truly sorry for what happened to your granddaughter, fucking terrible, mate!"

Bill scratched his head. "So you're not here to warn us off, then?"

Johnnie laughed. "Nah, to be honest, I know they are family, but I have disowned them. Truth is, I hate them, even my own boy. I lost all feelings for him. I never brought him up to deal drugs... of course, our kind have a way of life, wheeling and dealing, but not that shit, messing up innocent kiddies. Fuck 'em. If your boys take out my boys, then so be it. I, for one, won't shed a tear."

Bill, taken aback by this last statement, but also very relieved, asked, "So what do you want from me?"

"Well, Bill, I know you're a fair man, and I guess you have brought your boys up to be fair, so all I ask is they don't burn down me site. We have little 'uns on there and we ain't all bad."

Bill threw his head back and laughed. "Cor, Johnnie, you have listened to too many rumours. Look, mate, I give you my word. Your site will be left standing. No one, and I mean no one, other than those involved, will get hurt!"

Johnnie's shoulders relaxed and he sipped his tea. "I was just packing me bags ready to leave, then I thought I should pay you a visit. So glad I did. At least I can stay in me own van without sleeping with one eye open."

Bill shook his hand and, as soon as he had left, he got on the phone to Dan.

*

Dan had been in a meeting with the boys, planning how to stop the O'Connells once and for all. Fred wanted to go in all guns blazing as usual and Sam demanded he be the one to personally kick seven colours of shit out of Billy.

"Shush, it's Dad," he said in a serious tone. Even as grown men, they still had the utmost respect for their parents. He listened carefully and answered for all in the room to hear.

"Don't worry, Dad, you have my word!"

Fred rolled his eyes. "Don't tell me he wants us to leave it, after all those fuckers have put us through, especially our Ruby?"

Dan shook his head and smirked. "Dad is with us but on one condition. We keep it well away from the site."

Sam frowned. "As if we would!"

"The fucking mackerels ain't so stupid as to hide on the camp. They know we could bulldoze the place," said Dan, still smirking.

"They are hiding somewhere and, trust me, it's only a matter of time before someone squeals. I've got some of the lads with their ears to the ground. We have time and patience… well, maybe not you, Freddie boy. Patience is not one of your fortes." He laughed.

By the time the club opened, news arrived of where the O'Connells were hiding – a farmhouse in Kent. Fred rubbed his hands together. Right, now I am gonna rip a few heads off, he thought to himself. The brothers sat around the table in the office and, over a few brandies, plotted their revenge.

The door flew open and in walked Jack. He was dressed in jeans and a black jacket. He was tall and stocky but today, unlike his usual calm self, he was fiery-eyed and confident.

"So you know where they are?" His voice changed, deep and husky.

"'Ere, Jackie, you ain't coming, mate. This ain't your war. No need to get your hands dirty, you save that for the ring!" said Joe, who had been quiet throughout the discussion. He tended to take a back seat and listen to his brothers, knowing he wasn't the sharpest knife in the drawer.

"No disrespect, Uncle Joe, but this is more my fight than any of you. Ruby was my concern: my sister, my fight!" His voice was almost demonic, cold and harsh.

There was silence as they stared.

"I am going to take care of those scumbags myself, for Ruby!"

"Look, boy —" Fred didn't have a chance to finish.

"In case you haven't noticed, I am no boy. I might not be aggressive like you, Fred, but those lowlifes fucked me over, and my sister, and they won't see what's hit 'em, when I get hold of them!"

Fred smiled. "I call you boy, 'cos, Jack, you're our boy. When you're fucking fifty years old we will still call you 'boy'. I am well aware that you're a man. And, yes, I hate to admit it, but you could beat the shit out of me if you had to, but we can sort out those O'Connells ourselves, no need to get your hands dirty!"

Jack bit the inside of his lip and flared his nostrils. "You don't get it, do you? Those bastards planned our Ruby's murder. They knew Jesse was going to kill her. What fucking cunt does that to a kid: marries her, promises her the world, and then leaves her to die, just to get their hands on a club? And they thought Ocean would be a wealthy widower, all their fucking prayers answered. Well, I'm gonna answer their prayers because, when I get my hands on them, they'll beg to die, and I'll honour their pleas."

Sam stepped forward and put his arm around Jack's shoulders. "You have been through too much. This will haunt you!"

Jack shrugged his father off. "Not taking them out will fucking haunt me. I have seen a lot in my life. What fucks my head up is not being there at the right time to do anything. I wasn't there for Ruby, and look what happened to her! Well, I am going to do what's right – remove the nightmares, the thoughts that control me – 'cos there will be four less O'Connells, four less scumbags, four less cruel creatures roaming around. Trust me, I can help in more ways than you know!"

Dan nodded and put out his hand to shake Jack's. "Okay, boy, sit your arse down and listen to the plan."

He pulled up a chair, giving him the respect to have his say.

*

As the evening approached, Dan and Joe jumped into one car whilst Sam and Jack got in another, leaving Fred on his own. There was a whisper that the O'Connells had a Kent copper in their back pocket so they planned to send Fred along first. A vanload of heavies was to meet them there for back-up if need be. Strangely, the hideout where they were supposed to be lying low was a mile away from Francesca's house, which they used for Christmas holidays, meaning they knew the area well.

The farmhouse was surrounded by fields. A country lane ran across the front, with a turning five hundred yards up ahead. The only means of escape was the back field. No nearby houses overlooked the hide-out so the coast was clear. Fred slowly pulled up outside with his lights off. Dan and the others held back.

Suddenly, a police car thrashed around the corner and skidded to a halt. The officers jumped out of their car, almost ripping the door off, dragging Fred out.

Dan drove slowly past and laughed.

The police didn't catch who was in the other cars. They weren't the Vincents' famous red Mercedes with the private number plates.

One copper threw him heavily against the bonnet.

"What the fuck do you idiots think you're doing?" scowled Fred, who was itching to punch the fat one in the face.

"Well, look who it ain't. Freddie Vincent," he said, holding Fred against the car.

Fred laughed, which irritated the copper. "I don't know what you're laughing at, mate, but I think I can find enough on you to have a field day." He loosened his grip and allowed Fred to turn around. They stood face to face, both smirking.

"So what've you stopped me for then, officer?" asked Fred, raising his eyebrow.

"Oh, let me see, dodgy headlight, driving without due care and attention, drunk driving, wearing a bullet proof vest – take your fucking pick, son!"

"Bullet proof vest! I run a nightclub as security and it's keeping me warm." He laughed out loud. "You Kent police are all the same! Look at you, standing there in your flak jacket and combat jeans, thinking you're straight out of fucking Iraq. But you aren't though, are ya? No balls for the army, not even man enough for the fucking Met police – now, they take on real men, not fanny pieces like you!"

The burly copper smirked at the smaller copper and kicked Fred in the leg. The pain was sharp but he refused to make a sound. Instead, he smiled. "I wouldn't push it too far, Officer Trench!"

Trench stood back and looked uneasy.

"Yeah, mate, I know who you are, you silly little wanker. Before you even think of touching me again, I best tell you, I fucking know who you are, and what you are, and you may be the O'Connells' sidekicks, but, ya see, the Met police hate you weasel wankers, and would love to see the footage I have on you!"

The smaller policeman looked at the floor. Officer Trench frowned and Fred watched as the colour left his cheeks.

"You think we don't smell a pig in our clubs? They're rigged up with cameras, every bloody inch of the place. Shitting your fucking pants now, ain't ya?"

"You have nothing on me, Vincent!"

Fred straightened himself up and laughed. "Oh no? We fucking marked your cunting card years ago. Don't suppose your buddy over here knows ya like little boys!" He glanced at the other copper. "And you, ya scrawny bag of shit, Officer Rolland, we got enough on you – selling drugs to me punters! Ya see, us Vincents, we have this insurance – a library of footage, neatly lined up in our lawyer's office, get my drift?"

The two coppers were shitting hot bricks. He knew too much to be bluffing. No way could they chance on a nick.

"Go on then, Vincent, on your way. I will let you go this time, just slow down on the bends,"

Fred laughed. "Who the hell are you to fucking talk to me like that?" He paused, looking at their feet, which stood them on uneasy ground. "If I see your face or hear that either of you two cokeheads have been near or by, that footage is going straight to where you know it hurts, got it? Have I made myself crystal cunting clear?" he screamed, lurching forward.

Officer Trench nodded, along with Rolland, knowing full well he held the power to take them down in a flash. They had been warned not to mess with the Vincents, and hiding behind a uniform gave them no favours. They crept away and drove off into the night, not bothering to call Levi to give him the heads up. What should happen tonight was none of their business. Their own reputation and liberty were on the line and Freddie Vincent was not fucking around.

The farmhouse was rundown and barely inhabitable, but tucked neatly in a field. No one should have known their whereabouts as they had kept it a tight secret. Levi had made a deal with the coppers to keep an eye on the place. They had Noah with them, a tough traveller who no sane man messed with. Farley had taken a kicking when he'd refused entry to Noah that night at the club, but he was spared his life and got away with a broken nose, jaw and a cracked rib. However, that was a few years ago and now he was on side again with him. The O'Connells had lost a fair few friends and needed the backing of their fellow travellers. Many refused to get involved, as the Vincents were too big a fish to fry.

Noah was sitting on the old worn and torn leather armchair, and listening to the wind whistling through the cracks in the windows. The frames had rotted away and what was left barely held together. Billy was nodding off on the sofa – his fat head held upright by his wide neck. The cold didn't bother him; he was carrying so much blubber. His stomach spilled over his trousers and he walked around most of the time with his shoe laces untied. The rattle at the back of his throat when he snored was annoying Levi. He jumped up and headed for the run-down kitchen, which they had managed to half clean up to cook and eat in. The fridge was filled with beer cans, the sides had packets of biscuits and crisps, and the empty takeaway cartons were piled up.

They planned to keep their heads down for a few days and work out how they were going to turn this nightmare of a situation around. Ocean sat next to the fire, sharpening his knife. It made him cringe, knowing this was the only weapon he had, and he was unsure if he had the guts to use it.

Noah's phone pinged and Levi jumped. "Who was that, Noah?"

"My Rose, just saying goodnight." A half-cocked smile spread across his face.

"Right, boys, I'm starving, I'm gonna order a pizza," announced Noah. There was silence. Farley poured himself a beer and tried to stop his hands shaking. The looming threat had left him feeling uneasy and sick. Levi lined up a gram of cocaine along the kitchen surface. His nose was a real mess now and the only way to cope with his ugly face was to keep snorting the Charlie.

Noah dialled the number. "Hello, I want to order a pizza."

There was silence at the end of the phone and then a voice said, "For how many people?"

"Um, let's see… Levi, want a pizza?" asked Noah.

Levi shouted from the kitchen, "No!"

"Ocean, want pizza?"

He shook his head.

"Farley, what about you?"

Farley was feeling very sick and hollered back, "No way, I'd heave it back up!"

"And you, fat boy, I bet you want some?"

Billy laughed. "Yeah, too large meat feasts!"

Noah still had a grin on his face when he returned to the call. "Yes, three large meat feasts."

Fred joined his brothers further up the lane and clambered into the back of Sam's car with Joe. Dan stood having a fag, listening to Jack.

"Who was you talking to, boy?" asked Fred.

Jack smiled. "Are we ready to deliver pizzas?"

Sam ruffled his son's hair. "You little fucker, Jack. Who have you got in that farmhouse?"

"Noah. He wants the O'Connells fucked up. Said he will keep them there until I give him the okay. See, Dad, I ain't a little boy anymore. Ocean, Farley, Levi and Billy are inside with no guns and just a couple of knives."

"Are you sure you can trust him? He's another pikey," said Joe.

Jack laughed. "Well, we've got insurance just in case, but Noah has a burning grudge to bear, and it ain't with us."

Dan reached through the car window and playfully slapped his face.

"Give it fifteen minutes or they will smell a rat," said Jack.

"But are you sure about Noah?" repeated Joe.

"Noah said he will put the boot in, out of respect. He has his reasons for ensuring they never see the light of day, so he is going to open the door and let us in, but there is a backdoor. He has made sure it's unlocked, so we can go through the back as well... But Ocean's mine, all right? I want him!" said Jack.

Sam and Dan exchanged glances and then nodded. Jack had never seen his uncles or father in action. He had seen them fight at the gym, and admired them, especially Fred. Fast and furious, he called him.

Adam and Jason stood towering above the Vincents. They agreed to go in the back door just in case Noah had a change of heart. He was such a big lump. Dan tapped on the door.

"Go and get the pizzas, mush," directed Noah to Ocean.

"How do you know it's the pizza delivery?" Ocean was a nervous wreck.

"'Cos I fucking ordered it, cranky cunt!"

Ocean gripped his knife and turned the handle slowly, edging it open. Then Dan, with brute force, kicked the door in, sending Ocean on his arse. Billy was wide awake and struggling to get to his feet. Levi and Farley ran towards the back exit, to be rudely stopped by Jason and Adam.

Levi had the other knife and pulled it from his pocket, wielding it in front of Adam. "Come on then, fucker!" High on cocaine and cocky as fuck, Levi got a shock when Fred bashed him on the shoulder and he heard the jangle as his blade hit the stone floor. Fred seized him by the throat and dragged him back into the living room, throwing him on the floor.

All the men were now in the same room. The O'Connells looked from one to the other, knowing there was no escape, and praying it would be over quickly.

The Vincents stood staring, menacingly, in silence and Jack glared at Ocean with a sadistic grin on his face.

Noah got up. He hadn't moved from his seat until now. He was a huge bulk of a man, with scars across his face, thick sideburns and a thick, gold loop dangling from his ear. His hands were the size of concrete slabs. It stood to reason that the O'Connells thought they were safe in his protection. "Thank you, boys, now this is my fight!"

"What?" said Dan, totally bewildered.

"Yeah, Vincent, I am glad you came just to herd these cats, but I have a little issue of me own, see." His voice was deep and gruff and Dan grinned. He was going to watch this giant slaughter the O'Connells, pleased he didn't have to get his clothes dirty.

Ocean was cowering in the corner, covering his face, terrified, but Jack wasn't having it. He needed to let go of his built-up anger. Ignoring Noah, he reached down, pulled Ocean to his feet and punched him full force in the side of the head. Ocean wobbled but didn't go down. Jack snatched him by the collar and thumped him again, not letting him fall. Again and again, he hammered into his face until, finally, he couldn't hold the weight and let Ocean crash to the floor. All eyes were on him. Even the Vincents were shocked at his brute, relentless force. The O'Connells were cringing at the sound of broken bones and the sight of the pretty boy's face caving in. Jack wasn't even breathless. It was nothing to him. He had the power of ten men and stepped back, calm and collected, as if brutalising a man near to death was normal. Even Sam shuddered.

Noah didn't flinch. A cruel smirk spread across his face. He stared at Levi. "He got off lightly. You though, you perverted mush, ain't!"

Levi struggled to his feet and tried to back away. "Noah, what the fuck have I done to you?" His voice was cracking, ready to cry, as the coke had worn off.

"You know what you did. My dear little sister, gawd rest her soul."

Levi knew what he meant and prayed he could take the beating and live. No point in denying it. He did get her hooked. He had wanted her for himself, and the only way he could have a piece of her was by giving her freebies, but she had to give out for it.

Billy wasn't so cocky now. He was totally immersed in dread, his breathing tightened and pains shot down his arm as an odd, whining sound left his mouth. As Sam went to lunge at him, Joe stopped him. "No! Look, the cunt's having a heart attack!"

Noah looked away from Levi to watch Billy gripping his chest as his lips turned blue. Within seconds he slumped on the sofa. Sam spat on his face, the phlegm dripping from the end of his nose, but Billy didn't flinch. He was dead.

"Go on, boys, you can leave these two dead-beat mushes to me. I think it only fair I take 'em out the old-fashioned way, true Romany style."

Dan was not sure if he was being up front. "How do I…?"

"Don't worry, you'll hear the screams." With that, he pulled from his pocket two chunky gold knuckle dusters, diamond encrusted, with his sister's name on. He'd had them made and kept them for this special occasion.

There was a deep, thoughtful silence on the way home, until Sam said, "See, son, I told you this would bother you, haunt ya!"

Jack wanted to laugh. His father couldn't have been more wrong. "I only hope I've killed the cunt!"

*

There was no news or gossip until three days later when Detective Inspector James knocked at the door. Sam was nervous this time but not just for himself. He was very worried for his son, Jack. He had tossed and turned for two nights, worrying that Jack was now caught up in a war he was too young to handle.

"'Ello, Detective, what can I do you for?" He tried to make a joke.

DI James smiled. "May I come in? I need a chat with you and your boy."

Sam felt his throat tighten. This was it, they were going to get nicked. He knew the fight had been messy. Had all the loose ends been tied up? Shit, they shouldn't have trusted Noah. "Yeah, course, mate. Can I get you a drink?"

James saw Sam was nervous, too friendly, not his usual steel trait. "Yeah, why not? Let's make it a double. I fucking need a drink. Those Kent coppers are doing my nut in!"

Sam poured two large whiskies and sat opposite the DI.

"What's this all about then, guv?" he asked, perched on the edge of his seat.

James loosened his tie and sipped the drink. "I don't know, mate. There was an incident down in Kent. Levi, Farley and Billy O'Connell were found dead. A travelling man, called Noah, claims they set him up and took him there to murder him over a dodgy deal. Well, as it happens, two of them laid into him. Farley O'Connell stabbed him in the arm but, in fear of his life, he fought back." He took another mouthful of the neat whisky as he allowed it to burn the back of his throat.

"So, what's that got to do with us?"

"Well, apparently, a gypsy by the name of Ocean…" Sam nodded, waiting for the DI to get to the crunch line, "is claiming it was your boy who attacked him, and not Noah. Says you were all there."

Sam sniffed the air and smiled. "I won't lie. I do know of this Ocean and, yeah, I wanted the cunt dead but, if this Noah is putting his hands up to it then what are you doing 'ere?"

"It's those fucking Kent coppers. They ain't old school. They got two murders, one death by natural causes, and the other by a brutal beating. They can't nick Noah. He has a good enough case for self-defence. Both the two knives had Levi's, Farley's and Ocean's prints on 'em. There is a nasty wound in the back of Noah's arm which he couldn't have done himself, but they are bored shitless down there and want a nicking. With Ocean singing like a canary, they are after your boy."

Sam gulped back his whisky. "So, what now then?"

The DI smiled. "They called me in because you're on my patch. I told them if you have an alibi then I'm closing the case, and the chief agreed. They know the Crown Prosecution Service wouldn't have a leg to stand on."

Sam smiled and nodded. "Yeah, what day did you say?"

"Give me a list of names. I will get the statements, and then the Kent lot can go fuck 'emselves."

Jack strolled in, unaware that it was the DI sitting there. He stopped in his tracks. James looked him up and down, noticing the bruises on his knuckles. "Take my advice, lad, make sure you wear those boxing gloves before you go pummelling the punch bag. It'll do you no good to ruin your career. Ya gonna be a reigning champion one day."

Jack's face lit up. "I hope so. Train every day and most nights, unless I'm working."

"Right then, I'll be off. Don't you worry about a thing, Sam. You phone your alibis, and let them know I'm coming to take a statement and, after this case is closed, I'm gonna call it a day. Listening to those fuckwits in Kent has finished me off. Time to get out and fuck off to Spain."

As he heaved himself off the seat, Sam stopped him. "Hold up a sec, I've got something for you."

James frowned and watched as he opened a drawer and removed a bunch of keys and a piece of paper. "Here you go, it's yours!"

The DI stared at the keys, baffled. "What's this?"

Sam patted him on the back. "We all know, me and me brothers, that you have always seen us right. Behind the scenes, you sorted out our shit, one way or another. Ya have been good to us. We only wish we could have found out who hurt your girl…"

James jumped back, a lump wedged in his throat. "You knew?"

Sam gave him a sympathetic nod. "Yeah, we always kept our ears to the ground to find anything that could help you but never came up with a single clue."

He sniffed back a tear. "I always believed it was Charlie McManners. So, son, you perhaps helped out more than you realised!"

DI James gripped the set of keys and, through watery eyes, read the note. New owner – four bedroomed villa in Marbella.

He glanced up at Sam as the tears tumbled down his face. "If I had a son, I'd have wanted him to be like you." This was the first time ever, as a grown man, he had shown emotion in public, but he had been there over the years to see and hear of the ups and downs the Vincents had faced, especially Sam.

Sam hugged him and said goodbye.

Jack waited until his father closed the door. "So, Ocean ain't dead then?"

Sam grinned, "Nah. Son, the fucking state you left his face in, he will wish he had died. A man like that lives on his looks. Now he ain't got a face. That will haunt him for the rest of his life."

Chapter Twenty Three

Six months later

The rain poured. It was not the best day for the funeral but the wait had been long enough. The red tape was never ending. Now, after six months, the case was finally closed. The body was released for burial. It was a small gathering, with nothing too lavish.

Jack turned his coat collar up to stop the drops of water from going down his neck. Even the thick, warm material would not stop him from shivering. The tears streamed down his face. As the coffin was lowered into the grave he stood and stared. Visualising the corpse inside, he shuddered and said a few words quietly, for only her to hear.

The black limousine pulled up by the gates. Jack hurried over and the door was opened for him. There were a group of onlookers that Jack just about recognised but he didn't stop to speak, too intent on getting away. He said his goodbyes and couldn't bear to hang around.

"Get in, and out of that wet coat." He looked at his aunt and smiled. She was the mother he needed, not Jesse.

"Are you all right, my darling?" Francesca touched his cheek.

He nodded.

"Look, why don't you and Kizzy spend some time with me in the States?"

Kizzy's face lit up. She sat opposite Jack, gripping his hand. She had never been to America, or outside of England for that matter.

He suddenly had a sparkle in his eyes. "Yeah, I need a break and Kiz can meet our other family."

Francesca laughed. "Now there's an experience. Kizzy, queen of the gypsies, meets king of the mafia."

That brought a huge smile to Jack's face. Kizzy was delighted that the Vincents had accepted her. Their relationship, in those short six months, had grown so fast. It had been a roller coaster ride, that was for sure, but one she and Jack held on to together.

"You will love America, and my Uncle Sergio!" squealed Ruby. Her face was soft and sweet, like the charming three-year-old she once was. The realisation that terrifying evening, faced with her knife-wielding mother, told her everything she needed to know to be a loyal Vincent. No matter how far she had pushed her family, they would lay their lives on the line for her. She wasn't hidden from their secrets, she understood it all – the need to be an essential part of the pack. She would never look back or go it alone. No one would come between her and her family. She looked at her aunt and smiled. Francesca had sat, day in day out, by her hospital bed, all through her recovery, physically and mentally. The psychiatrist had worked with Ruby, restoring her back to normal, all with the help of her family, every single one of them.

She recalled the words her aunt had said as she had sobbed into her arms and pleaded for forgiveness. 'Ruby, we were wrong for hiding the truth about your past, your mother, and what I did. It was our fault that you went in search of her and it was our fault you took solace in the arms of a man so far removed from us. You were looking for something missing in your own life. I did the same thing. I never waited to find the truth about my husband – too much in love, I suppose. We make mistakes on our journey, but it shapes us into the person we become. Look at you now. You are still young, beautiful, and have experienced the worst of people. Now you can see the best. It's the ugly characters who really highlight the good ones.'

When they reached their home and everyone stepped out of the car, Jack lifted his sister, helping her with the cumbersome crutches. Even six months on, the nerves in her leg were still damaged. Ruby whispered, "Was you praying for Jesse, Jack?" Jack turned and, with a cold expression, he said, "No, I told her to rot in hell!"

"Me too!" she whispered.

The tears he cried were not for his mother but the years of sadness she had caused them. Now, he had a new life: he could look to the future with more confidence and no more nightmares. Jesse, the boogie man, lay six foot under and he could sleep soundly, knowing she couldn't ever harm them again.

He winked at his sister and then he turned to his aunt. She had the same expression as Ruby. That cool demeanour with eyes that could melt your heart. He knew she wasn't like his mother. She was just lost for a while, but now she was back. A true Vincent.

They say it's the alpha female who really leads the pack!